Love, Money, and Revenge

"I HAVE NEVER MADE LOVE BEFORE YOU ARE MY FIRST"
"YOU ARE MY FIRST TOO"

ROBERT CORY PHILLIPS

Order this book online at www.trafford.com
or email orders@trafford.com

Most Trafford titles are also available at major online book retailers.

Printed in the United States of America.

ISBN: 978-1-4907-4995-2 (sc)
ISBN: 978-1-4907-4997-6 (hc)
ISBN: 978-1-4907-4996-9 (e)

Library of Congress Control Number: 2014919170

Trafford rev. 01/15/2015

 www.trafford.com
North America & international
toll-free: 1 888 232 4444 (USA & Canada)
fax: 812 355 4082

Contents

Epigraph

The enjoyment of writing this book was to meet all the people that I did not know. They became my friends as we eat supper, talked, laughed, and even cried together.

Loaner became my favorite. As a puppy we had fun as he grew up. He learned to protect and love Guyiser. The ladies in this book were awesome. They taught me about the different types of love. Cindy was my first love. Fun-loving, exciting, and to me, very interesting to be with. And then there was Carla. I knew her in my life.

Sadness came to me when the father, Mr. Blackman, died. He also was a man in my life that I knew a long time ago.

Thank all of the people in this book for giving me your time and all the good times. I will never forget you.

I loved the ending of this story.

Acknowledgments

I wish to thank the television media, the newspaper press, studios, directors, reporters, and crews for stretching the imagination. You were all very helpful --- Thanks.

I also thank Cory Brandon for his research material.

Thanks to Mrs. Sherry Jolly of Executive Aid Secretarial Service in Nashville, TN for her edit, proofreading, and suggestions.

To my publisher, Trafford Publishing, and the entire staff for their time, help, and believing in this novel.

Robert Cory Phillips

About the Author

Born in Nashville, Tennessee, and moved to Hollywood, Robert Cory Phillips has been a professional photographer 22 years of his life. Working in film, video, shooting stills on the sets of major films and commercials has awarded him many years of pleasure. He was a player in a group of screenwriters where he added warm, touching laughter dialog to many scripts. As an actor in Hollywood, he surrounded himself with the friendship of actors and actresses. His talents spread to writing. American Literary Press quickly published his children's book. Love, Money, Revenge brings it all together for him. His experience with the rich and famous, with on-set photography working with directors, camera crews, art department, magazines, editors, and the little people have filled and enriched his life. Today he enjoys his home in Nashville, Tennessee where he can relax and with passion write. His following of readers can enjoy his work and can be seen everywhere.

His certificates of achievements include his work at the Tennessee Baptist Children's Home in Brentwood,

Tennessee. He is a graduate of the Learning Tree University in Woodland Hills, CA, and the Oxford Theater and the School of Arts and Brooks Collage, Calif.

Love, Money, and Revenge

Blood trickled from his mouth. His face was swollen from the beating he had received. Guyiser quickly grabbed the shotgun from the ground. "Get back. Get against the wall." The man backed up with his hands in the air. Guyiser walked to him and shoved the shotgun into his neck. "You killed my father, didn't you?"

"Please mister, don't shoot me."

"Why? Why did you do it?"

"He owed us money for a drug deal."

"That's a lie. You're lying."

"It's the truth. We bought pot from him and he called the cops and told them where it was." Guyiser moved the shotgun to his stomach. "Please don't kill me. I'll do anything you say. I'll go away.

You'll never see me again." Guyiser stared at him. He could only see his dead father's face.

"Well, you're right about one thing. I'll never see you again." Guyiser squeezed the trigger on the shotgun. The shot echoed in the alley. Guyiser watched the man slide down the bloody wall.

Trash And Treasure

Part 1

Throw it away,
We'll get a new one
Another day...
Look Dad, what I have found,
It was just lying on the ground.
That's money, son. That's not trash.
We'll take it home
And polish the brass.

Guyiser Blackman, a self-made billionaire, was taught by his father to think outside of the box.

As a shy, quiet, poor young man, at the age of seventeen, he would watch his father go through the streets and alleys picking up what others had thrown away as trash. His father would spray-paint things gold or silver and give them new life. Then he would sell these chairs, picture frames, jars, flowerpots, bricks, shoes, lamps, and anything else he would find. Guyiser and his father would take some money and go to garage sales all over town to buy things. They would bargain for things left over. Then, they would take their things home, fix them, paint them, and resell them for a small profit.

Counting money at the table at night, Guyiser would hear his father laugh and smile and say, "Get it at the bottom, sell at the top." Guyiser would go to sleep at night with the moon's glow coming in his window and the sound of his father's voice echoing in his thoughts.

In the early morning's sun, Guyiser would dress in his plaid shirt and bibbed overalls and go to his peaceful place on the thirty-five acre farm. There he would climb a tree and sit on a board seat he had made watching their two cows and the birds. His tree house was like an island in the middle of the ocean. A small leather pouch hung from a limb. Once a week he would climb the tree and put pennies, nickels, dimes, quarters, and a few dollars in the pouch. This was his money that he had earned helping his father.

As time passed, the money in the pouch grew. Guyiser would run to his tree, kicking and smiling. He would scramble up the tree and sit down to count his money. "Thirty-one, thirty-three, thirty-six dollars and forty cents." With a big grin on his face, he would think about getting another leather pouch. This was his secret, and not even his father knew about the tree or the pouch.

The 35-acre farm was mostly tall skinny trees on rolling hillsides with gullies where creek water ran. The few acres on the flat land had corn that grew to be sold at the market place. Guyiser's mother always had a garden with tomatoes and green beans and strawberries that she would preserve and make jam and jelly. She loved to make marmalade from the apples she would gather from the six apple trees. This was a way of life that had been passed down to her from her grandmother to her mother and to her. Guyiser loved to sit at the kitchen table and watch her. She would take a spoon of jam and say to Guyiser,

"Taste this. Is it good?" She would smile her warm loving smile and say, "Guyiser, did you make your bed?" Guyiser loved to hear her soft voice.

And when she died, Guyiser could see changes happening. The smell of the kitchen disappeared. The garden vanished. Apples fell to the ground. His father would sit and stare and drink cheap wine. The corn fields died. He saw his father almost giving up. Feed the cows. Feed the chickens. Sit, stare, and drink cheap wine. The old farm house would never be the same and Guyiser knew that.

Guyiser did have many great memories of his mother. The way she would stand on the porch and wave to him when he left for school and she was always standing there when he came back. But that was then, and this is now.

Guyiser woke up to the smell of breakfast, it was a beautiful warm sunny morning. Putting on yesterday's bibbed overalls and water on his hair, he wandered into the kitchen where his father sat at the table. "It's about time. You going to sleep all day?" He said "Sit down." Guyiser looked at this man with an old wrinkled face and dirty fingernails, a shirt with missing buttons, boots with broken shoestrings, and food on the table. The old man is still trying, he thought. "I'm going into Nashville later, you wanta come?" To Guyiser, it was a great time to get away from the farm and Centerville. Centerville only had twelve stores and a road around the courthouse. So to go to Nashville was like going to another world even though it was only forty-two miles away. The Grand Ole Opry, country music, country singers, city people, bright lights, and stores of all kinds lured him.

"I'll wear some clean clothes, comb my hair, and clean the mud off my boots," Guyiser said excitedly.

"Yes sir, I really want to go."

Nashville, Tennessee, was growing like no other city. New homes were being built. Old roads were being widen and paved. There were jobs for everybody. It took about an hour and a half to drive to the big city in their old truck. Mr. Blackman wanted to buy some cow feed that Centerville didn't have. Plus, it was cheaper by the pound in Nashville.

As they rode down the bumpy old road, all Guyiser could think of was the big buildings, the city people, cars, and a life he could only imagine. All of a sudden, there it was—a sign on the side of the road, "Nashville City Limits." Guyiser's heart beat fast as he pointed to the sign. "Look, Pa!" It was a six-mile drive into Nashville to reach the courthouse where the feed store was.

Mr. Blackman laughed as Guyiser waved to people he did not know. "You like it here in the big city?" A big smile on Guyiser's face said it all. "Yes sir, I wished we lived here."

The smell of the cattle stockyard and feed store was strong in the air. As they parked the truck Mr. Blackman said, "Well, we're here. You wanta walk around while I see about the feed?" Guyiser jumped from the truck with a boyish smile. "But don't go far. I'll need your help, you hear me?" Guyiser stepped on the sidewalk. His head was like a doorknob, turning in all directions. *So much to see! Country music stores, clothes stores, guitar stores, eating-places, a bicycle shop, and boot repair shops. People looked like country singers with their western shirts and boots.* There was a car with horns on the hood and a truck with a shotgun hanging in the back window. This was not Centerville at all. He walked up one side of the street and down the other. Then he saw another street. Actually, it was an alley. Being an alley cat like his father, he decided to walk down it. A dog barked, but he kept walking. Trashcans were full, empty boxes were piled up. A cat ran in front of him. Then he saw something that made him walk faster. It was a pile of bicycle frames behind the bicycle shop. Some were bent. Some were broken. Some had missing parts. Guyiser saw a gold mine. He ran down the alley, turned the corner, and went to the bike shop. He stood looking in the window. The sign over the door read, "Gibson's Bicycle Shop." His eyes were glued to a bike in the window. It was a black bike with chrome fenders. It had a horn and colored streamers hung from the handlebars. The shiny whitewall tires made it stand out. It was the most beautiful thing he had ever seen. Blood rushed to his head, his heart pounded, and as he stood there, an unusual feeling came over him. There was something telling him to go in. It took a few minutes before he opened the door.

A little bell tinkled as the door opened. A jolly older man wearing an apron and small glasses walked up to Guyiser. "Hi, young man, my name is Gibson. Can I help you?"

Guyiser just stood there looking at all the bicycles. There were bikes in all colors---big ones, little ones, and tricycles.

"No sir, I just want to look, if that's all right. But, I would like to talk to you."

Mr. Gibson just smiled. "Help yourself. Look all you want, and there is candy in a jar on the counter over there." He turned and walked into a back room. Guyiser looked at the glass counter. It was full of parts, locks, chains, horns, streamers, and handle bar grips. He walked to a bike and touched it. He looked to the back room. Mr. Gibson was working on a bike. Before he knew it, he was sitting on the bicycle. He could feel the speed and the air rushing past him. *This is for me,* he thought. Then he looked at the price tag hanging from the handlebars. The price was sixty-eight dollars. Guyiser thought about the leather pouch. He didn't have that much money. He stood looking at the bike.

Mr. Gibson came to him.

"Too much for you? Tell you what. I'll make you a good deal."

Guyiser kept looking at the bike. "Sure is a beauty, but no sir. Mr. Gibson, I saw a bunch of bikes in your alley. Are they free or for sale?"

Mr. Gibson laughed. "No son, they're scrap and parts I use sometimes. But, if you want to fix them up, I'll sell you some. You'll have to work hard to make them look good. I don't have time to fix them."

"Sir, that's what I'm good at, fixing things. Guyiser thought for a moment. "It's a deal. Mr. Gibson, but I don't have the money with me right now. It's in the tree, but I'll buy them. Consider them sold."

Mr. Gibson was puzzled at Guyiser's answer, but patted him on his shoulder.

"What's your name, young man?"

"Guyiser, Guyiser Blackman, Sir."

"You know, Guyiser, you'll need some parts."

"Yes sir, I looked them over. They need a lot more than parts, a lot of work to… Sir, I'm so excited! My dad will bring me back and I'll get them then. And pay you too… Is that all right with you?"

"Sure Guyiser, they're yours."

Guyiser left the store feeling like a new person. Excitement swelled in his chest. Like his father, he was now a businessman. He had just made a deal and could not wait to tell his father. *Make a plan; work a plan was his thought. I'll fix a place in the barn to work on the bikes. I'll make a big sign saying, "Guyiser's Bike Shop." I'll buy cheap and sell high. I'll buy at ten dollars and sell at forty dollars. No, I'll buy at three dollars and sell at thirty dollars. I'll be rich!*

Mr. Blackman had just finished paying for the grain when Guyiser ran into the feed store. "Dad, wait till you hear!"

"Help me load this grain in the truck."

"I will Dad, but just listen."

"Now boy, it'll be dark time before we get home. We'll talk later."

It was a long ride home. Guyiser sat looking out the window as the truck went down the road. The sun was setting in their eyes as Mr. Blackman spit out the window. "So what's all the commotion about? You meet a girl?"

"Better than that. I made a deal. I met a man. His name is Gibson. He owns a bike shop, and we talked and we made a bicycle deal." Guyiser laid out his plan to his father. "I'll do all the work. I'll do all my chores on the farm and work all summer on the bikes. I know I can sell 'em, I know!"

The ride ended at the barn. Mr. Blackman turned to Guyiser, "You're a smart boy, Guyiser. Maybe it'll work. Tell you what, I'll help you any way I can. How's that?"

"Thanks, Dad. Could we pick 'em up next week some time?"

With a nod of his father's head and a smile, he opened the truck door. "Let's get this feed unloaded. Those cows and chickens are hungry."

The weekend came and went. Guyiser and his father had worked hard at the swap meet and were happy with their sales. It was late Sunday night as they sat around the kitchen table talking and laughing about the customers. Mr. Blackman pulled out his brown paper bag and poured out all the money on the table. He spread it out as Guyiser watched. "You count the change, and I'll count the bills. The count should be better than last week's."

Guyiser took out a black notebook from the drawer. "I counted eighteen dollars and fifty cents. How much you count?"

Mr. Blackman looked at Guyiser, and then at the stack of dollar bills. He leaned back in his chair and patted his stomach. "We did real good. Put down in that book that we made three hundred seventy-two dollars and fifty cents. Your share, I figure, is fifty-six dollars." Guyiser didn't know how he figured this out, but he was happy. As Guyiser counted his money, he thought about the alleys they had worked in. He looked at the cuts on his hands from broken glass and the trash he had plowed through. But it was now all worth it. He looked at his father drinking cheap wine from the bottle. "Can we go back to Nashville soon? I want to pick up some of Mr. Gibson's old bicycles."

Mr. Blackman looked at the almost empty bottle, "I think about Wednesday, yeah, Wednesday."

It was eleven o'clock Sunday night. The movie had just ended on T.V., and the news was coming on. Guyiser lay on the floor counting his money and watching a woman reporter. "And now, to our local news. Nashville is growing faster than any city in Tennessee. New jobs for more people, more housing, and more children mean more schools, and more buying power for stores..." Guyiser looked at his money. *Kids need bicycles.*

Monday morning Guyiser opened the barn doors and looked at all the mess. Where to start?

His mind was whirling: *A large work area, a storage area, a sales area,* -- make a plan, work a plan. He could see bikes over there. An office over there. A work area here. *It's perfect. It's perfect!*

Guyiser worked all day in the barn cleaning out cow shit and moving chicken pens. With scraps of boards and planks, he nailed up holes in the walls. *Some paint would look good in here. A rack for the bicycles. A four by eight sheet of plywood would make a good worktable, and I'll hang tools on the wall.* All night he worked. Tuesday morning he woke up in a haystack in the barn. So much to do. All day he nailed things, made things, shoveled stuff, raked stuff, and painted walls. The sun was almost down. Guyiser sat on a bale of hay looking at what he had accomplished. He was pleased and wanted to show his father his new bike shop.

Standing outside the barn, Guyiser and his father looked over the double doors of the barn. "This is where my sign is going. Now I want to show you my bike shop." With pride, Guyiser swung open the large doors. "Come on in and check it out." As they walked through the barn, Guyiser did not say a word; he only looked at his father's face. "You know there's a leak over there. It leaks over here too, but we can fix them."

Mr. Blackman smiled from ear to ear, "I'm proud of you, boy. You did good, but where is my office?" Guyiser punched his father's arm. His father punched him back, and soon they were hugging. "We'll go into town tomorrow and see your Mr. Gibson."

"Thanks, Dad, I love you."

Wednesday morning's sun came brightly over the hills of the farm. Guyiser sat in his tree as the cool morning air gave him a chill. The day's sun became brighter and brighter. Guyiser sat looking at his leather pouch. He now had over forty-five dollars. He counted it out. With what his father had given him, he had one hundred and one dollars and eighty cents. He didn't know what the bikes would cost. *I hope I can buy maybe five bikes and some parts and some paint.* He climbed down the tree and ran to the house. Mr. Blackman was sleeping on the couch as Guyiser came in.

"Wake up, Dad. It's Wednesday, and we got to go to town."

After some coffee and biscuits with honey and syrup, the old truck was on its way down the bumpy, dusty old road. They were singing as they rode along, "We'll be coming 'round the mountain when we come, we'll be coming 'round the mountain when we come." Guyiser broke into his own version: "We'll be hauling some old bicycles; we'll be hauling some old bicycles, when we come." They both broke into laughter.

Mr. Blackman spit out the window and turned to Guyiser, "Now whatever you do, don't spend all your money. Save some for a rainy day. You might need something you don't even know about, you hear me?"

"Thanks, I'll remember that." It wasn't long before they reached the top of the hill of Nashville. Guyiser stuck his head out the window and read the sign, "Nashville City Limits." "Yahoo! Yahoo!"

Nashville streets were busy as they drove into town. Guyiser could see the sign of the bike shop.

"There it is Dad, there!" Mr. Gibson was sweeping the sidewalk as they parked. "Mr. Gibson, good morning, sir. You remember me?"

"I sure do. You're Guyiser Blackman. How are you?"

"I'm fine, sir. This is my Dad."

"Mr. Blackman, nice to meet you. You have a smart young man here. Ya'll come on in." The little bell tinkled as they walked in. "So, what can I do for you today?"

Guyiser smiled at his father and at Mr. Gibson.

"I want to buy some of those bicycles out back. I got a place to work on them in our barn. I want to fix 'em up and sell 'em like you do."

Mr. Gibson looked at Mr. Blackman and at Guyiser. "So you want to be my competition; well, competition is good for business." Mr. Gibson grinned, "What do you need?"

Guyiser was ready for his questions, "Sir, I would like to start with five bicycles, two girls' bikes, and three boys' bikes. How much would you charge me for the frames and parts I need? Your bikes sell for sixty to eighty dollars new, so your old bikes should be at least half that."

Mr. Gibson was surprised at Guyiser's answer. He looked at Mr. Blackman and laughed, "You do have a smart boy here. Well, let me think, Guyiser. Why don't you go out back and pick out what you want. We'll see what you need, and I'll come up with a price for you. How's that?"

Guyiser shook his hand, "Yes sir!" Guyiser was excited. He ran out the back door and started looking through the bikes.

Mr. Gibson turned to Mr. Blackman, "I never saw a boy wanting to fix and sell bicycles. Most boys just want to ride 'em."

Mr. Blackman smiled, "Well, he's kind of an unusual boy."

It didn't take Guyiser long to pick out five bicycles. Some had wheels, some had chains, some had handlebars, but in all they were in good shape. But all of them needed something. Mr. Blackman stood looking at the bikes Guyiser had picked out. "What do you think, Dad? I can fix them like new."

"Looks like a lot of work to me. Let's see what Mr. Gibson has to say."

Mr. Gibson was a man in his sixty's. He was a good church-going man. He loved children. Each year at Christmas time, he would almost give away bicycles to poor kids. He was a rich man who had made his money a long time ago. He owned his shop and the ground it stood on. So, to help other people made him feel good.

Guyiser and his father stood looking at the bikes when Mr. Gibson came out. Guyiser was smiling with excitement, "Well, sir. This is it. What do you think?"

Mr. Gibson walked around looking at the bikes. "Yep, ok, yeah. Are you sure this is what you want? You'll need some fenders, chains, grids, spokes, and maybe a few horns, reflectors, some streamers … Come on in and we'll figure this out." The three of them went in and sat at a small table. Mr. Gibson took out a notepad and began to write down things and numbers.

Guyiser watched as Mr. Gibson added, subtracted, and doubled. He tore the paper from the pad and slid it over to Guyiser. Guyiser looked at his father, at Mr. Gibson, and at the paper.

After several minutes, he shook his head and looked at Mr. Gibson, "I can't believe your price for five bicycles and parts. Are you sure you didn't make a mistake in your adding?" Guyiser looked at the paper again, "This paper says you want a hundred dollars for five complete bicycles."

Mr. Gibson took the paper back, "Don't you think that's fair? It that too much?"

Guyiser stood up and grabbed Mr. Gibson's hand, "No sir. I think that's very fair."

Mr. Gibson added, "You know that's a lot of work for you. It'll take you a couple of months to put them together, and then you'll have to sell them."

Guyiser looked at his father and at Mr. Gibson. "Sir, when I finish with them, they will sell themselves." Mr. Gibson liked Guyiser and his energy. He stood on the back steps watching Guyiser and his father load and tie down the bikes. Guyiser went up to Mr. Gibson and pulled out the leather pouch of money and started to count, "Here's the hundred dollars you wanted."

Mr. Gibson took the money and noticed Guyiser was holding a dollar and some change. "Son, you're going to need some extra things, you know. Here, take this twenty back. It will be a loan. Pay me later."

Guyiser slowly took the money, "Are you sure?"

"I'm sure. Do you need anything else?"

Guyiser looked at the bikes in the truck.

"Well sir, I could use a spoke wrench."

Mr. Gibson smiled and reached into his apron, taking out a small tool. "Here, I'll loan you this one, but I want it back." He laughed, "Thank you, Guyiser, for doing business with me. Let me know how you're doing, ok?"

Guyiser's father called to Guyiser and Mr. Gibson, "Nice to meet you, Mr. Gibson. Everything is tied down, Guyiser. You drive the truck down to the end of the block, and I'll meet you there." Guyiser waved to Mr. Gibson and looked back at all the bicycles as he slowly drove away. His father stood on the corner with a brown bag in his hand. Guyiser stopped and Mr. Blackman got in and patted the bag with a smile.

"Something for you, something for me." Ten miles down the road, Mr. Blackman pulled out a bottle of wine and took a big drink.

Guyiser looked at him but did not say a word.

The hot old sun was high in the sky as the truck turned into the farm's dusty driveway. "I'll unload, Dad. I know where everything goes."

His father nodded and walked to the house. "Feed the chickens, Guyiser." It took about two hours to unload and put everything in its place. Guyiser sat on a bale of hay, looking at the bikes. *It's looking like a bike shop*, he thought.

Weeks turned into a month. Guyiser and his father were busy almost every day going through alleys looking for things they could fix and resell. At night, Guyiser would work on the bikes. He was good at fixing things, so bike after bike became easier for him to repair. By the end of the month, he had repaired and completed two bikes and had almost finished the third. They looked great. He had names for them. One he called Speed Man and another he called Faster. The girls' bike he called "Lady Thriller." One bike was all black. It had no fenders but had knobby tires for off-road riding. This was his tough bike, and he named it "Mountain Man." There were four bikes he would always build and carry in his line of bicycles.

One evening Mr. Blackman came into the barn where Guyiser was working on his Mountain Man bike. "My, my, you're really serious about this, ain't you?" He looked at the girls' bike, "Lady Thriller." "That's a good name when you are going to start selling them."

Guyiser tightened a spoke and spun the wheel. "I want to finish one more; then I'll put out some flyers."

"Well son, I like what you're doing. Keep it up."

It was Sunday afternoon, some weeks later. Guyiser sat looking at his first four finished bicycles. He had found great pride in his work. All of the bikes were perfect. They stood on their kickstands all shiny. Guyiser sat eating an apple and looking over each one of them.

A horn sounded. He went to the door and saw a truck coming in the driveway. As the truck got closer, he could see it was Mr. Gibson. Guyiser ran to meet him and as he stopped, he said, "Mr. Gibson, what a surprise! It's good to see you." Mr. Gibson, with cane in hand, got out and shook Guyiser's hand. "Come on in, sir."

Mr. Gibson looked at the sign above the barn doors, "Guyiser's Bike Shop." "I like it. How are things going?"

"I'm great, sir. And things are going great, too. Come on in." Mr. Gibson was amazed as he entered the barn. He looked at the four beautiful bikes standing side by side. He saw a work area with a bike upside down Guyiser had been working on. He saw some tools on the wall and heard a radio playing music. In a corner was a small desk with a lamp.

"You know, Guyiser, this reminds me of my first shop. I'm impressed, really impressed. I think your work shows what kind of man you are."

Guyiser watched him walk around, looking at everything. "I'm glad you're here, Mr. Gibson. I'm at a place where I could use some advice. Could we sit and talk a minute?" Bales of hay were their chairs.

"Anything I can do, Guyiser. Just ask."

Guyiser gathered his thoughts, "Well, I'm ready to sell my bikes, and I have a flyer made up. I'll show you."

He went to his desk and got the flyer, handing it to Mr. Gibson.

Mr. Gibson studied the flyer. "Not bad, but you should say 'their bikes, seventy dollars, my bikes, fifty-five dollars.' I like your four groups. "Lady Thriller," that's great and "Mountain Man" should sell. Put all sizes on the flyer. But as I sit here, I see you selling your entire stock fast, then what? You need more bicycles. You need an inventory of bicycles. Tell you what. Next week sometime, come to my shop and get five or six more frames and parts. I'll give you credit. Pay me later. I believe you will make a good business partner."

Guyiser sat there not believing what he was hearing. He was getting more bikes and credit. He was getting a friend. "Mr. Gibson, I don't know what to say." Mr. Gibson looked around the barn and at Guyiser. "You don't have to say anything, Guyiser. I can see. I can see."

With new flyers, Guyiser rode one of his new bicycles to Centerville. He put flyers all over town. He went to the high school. He gave out flyers to kids playing in the streets. He put them in mailboxes and left some at gas stations. It was late evening when he returned with sore legs. He put the bike in the barn and went to the house. As he entered the house, he saw his father sleeping on the couch. The T.V. was on and an empty bottle of wine was on the floor. Guyiser closed the door and went back to the barn. He lay down on the hay and soon fell fast asleep.

It was Tuesday morning. Nashville's sky was a sunny blue as Guyiser and his father parked in the alley behind Mr. Gibson's Bike Shop. Guyiser's eyes grew wide open as he saw the bicycles. They were in better condition than the ones before. There were red, blue, and white ones, and they looked great. Guyiser knocked on the back door and was excited to see all the bikes. At the click of the door, Mr. Gibson opened it. "Well, Guyiser. It's good to see you." He waved to Mr. Blackman sitting in the truck.

"Good morning, Mr. Gibson. I'm back like you said."

"Well, there they are. Help yourself. Oh, yes. I have some baskets for the bikes to give you." Mr. Gibson heard the little bell tinkle. "Customer got to go."

Guyiser quickly picked out six bikes. *Wow! These don't need so much work.*

He started loading them into the truck.

Mr. Blackman got out of the truck. "Need help?"

"No, Dad. I can handle these."

Mr. Blackman started walking down the alley.

"I'll be back. Going to the store." Guyiser knew what for.

Mr. Gibson came out with five new bicycle baskets, "Here, these will make the bikes look good and will help to sell them. Just sign my paper for 'em." Guyiser read the paper and signed it.

Six bikes, five baskets, and parts. "Wow! These are just what the bikes need. Thank you, sir"

"Yep and here are some streamers. Ain't they pretty?"

Guyiser took them and held them up, "Really pretty. Oh, Mr. Gibson, I did what you said about the flyers.

I passed them out everywhere. Grand opening in two weeks."

Mr. Gibson could see Guyiser's excitement. "You'll do good, Guyiser. Don't worry about a thing. I have a customer, so I have to get back. Good luck and I'll see you later." Guyiser looked at all the bicycles. Yeah, Good Luck.

Days and nights passed as Guyiser worked in his shop. The more he worked on the bikes, the more he enjoyed standing back and looking at what he had made. He now had a real bike shop. He had made a future for himself and still had many dreams. He went outside the barn and closed the doors. He wanted to see what his customers would see when they entered his shop. Slowly he opened the double doors. He stood looking at eight shiny new bicycles of red, blue, gold, silver, and black. There were boys' bikes, girls' bikes, and a tricycle. He amazed himself. He looked at the work area, his small office, and a counter he had built. A sign on the wall said, "Welcome." A little tear came to his eyes. He was so happy as he took a big breath.

Supper that night was breakfast. They sat at the kitchen table eating eggs, bacon, biscuits, gravy, and syrup washed down with coffee and milk. Guyiser was a little sad. "Dad, do you miss ma?"

Mr. Blackman was surprised at this. He looked at Guyiser and kept eating, "Sure I do. Why do you ask something like that?"

Guyiser stood and put his plate in the sink. "I don't know. I just wish she were here with us. I'd like her to see my shop."

Mr. Blackman leaned back in his chair. "Guyiser, I think she is here. You know you have a lot of your mother in you. It shows in things you do, in the way you think. That's what makes you special, and you are special to me, son."

The First Sale

Part 2

"I'm on my way," he was heard to say,
The sun was bright on this special day.
Two bikes down and a million to go,
I can do it, I know, I know...

The big day finally came for Guyiser Blackman's "Grand Opening." It was eight o'clock on Saturday morning as a cloud passed by the sun. Guyiser sat on a bale of hay outside the barn eating an apple and looking down the dirt driveway. The parking area was raked smooth and ready for cars and trucks. He sat waiting and waiting. Nine o'clock came. He heard and then saw a truck coming over the hill in a cloud of dust. Guyiser stood up and watched the truck pass the driveway and disappear down the road. It was ten twenty as Guyiser looked at his pocket watch.

Another truck topped the hill. He closed his eyes and crossed his fingers. As he opened his eyes, he saw a truck pull into the driveway. There were two boys standing in the bed of the truck waving. The truck stopped and the two boys jumped out. A man got out as the boys ran to Guyiser. "Hi, is this your bike shop?"

"Hi guys, yes it is. Come on in." The boys ran inside as the man walked to Guyiser.

"We saw your flyer and wanted to see your bicycles, but we're just looking."

"Yes sir, help yourself."

It didn't take long until the boys found bikes they liked. "Daddy, I want this one." It was a Mountain Man bike. The other boy liked the silver bike called Speed Man.

Guyiser went to one of the boys. "Here, let me adjust the seat for you, and you can ride it around in the parking area." The other boy was already riding around.

The man turned to Guyiser, "How much?"

"Well, for both it will be a hundred and ten, but it's my grand opening so I'll take off ten dollars."

The man thought for a second, "Sounds good to me, but I don't want the boys to know I bought 'em. I'll pick them up later. I want to surprise 'em. Hold them for me. I'll pay you Monday when I pick 'em up."

Guyiser was happy with the sale, but he thought about it for a minute. "I'll be glad to hold 'em for you, but I need a small deposit."

The man reached in his pocket and gave Guyiser two twenty dollar bills. "Is that good?"

"Yes sir, that's fine." Guyiser went to his desk and wrote a receipt stating that forty had been paid and there was a balance of sixty. They shook hands.

"Let's go, boys." The boys put the bikes back in the rack.

"But Daddy, we liked both of them."

"Not today. We're just lookin'. Let's go." The man winked at Guyiser. "Thanks."

Mr. Blackman was sitting on the front porch swinging and drinking from his bottle. Guyiser came running to him. "I did it. I sold two bikes." He was waving the two twenty dollar bills.

"I adjusted the seat for 'em, and they rode the bikes, and I did it!"

It was one o'clock. Guyiser sat on his bale of hay thinking about his first sale and looking at the money. A car pulled into the driveway and up to the barn. A girl and her mother got out and walked to Guyiser.

"Hi, I got your flyer in our mailbox. Have you got a girl's bicycle?" Guyiser's mouth dropped open. The girl was beautiful. She had long blond curly hair with two pink bows in her hair. She had on a blue and pink dress with flowers on it. She wore white shoes and socks. Guyiser took all of this in as she spoke.

"My name is Cindy. Are you Guyiser?" Guyiser could not speak.

Her mother spoke to Guyiser, "Are you all right?"

"Yes ma'am, I huh, I'm, Yes ma'am. I have girls' bicycles. I'll show you." Guyiser motioned them in. They walked in and looked around. Cindy and Guyiser kept looking at each other. She could see that they were about the same age.

"Don't you go to school in Centerville?"

Guyiser nodded, "Not all the time; just one or two days a week. Do you?" Cindy nodded yes. Guyiser looked at the bicycles. "This is one of my girls' bicycles. I call it my "Lady Thriller." I have three to choose from. There's a red one, a blue one, and a white one with a basket, but I can put a basket on any one you like." Shyness came over Guyiser. He thought he was talking too much.

Cindy looked at all the bikes. "Oh, I like this blue one. What do you think, Mother?"

She looked at it, "Well Honey, you're the one who will ride it. Whatever you say is fine."

Cindy turned to Guyiser and smiled, "What do you think?"

"Blue is my favorite color. I think you would look great on it. I'll adjust the seat for you." Guyiser went to get his wrench.

"Cindy, he's cute. A little shy, but cute."

They giggled. "I know, Mother."

Guyiser raised the seat. "Try that." Cindy got on the bike and rode out of the barn. Guyiser watched her every move. He had had a date before and had been around girls, but Cindy was different. She had spirit and beauty with her candy blue eyes and great smile. Her mother and Guyiser watched Cindy ride around the parking area. She got off the bike and walked back to them.

"I like it. It rides so smooth. Can I have a basket?"

Guyiser smiled really big, "You sure can."

"I like it too, Honey. Mr. Guyiser, how much?"

Guyiser was looking at Cindy. His mind was on her, not on the bike. "How much? uhh, only fifty dollars." He turned to Cindy, "And I'll deliver it free." The sale was made.

Cindy's mother wrote Guyiser a check. Guyiser looked at the check she had signed. "Thank you, Mrs. Taylor. It's been a pleasure meeting you." Guyiser shook Cindy's hand. Her hand was soft. He could feel blood rushing to his head. "When can I see you again? I mean when can I deliver the bike?"

Cindy looked at her mother, "Well, tomorrow about two o'clock, and you can have supper with us."

This was too much for Guyiser. He squeezed her hand. "That would be great."

With a red face and a big smile, "That would be great."

"Oh, we live just two miles down the road on the left. It is a big white house. See you tomorrow."

The sun finally set and a quarter-moon came out. Romance had struck Guyiser. The sale of bikes crossed his mind but as Guyiser fell asleep, only Cindy Taylor was on his mind.

Clouds had rolled in over the hills that Sunday morning. It looked and smelled like rain was coming. Guyiser sat at his small desk in the barn writing in his sales book. His leather pouch was no longer in the tree house, but it was hanging on a nail behind him.

He opened the pouch and reached into his pocket. He pulled out the two twenties and the check. He sat looking at them. "I'm on my way," he shouted as he put the money in the pouch.

Guyiser sat at his worktable making a sign. "Bike shop closed on Sunday, open Monday." He walked down the driveway and put the sign on the gate. He ran back to the house as Mr. Blackman came out. "Dad, I've sold three bicycles and going to deliver one today. Can I use the truck?"

Mr. Blackman stumbled down the steps with a bottle in his hand. He looked at Guyiser and saw the joy and excitement on his face. "I'm proud of you, boy. Sure you can—just be careful."

Guyiser went to the barn. He dusted off the blue bike and loaded it in the truck. He sat on a bale of hay looking up at the sky. *Yep, it's going to rain tonight.*

It was one thirty on Guyiser's pocket watch.

He climbed into the truck. His hair was combed, his boots were clean, and his light blue shirt and blue jeans were pressed. The ride was only two miles down the road, but he didn't want to be late. He drove slowly as he thought to himself. *Maybe I shouldn't stay for supper. I should just deliver the bike, say thank you, and just leave. But, I don't want to be rude.*

The ten-minute ride took twenty minutes as Guyiser turned into the Taylor's driveway. He parked and honked the horn. Cindy appeared at the door. "Hi, Guyiser." She walked to the truck as he got out.

"Hi Cindy, you sure look nice today. I mean you looked nice yesterday, but you still look nice today." They stood looking at each other.

"You look nice too, Guyiser." Guyiser could not speak. He only stood there red-faced with his hands in his pockets. "I'll get your bike down." He climbed into the truck's bed and untied the ropes. He lifted the bike down to the ground and jumped from the truck.

"It's beautiful," said Cindy as she walked around touching her new bike. Maybe we could go for a ride together sometime."

Guyiser grinned, "Yeah."

Mrs. Taylor came out on the porch, "Hi, Guyiser. You two come on in. Supper is on the table." With that, she went back in the house.

Guyiser sat at the table looking at all the food.

He saw fried chicken, mashed potatoes, corn, beans, cornbread, stuffing, iced tea, and banana pie. It had been forever since he had seen a table set with all this kind of food. They all sat looking at each other. Mrs. Taylor said the blessing. Small talk and laughter made the food taste better. Mrs. Taylor handed Guyiser the bowl of mashed potatoes. "So, Guyiser, what do you want to do when school is over?"

This caught him off guard, "I don't know, ma'am. Maybe I will keep working in my bike business."

Cindy looked at Guyiser, "I want to go to college to study communications. I want to work in T.V or radio broadcasting, you know?"

Mrs. Taylor stood and picked up some dishes, "More pie, Guyiser?"

Guyiser smiled and patted his stomach, "I've had plenty, thank you ma'am."

"So why don't you two go sit on the porch? I'll clean up."

Cindy and Guyiser stood up. "Everything sure was good, Mrs. Taylor. Thanks for having me over."

"Come on, Guyiser. Let's go out. Mother loves to clean up."

The old swing made a squeaking sound as they sat swinging. Cindy looked to the sky. "It's going to rain."

Guyiser was looking at her. "Yep, we could use some rain." They sat swinging and looking at the clouds.

All of a sudden, Cindy jumped from the swing, "Let's go to the barn. There's something I want to show you." Cindy grabbed Guyiser's hand, "Come on."

They ran to the barn and went inside. The smell of the hay mixed with the smell of the coming rain. Cindy led Guyiser into a cow stall. His eyes opened wide as he saw a mother dog and her five puppies in the hay. Cindy sat down and petted the mother. "This is Mandy and her pups." She picked up one of them. "They are so soft; I just love them." Guyiser sat down, looking at the pups having their dinner. Cindy kissed the pup she was holding. "These are German Shepherds, and they're only five weeks old." Cindy handed the pup to Guyiser, "He's a he." The pup was soft. His fur was black, brown, and white. He had silver feet. The pup licked Guyiser's face. "He likes you. Do you want him?" Cindy became a little sad. "We have to give them away."

Guyiser looked at Cindy and the pup.

"I've never had a dog. I wouldn't know what to do with him."

"Silly boy, there are lots of things to do with him. You can play together, you can teach him tricks, and you can talk to him. He can be your friend."

Guyiser held the pup high in the air and looked him over. A friend. I don't have a friend. "I don't know if I can keep him, Cindy. What would I call him?"

Cindy looked at the pup and at Guyiser. "Well, if you don't know if you can keep him, just call him "Loaner." Guyiser and Cindy laughed.

Guyiser held the pup close to him. "Loaner, that's a good name. Are you sure I can have him?"

Cindy and Guyiser again sat on the porch swinging. Guyiser was holding his new friend. "It's been a great day. Thanks for inviting me. Your mother is great, too." Guyiser stroked the puppy's back. "Can I tell you something?" Cindy nodded with a smile on her face. "I sure do like you. I never had a girl for a friend."

The moment was silent. Cindy straightened her dress and looked to the sky. "Well, I never had a boy for a friend before." Two large dark clouds bumped together, and the sound of thunder echoed in the sky. Guyiser looked to the sky. "It's getting dark and I smell rain real strong. So, I'd better get going, me and Loaner. Maybe I can see you soon, if that's all right with you." They stood up looking at each other.

Cindy petted the puppy. "That would be nice." She leaned over and kissed Guyiser's cheek. "Good night, Guyiser, and take good care of Loaner."

Guyiser ran down the steps and got into the truck. Raindrops hit the windshield as he drove away with Loaner on his lap. Guyiser's thoughts were on Cindy and her kiss. The rain came down hard. Her smell, her touch, her laughter all echoed in his head. Loaner made a small whimpering noise. "Don't worry, little fellow. I'll take care of you." The thunder crashed as the truck stopped at the barn.

Guyiser sat in the truck petting his new friend. "It's only rain, Loaner. Let's go inside." Guyiser put Loaner in his shirt and ran to the barn. Inside the barn, it was a little cold. Guyiser made a small nest in the hay and put Loaner in it. "This will be your new home, pal. Are you hungry?" Loaner was shaking in the hay. "You look cold. I'll get you a blanket." Guyiser started to leave but stopped at the door. Loaner scrambled from the hay and ran to Guyiser's feet. He picked up the puppy and kissed him. "You're right. Let's go in the house."

The rain was beating down on the tin roof of the porch as they went in. Mr. Blackman had made a fire in the fireplace and a warm glow filled the room. Guyiser looked around and saw his father sleeping in his favorite chair. The T.V. was on and a woman reporter was saying, "…and the storm is here for at least two days."

Guyiser went to his room and put Loaner on the bed. Loaner whimpered. "I'll be right back." In the kitchen, he got a bowl of milk and a ham bone and then returned to his room. Loaner let out a small bark as Guyiser put him on the floor by the food. He watched Loaner lick the milk and chew on the bone. Loaner's little tummy was full as Guyiser picked him up and put him on the bed. They had fun playing together. With the rain hitting the window and the fire making the house warm, the conditions for sleep were good. Little Loaner was tired out and went to sleep beside Guyiser's warm breath. Guyiser rubbed the soft fur of Loaner and soon fell asleep, too. The bond between Guyiser and Loaner had begun.

The smell of coffee and eggs and bacon cooking filled the morning air. The rain was still coming down and hitting the tin roof. Guyiser woke up to his new friend licking his face. He smiled and pushed the puppy away, but he came back with a small bark and some more licking. "All right, all right, I'm awake." Guyiser lay there putting his thoughts together. A knock on the door made Loaner's ears perk up. He let out a little bark.

"Wake up, Guyiser. Breakfast is ready."

Guyiser stood at the kitchen door with his puppy in his arms. Mr. Blackman was already eating. "Good morning, boy." Mr. Blackman looked up to see Guyiser standing in the doorway. Then he saw the puppy. "What's you got there?" Guyiser, not sure of his father's voice and held the puppy out to his father.

"It's a puppy, Dad. I got him last night. His name is Loaner." Mr. Blackman reached out for the puppy. Guyiser, still not sure of his father, walked to him.

Mr. Blackman took the puppy and looked him over. "He's gonna be a big dog, and I think he's hungry. Give him some eggs and bacon so he'll eat like us." With that, he handed the puppy back to Guyiser and went back to eating his breakfast.

It was eight o'clock that Monday morning. The clouds were still there, but it had stopped raining. Guyiser was working on a bicycle in the barn. Loaner was watching him and chewing on some hay. A small radio was playing music. Guyiser walked over to his desk and sat down. Loaner came over and sat at his feet. Guyiser picked the puppy up and put him on the desk.

He looked at Loaner and thought of Cindy. He looked around the shop and back to Loaner. *We're gonna be all right, Loaner.*

There was a sound of a truck pulling up to the barn. When it stopped, he saw his customer, Mr. Thomas. Guyiser went to greet him. "Good morning, Mr. Thomas. Kind'a wet out there; come on in."

Mr. Thomas entered the shop. "Sure is and was bad last night. I came to get the boys' bicycles, and you know, I want one for myself so I can ride with them."

Guyiser led him over to the bike rack. "Here are your boys' bikes ready to go."

Mr. Thomas looked them over. "Yep, a Mountain Man and a Speed Man." Mr. Thomas walked over to the other bicycles. "That one there, the one called "Faster", that's for me." He looked at Guyiser and winked. "I'm a fast man." They laughed. "And I want two of those baskets."

Guyiser got the baskets off the wall. "Yes sir, I'll put them on for you."

The bikes were loaded on the truck and tied down. "What do I owe you?"

Guyiser went to his desk and wrote out a receipt. As he handed it to Mr. Thomas, he said, "Your balance was sixty dollars, your bike is fifty, and the two baskets are eight each. This gives us a total of one hundred twenty-six dollars."

Mr. Thomas pulled out a wad of money. "Here you are. He looked at Loaner. "He's going to be a big dog. German Shepherd?"

"Yes sir."

"I should get the boys one—builds friendship. Well, got to get down the road. Thanks, Guyiser."

Guyiser shook his hand. "Thank you, Mr. Thomas. It's been nice meeting you. Take care." Guyiser waved as his first customer drove away.

The leather pouch was getting fat. Guyiser hung it back on the nail. He turned back to his desk and wrote in his book. Sold another bicycle. He felt something at his feet. It was Loaner looking up at him. He had caught a small field mouse. The puppy made a little bark.

Guyiser picked up Loaner and held him. "Well, thank you, little friend."

The rain started again. Guyiser knew that business would not happen today. This would be a good day to work on his bikes. Mr. Blackman knocked on the door and came in. "It started again." He shook the rain off his hat. "I got to go into Nashville to do some business, so you and this little dog stay here and watch things, okay?"

Guyiser was putting a chain on a bike. "Okay, Pa. I've got plenty to do around here." The thunder was loud as Mr. Blackman drove off down the muddy driveway. Guyiser put another log in the old potbelly stove and went back to work.

Darkness fell and so did the rain. Guyiser and Loaner were in the house playing. The T.V. was on and fire in the fireplace made the house warm. Guyiser looked at his pocket watch. It was six thirty. Loaner tugged on Guyiser's pant leg. "You hungry? I am. Let's go in the kitchen and see what we can find."

The rain came down heavy on the tin roof as Guyiser made a sandwich and watched Loaner chew on a ham bone.

The fireplace crackled as Guyiser sat in his father's chair with Loaner on his lap. "Hey, little fellow, I wonder where Dad is?" Loaner rolled over and went to sleep. Guyiser watched a movie until he dozed off. Later, he barely heard the eleven o'clock news. "The rain is still here and won't go away." The fire in the fireplace went slowly down. The long day had ended.

The morning news was on as Guyiser rubbed his eyes. The sky was cloudy gray, but the rain had stopped. Loaner barked at the door and ran to Guyiser.

Guyiser looked around and shouted for his father. "Pa, you home? Pa!" There was no answer.

The house was cold. Guyiser started a fire in the fireplace. Loaner barked again. "You want to go out?" Guyiser opened the door as Loaner ran out. Guyiser watched him for a moment and turned to hear the T.V., "Roads are washed out from Memphis to Nashville. People have been caught in flash floods. Three are reported dead." Guyiser's heart dropped. He went out on the porch and looked down the driveway. Guyiser and his father were very close since his mother's death.

While looking down the road, he realized how little he knew about his father. His father was a goodhearted man. He didn't talk about his life. He didn't talk about his business. He was an easy-going man, and if someone needed something, he was there. Guyiser stood on the porch worrying about his father. He tried to assure himself. You're okay, Pa. Come on home. Loaner barked at Guyiser. "You hungry again?" Guyiser picked him up. "Look at you, all wet and muddy." They went into the house. "Let's get you cleaned up." Guyiser was washing the dishes when Loaner started barking again. He ran to Guyiser and then to the door. He kept barking. "What now? You want to go out again?" The old truck pulled into the driveway and up the muddy road honking as it neared. Guyiser ran to the door and saw the truck park. "Pa, Pa, you're home. Where have you been?" Guyiser ran to his father and hugged him. "I've been so worried."

Mr. Blackman smiled and laughed. "I'm all right, boy. Had to spend the night in Nashville. The roads here are washed out. Help me unload this stuff. I got some dog food for your dog and food for us."

That evening they sat around in the living room. Mr. Blackman was watching a movie, Guyiser was reading a book, and Loaner was playing with a rubber ball. Guyiser looked at his father, "I'm glad you're all right. I love you, and I was scared for you, Dad."

His father was still watching T.V. A few minutes had passed. Mr. Blackman went to the fireplace and put a log on the fire. He went back to his chair. "You know, it's your birthday next month. What would you like for your birthday present?"

Guyiser was surprised. He put down his book and looked at his father. "I forgot about that. I got my bike shop." Loaner barked. "I got me a dog. I met a girl. I got you. I don't really need anything—maybe a shirt and jeans, but not overalls. I don't like overalls anymore. They make me look funny."

Mr. Blackman leaned back in his chair and closed his eyes. "Well, if you think of something, let me know."

A week passed by fast. Guyiser had all the bikes ready for sale. The rain had passed, but a chill stayed in the air. The leaves on the trees were changing color. Loaner's short legs were getting longer. Guyiser and Loaner often ran in the fields. However, Guyiser missed something. Every time he looked and played with Loaner, he saw Cindy. He sat on a bale of hay with Loaner at his feet. "What say you and me go see Cindy and your mother tomorrow?" Loaner jumped on Guyiser's legs and barked.

The dull sun was trying to peek out, but the gray skies were still there. Guyiser was playing with Loaner in the field. He was teaching Loaner to sit, fetch, stay, and to be his friend. Loaner was learning fast to respond to his master's voice, whistle, and hand commands. The old tree house stood tall as Guyiser climbed up the branches to the board seat he had made. He laughed at Loaner as he looked down watching the big puppy circle the tree. The leaves were a beautiful red and yellow. They would fall off when the wind blew. Guyiser teased Loaner, "Come on, boy. Climb." Loaner jumped on the tree and barked. All of a sudden, Loaner changed his attention to something else. He ran from the tree a few feet and began to bark and bark. Loaner looked at Guyiser and continued barking. "What is it, boy? You see a rabbit?" Guyiser looked around as Loaner's bark grew stronger. Then he saw what Loaner was barking about.

He saw two men walking around the tree line way over in the west field. He watched for a minute, but he couldn't tell what the men were doing. They were too far away. Guyiser climbed down from the tree. He called to Loaner who was still barking. "Good boy. Come on, Come on." They ran back to the house and ran inside. "Dad, where are you.? Mr. Blackman was in the kitchen at the table, looking through a catalog. "Dad, there are two men down on the west side in the trees."

Mr. Blackman quickly got up and ran to the fireplace. His shotgun hung above it. He quickly loaded it with two shotgun shells. He grabbed his coat and turned to Guyiser, "You stay here! Stay here, you hear me, boy?" With that, he ran out of the house. Guyiser went to the window and watched his father run toward the west part of the farm. His father disappeared over the hillside. It took Mr. Blackman a while to run over the hills and into the fields. As he topped the second hill, he saw the two men in the tree line. He knew what they were doing. With shotgun aimed at the men, he approached them. The men saw him coming. "Looking for something? I ask you, you looking for something?" Mr. Blackman raised the shotgun and aimed it at them. "You trying to rip me off, ain't you?" The two men looked at each other. "But I already harvested it all. Is that what you're here for?"

The men stood there with empty bags in their hands. "No, Blackman, you got it all wrong. We came to buy."

Mr. Blackman cocked the hammer on the shotgun. "Buy, my ass. Get off my property or I'll shoot you where you stand. Now get!" The men turned and walked away. They climbed the fence, got in their truck, and drove away. Mr. Blackman stood there and watched them until they were out of sight. Guyiser opened the door as Mr. Blackman stepped on the porch.

"What did they want, Pa?"

Mr. Blackman entered the house. He went to the fireplace and hung the gun back in its place. He turned to Guyiser and took off his coat. "Hunters, just hunters. Lost. It's okay." Mr. Blackman went back to the kitchen, sat at the table, and continued looking at his catalog.

Guyiser could feel that something was wrong. His father's voice was angry, and besides, it was not hunting season. Nevertheless, he let it go. He and Loaner headed for the barn. Inside, Guyiser got a Mountain Man bike from the rack. "Let's go visiting, Loaner."

The dog barked and ran to the door. As Guyiser rode down the road singing, Loaner ran ahead of him. A short fifteen minutes later, Guyiser saw the Taylor mailbox. He rode up the drive to the big house. It was a nice big house with a white picket fence. Mandy barked and ran to meet them. Loaner and Mandy jumped on each other and ran off playing. Guyiser went to the door, brushed his hair back, and knocked. He was surprised when Mrs. Taylor opened the door. "Hi, Mrs. Taylor, how are you?"

Mrs. Taylor saw that Guyiser was surprised and nervous. "Guyiser, what a surprise. I'm fine. Please come in."

Guyiser just wanted a quick visit. "Oh, no thank you, ah, I was just passing by. Cindy here?"

He waited for a yes answer.

"No, I'm sorry, Guyiser. She and her dad went into town to the post office."

Guyiser tried to smile, "That's okay. Just tell her I came by. Thank you, Mrs. Taylor. Bye." Before Mrs. Taylor could say anything, Guyiser was off the porch and on his bike. She watched as he called to Loaner and rode away.

Guyiser sat at his desk in his shop looking around and thinking. He had closed both barn doors. *I need a window so I can see out and see the road. Right there.* He pointed to the boards beside the doors. *That's my project for today.* He went to the shed out back of the house. There he found a large window frame with glass in it. Perfect! Inside the barn, he traced the window frame. Then, he got a saw from off the wall and began to cut some boards. The boards would be a border to hold the window in place. With a hammer, a few nails, and some creative planning, it would soon be finished. Loaner watched as Guyiser hammered in the last nail. He went back to this desk and sat down, looking at his latest accomplishment. Loaner jumped up on the windowsill and looked out. Guyiser sat there smiling and feeling proud of himself.

There was no business that day. *Where are the people? I'd better make a plan. I need to see Mr. Gibson and pay him some money. I need some customers. I need to cut some wood for the fireplace and here. I need to build a fence for the cows. I need a big sign for the gate. I want to see Cindy!*

It was five fifteen that evening, and it was already getting dark. Supper was finished, and Mr. Blackman sat in his favorite chair flipping through channels. Guyiser was putting the food away and washing dishes. Loaner was lying by the fireplace looking at Mr. Blackman. "Dad, what say we go to Nashville tomorrow? I need to see Mr. Gibson." He went into the living room and sat on the couch. "What say?"

Mr. Blackman flipped a few more channels, "Sounds good to me. I need to go in anyway." Mr. Blackman stopped on Channel 4.

The news reporter was a pretty, blond woman. "Thanks for joining us. Here's the "News at Six."" Guyiser stretched out on the couch. *That could be Cindy!* The reporter continued. "A large "pot" bust scored 85 pounds of the stuff in a warehouse in Nashville today. Police say no one was caught."

Mr. Blackman changed the channel. "I'm going to check on the cows." He stood up and went to the door. "Hey, dog, you wanta come; come on." Loaner wagged his tail as he got up and went out with Mr. Blackman.

It was a cloudy morning as the sun tried its best to appear. Guyiser and his father piled into the truck with Loaner in the middle. It was quite a ride. While Guyiser was petting Loaner and making his plan of what to tell Mr. Gibson, Mr. Blackman was totally in his own world. It took what seemed like forever to make the top the long uphill climb. There again stood the sign, "Nashville City Limits." The long ride down the hill ended in Nashville. Guyiser could see "Gibson's Bike Shop" sign as they rounded the corner. "Well, we made it. I'll drop you off at Gibson's.

I got to go to the hardware store. I'll pick you up later." The truck stopped and Guyiser and Loaner got out.

The little bell rang as they went in to the shop. Mr. Gibson was putting a new bike together. "Guyiser, good to see you. Who is your friend?" It seemed like Mr. Gibson was always in a good mood.

"Hi, Mr. Gibson. This is Loaner, my dog."

Mr. Gibson held out his hand to Loaner. Loaner smelled and licked his hand. "He's a fine looking dog. Come on in and sit a while." The shop smelled of warm rubber and of new bikes. "So, what's on your mind today?" They sat in rocking chairs by the potbelly stove.

"Well, sir," Guyiser reached in his coat pocket and pulled out his leather pouch, "first, I want to pay you some money." Guyiser continued, "I sold some bikes."

He opened the pouch and pulled out the cash and check.

"But my problem is that I have no more customers. I have put together all my bikes and they look great. Now, I need business. What do I do?"

Mr. Gibson looked at the money Guyiser had brought. "Well son, the first thing you do is open a bank account. Start building your money and credit. And now for customers," Mr. Gibson rocked in his chair, "A couple of things. The weather has been bad. That keeps people at home. You sell more bicycles in good weather. Remember, you're selling bicycles— not food. People buy food every day. Bicycles are for kids." Mr. Gibson continued, "I have a lot of slow times. When it's slow, I repair bikes. I make up ads and flyers. You know, I sell more bikes during special times of the year like kids' birthdays and summer time, but I sell most of my bikes at Christmas time. That makes my whole year. I'm glad it's coming up soon." Guyiser listened hard to every word and started feeling better. Mr. Gibson shook his finger at Guyiser, "Start your ads and flyers now! And, at Christmas, you'll sell everything. I'll even let you have some of my inventory to sell."

Guyiser had never even thought of the things he was hearing from Mr. Gibson. His mind went wild with ideas. *Christmas ads and flyers. Christmas lights on the barn. Free Christmas trees with the purchase of a bike.* As he rocked in his chair, he could see it all. Mr. Gibson had sparked a fire. Guyiser now knew what he had to do. Loaner was lying at Guyiser's feet. He raised his head and barked as the doorbell rang. It was Mr. Blackman. "There you are. Hello, Mr. Gibson."

Mr. Gibson stood and shook hands with Mr. Blackman. "Hello to you."

Guyiser stood saying, "Dad, you ready to go? I gotta get back. There's a lot of things to do."

Mr. Blackman could see the excitement in Guyiser's face. "Sure boy, let's go." They said their goodbye's and left the store. The ride home was long.

Guyiser was staring straight ahead. "Dad, what is today's date?"

Mr. Blackman had a bottle of wine between his legs. He took a drink, then thought, "Well, it's the 5th day of October." Guyiser counted on his fingers, *October, November, and December. Three months.*

The day was cold and muggy as the truck turned off the road and into the driveway. Guyiser looked to see smoke coming out of the smoke stack of the barn.

They parked the truck in front of the house. Mr. Blackman went in as Guyiser and Loaner headed for the barn. Guyiser opened the door and to his surprise, he saw Cindy standing there. Loaner barked and ran to her. She looked so pretty as she stood there in her powder blue turtle-necked sweater and jeans. Her long blond hair shown with a glow around her head from the fire in the stove. "I hope you don't mind me making a fire."

Guyiser could feel the warm air and the softness in her voice. He went to her and took her hand. "Mind? Heck no. Gosh, it's so good to see you."

Cindy smiled that angel smile of hers and squeezed Guyiser's hand. "I missed you. Mom said you came by." She looked at Loaner.

"Boy, he has grown. How you two getting along?"

Guyiser looked at Loaner and said, "Me."

Loaner walked to Guyiser's side and sat down.

Cindy looked at Loaner and then at Guyiser. "Wow, that's great. Can I try it?" Guyiser nodded. Cindy looked at Loaner, "Me." Loaner did not move.

Guyiser laughed, "He's my dog." And with a smile, "Let's sit down." They sat at the worktable. As they talked, Guyiser told Cindy about Mr. Gibson and his advice. Cindy was excited for Guyiser and wanted to help him with his Christmas ideas.

"I'll bring my sketchpad, some paper, and colored markers in the morning and help you."

Guyiser lit up like a Christmas tree with delight as Cindy talked. "I'd be proud if you could help me, Cindy." They joined hands across the table.

They sat there in silence looking at each other.

Cindy spoke first, "I have to go now. But, I'll see you in the morning." The stood and went to the door. Guyiser watched out the window as Cindy rode her bicycle down the driveway and out of sight.

Another cold morning had opened its eyes as the sun came out over the hills of Tennessee. Guyiser was chopping wood of a big tree that had fallen. Loaner was out running in the fields. Mr. Blackman was throwing hay out for the cows and feeding the chickens. The woodpile was growing as Guyiser kept swinging the ax. Cindy opened the driveway gate and rode up to the barn. She looked for Guyiser and saw Mr. Blackman. "Need some help?" He turned to see Cindy. "Hi sir. I'm Cindy Taylor, a friend of Guyiser's."

Mr. Blackman put down the bushel of chicken feed and walked to her. "Hello there. Nice to meet you. I've heard good things about you." Mr. Blackman looked her over. "I met your daddy in Centerville one time. Guyiser's over there chopping wood behind the barn. Go on over."

Cindy could hear the chopping as she stopped by the barn and watched Guyiser working. His strong arms swung hard as he cut limbs and chopped at the tree. She knocked on the barn, "Hey big boy, what are you doing?"

Guyiser turned to see Cindy leaning against the barn. A big grin came on his face as he put down the ax and walked over to her. He took her hands and kissed her on the cheek. "My, you're a sight for sore eyes!" They looked at each other. "Let's go inside where it's warm. It's cold out here." Guyiser squeezed her hands.

"It's good to see you this morning. I thought about you last night."

Cindy looked at Guyiser, "Me too."

Once inside the barn, Guyiser put a log in the potbelly stove. Cindy was sitting at the worktable where papers and colored markers lay spread out. "Want some hot chocolate? I brought some with me." Cindy took the thermos and two cups from her backpack. Guyiser just stood there watching her as she poured the hot chocolate. She was wearing a pretty, pink soft sweater, which accented her long curly blond hair and pink fingernail polish. Cindy looked at him with her candy blue eyes and an engaging smile that would make any man melt. She held out the cup as Guyiser walked to her.

He held her hand and the cup and looked into her eyes. "Thank you, my lady." He took the cup and bowed to her. About an hour later, Guyiser was writing words that would express Christmas and his bike shop. Cindy was drawing pictures in her sketchpad. She had drawn a picture of a Christmas tree trimmed with lights, red ribbon, and a star at the top. There was also a picture of Santa Claus with a pack on his back. She had just started drawing a large animal when Guyiser slid close to her. "What's that?" Guyiser laughed.

Cindy looked at him, "You silly thing, it's a reindeer." She added the antlers. They laughed together and looked at each other. Then it happened. The kiss. A short one. Then the kiss again, longer—it was the kiss that told that they were going to be lovers. It was a long moment, kiss after kiss. Guyiser's hand roamed under Cindy's sweater.

A loud knock on the barn door and Loaner's barking brought the moment to an end. Mr. Blackman and Loaner came in. Mr. Blackman held up a rabbit. "Look what Loaner caught! Rabbit stew for supper tonight."

Cindy turned to Guyiser, "I have to go. You understand." Cindy stood and put on her coat and scarf. "I'll see you tomorrow, okay?" She walked past Mr. Blackman and Loaner.

"Nice to meet you, Mr. Blackman. It's late and I have to leave." With that, Cindy disappeared out of the barn and down the driveway.

Cindy lay in her bed wide awake that night. Guyiser and his kisses kept running through her mind. She thought of his strong arms around her, the laughs they had shared, the fun of working together, and his warm breath, as they were so near to each other. She thought of the excitement she felt watching Guyiser chopping wood. She rolled on her side looking out her bedroom window. *Could he be the one?* Cindy closed her eyes and fell asleep.

The fire in the potbelly stove warmed the old barn as Guyiser stood at his worktable drinking his coffee and looking at the sketches Cindy had drawn. His eyes lingered on the reindeer, and he heard their laughter. Her warm kisses were still on his mind. Guyiser went to the window and looked down the long driveway. Loaner jumped on the windowsill and barked. Guyiser petted his head, "I hope she comes here today." Loaner looked at Guyiser and barked again.

It was eleven o'clock as Guyiser sat at his worktable cutting out the drawings and placing them around his words for his ad and flyer. *The ad looks great*, he thought. "Christmas at Guyiser's Bike Shop." The ad went on the say, "Free Christmas tree with your new bike. Bring your saw or ax and "You Pick Your Tree." The 35-acre farm had pine and cedar trees all over it. The final ad, with Santa, packages, a Christmas tree, and the reindeer stood out. *Cindy, you're amazing*, he thought.

Guyiser's plan was coming together. He was excited about the flyer. He went outside the barn and stood looking at the big brown building. Loaner sat at his feet. *I'll put lights across the top and down the sides. I'll put lights all around the doors and the window. Maybe I'll put lights along the fence and put a snowman over there. I'll have a sign for over the door, 'Santa's Workshop.'* The kids will love that.

"What do you think, Loaner?"

Mr. Blackman came out of the house and saw Guyiser looking at the barn. He buttoned his jacket and walked over to his son. "What you doing son?"

Guyiser pointed up to the barn. "Making a plan. I want to put Christmas lights there and over there, too. Is that all right with you? Mr. Gibson says Christmas time will sell lots of bikes."

Mr. Blackman put his hands in his coat pocket, looking at the barn. "It's all right with me. I'll even help you. Oh, yeah," Mr. Blackman pulled something out of his pocket, "this is for your dog." Guyiser reached for the small paper bag. He opened it and took out a thick black leather dog collar. It had shiny spike studs on it. Mr. Blackman pointed to the collar. "In case he's in a fight—he'll be protected."

Guyiser hugged his pa. "Thanks, Dad. You do love him, don't you?" Mr. Blackman did not say anything but watched as Guyiser put the collar on Loaner. Loaner was not a little puppy anymore. He had grown into a beautiful German Shepherd. The collar made him look awesome. Loaner ran around them, barking. He seemed happy with the collar and the attention they gave him.

Guyiser stood in the barn by the window. He looked at his pocket watch. It was 3:30 in the afternoon and it was cold. The sky was gray on this October day. He went to his desk and looked at the calendar. He turned the page to November. *Well, let's see. If I pass out flyers this week and again this week, I can place the ad in the Centerville paper on the 20th right before Thanksgiving. I'll place the ad again on December 18th and run it for one week.*

Loaner began to bark and run to the door. Cindy knocked and went in. "Hello, you here?"

Guyiser waved his hands. "Here, here."

He went to Cindy and grabbed her hands.

"I'm sorry I'm so late. School will be out for the holidays soon, and we are having exams."

Guyiser's dull cold day turned warm. "Well, I know you'll pass. Come on in and get warm."

They sat at the worktable talking about the ad and making plans for the barn decorating. The previous day did not come up, but when they looked at each other, they knew. "The ad looks great Guyiser. I want to help you with everything."

Guyiser's confidence began to grow.

"You sure can."

Cindy became excited about the project. "I'll make 100's of copies of the flyer at Daddy's hardware store, free. Then we can ride around passing them out to everybody. And, I have a friend at the Centerville Newspaper. And, we have extra Christmas lights at home, and," Guyiser could not control himself. He grabbed Cindy, kissed her forehead, her cheeks, and then her lips.

The two stood at the doors of the barn. "Thanks for coming today." Guyiser tied her scarf around Cindy's neck.

Cindy put her arms around Guyiser's neck. "No, thank you." She kissed Guyiser, ran to her bicycle, and rode away.

For the next two weeks, Guyiser and his father made the rounds looking for things they could resell. An antique store that Mr. Blackman knew of was closing. He made a deal with the owner on all kinds of things. They hauled things from the store for days. There were old trunks, mirrors, pictures, chairs, tables, dishes, fans, and boxes of whatnot items. Mr. Blackman was happy with his find. He knew he had enough to sell for months.

It was late October as Guyiser and Loaner were playing in the house. Mr. Blackman had gone into Centerville to buy some tarps to cover the chicken house. Loaner barked and ran to the door. A station wagon pulled in the driveway and stopped at the barn. Guyiser put on his coat and went out. A man and his wife got out as Guyiser approached. "Good afternoon. How are you today?"

The man spoke up, "You open today? We're looking for bicycles for our boys."

Guyiser opened the door. "Yes sir, come on in." Inside they looked at the bicycles.

"Our boys are three and five. We need one with training wheels and one without."

Guyiser went to the bike rack and pulled out a shiny red bike with chrome training wheels on it. He rolled it over so they could have a better look. "Your three-year old could ride this one for years."

The woman looked at the bike and tooted the horn. "I like this one, Frank."

Guyiser went back to the bike rack and pulled out a Mountain Man bike. "How about this one for your older boy?"

As he rolled it over to them, the man shook his head, "No, it's too big for him."

Guyiser thought for a moment and then went back to the bike rack. "I think I have one just his size." He walked to the worktable. There was a small bike with chrome fenders, a horn, and a light. The streamers on the handlebar grips were colorful. As he rolled it to them he said, "This bike is the right size I think, and it doesn't have a crossbar. That's a safety feature in case he falls. I can add a basket on the front for carrying things."

The man walked to the bike and stood beside it. "It's the right size okay. What do you think, Hun?"

His wife looked at the bike. She thought of a bicycle she had had as a little girl. "Oh, he'll love it!"

Guyiser turned to the man. "It looks kinda like a girl's bike."

Guyiser looked at the bike.

"That's because there is no crossbar in the center."

The man looked at the bike again. "Well, I guess he could get on and off easier. How much?"

Taking the check, Guyiser went to his desk and wrote a receipt. "Did you want a basket?" He smiled at them.

They loaded the bikes into the station wagon. They shook hands, said goodbye, and drove away. Guyiser stood by the barn and waved to them. He looked at the check. Two more sold! He went to his desk and wrote in his book. Sure, it was a small girl's bike, but his salesmanship had paid off and everyone was happy.

Mr. Blackman had not gone to Centerville. Instead, he had gone to Nashville to see Mr. Gibson.

The small bell rang as Mr. Blackman entered Gibson's Bike Shop. Mr. Gibson greeted him with a warm handshake. "Well, this is a surprise. Come on in." He looked at the door.

"Where is Guyiser?"

Mr. Blackman informed him that he was home, and he had come to talk with Mr. Gibson. The two men sat in the store and talked. Mr. Blackman spoke first. "It's Guyiser's birthday next month and I got something for him. I would like to leave it here at your shop." He went on explaining his surprise to Mr. Gibson who gladly agreed to help. Everything was set.

On the way back home, Mr. Blackman stopped and bought his tarps. He left the store and climbed into his truck. Two men came up to the truck. "Blackman, we want to talk to you." He saw anger in the man's face and voice. "You turned us in, didn't you? We lost a lot of money because of you. The cops took it all."

The second man spoke up, "And you're gonna pay us back."

Mr. Blackman reached under the seat for his gun. "I didn't turn anybody in. People could smell your pot all over the block. It's your own fault. You're just stupid!" The two men saw the gun in his hand and backed off.

"We're gonna get you, Blackman. You keep lookin' over your shoulder. We'll get you." The two men backed off and walked away. Mr. Blackman sat in his truck and watched them. A small smile crossed his face as he started the truck and drove away.

Cindy's bicycle basket was full and running over with 100's of flyers and Christmas lights as she peddled up the driveway to Guyiser's shop. Guyiser ran to meet her. They kissed and walked to the barn. Inside, they sat at the worktable looking at the finished flyers. "This is great, Cindy. This colored flyer will attract everybody." Cindy was as excited as Guyiser was. "I added this." She pointed to the flyer. 'Highway 70 to Guyiser's Bike Shop. Just west 7 miles from Centerville. Merry Christmas.'

Guyiser turned to Cindy, "I love it! And you for all this work. Thank you."

She picked up one of the flyers and looked it over. "I'm glad you like them. If you want, we can start passing them out next week. School is out for me, and I want to help you, okay?" The look between them told it all. "I gotta go. Mother wants me to go to the store with her." She got on her bike and rode down the road waving at Guyiser. "See you later."

Guyiser stood and watched her ride away.

"See you later," he whispered.

November came in with the coldest temperatures ever. The cloudy gray sky blanketed the hills of Tennessee. Guyiser and Loaner were rough housing on the floor. Loaner was so strong. He could pin Guyiser down with his strong legs and weight. Guyiser lay with Loaner on top of him. He looked his dog straight in his eyes. "When you hear the word protect me. "Now," Guyiser whispered, "Now!" Loaner's ears went back; his strength grew along with his increasing growling. His mouth opened. His long white teeth increased the threat. His growls were now more furious. His eyes pinned Guyiser. He could feel the threat in this monster dog. Guyiser quickly spoke to Loaner. "Me, Me! Relax Loaner.

Loaner slowly relaxed his growl. His eyes changed. His large mouth closed. His tense muscles began to relax. Loaner got off the top of Guyiser and barked in triumph. He circled Guyiser and lay down beside him. Guyiser felt relieved about what had just happened. He petted Loaner and gave him praise. "Good boy, Good boy." He could only think, Wow!

The warm fireplace crackled as Guyiser got off the floor and went to the window. The T.V. was on and a woman reporter could be heard in the background, "And now to the weather report. John, what's happening?" The camera changed to the map of Tennessee. "Hello, everybody. Get out your shawls and bundle up. It's coming." The man pointed to the map. "Snow flurries are coming from the northwest and…" Guyiser saw his father's truck pull into the driveway.

Mr. Blackman stopped and waved to Guyiser. Guyiser put on his coat and hat and went to help his father.

"Well, I got the tarps. Help me cover the chicken house before it gets dark." They worked fast in the cold air and soon the job was finished. "That's good, boy. The chickens will be a lot warmer now. Let's go in; I'm freezing."

They sat at the kitchen table eating some good warm stew Guyiser had made. Mr. Blackman said, "And if you see anyone or anything strange around here, you let me know right away." He turned to Loaner, "You hear me?" Loaner barked at Mr. Blackman.

The next morning's weather had not changed. The cold smell of snow was in the air. The fire in the potbelly stove made the barn warmer than outside as Guyiser and Loaner walked around inside. Guyiser stood looking at all of his bikes. He pulled a large bike out of the rack and rolled it to the center of the barn. He stepped back and looked at the standing bicycle. He had seen a boy riding his bicycle pulling a little wagon with a long rope. Guyiser went over to his worktable and sat down. He got a pencil and paper and began to draw. *What if I could design a two-wheel wagon that could fit easily on the bike's back axle? It could haul kids, or wood, or groceries, or anything.* He looked at the bike again. He continued to draw. A picture appeared on the paper. Not bad, he thought. He looked at the bike again. Ideas began to pop into his head. *What if the spokes were all different colors? What if the frame were painted with that glow-in-the-dark paint for riding at night?*

What if the seat were designed to carry two people? Guyiser didn't know it, but his ideas would change the future of bicycles. And his future.

How about safety features for bikers—things like helmets, or kneepads, or arm pads? His mind was floating in a sea of ideas. He looked at all the bicycles again. *Let's see,* he thought, *I have four named bikes— Mountain Man, Lady Thriller, Speed Man, and Faster.* His father kept coming to his mind, and he could hear him saying, 'Take something, and make something out of it, boy.' *I know,* he thought. *I'll put decals on the bikes like cartoon characters, tigers, monkeys, bears, and things that are fun for kids.* The day was a long day. Guyiser stretched out on the hay and watched the fire burn in the potbelly stove.

With Loaner by his side, he took a nap.

It had been a long week as Guyiser sat at his desk. He was marking off the days that had gone by on his calendar. It was the 13th of November. He and Cindy were going to pass out the flyers tomorrow.

Guyiser looked at the bicycles in the rack. He had sold two more bikes during the week on lay-away. *I need more bicycles*, he thought. Guyiser stood by the potbelly stove getting warm and looking at his flyer. Loaner ran to the barn door barking. He ran to Guyiser barking and back to the door barking. "What is it, boy?" Guyiser went to the door and opened it. Just as he did, he heard gunfire in the west field. *Hunters again*, he thought. Guyiser put on his coat and hat and ran out. Loaner kept barking as they ran through the field. Just as they topped the hill, he saw something in the tree line. They ran to it. Guyiser could see it was a cow. The cow was dead. It was Bell, his pet cow. He had grown up with this animal. He dropped to his knees crying as he touched his friend. Bell and Hay had been family pets. *Who would do a thing like this?* He looked to the sky and cried out loud, "Why, God, why?"

Guyiser cried all the way back to the house. Tears rolled down his face as he opened the door and called to his father. Mr. Blackman appeared at the kitchen door. "Dad, it's Bell. Somebody shot her. She's dead."

Mr. Blackman was in total shock. He grabbed his shotgun from the fireplace. "Show me, boy." They walked in the field to where Bell lay dead. Guyiser began to cry again. Tears came to Mr. Blackman's eyes as they stood looking at their pet cow. "Your ma loved this cow." Mr. Blackman looked around the field. "Where is Hay?"

Guyiser spoke through tears, "She's at the barn, she's okay."

They stood by the grave they had dug as Mr. Blackman pounded a wooden cross into the ground.

They said a prayer. Mr. Blackman put his arm around Guyiser's shoulder as they walked in the cold air back to the house. The house felt cold as they walked in. Something had been taken from them.

Night fell as Guyiser spoke to his father. "I'm going to bed, Pa. Good night."

Mr. Blackman sat in his chair staring into the fireplace. Tears filled his eyes as he thought of his wife and the cow. "Good night, boy."

It was around ten o'clock the next morning as Cindy and Guyiser sat in the barn talking about Bell's accident. After a while, Cindy turned to Guyiser. "Let's go pass out these flyers. Maybe that will help take your mind off this." Guyiser agreed. They loaded their bicycle baskets with flyers, and off they went.

They passed out flyers everywhere. Every mailbox all the way to Centerville got one. They even put flyers on telephone poles along the way. They laughed and talked as they rode together. Cindy had many friends in town. The flyers were put in most all the shops and stores. Some were put in the windows. If anyone lived in or around Centerville, they would know about the Christmas sale at "Guyiser's Bike Shop." The two stopped in a restaurant and had lunch. Then they walked around the streets passing out the flyers to people walking around. Happy with their work in Centerville, they started their ride back home. One main stop remained. That was the schoolhouse. They put flyers everywhere—in trees, parking lots, doors, windows, everywhere. They laughed as Cindy put one in the principal's mailbox. She grabbed Guyiser's hand. "Let's get out of here." They rode away laughing and having fun.

It was four miles from town as they were walking their bikes up a hill. They were singing Christmas songs, laughing, and flirting with each other. Guyiser looked up the road to the top of the hill. There he saw a truck parked. They continued their walking and singing. The truck raced its motor and raced down the hill. Guyiser looked up to see the truck coming down. As it got closer, Guyiser saw the truck cross the center of the road and head right for them. He shouted to Cindy, "Get off the road!" She looked up to see the truck speeding toward them. Guyiser and Cindy pushed their bikes off the edge of the road and jumped into the ditch. The truck roared by, throwing rocks and gravel at them. Guyiser looked up to see the truck speeding away. "Cindy, are you all right?" He held her as they were both shaking. Loaner was hit with rocks and gravel, but he was all right.

At the house, they sat at the kitchen table telling Mr. Blackman what had happened. "But you didn't see who was driving? Or what kind of truck?" Mr. Blackman was asking.

"No, it happened so fast. We just jumped for our lives."

Mr. Blackman looked at Cindy, "Well, I'm glad you two are all right." He looked in his coffee cup and heard a voice in his mind. 'We're gonna get you, Blackman.' The thought lasted several minutes before Mr. Blackman came back. With a smile on his face, he turned to Guyiser. "Guyiser, I'd like to speak to Cindy alone for a minute, okay? Go put a log on the fire." Puzzled, Guyiser looked at Cindy. He got up and left the room. Mr. Blackman watched as Guyiser left. He then turned to Cindy with a smile, "You really like each other, don't you?" Cindy smiled and nodded. "Well, I'd like to ask you for a favor."

Cindy smiled and nodded again. "Sure, Mr. Blackman, anything."

He reached out and touched her hand. "Well, it's Guyiser's birthday on the 18th and I'd like you to go into Nashville with us for lunch." Mr. Blackman continued, "I got him a present you can help him bring back."

Cindy became excited with the idea. "Sure, Mr. Blackman, anything for Guyiser." They shook hands.

"We'll leave about ten o'clock next Tuesday, okay?"

Guyiser and Cindy stood on the front porch talking about the day's events. "It's been an unusual but interesting day, Guyiser. We did get the flyers out." Guyiser hugged Cindy tightly and kissed her. Cindy returned the kiss. "I gotta go now. I have to do a lot of studying and I have things to do. I wish I could stay longer, but I'll see you Monday or Tuesday for sure. Love ya." With that, she got on her bike and rode down the driveway.

Guyiser watched her. He then turned to Loaner, "You, you go with her and protect her all the way home, understand?" Loaner barked at Guyiser and ran after Cindy.

Mr. Blackman and Guyiser were sitting at the kitchen table playing checkers. Mr. Blackman jumped two of Guyiser's checkers and smiled as he picked up the pieces. "You really like that little girl, don't ya?"

Guyiser just smiled and nodded. His father continued, "You know, Guyiser, we never had that talk about the birds and the bees." Guyiser looked at him quickly, unprepared for what he had just heard. Mr. Blackman continued, "I'd hate to see anything happen to her, or you. You know what I mean?"

Guyiser explained to his father that he knew about the birds and the bees. "I like her a whole lot, and nothing is gonna happen to her, I promise." He moved his checker, "Check."

Mr. Blackman looked at the board then at Guyiser. With a smile on his face, he said, "You win, boy! I'm proud of you."

A bark and a scratch on the door sent the message that Loaner was home. Guyiser let him in. "Everything all right, boy?" Loaner barked at him and went to his blanket to lie down. "You're such a good dog. Good boy, Good boy."

The morning air in the house was freezing as Mr. Blackman was building a fire in the fireplace. It was five thirty when he turned on the television. The sky was dark as he stood looking out the window. His hot coffee felt good going down as he sat in his chair. The weatherman was waving as he spoke. "Good morning, everybody. It's cold out there and as we told you last week that it was coming—now it's here. A blanket of snow fell last night." Mr. Blackman could hear the weatherman, but his mind was on the day before. The weatherman continued, "It won't last long, but there is more on the way." Mr. Blackman finished his coffee and closed his eyes.

Guyiser was still asleep with Loaner beside him. Loaner heard the T.V. and knew Mr. Blackman was up. He jumped off the bed and ran to the living room. He went to Mr. Blackman and licked his hand. Mr. Blackman opened his eyes, smiled, and petted Loaner's head; then he closed his eyes again. Loaner went to the window and jumped up on the windowsill. He saw the white ground and did not understand what it was. He ran back to the bedroom and jumped up on the bed. Wagging his tail, he started licking Guyiser's face. He playfully jumped on Guyiser and barked. Guyiser rolled over and covered his head. Loaner bit the blanket and pulled it back. Guyiser opened his eyes and looked at Loaner. "What do you want?" Loaner barked and jumped off the bed. He stood looking at Guyiser, barked again, and ran out the door. Guyiser slowly got up and put on his pants and shoes. He threw a blanket around his shoulders and went into the living room. Mr. Blackman was napping. Loaner stood by the window and barked. Guyiser went to the window and looked out. The sky was still dark gray, but his eyes lit up to see the white blanket on the ground. "Snow! It snowed last night, Loaner. That's snow." This was Loaner's first snow, and he wanted to investigate the white stuff. "You want to go out?" Guyiser opened the door and Loaner ran out. Guyiser went back to the window to watch Loaner's reaction.

Loaner ran in the snow, stopped, smelled the ground, and ran again. Guyiser watched and stood there laughing. He turned to see his father watching T.V. Mr. Blackman sat with his eyes closed. "Good morning."

"Morning, Dad, Did you see the snow?"

Mr. Blackman looked at his empty coffee cup and got up. "Yep, and there's more on the way." He went to the kitchen. Guyiser stood looking at the T.V. as the woman reporter spoke. "Thanks, John. We'll check in with you later. In our local news, did you know it is against the law to put things other than mail in a mailbox? Police say, 'Don't do it.', but they will let it slide this year as long as it doesn't happen again. So Merry Christmas law breakers." Guyiser's eyes were wide open. That was us, he thought.

Guyiser and his father had the truck loaded with some great antiques. "You think anybody will be at the sale?" Guyiser asked his father.

"Oh, yeah, people love swap meets in any kind of weather. Why don't you bring some of your flyers with you?" Guyiser ran to the barn to get them. The three of them piled into the truck and headed to the swap meet.

It was about 7 o'clock and dark as the truck pulled up to the farmhouse. They unloaded the few things that they did not sell and put them in the shed. Inside the house, Mr. Blackman sat at the kitchen table counting their money. Guyiser was building a fire in the living room. He came into the kitchen and sat down with his father. He watched him counting the money. "Antiques sell pretty good. Here's your share." Mr. Blackman said handing Guyiser some money.

"Thank you." Guyiser could still not figure how he figured his share, but he would put it in his pouch anyway. Mr. Blackman got up and put the money in his pocket, and then poured dog chow in Loaner's large bowl. Loaner was hungry as they laughed and watched him eat.

Sunday was a slow day. Most of the snow had melted. Guyiser and his father sat around the living room watching T.V. and playing checkers. The Titans were playing the Raiders. It was the fourth quarter, and the score was Titans 34, Raiders 3. The two cheered as Tennessee kicked a field goal. "I guess we win, Pa." Guyiser stood up and looked at the shotgun over the fireplace. "Mind if I take the gun out? Maybe Loaner and I can get a rabbit or two."

Mr. Blackman looked at the gun, "As long as you clean it and are careful."

Several hours had passed. Mr. Blackman was outside feeding the cow Hay. The chickens clucked as he threw feed to them. He looked up to see Guyiser and Loaner coming over the hill from the field.

Guyiser saw his father in the distance and held up his arm with two rabbits in his hand. Mr. Blackman smiled and went back to the house. He put a log on the fire and went to the kitchen window. Guyiser was cleaning his catch as Loaner watched. Mr. Blackman felt proud of Guyiser. He was tall, good-looking, smart, and strong. He also felt proud of himself for raising Guyiser to be a good person who cared about other people.

The smell of the warm stew filled the entire house, and the warm fireplace made it a perfect day. They sat in the living room, Mr. Blackman in his favorite chair and Guyiser stretched out on the couch. Loaner lay by the fireplace. It was a true picture of peaceful happiness. Mr. Blackman looked at Guyiser who was almost asleep. "Hey, wake up." Guyiser stirred and looked at his father. Mr. Blackman continued, "We got to go into Nashville Tuesday. I got some business to attend to. You can see Mr. Gibson." Mr. Blackman got up and went to his bedroom. "Good night, you two." Loaner rolled over to see Mr. Blackman's door close. Guyiser drifted off to sleep.

Monday morning found Guyiser in the shed. There he found a large sheet of plywood, a 4' x 8' sheet. This would be his sign with arrows pointing to his driveway out by the road. *I'll paint it red on both sides with white letters and white trim around the edges. Cindy is the artist, and she can put the words and her drawings on it. I'll put it up high so people can see it from both directions. Make a plan, Work a plan*, he thought. He took the plywood to the barn and began to paint. While it was drying, he thought he could climb up on the barn's roof and begin to put up the Christmas lights. After several hours, he ran out of lights and needed more. *I'll buy more tomorrow in Nashville, he thought. Boy, this is a lot of work!*

Snow began to fall that night. Guyiser stood by the window and looked toward the barn. The small light was on over the barn doors. He could see the snowflakes falling. He could hear the snowflakes whispering to each other as they fell to the ground. *The mystery of God*, he thought. He could hear his father's wise voice. He could feel the warm love of his mother. He could see Cindy's glowing face and feel her warm blue eyes giving him love. He could see Mr. Gibson's jolly soul and friendship. Guyiser looked down at Loaner who was sitting by his side. "And you my friend, and you my friend." The blue-white snow kept falling.

The snow had covered the ground and was beautiful that morning as Mr. Blackman stood looking out the living room window. Sipping his coffee, he saw Cindy coming up the driveway. She stopped by the truck and put a package under the tarp. Then she came to the house and knocked on the door. Mr. Blackman greeted her, "Hi, pretty girl, come on in. You're just in time for breakfast." They sat in the kitchen talking and eating. Loaner barked at Guyiser and ran into the kitchen. He ran to Cindy and barked again. Mr. Blackman looked at Cindy, "Why don't you go get him up?" Cindy smiled and left the kitchen. She stood by his bed and grabbed the pillow from under Guyiser's head. He opened his eyes to see Cindy standing there. She hit him with the pillow and laughed.

"Wake up, big boy. Breakfast is ready."

Guyiser grabbed her arm and pulled her down on the bed with him. "Wow! What a great way to wake up."

She kissed him and smiled, "Get up." With that, she went back to the kitchen.

Soon they all sat talking and laughing as they finished breakfast. Cindy stood up and tapped her coffee cup with her spoon. "You attention, please. My parents and I would like to invite both of you and Loaner to join us for Thanksgiving Day." Cindy continued. "They really want you to come. So plan on it!"

Mr. Blackman turned to Guyiser. "It sounds good to me, what do you think?"

Guyiser reached for Cindy's hand and squeezed it. "What can we bring?"

Out on the porch, Cindy made a snowball, threw it at Guyiser, and ran to the truck. Mr. Blackman also made a snowball and threw it at Guyiser. Laughing, they piled in the truck with Loaner in the back. The old truck turned onto the main road with white smoke trailing. The trip to Nashville was a long one. The closer they came to town, the more cars and trucks there were stuck on the side of the road. Mr. Blackman drove slowly and safely even though they slid from time to time. The streets of Nashville were busy with snowplows clearing them and trucks dumping salt along the way. The snow had not stopped people from working or shopping. Shop keepers had hung the Christmas lights early this holiday season. As they rode along, Cindy and Guyiser pointed to different light designs and signs.

The restaurant was only a few blocks away from Mr. Gibson's Bike Shop. The truck pulled into a parking spot. The wind was strong; the snow was swirling as they entered. They sat at a booth by the window. There was a fireplace with warm air making the food smell like home. A friendly old woman took their orders. As she disappeared, they looked out the window watching it snow. "I love this time of year," Cindy said. "The trees, the snow, the icicles, and the lights. How was your Christmas, Mr. Blackman, when you were a young boy?"

Mr. Blackman looked out into the falling snow. They watched him thinking. "Well, my ma liked to can stuff like peaches, apples, beans, and the like. She always made a fruitcake at Christmas. I'd stand in the kitchen and lick the bowl. My pa and I would go hunting a lot. As far as presents, there wasn't much. In fact, we were pretty poor, but we had enough to go around.

And we had each other. We always had a tree by the fireplace. Pa would put cotton on it." Mr. Blackman smiled, "That was a long time ago."

The little woman came back with their food. "Let's see, you wanted the chicken, and you wanted barbeque. I'll bring your catfish plate right back."

Guyiser spoke up, "Don't forget the soup and bone for my dog." They all laughed.

"Oh, I didn't forget, sonny," she said as she walked away.

The three of them were full as they stood on the sidewalk in the snow. "Let's get in the truck," Mr. Blackman said.

Cindy looked at Guyiser. "Let's walk."

Guyiser needed to go to the bank and stop at the five-and-dime store to buy some Christmas lights.

"We'll walk, Pa. We'll meet you at Mr. Gibson's. Come on, Loaner."

Mr. Blackman got in the truck and watched them walk down the street. He reached under the seat and got his pistol. He put it in his pocket.

Mr. Gibson sat by his stove looking out the window at the falling snow. The little bell rang as Mr. Blackman came in. "Afternoon, Mr. Blackman."

"Afternoon, Mr. Gibson. How do you like this snow?"

Mr. Gibson laughed and pointed to the stove. "As long as I'm warm, I don't care."

They sat and talked for a while, then Mr. Blackman said, "Is it out back?"

Mr. Gibson nodded, "Yes, it is and it's beautiful."

The little bell rang again and Guyiser and Cindy came in. "Burr, it's cold out there. Hi, Mr. Gibson, this is Cindy Taylor, my girlfriend."

He looked at Cindy for her approval.

"Hi, Mr. Gibson. I'm glad to meet you. Guyiser has told me all about you."

"My pleasure, young lady. Come on in and get warm." The gathered around the warm stove talking and laughing at Mr. Gibson's jokes about the snow that gave Santa Claus a cold. "Yep, that was in 1900 and something; I can't remember." They all laughed again.

"Mr. Gibson, I'm going to need some more bicycles. I think my flyers and ad will bring a lot of customers for my Christmas sale. You have some more out back?"

Mr. Gibson laughed like Santa. "Ho, ho, ho. Don't worry about bicycles. By the way," He got up and went to the counter. He picked up a gift box and handed it to Guyiser. Mr. Blackman handed Cindy her package. Mr. Gibson looked at Mr. Blackman.

"Your father said it was all right. Happy Birthday!"

Guyiser started ripping off the paper from the long box. His eyes widened and his mouth dropped open. "A gun, a 20GA shotgun!" He grabbed Mr. Gibson and gave him a big hug. "Thank you sir, thank you." He turned to Mr. Blackman and Cindy. "Look! Look at what I got!" Guyiser went to his dad and gave him a hug. "Thanks for letting me have this."

Cindy spoke up and held out her present. "Happy 18th birthday, boyfriend."

Guyiser looked at the gift box wrapped with a bow and a card on the top. He handed the shotgun to his pa and sat down to open Cindy's gift. He carefully took the bow off and read the card.

"To our first birthday together and many more to come. Love Cindy" He looked up at her. To him, the card would have been enough. He continued opening the package. As he took the top off, he saw what he had always wanted. It was a beautiful black leather jacket. "Oh, Cindy, Oh, Cindy," he said as he held it up to show everybody.

Cindy moved the tissue paper. "There's more."

Guyiser looked to see a bright red wool scarf and a pair of black leather gloves. Overjoyed, he jumped up and put the coat on. "It fits perfect. Look, Dad."

Cindy put the scarf around his neck and smiled, "You look so handsome."

Guyiser kissed her. "Oh, Cindy, thank you!"

Mr. Gibson spoke up, "Why don't you go out back in the snow and see if it keeps you warm?"

Guyiser grabbed Cindy's hand and headed to the back door.

Mr. Blackman stopped them, "Oh, Guyiser, I got you a present too." He reached in his coat pocket and took out a small wrapped box. "Here, son. Happy Birthday."

Guyiser took the small box and tore off the paper. He looked at his father and opened it. He was puzzled at what he saw. "Keys?" He held them up, looking at them. "Keys?"

Mr. Blackman opened the door. "Go on out, boy." Guyiser stepped out the door and looked in the parking lot. There sat a big, new, beautiful red Ford truck.

Guyiser could not believe his eyes. "For me?" He lit up as a Christmas tree covered with hundreds of lights. He ran to it and began touching it all over.

"Really, Dad, for me?" He ran to him with tears in his eyes. They stood looking at each other.

Mr. Blackman smiled. "You need something to carry all those bicycles around in."

Guyiser hugged him again and stood crying. "I love you Dad, I love you so much."

Mr. Gibson and Mr. Blackman looked at each other remembering their first trucks and understood the joy Guyiser was feeling now. "Why don't you two go ahead and head back to the house? I'll take the gun and Loaner with me."

Mr. Gibson spoke up, "And come back next week and get a bunch of bicycles."

Guyiser and Cindy ran to the new truck and drove away. Mr. Blackman waved and shouted to them, "Drive slowly, take your time." He thanked Mr. Gibson for everything and left the store with Loaner. In his truck, he took out the gun and put it on the seat. "Let's ride around town a bit, what you say, Loaner?"

Loaner looked around and barked.

The snow had all but stopped. The truck drove up one street and down another. An hour passed and there was no sign of the two men he was looking for. Mr. Blackman petted Loaner, "Let's go home. It's getting dark."

Guyiser and Cindy parked on the side of the road. The Taylor's had decorated their mailbox with ribbon and bows, but now it was covered with snow. Guyiser put his arm around Cindy. They kissed as the radio played their favorite music, and the heater's warm air fogged the windows. "Do you want to drive down to the lake?"

Cindy snuggled in Guyiser's arms. "Why? I like it here."

"Well, we could watch the water freeze."

"Not tonight, birthday boy. I have to go in. My parents will be worrying. It's dark."

Guyiser kissed her forehead. "I guess you're right. Pa will be home soon, too. What say I pick you up tomorrow? I got a truck now!" He petted the steering wheel.

"You sure do. I like your truck, too. And the smell of your leather jacket, besides it looks great on you.

You're getting to be quite a catch." She kissed Guyiser long and tender. "Boyfriend, take me home." Guyiser watched her go up on the porch and to the door. Cindy turned and threw him a kiss before she went in.

He sat there thinking about her. As he pulled into his driveway and parked, he thought about his wonderful day.

The snow began to fall again. Inside the house, Guyiser built a fire and hung his new jacket. He stood there rubbing it. He put the red scarf and gloves in the pockets. He could see Cindy's happy smile as she handed him the present. Guyiser went to the window to look out at his new truck. Mr. Blackman pulled off the road and up the driveway. He and Loaner played in the snow as they walked to the house.

Later that night, they sat watching T.V. and talking. Guyiser went to the window again and stood there looking at the falling snow and his truck. Mr. Blackman got up and went to the window. "You know, I saw a metal carport at the swap meet last week, roof, and all. I bet I could buy it for about $50."

Guyiser was still looking at the truck. "God I love that truck." He hugged his dad. They went back and sat down. Guyiser began watching T.V. and thinking. Mr. Blackman went to the kitchen and returned with a bottle of wine. Guyiser sat watching him drink. "You know my sale starts the end of next week, and I could use your help."

Mr. Blackman took a drink. "Sure, boy. I'll help you."

Guyiser continued, "Would you be my Santa Claus?" His dad quickly turned and looked at Guyiser. "I'll get you a Santa suit with a hat and a beard. The kids would love it. What do you think?"

"Me? Santa Claus?" He took another drink. He sat there thinking. "I've done a lot of things in my day, but I never been a Santa Claus. But it might be fun. Can I sit in a big red chair?"

They started laughing. "Anything you want, Dad."

Television

Part 3

A magic box full of pictures and
A fantastic fantasy world. A place
Of learning. A place of dreams. A
Place of truth, or so it seems...

The Taylor house, big as it was, looked even larger with a foot of white snow on the roof. Smoke poured out of the chimney, making it warm with the holiday season. Inside, Cindy and her mother were putting up some of their Christmas trinkets. Cindy was decorating the stairway banister as her mother gave instructions, "Put some there. Yes, that's pretty, and over there."

Cindy kept saying, "Yes, Mother. Okay, Mother. Yes, Mother." To Mrs. Taylor, Cindy was still a little girl, even though Cindy was a mature young woman and was soon graduating from high school. She was on the debate team and had worked on the high school newspaper. Her grades were the highest in her school. Mr. and Mrs. Taylor were very proud of her. They were also proud of her independence and dedication to anything she set her mind to do.

Cindy's parents had given her knowledge and direction to know right from wrong. As an only child, she had been given all their love. Yes, Cindy was a little spoiled, but that only added to her bright and shining outlook on life. Angels protected her and God was in her heart. Cindy had a gift of being able to weed out and see through people who were not truthful. She could discern their motives. To her, the value of truth and the understanding of what was not true would rule her life.

Cindy's parents had also given her a bit of a wild side. She had a lot of "tomboy" in her. She could throw a football as well as a boy. Cindy also rode horses bareback. She could pitch hay with her cousins all day and later win at arm wrestling. Apple trees were her favorite tree to climb. She especially liked the big, red juicy kind. Cindy loved to dance and to act silly. Her smile had a "Let's try it" and "Devil beware" in it. 'To experiment was to learn' was her motto. *Would that rope hold me? How long can I hold my breath under water? What does that taste like?*

What does a kiss feel like? Drugs and alcohol are a 'No.' Cindy had seen the effects of both and had been educated in this area. She was also educated in sex education. Like all boys and girls, she was curious. She knew sex involved love, respect, and would be a very special part of her life.

Cindy hung her last bell on the banister. "Let's finish this later, Mother. I need you to help me." Cindy put the Christmas box in the corner. "Let's go in the kitchen." At the table, Cindy took some papers from her purse. She excitedly showed them to her mother. "This is an application from a television broadcasting school in Florida. I sent a letter to them with my grades and interest in television. This letter says they want me. All I have to do is fill out this application. Isn't it great? This is what I have always wanted to do!"

Mrs. Taylor read the letter. "But, you will have to move to Florida!"

Cindy was ready for this. "Only for six months, and when I finish their school, they guarantee an apprenticeship at a T.V. station. Maybe it will be in Nashville. Oh, Mother, say 'Yes'."

Mrs. Taylor looked Cindy in her eyes. "Is this something you really want to do, I mean television?"

Cindy squeezed her mother's hand, "Yes, Mother. I've always dreamed of it. It's like college and a career. It's a way I can help people—a way I can make a difference in this world by traveling and reporting news all over the world."

Mrs. Taylor had always supported Cindy.

However, this was big.

Her little girl was growing up. "Tell you what. Let's talk it over with your father and see what he says, okay?" Cindy knew it would be acceptable. She and her father were very close. She knew that a hug and a few tears on his shoulder would be all it would take. He would say, 'Yes!'.

Supper was always a special treat at the Taylor house. Even for the three of them, Mrs. Taylor loved to cook. Just in case company dropped in, she always made extra. This family talked a lot. They all had something to say. Mr. Taylor always had new customers who came into his store. Mrs. Taylor heard a rumor about their neighbor who may be having a baby. Or maybe Bennie, their rooster, looked sick, or tomorrow night they were having a new flavor of jello. Cindy's life was, 'He said, she said,' and of course, Guyiser's new projects.'

They had just finished supper when Mrs. Taylor turned to her husband. "Ben, Cindy has something to tell you. And I told her that we all should talk about it."

Cindy reached across the table and held her father's hands. She took a deep breath and started, "Daddy, I have a great opportunity to do something constructive with my life. Something I have given serious thought to. And with your and mother's support, my life's dream can come true."

He looked at Mrs. Taylor and at Cindy. "Go on."

Cindy continued, "I have always wanted to work in the television industry and now I have the chance." She showed the papers to her father. "I have been accepted by the 'Television Broadcasting School of the Arts.' It is a six-month course, which included a guaranteed apprenticeship at a television studio."

Mr. Taylor became interested in the idea. "What would you do? Television is big."

"That's the exciting part, Daddy. I could be a writer, an engineer, a reporter, or even a producer of a show. There are dozens of things I could do! Besides, after the course, I'll have a choice of what I want to do. I could even work in Nashville at a T.V. station." Cindy always sparkled with excitement whenever she spoke.

Mrs. Taylor interrupted, "Now tell him the bad part."

Cindy looked at her. "It's not a bad part." Turning to her father she said, "The school is in Florida. I can come home on weekends and call you all the time. This is a great opportunity for me. Daddy, please think it over and say 'Yes.'"

"Your mother and I will think it over. However, no promises. We love you and want the best for you."

Guyiser slept in a little late. He got up, dressed, and went to the living room. The fireplace was burning warm and bright. Guyiser went to the window and looked at his truck. It looked like a cherry in vanilla ice cream. *Where is everybody?* He went to the kitchen. Coffee was on the stove. He next went to the window. There was his father and Loaner. Mr. Blackman was throwing feed to the chickens. He threw a handful at Loaner. Loaner jumped around playfully in the snow and barked at him. Guyiser poured himself a cup of coffee and went back to the living room. He turned on the T.V. and sat down sipping his coffee. 'Breaking News' came on. "There was a 12-car pileup on highway 70 last night. It seems a tractor-trailer slid into a snowplow causing cars and trucks to slip and slide into each other. The operator of the snowplow died at the scene. Several people were rushed to the hospital. Police say,…"

Mr. Blackman and Loaner came in. "Dad, did you see this?"

His father took off his coat, and looking at the T.V. said, "Yep, bad accident. I knew the man." Loaner ran to the kitchen.

Guyiser looked at his father. "I'm sorry." Mr. Blackman shook his head and went into the kitchen, too. Guyiser looked at his watch. It was eight thirty. He put his coat on and went to his truck. He started it up and turned on the radio and heater. He scraped snow off the windshield. After letting the engine run,

Guyiser went to the barn. Inside, he built a fire in the potbelly stove.

Mr. Blackman and Loaner came to the barn. "What you gonna do today, boy?"

Guyiser pointed to the big sheet of red plywood. "Cindy and I are gonna finish this road sign and maybe hang some lights up. What are you gonna do?"

"Well, I figured me and Loaner would drive around the property line and check the fences. Make sure they are all up." Loaner barked and looked at Mr. Blackman. "You ready, boy? We'll see you later." They left the barn. Guyiser looked at his watch. *Nine forty-five. I better go get Cindy.*

The truck was nice and warm as Guyiser pulled into the Taylor's drive. He pulled to the house and tooted his horn. Cindy and her mother came out. Guyiser went to meet them. "My, my, that sure is a pretty truck, Guyiser. Happy birthday to you."

"Good morning and thank you, ma'am. Hi, Cindy, you ready to go?" Guyiser looked her over. She stood with her beautiful smile. She had a black turtleneck sweater on, which accented her long blond curly hair. Her powder blue jacket and jeans looked great with her white boots.

Guyiser took a deep breath, looked at Mrs. Taylor, and then back at Cindy. "You sure do look pretty today." He held out his hand to Cindy. They ran to the truck and got in. Cindy waved to her mother, and Mrs. Taylor waved back as they drove away.

The barn was nice and warm as Guyiser and Cindy laughed and talked as they worked on the sign.

They stood back and looked at it. "Now, that will get some attention," Guyiser said. "You framed everything in just the right place." Guyiser looked at Cindy and kissed her. "And your Santa with his little glasses is perfect. Oh, did I tell you? Pa is going to dress up as Santa Claus for the sale." They laughed and laughed. Cindy took her red paintbrush and dabbed Guyiser's nose. "And Rudolph." They laughed and kissed again. "Let's finish the other side now. I have to go soon. Mother wants me to help her decorate and to go to the store and things. And I want to stay on her good side."

About an hour later, they again stood back to see their work. Cindy held up her brush like an artist measuring his work. "You know, I think I like this side the best. What do you think?"

Guyiser held up his brush pretending to measure.

"I like both sides the best!" He quickly dabbed some white paint on Cindy's nose. "But most of all, I like you the best." They hugged each other and kissed and kissed. Guyiser's hands were rubbing Cindy's butt as they kissed. She broke the kiss by looking in Guyiser's eyes. "That feels good, and I wish I could stay longer. But, I have to go, okay, boyfriend?"

They sat in the truck at Cindy's house kissing goodbye. The kisses became more passionate and Guyiser's hand roamed under Cindy's sweater. She could feel his warm hand under her bra and was too caught up in the moment. "Oh, Guyiser," she said as her hand squeezed his thigh. "Not now."

With that, Cindy got out of the truck and ran up the steps to the front door. She stood there a moment and then went in.

With that, Cindy got out of the truck and ran up the steps to the front door. She stood there a moment and then went in.

Guyiser sat in his truck thinking before going to the barn. His mind was fresh with the taste of her kisses. He could still feel her warm, firm, breasts. He could hear her soft purr and her soft voice. He could feel her hand on his leg. He could smell her perfume and the scent of their love.

Guyiser sat at his desk in the barn looking at the big red sign. Cindy was everywhere he looked. He needed to clear his mind. He left the barn and began to walk. Soon he came to his tree house. He climbed the tree and sat on the board. The tree had shed all its leaves. He looked over the fields. They were white and pure. There was not a footprint anywhere. Guyiser leaned back against the tree and started to become at peace with himself.

Darkness began to set in, and the snow began to fall again. Guyiser climbed down the tree and walked back through the field to the house. He saw his father's truck in front. Loaner came running to him. They played for a while in the snow. Mr. Blackman sat in the kitchen having a glass of wine as Guyiser and Loaner came in. "Dad." Guyiser took his coat and hat off and went into the kitchen, "It's starting again." He went to the window and looked out. "Were the fences all right?" He sat down.

Mr. Blackman took another drink. "Not bad. A tree had fallen on the fence in two places, but not bad. We did see some deer out back.

Guess I'll put a few blocks of salt out for 'em."

Guyiser tapped his fingers on the table. "Pa, can I talk to you?"

Mr. Blackman leaned back in his chair, "Sure, boy. What's on your mind?" Guyiser continued tapping his fingers. "It's about Cindy and me. I can't get her out of my mind. She is everything a man could want. And we are good together. And I want to know what love is. Can you tell me?" Guyiser looked at his father and searched his face. "Tell me about you and ma. You loved her."

Mr. Blackman leaned on the table and poured another drink. "You know, Guyiser, love comes in many forms." Guyiser listened intently. "Some people love their jobs. Others love their pets. Some people are in love with their possessions. A preacher loves God; he's married to God. Me and you love each other." Mr. Blackman took a drink and continued. "You love your bicycles and your truck, and maybe you love Cindy." He touched the ring on his finger. "As far as your mother, I knew the minute I touched her hand and she touched me. I respected her; I honored her thoughts. I could feel her heartbeat, even if we were miles apart." Mr. Blackman looked into Guyiser's eyes. "And I knew she loved me and that we would never part, no matter what. Our love was still growing the day she died." Tears came to his eyes.

Guyiser reached across the table and held his father's hands. "I think I kinda understand now. Love is everywhere and when it is between two people, it's stronger than life itself. Thank you for loving me and thanks for talking to me. I love you, Dad, I really do love you."

The worktable in the barn was full of boxes of Christmas lights and decorations. "Eighteen, nineteen, twenty. I measured the driveway," Guyiser said, "and it takes five strands on one side and five strands for the other side. The rest are for the outside and inside of the barn." Mr. Blackman and Guyiser stood looking at all the lights. Mr. Blackman finished his coffee, "Well, let's get started." Loaner ran around the fence as they nailed the lights along the fence rail. After a couple of hours, they had finished. They would tackle the barn next.

Guyiser, holding the ladder, shouted up, "You O.K. up there?" The view from the top of the barn was beautiful. Mr. Blackman could see all the fields covered with snow and with sprinkles of trees. It was like looking at a Christmas card. Then something caught his attention. About a half mile away, he saw a truck parked on the top of a hill on the main road. He could not see anybody, just the truck. He finished nailing the lights up and climbed down the ladder.

"I'll be back in a while." He went in the house to get his shotgun. He walked passed Guyiser. "You stay here.

Come on Loaner!" Guyiser stood holding a strand of lights.

"What is it? What did you see?"

"You just stay here!" Guyiser stood there watching as the two walked through the field of snow and disappeared over a hill. They were soon at the north side of the field. Mr. Blackman climbed over the fence and walked to the road. The truck was gone.

He stood looking at the tire tracks in the snow. Guyiser was in the house standing by the fireplace as Mr. Blackman and Loaner came in. "What was it?"

"Hunters, I guess. They were gone when we got there." Mr. Blackman hung his gun up and went to the kitchen. He returned with his bottle of wine. "Let's go finish with them lights."

They hammered and hung lights all around the frame of the barn. Guyiser looked at his shaking father. "Go on in Dad and get warm. I can finish the doors and window." Mr. Blackman handed the hammer to Guyiser, shook his head, and walked to the house.

Again, the snow began to fall as Guyiser entered the house. His father was sitting in his chair, cleaning the shotgun. Guyiser shook the snow off his coat and hung it up. "I can't wait 'till it's dark and we can turn the lights on and see 'em." He took the shotgun and looked down the barrel. "Looks good and shiny."

"Yep, you gotta keep 'em clean. You want to try yours out tomorrow? Thought we could go huntin' and I might teach you something'."

They had breakfast for supper that night. It was not unusual to have eggs and ham with biscuits and gravy. In fact, this was their favorite meal. Night had fallen, and it was still snowing. They stood outside the barn. Guyiser began to count, "One, two, three!" He plugged the extension cord into the light strand. All of the lights lit up. Guyiser and his dad and looked down the driveway. "Looks good. Let's walk to the road and get a better look."

They stood on the main road looking at their work. The long driveway was all lit up. The lights led to the big parking area. The barn was a big silhouette of colorful lights in the darkness. The lights around the barn door and window were blinking. The two stood there in amazement. "Wow! Wow!" was all Guyiser could say.

Mr. Blackman had not visualized what Guyiser had. "I never thought the old barn could look like this. You sure made a good plan, son. It sure is pretty."

"It's just the way I saw it. Wait 'till Cindy sees it. It was her idea, too."

Gunfire could be heard echoing in the hills. Loaner was barking and jumping around in the snow. "Anyone can hit a still target. But, if a rabbit is running up a hill, you have to shoot over his head. And, if he's running down a hill, you shoot in front of him." Guyiser stood with his shotgun and listened to his dad. Mr. Blackman continued. "Now, you try it." Guyiser raised his gun. Mr. Blackman swung a tin can hanging from the tree branch. The tin can was on a long string, which swung back and forth. Mr. Blackman stepped back, "Fire!" Guyiser followed the swinging can. Looking down the barrel, he fired. The can flew off the string and into the air.

"Good shot, Good shot." Mr. Blackman picked the can up off the ground. "Good shot!"

It is about eight o'clock the next morning as Guyiser stood looking out the living room window. He saw several of the local farmers with their tractors on the main road pushing snow off the road. Mr. Blackman and Loaner were finishing breakfast.

"Dad." Guyiser went to the kitchen, "Dad, I need to see Mr. Gibson and get some bicycles. Think I'll go in early so I can get back before it's too late. That okay with you?"

Mr. Blackman dipped his biscuit in the gravy and took a bite. "Sure, boy. You want me to go with you?"

Guyiser stood and put his plate in the sink. "No, thanks, it won't take me long."

His father walked to the living room and sat down, "Okay. Drive carefully and I'll be right here." He patted his chair.

The road to Nashville had not been too bad. Besides, having Loaner along to keep Guyiser company was a big help. Mr. Gibson was putting a shipment of bicycles and parts in his storeroom. Guyiser picked up a big box. "Where do you want this box?"

"Put in over here. That's perfect. Let's sit down. I'm not as young as I used to be." They sat by the stove relaxing and talking. "Did you find anything out back?"

"Not much to choose from." Guyiser rocked in the rocking chair. "Not much, but a few."

Mr. Gibson looked at his bikes. "I want you to take about eight or nine of these bicycles. They're new and ready to go."

Guyiser looked at the bikes. "You sure? These bikes cost more money."

Mr. Gibson laughed and just rocked. "Don't worry, Guyiser. It's the Christmas holidays. People will buy anything. Just hang a sale ticket on the handlebars. That's business." He thumbed his nose. "You'll learn," and he laughed, "Ho, Ho, Ho."

Guyiser tied down all the bikes in his new truck. Mr. Gibson came out with ten new baskets. "Take these, too. How much you selling 'em for?"

Guyiser took the baskets. "Eight dollars."

Mr. Gibson laughed. "Twelve dollars each. Remember its Christmas." He laughed again, "Ho, Ho, Ho."

Guyiser shook his hand. "Are we square with what I owe you?"

"Everything is just fine."

Guyiser got in his truck and turned to Mr. Gibson. "If you get a chance, come out to see my shop."

Mr. Gibson waved, "I'll do that, Guyiser."

Guyiser and Loaner sang and barked all the way home. It was five thirty when they pulled into the driveway. Guyiser backed up to the barn and went in. He built a fire and looked around the barn. I need more space. I'll take my worktable down. He made his plan. *I'll put my lay-a-ways over here and the small bikes over here. I'll scatter the boys' and girls' bikes so people can walk around and see 'em.* Good. Guyiser rolled the last bike into the barn and stood it by the door. He walked around looking at all the bikes. Baskets were hanging around on the walls. Extra parts and items were on the tabletop. As he looked around the large room, he thought, *I really did it. This really looks like a bike shop.* He jumped up and shouted aloud, "I'm a business man! Yes, I am."

Thanksgiving morning was an exciting morning for Guyiser. Tomorrow, his sale would start. Everything was ready. The sign by the road, the Santa suit, the lights, and all the beautiful bicycles were ready. Guyiser knocked on his father's bedroom door. "Wake up, Dad, It's six o'clock." He sat at the kitchen table as Mr. Blackman stood in the doorway yawning. "Your coffee is ready."

Mr. Blackman sat drinking his coffee. "Why so early? I could have slept another hour."

"I know, but Cindy said to come over about eleven o'clock, and I thought we would drive into Centerville. I need to pick up a few things." All the chores were finished as Guyiser, Loaner, and Mr. Blackman drove to Centerville. Not much was open as they drove around the courthouse and into the gas station/market/ auto and tractor sales and looked for a place to park. As they stopped and parked, Mr. Blackman turned to Guyiser, "Again, what are we here for?"

As they entered the store, Guyiser said, "A gratitude present for inviting us to their house. Don't you know your manners?" Inside, they walked around looking for something. Guyiser found a pretty box of candy with a ribbon around it and a bunch of mixed flowers. He stood paying for his gifts as Mr. Blackman came up to him. He held up his find—a gallon of eggnog and a bottle of Jack Daniels. They laughed and left the store with their presents.

As they pulled up to the Taylor's big house, Mr. Taylor was shoveling snow off the porch steps. He put the shovel down and walked to them. "Good morning, Mr. Blackman. Good to see you again. And you must be Guyiser. My house rings with your name." They shook hands. "Cindy talks about you two all the time." Loaner barked. "And look at this dog. Loaner, right?"

Guyiser smiled and watched Loaner run off to the barn. "Yes, sir. And thanks for having us over."

"It's our pleasure. Come on in, Come on in."

Mrs. Taylor and Cindy greeted them and invited them into the living room. Cindy went to Guyiser with a warm kiss on his cheek. "Thanks for coming."

Guyiser handed her the box of candy. "For you. Mrs. Taylor, for you." He handed her the flowers.

"Why, thank you, Guyiser."

Mr. Blackman held up the eggnog and the Jack Daniels. "And this is for everybody." They all laughed and the day began.

The three men sat in the living room talking about this, that, and the other thing. Cindy came in and put a log in the fireplace and then sat on the arm of the couch beside Guyiser. He held her hand. "You look great today." He looked at Mr. Taylor, "And the decorations and your house look really pretty."

"Yes, Cindy and her mother do this every year."

Mrs. Taylor appeared in the doorway. "It's ready. Come and get it." They all went into the large dining room. The table was beautiful. Candles were lit and food filled the table. They all sat eating, talking, and laughing.

As they finished, Mrs. Taylor brought in dessert— pumpkin and banana pies.

After dinner, they all relaxed in the living room. Cindy was playing Christmas songs on the piano. Mrs. Taylor was singing. "Come on. Join in, everybody. Jingle bells, Jingle bell, Jingle all the way."

The evening was perfect.

Guyiser stood by the fireplace. "And now, I would like to invite you to my Christmas lighting at my new bike shop, which opens tomorrow!" They all clapped.

They parked on the roadside at the gate of the driveway. Guyiser got out and ran up to the barn to plug in the lights. All the lights came on. As he ran back to the road, he could hear the oo's and ah's. Guyiser ran to Cindy. Everyone clapped and cheered.

Mr. Blackman poured Mr. Taylor a shot of Jack. "Come on up and see his shop." They walked up the driveway, talking and having fun. Mr. and Mrs. Taylor even stopped and threw snowballs at each other. Inside the barn, they stood looking at all the shiny new bikes.

There were big ones, little ones, red ones, blue, white, black, and green. All of the colors sparkled as the lights blinked and winked hanging around the walls.

Cindy and Guyiser stood holding each other. "Everything is just beautiful, Guyiser." Mr. and Mrs. Taylor walked around the room, looking at everything. Mrs. Taylor pointed at the bikes. "I take that one, and that one, and that one." They all laughed. After talking for a while, the Taylor's said they should get back. Mr. Blackman walked them to their car. Cindy and Guyiser lingered behind, kissing. She asked Guyiser to pick her up about eight o'clock the next morning. They kissed and ran down the driveway.

Guyiser lay in his bed that night. He was seeing things that had happened that day. The encouragement from everyone made him realize that what he was doing was what he loved to do. His bike shop had started with a few broken bicycles and had grown into a real bike shop. This was something he could see, something he could touch, something he could love doing. His father's support, Mr. Gibson's encouragement, and of course, Cindy, were all factors in his life. Tomorrow, and the rest of the month, will be the telltale for the rest of his life. He reached out and touched Loaner, "And you, my friend."

"Thanks for joining us. This is the six o'clock morning news." Guyiser stood looking out the living room window. The dark, gray clouds were drifting to the northeast. He turned to the T.V. "It's not over yet, but the afternoon may see some sunshine." It had been some time since he had seen any sun. Guyiser finished his coffee and went to his shop. Excitement filled the air as he opened the barn doors. All the pretty bikes seemed to say, "Good morning." He made a fire and turned on the radio. He sat at his desk looking around and thinking. The music and warm fire soon made the bike shop come to life. Guyiser looked at his watch and walked outside. Mr. Blackman and Loaner were out back feeding the animals. Guyiser waved and walked to them.

Mr. Blackman spoke first. "It might be a pretty day today. It's gettin' lighter. Are you all ready for your sale?"

Guyiser reached in the bucket for a handful of feed. He threw the feed at Loaner. Loaner jumped around and jumped up on Guyiser. "Yes, sir, all ready. Going' to get Cindy now. Be right back. You stay, Loaner." Loaner grabbed Guyiser's pant leg and shook his head and growled. "No, Loaner, I don't want to play."

Loaner let go and ran to Mr. Blackman.

He started grabbing his pant leg. Mr. Blackman shook his leg. "Must be a rabbit out there. We'll see you later." Guyiser went to his truck and drove away.

Cindy stood looking out her living room window. The big red truck pulled into the drive and up to the house. She opened the door and shouted to her mother, "Bye, Mom. See you later." She stood on the porch as Guyiser came to meet her. He stopped at the bottom of the steps with his eyes wide open and mouth agape as he looked at Cindy. She was dressed all in white and red. She wore a white fuzzy long-sleeved sweater with a short white skirt. There was a long red scarf around her neck and a red Santa hat on her head. She wore white boots on her feet with white fur around the tops. All around on the bottom of her skirt there were little bells.

Cindy picked up her backpack and walked down the steps with a big smile on her face. "What do you think?" She said as she modeled for Guyiser. He was speechless. With each step she took, the little bells jingled. She shook her skirt and all the little bells jingled together. Cindy's big blue eyes, long blond hair, and pink lips were all a perfect match. "Mother sewed all the bells on. You like?"

Guyiser finally spoke, "I like everything I see. Are you Cindy, or are you a Christmas angel?"

Cindy kissed him. "For you, I'm both. Let's go." Guyiser stopped at his gate and put up an 'open' sign.

Inside the barn, they looked at each other. "You look so handsome today."

Guyiser shook her skirt. "Tell your mother thanks for the bells. Now I can keep up with you." They laughed and went to the window. Looking out, they saw Mr. Blackman and Loaner coming across the white field. He was carrying two rabbits. Loaner was running around and playing in the snow. Guyiser looked down the road. "Well, we're open. Where are all the customers?"

Cindy laughed. "It's early, Guyiser. You must be patient – about everything." She turned and went to her backpack. "Chocolate?" The two sat around the potbelly stove talking. Guyiser started laughing and laughing. Cindy looked at him. "What's so funny?"

Guyiser chuckled. "Do you mind me asking you something?" He looked at Cindy. "What color panties are you wearing?" He laughed again.

Cindy was surprised at his question. She sat there looking at him but would not be overcome.

She stood up and stepped in front of him. Slowly she lifted her skirt. Guyiser could not believe this was Cindy. "Pink." Guyiser could not say anything. He just sat there looking at Cindy's pink panties. "Are you happy now? They match my bra." She smiled and started laughing. She had surprised Guyiser and had won that conversation.

Cindy stood at the window. "Guyiser, there's somebody coming." He ran to the window. She went to the door to greet the people. A man and a woman got out of their car and walked to her.

Cindy shook her skirt and the little bells rang.

"Well, well, good morning, Cindy. You look all Christmassy."

She held out her hand, "Why, Mr. and Mrs. Wilson. It's good to see you again. Come on in. How is Tony? Oh, this is Guyiser Blackman. This is his shop."

They greeted each other and walked looking at all the bikes. "Oh, Tony is fine, but he lost his bike at school. Someone took it. I like this one, John."

Mr. Wilson came to see the bike. "It's okay, but look at this one over here." Mrs. Wilson went to see the bike he was talking about.

Cindy winked at Guyiser. She went to the bike and pulled it from the rack. "This is called 'Faster'. It had a royal blue frame with chrome fenders, streamers, and a horn. "Is it the right size? The seat is adjustable."

The Wilson's looked it over and looked at each other. "Yes, it's fine. We'll take it. Can we pick it up later?"

Cindy started writing in the sales book.

"Sure, no problem. How about a basket?" she said pointing to the wall. "He can carry his school books and things. They're only twelve dollars. Oh, one more thing." Cindy went to the counter and held up a long, silver chain with a lock and key. "He can lock this one up. Just five dollars."

The Wilson's looked at each other. Guyiser stepped in, "No, the chain and lock are presents." He smiled and stepped back.

"Why, thank you. Cindy, write us up. You take a check?"

Cindy smiled as she wrote, "Sure, Mr. Wilson."

Mrs. Wilson was still looking around. "Do you have any tricycles? Our granddaughter wants one."

Guyiser showed her the two tricycles he had. "Oh, they're cute, John. Let's get one later."

As the Wilson's drove away, Cindy wrote on the bike's ticket, "Sold". She ran to Guyiser and threw her arms around his neck. He hugged and kissed her. "You were great! You sold a bike and a basket. Let's see, I owe you."

Cindy grabbed his face, "A big kiss—that's my reward."

Mr. Blackman and Loaner came in the barn. "Is that all you two do is kiss?" He smiled as he kicked snow off his boots.

"Guess what. Cindy sold a bike and a basket."

Mr. Blackman looked over the bikes.

"Good for you, Cindy. That's one down. You two gettin' hungry? We're having rabbit stew with beans, carrots, and potatoes and cornbread. That sound good to you?"

They nodded their heads 'Yes'. Cindy took Mr. Blackman's arm. "I'll cook some night this week for you, okay?"

He stepped back and looked at her. "My, you sure look pretty, my, my."

Cindy looked at Guyiser and back at Mr. Blackman. "Pink," she said, "Pink." They burst out laughing.

The sun did come out that afternoon. It made the snow even whiter. Blue skies replaced the gray clouds. The air was still biting cold, but Cindy and Guyiser decided to go out and roll a snowman. They started a small snowball at the beginning of the driveway and by the time they had rolled the snow to the barn, it was very big and round. Laughing and playing, they enjoyed the sunshine and the blue sky. Loaner sat watching them add the eyes and nose to the snowman. Cindy put a broomstick in the snowman's arm. When they were finished, the snowman stood about six feet tall. He had on a hat, scarf, and a happy face. Mr. Blackman come out of the house carrying a camera. "I've been watching you two. Let's get a picture of you two with your snowman. Loaner, you too." Mr. Blackman snapped away, "Now, you two by yourselves." He kept clicking. "Okay, now kiss. That's good."

Cindy ran to Mr. Blackman. "Now, you, Guyiser, and Loaner." She took the camera and began to take picture after picture. "Now, you two kiss."

They all laughed and began throwing snowballs at each other.

In the barn, they sat by the stove on bales of hay talking. Guyiser went to the window and looked out, "I thought there would be a lot of people."

Mr. Blackman went to the barn door and looked out. "Don't worry, Guyiser. Most people will come out this weekend. Then you'll get busy. I'm Going' to the house to check the stew."

Cindy walked to the window with Guyiser. "He's right. Don't worry. It's five o'clock. I should go. Take me home? I've had a great day."

Night had fallen as Guyiser put the lock on the barn doors. He stood looking up at the stars in the sky and at the beautiful white fields with their bluish glow. He and Loaner walked to the house. Inside, Mr. Blackman sat eating. "This stew is really good tonight, boy. I added some hot sauce." Guyiser sat looking at the bowl of stew. "I guess you're right, Dad. People will come."

The sun was bright as it came over the east hills and mountains of Tennessee. The sky was clearing as the night fog faded away. Guyiser lit a fire in the big barn. He went back to the house where his father was watching cartoons on T.V. Mr. Blackman was laughing aloud. "That cat and Tweedy Bird just kill me."

Guyiser went to the kitchen. He washed last night's dishes and poured himself a cup of coffee. He was sitting at the kitchen table when Loaner ran in barking. He stood there barking at Guyiser and then ran out. He returned barking and grabbing Guyiser's pant leg. He shook his head and ran out again. Guyiser went to the living room where Loaner stood on the windowsill looking out and barking. He went over to the window. His eyes opened wide as he saw a truck and a car pull into the drive and park at the barn. Guyiser put on his coat and scarf and called to his father in excitement, "Pa, people are here!" He ran to the barn shouting, "Good Morning, And Good Morning."

To Guyiser, people were everywhere, even though there were only five people in his shop looking at his bikes. Mr. Blackman came to Guyiser, "I told you not to worry. I'll go get Cindy. You take care of your customers." He smiled and patted Guyiser's shoulder as he left.

Cars, trucks, people, and kids came all through the day. Cindy and Guyiser greeted them all with big smiles and wishes for a happy Christmas. Some people were just looking. Others were buying. The lookers all said they would be back soon. Cindy and Guyiser were taking orders and writing "Sold" on each bike's sales ticket. Mr. Blackman came out of the house wearing his Santa suit. Children gathered around him all day and into the evening. He always asked them what color of bicycle they wanted. The kids and parents all had fun with him. Some parents took of pictures of their kids and Santa sitting by the snowman. Cindy would sit on Santa's lap holding a baby for pictures.

It had been a great day's fun as Guyiser, Cindy, and Santa sat at the desk looking at the sales book. Cindy had sold three bikes and Guyiser had sold four.

Guyiser was very happy with the day's events.

Mr. Blackman sat in the big red truck waiting for Cindy and watching the two lovebirds kiss goodnight. The sun was going down over the hill as she got into the truck and they drove away. Guyiser plugged in the Christmas lights. He was putting the sold bikes in the corner when another truck pulled up to the barn. Four kids jumped out and ran to the barn.

"Where's Santa? Where's Santa?" the kids called out. Guyiser told them he had gone home and he would be back tomorrow.

The father was looking at all the bicycles. "When will he be back?" Guyiser told him that Santa would be there all day tomorrow. "Good enough. We'll be back tomorrow." The man and kids climbed back in the truck and they drove away. Guyiser stood in the driveway waving to the kids. "See you tomorrow."

Guyiser sat at his desk looking at a flyer. Santa and Cindy had been good for his business. If the next few days were good, December would be a great month for sales.

The next few days were great. All of Cindy's and his work were paying off. They had all of Centerville and the surrounding area talking about Guyiser's Bike Shop since there was not a bike shop in that town. The five-and-dime store did sell a few bikes. If people wanted a bike for their kids, they would have to drive all the way to Nashville.

It was the first Sunday of December. Guyiser was putting all the sold and lay-a-way bikes in the back of the barn. Cindy and Santa were busy showing bicycles to prospective customers and playing with the kids. Cars and trucks were coming and going all day. Everybody was in the Christmas spirit. It was late in the day when Mr. Gibson pulled into the Blackman's driveway. He sat in his truck watching all the people and kids going in and out of the barn. Santa sat in his big red chair laughing with the children. Mr. Gibson got out of his truck and went in the shop. Inside he saw Cindy and Guyiser showing bikes to customers. He went over to the stove and sat in a rocking chair. He looked around the large room at everything. He spotted Guyiser, smiled, and waved at him. Guyiser waved back and walked over to him. "Mr. Gibson sir, it is so good to see you. How are you sir?"

Mr. Gibson shook his hand. "Couldn't be better. Guyiser, I am really impressed. You took this old barn and turned it into a real store. And all these customers and kids! I'm really impressed. How's business?"

"Mr. Gibson, my sales and lay-a-ways are more than my stock. I can't believe it."

Mr. Gibson rocked in the chair, "Well, son, I knew this would happen. You put a lot of thought and work into this place. And Cindy and your Santa Claus were great ideas. How many bicycles do you have left?"

Guyiser looked at the bikes, "Eight, nine, one tricycle, and four baskets."

Mr. Gibson laughed and got up. "Let's go outside. I have something for you." Guyiser followed him outside and to his truck. Mr. Gibson pointed to his load. "I just knew that you would do well, so I brought you ten new bicycles in boxes and some extra things." He stood there smiling as he watched Guyiser's face. Guyiser was touching the boxes in disbelief. He grabbed Mr. Gibson with a big hug. Mr. Gibson continued, "And you'll need more bikes the closer it gets to Christmas."

Guyiser grabbed his hand and kissed the old man's cheek. "I don't know how to thank you."

Guyiser could see the lights blinking and could hear Santa's Ho, Ho, Ho's as he unloaded the truck. Mr.

Gibson handed him the last box of extra things. "I have to get back to Nashville. It's getting dark."

Guyiser hugged him again. "Thank you so much Mr. Gibson. I'll be in Nashville soon and settle up with you."

Mr. Gibson got in his truck and waved.

"Don't worry about it." He drove away waving.

It had taken a few days, but the snow clouds were back. Guyiser walked around his shop with a clipboard. He was trying to count the bikes that were sold and the ones that were not. He was also sorting out the old bikes he had started with from the new bikes Mr. Gibson had just given him. He wanted to keep the baskets for eight dollars separate from the twelve dollar ones. Then he needed to keep track of all the extras he sold to go along with the bikes. Nothing was adding up. He knew he had no idea how much money he had made. Nothing matched even though he went over and over the figures. Nothing added up.

It was Monday morning and Cindy was going to ride her bike over to Guyiser's house. He sat at his desk trying to figure things out. This was really bothering him. He was also bothered about not being with Cindy. She would come in the morning and leave in the afternoon. He missed their playful times. He missed her touch and warm smile. He missed looking in her blue eyes, their bike rides, and her calling him 'boyfriend'. Rage came over him, and he threw the clipboard flying across the room. Cindy came in just as the clipboard hit the wall. She looked at the scattered papers, the broken clipboard, and then at Guyiser. He ran to her and hugged her tight. Her perfume and warm face flooded his mind. "Oh, Cindy. I've missed you, I've missed us," he whispered.

Cindy could feel that he was upset.

"Are you all right? What's wrong? I'm here for you." They sat by the stove talking. "What is it, Guyiser? I've never seen you this way." She held his hands.

Guyiser looked at her hands. "Cindy, I'm not smart. You're good in school. High grades and all. I can't do figures good, and I'm a poor reader. Pa is the same way. My mom used to read to us. She helped me with schoolwork. I wasn't good in school. My teachers said I had something called dyslexia or something like that. Sometimes, the numbers get mixed up. And words come out wrong when I read. That's why I quit school. And now I can't keep track of the bikes that are coming and going. I don't even know how much money I have made. But I do know it is a lot. And you, I'm afraid I might lose you." Tears began to roll down Guyiser's face.

Cindy sat in Guyiser's lap. She hugged him close and kissed his tears. "Guyiser, you are my first love. I miss you when we are not together. I pray that I don't lose you. I want us to always be together. Even if we're apart, we have something called love. Look at me. As far as those silly numbers, I'll help you with them. I understand and we can read together. Please let me be a part of your life." She smiled and kissed him. Guyiser looked into her eyes. A huge weight had been lifted from his shoulders. He now knew he could tell her anything and she would not judge him. "Now, go pick up that clipboard and those papers." He kissed her and went to pick them up. He stood looking at the clipboard and papers. Then he turned and looked at Cindy, smiling.

That Monday morning started out slow. Cindy sat at Guyiser's desk. He was looking over her shoulder. She was drawing lines on the paper. Cindy looked at Guyiser, "Now, this is your inventory list. In this column, you put bikes you get from Mr. Gibson and in this column; you put bicycles that are sold. At the end of the week, subtract this line from that line. That will tell you how many bikes you have sold and how many you still have for sale. Do the same thing with baskets and extra parts. And if you get confused, I'm here to help you."

Guyiser watched and listened to everything Cindy said. "Oh, I get it."

Cindy smiled at Guyiser. "I knew you would. Let's count everything you have now. And next Monday we will re-count everything and put those figures down on this list, okay? That way you will know how much money you made that week." They started counting. As Cindy counted the inventory Guyiser marked the numbers on the list. They laughed and played as they worked. "Now, when you hit the big time, you will have someone to do this for you. And they will put everything on a computer so you will always know what you have and what you need to order."

Guyiser learned a lot about business that day. He learned things that would stay with him the rest of his life. Cindy had given him confidence and direction. His father had given him vision. Guyiser could take an idea and make it come to life. In his early years, his mother had given him creativity. She could take an old bed sheet and make an apron, napkins, curtains, tablecloths, and all kinds of things.

Guyiser stood by the window. Mr. Blackman opened the door and called out, "Look what I got!" He had cut down a Christmas tree. "Something for your shop." Guyiser and Cindy decorated the tree with everything they could find. The day had been fun for everybody. Clouds began to drift in. Cindy was gone, and Guyiser sat looking at the Christmas tree. Loaner licked his hand, wanting attention. "Good boy. Yes, I love you too."

Cindy was helping her mother do things in their house. Elvis Christmas music was playing on the stereo. A fire burned warm in the fireplace. The smell of food cooking filled the house. The Christmas tree blinked with all the colored lights. It was a country 'Home Sweet Home.' Mr. Taylor had just come home. "Hello,

I'm home." Mrs. Taylor gave him a kiss and a hug. "Is this what you wanted?" He held up a big ham.

"It's perfect." Mrs. Taylor took the ham and went into the kitchen. Mr. Taylor followed her.

"Where's Cindy?"

"She's upstairs in her room." Mr. Taylor went to the stairs and called to her.

"Hi, Daddy. How was your day?" she said as she kissed him.

"Oh, just another day. I saw six deer on the way home. Oh. By the way, I have something for you." He handed her an envelope. "From the broadcast school."

Excitedly, she grabbed the envelope and ran to the couch. She sat down, tearing it open.

Dear Cynthia Taylor,

We received your application and would like you to join our staff in the training of the broadcast media.

Cindy looked up to her father. "Daddy, I'm in!" She continued reading,

Classes start January 15th and run for a six-month period. You have options for living quarters. You may live off campus or stay with us in the safe and protected environment of the school. This is a female dorm, which includes food and all books. Thank you for choosing our course in media

relations. Please report to Janice Roads, your counselor, on January 15.

Roger Hillman, Director
American Broadcasting-Television & Radio
of the Arts

"Daddy, that's just a month away." Mrs. Taylor heard the excitement and came into the living room. "Mother, look!"

Mrs. Taylor read the letter. "Oh, Honey, we're so proud of you. Your father and I talked it over." She started to cry. "But you're going away."

Cindy hugged her mother and father. "But, not for long. I'll be back in July. Time will go fast. And, I'll call all the time. Thanks, Daddy." Mr. Taylor had a tear in his eye. "I love you both so much."

Supper was full of talk and excitement.

Mrs. Taylor was making a list, "You'll need new clothes—skirts, dresses, and two blazers, and maybe a suit and new shoes and jewelry. You want to look professional. Oh, you'll need a briefcase."

Mr. Taylor spoke up, "You might want to change your hair style. Looks are important."

Cindy started laughing. "This is school. I'm not a reporter yet, but I know what you mean. Thanks, you two." She went to her room and lay across the bed. Her first thoughts were about telling Guyiser. *How would he take it? I'll write him every day. It's only for six months. He'll understand.* It started to dawn on her. *Six months.*

Six months. However, on the upside, I'll be doing what I want to do—television. She smiled and closed her eyes. *"Now for today's news. I'm Cynthia Taylor in New York. I'm Cynthia Taylor, reporting live from Nashville, Tennessee."* Cindy burst out laughing. Hugging her pillow and rolling around on the bed, "I can do it!" she shouted.

'Guyiser's Bike Shop'. Guyiser stood looking at the big sign over the barn doors. The lights blinked and blinked. Business was really picking up. Every day there was traffic with kids and cars. Mr. Blackman was having a good time running around in his Santa suit. Cindy and her bells attracted all the boys and girls. Loaner would sit by the snowman watching everything. It was three o'clock. Guyiser went to Cindy. He grabbed her and hugged her tightly. "What do you say we go into Centerville tonight and have a good steak supper and see a movie?"

Cindy was surprised at Guyiser's aggressiveness, but she liked it. "Well, boyfriend, I'll have to think it over.

Okay? I thought it over and the answer is 'Yes'."

"Good, I'll take you home now and pick you up about six thirty. Seal it with a kiss?"

Guyiser returned to finish the day. Santa was sitting in his chair. "Dad, I have a date tonight. Can you handle things here?"

Mr. Blackman let out a loud, "Ho, Ho, Ho. Who with? Ho, Ho, Ho. Sure, I can, boy. Go have some fun. Ho, Ho, Ho." Mr. Blackman was really into his

Santa thing. Guyiser went in the house to clean up and change clothes. He stood in the bathroom in a white shirt looking in the mirror. He put a tie around his neck and after a few tries; he had tied a pretty knot. Guyiser stood looking at himself. *Well, you're not so bad after all.* He combed his hair just right and smiled at his reflection in the mirror. *Not bad at all.* He left the house and walked to the barn. Mr. Blackman saw him coming. "Well, well, you look pretty good, tie and all."

Guyiser adjusted his tie, "Thanks, Think she'll like it?"

"I'm sure of it, you two go have fun. You hear me?" Guyiser went to his truck and drove away.

Guyiser walked up to the Taylor's door and knocked. Mr. Taylor opened the door, "Hello, Guyiser. Come on in. Come on in. Cindy is almost ready. You know how women are." They laughed. "Sit down, sit down." Mr. Taylor called to Cindy, "Guyiser's here." He went back and sat down. "Cindy tell you the good news?"

Guyiser shook his head. "News? No, sir."

"Well, I guess she'll tell you later. We're really happy and proud of her." Cindy came down the stairs wearing a beautiful dress and carrying her coat.

Guyiser walked over to meet her. "Cindy, you're beautiful. I never seen you in a dress."

Cindy looked Guyiser over. "And look how handsome you are. We make a good-looking couple. Ready? Bye, Daddy. Tell Mom bye."

"Bye, Mr. Taylor. I'll have her home early."

They drove down the drive and turned toward Centerville. They talked and laughed about the houses all lit up along the way. "Your dad told me you got some good news. What is it?"

Cindy froze. She didn't know her father had mentioned it. "Oh, it's nothing. I'll tell you about it later." She moved closer to Guyiser. "Let's just enjoy tonight."

They entered Centerville and rode around looking at all the lights and decorations. The restaurant was not too busy as the waitress showed them to a booth by a fireplace. They   sat there making small talk. Soon they ordered. Guyiser felt something was wrong with Cindy. "You, you're pretty quiet tonight. Some'em on your mind?"

Cindy reached for Guyiser's hands. Just then, the waitress came with their food and drinks. Cindy released her hands and leaned back. Guyiser was enjoying his steak when he noticed Cindy was just picking at her food. "You know, you said you were there for me. And I'm here for you. You know that?" They had finished their meal and were standing outside of the restaurant. Guyiser took her hand. "Do you want to walk around town and see things, or do you want to go to a movie?"

Cindy squeezed his hand. "I think I just want to go home. I'm sorry."

Guyiser turned her chin and looked in her eyes. "Is it something I did or said? I wish you would talk to me."

Cindy turned away. "No, no, it's not you. You're great to me and for me. I'll tell you tomorrow."

Guyiser put up his hands. "Okay, okay. No Pressure."

It was a quiet, short ride back to the Taylor's house. Cindy put her arms around Guyiser and kissed him good night. She got out of the truck and walked around to his side. She reached in and kissed him again. "I'll see you tomorrow. Sweet dreams." With that, she ran to the house and went in.

Cindy lay in bed staring out the window. It wasn't that it was hard telling Guyiser about the school and going away for a while. It was the thought of leaving him.

She was feeling love for him. She knew she would not be with him. He would not be there.

She kept telling herself, *It's not forever. It's only for a little while. That's right! It's only for a short while, and we will be back together.* With that thought, sleep finally came.

It was nine o'clock. Smoke poured from the barn's chimney on this cold day. Guyiser was showing a family two bikes. "I know your twins will really like these. You want to pick them up on the 23rd, right? Thanks a lot and we'll see you then." Their truck drove down the driveway as Cindy was coming up on her bike.

Guyiser stood watching Cindy ride up the driveway. Her little bells were ringing as she peddled. He ran to meet her. "Hi, girlfriend." They walked to the barn talking about how cold it was. Inside, they stood by the warm potbelly stove. "That truck that passed you was the Smith family. They said to say hello to you. They bought bikes for their twins."

Cindy sat down in the rocking chair. "Yeah, they're a great family. I know them from church."

Guyiser went to the window. Looking out, he said, "It's snowing again. I hope it doesn't stop people from coming out." He walked back to Cindy and the stove.

"Guyiser," Cindy took a deep breath, "there's something I have to tell you. I thought about it and you all last night." Cindy took an envelope from her backpack and handed it to Guyiser. He stood puzzled and took the envelope. He looked at Cindy and then opened it. Guyiser looked it over and began to read. 'Dear Cynthia Taylor,' He read on. Then he looked at Cindy and read aloud. 'Please report to Janice Roads, your counselor, January 15th.' Guyiser looked at Cindy. "Why didn't you tell me about this? This is great news. Something you have always wanted."

Cindy stood up puzzled. "But, but."

Guyiser grabbed her and swung her around. "My girlfriend in broadcasting! This is great." He kissed her over and over.

"But, I thought..."

"Oh, Sweetheart, in my mind, I've see you on T.V. a hundred times. I'm so proud of you."

Cindy took the letter from Guyiser.

"But, I'm going away."

Guyiser kissed her again. "But not for long. And Florida is not that far away. I can even go down there and visit you." He sat her down.

"Guyiser, I thought you would be upset. I've worried about telling you for days."

Guyiser knelt down beside her. "Look around, Honey. You see this bike shop. If it weren't for you, I'd still be helping my dad sell stuff on weekends. I'm doing what I want to do. And, I'm happy. Why shouldn't you be happy? I'm not losing you. In fact, let's look at the big picture." He stood up and smiled at Cindy. "I can see it now. I'm sitting in my penthouse office watching my wife on television as she tells the world important things. What could be better than that?"

Cindy stood up and hugged and kissed Guyiser. "I love you, Guyiser Blackman, and nothing could be better than that."

A horn sounded outside the barn. Guyiser went to the door. A man and a woman got out and came in. "You open?"

Guyiser remembered them. "Why, Mr. and Mrs. Wilson, come in, come in."

Mrs. Wilson looked around. "You still have that tricycle we saw last week?"

"Yes, ma'am. Did you want the red one or the blue one? Mrs. Wilson turned to her husband. "What do you think, John?"

"I like the red one."

Guyiser turned to Cindy, "Cindy, would you mind writing them up? I'll load the tricycle."

The snow fell all day. Cindy and Guyiser sat and talked about her school. Business had stopped for the day. Cindy felt like a new person. She and Guyiser felt even closer as they talked about their futures. "Yes, I'd like to have several bike shops in Nashville. I also have ideas about bike products. I hope Mr. Gibson can give me suggestions on that. He's a pretty smart old man, you know." Guyiser started laughing. "I just thought of something funny. Maybe you could advertise my bike shops on your T.V. show." They both started laughing and laughing.

Cindy turned serious. "And now, for today's news. Guyiser's Bike Shop has a sale going on." They burst out in laughter again. She stood by the window. "It's getting dark. I'd better go."

Guyiser came and stood hugging her and looking out the window. "I'll take you home. It's been another great day with you." Soon Cindy was on her porch waving and throwing kisses to Guyiser. The snow continued to fall as he drove home.

Guyiser pulled into his driveway and stopped. He sat in his truck looking at the lights along the drive. They led to the large barn, which was lit up with all the lights Guyiser had put on it. He watched the snow fall. The picture he saw seemed like a dream. He sat there seeing all the faces of the kids talking to Santa. He could hear the little bells on Cindy's skirt. He could see her smiling face as she wrote up sales. Loaner ran down the driveway barking and jumped in the back of the truck. Tears of joy and happiness came to his eyes. I've got it all.

Mr. Blackman was putting lights and cotton balls on the Christmas tree as Guyiser came into the house. His father stepped back from the tree. "What do you think?"

He was pleased with his work. "You're tall, put this star on top."

Guyiser did and stepped back by his dad. "It's the prettiest tree in the county, you know that?"

Mr. Blackman watched the lights blinking. "Yes, it is, even if I do say so myself."

Father and son sat watching T.V. and the blinking lights on the tree. "You want some more popcorn?"

"No thanks. I'm Going' into Nashville in the morning. You want to come?"

Mr. Blackman put the bowl of popcorn down. "No, I got some things around here to do. I'll watch the shop for you."

Guyiser stood up and stretched. "Okay I'm Going' to bed. Good night."

The snow had fallen all night. As Guyiser and Loaner rode down Highway 70, the chains on his tires chewed the snow. He drove slowly down the hill. In the distance, Guyiser could see a man in a suit and a long coat waving his arms. The closer he came, Guyiser could see a station wagon on the side of the road. The man kept waving his arms. Guyiser pulled in behind the car and stopped. The man came to the window as Guyiser rolled it down. "I'm glad to see you, young man. I have car trouble and I'm freezing."

Guyiser saw that the man was cold. "Come on and get in."

The man ran around and got in the truck. "Thank you, thank you. I've been here for hours. Loaner licked the snow from his coat. "Nobody out today."

Guyiser reached and turned the heater on high. "What's the problem?"

The man put his hands to the heater. "Well, I pulled over to clean the windshield. I got stuck and then the battery died. Won't start. You going to Nashville?"

Guyiser nodded. "You?"

"No, I'm going through Nashville to Alabama. Here's my card."

Guyiser took the card. "Well, Mr. Bagwell, maybe I can help you."

The man smiled. "Well, if you can, I sure would owe you."

Guyiser pulled the truck beside the car.

"You stay here and get warm." Guyiser got out and zipped up his coat. He picked his jumper cables out of the back of the truck. He hooked them up to the truck's battery and on to the car's battery. Then he got in the station wagon and in a few minutes, the car started. Guyiser turned the heather on high and got out. He unhooked the cables and the shut the hoods. When he got back in his truck he said, "You're right! It's cold out there. Let it sit for a while to build up the battery." Guyiser pulled in front of the car and backed up close to it. He got out, took a long chain from the back of his truck, and hooked it to both vehicles. Mr. Bagwell got out of the truck and climbed into his car. Guyiser came to his window. "I'll pull you out now. You ready?" He got back in his truck and put it in gear. Slowly, the car started to move toward the road. Guyiser's truck had no problem pulling the car. On the road, Guyiser unhooked the chain and went again to Mr. Bagwell's window. "We're about twelve miles from Nashville. Stay behind me and drive in my tire tracks. We'll stop at a big gas station up ahead, okay?"

Mr. Bagwell shook Guyiser's hand. "I won't forget you for this." They drove very slowly for an hour. At the edge of Nashville, Guyiser put his turn signal on and pulled into a large Standard Service Station.

They parked and go out. "Well, we made it." They shook hands again. "You should buy another battery. That one's got a bad cell, I think." Guyiser looked up to the sky. "And, there's more snow coming. You should get them to put chains on your tires."

Mr. Bagwell agreed. "That's exactly what I'll do.
Come on, can I buy you a cup of coffee?"

They sat at the counter having pie and coffee. "I saw a lot of toys in your car. For your kids?"

Mr. Bagwell shook his head. "No, my kids have all the toys they need. My company in Birmingham distributes toys all over the South."

The service attendant came to them. "Mr. Bagwell, your car is ready. We put in a new battery, put chains on, and filled it up with gas. We also added some anti-freeze. You're ready to go. Here are you keys, and thank you, sir."

Guyiser got up. "Speaking of going, I guess I'd better go, too. Mr. Bagwell, it's been a pleasure meeting you."

Mr. Bagwell stood up. "No, it's been my pleasure. What do I owe you, son?"

Guyiser shook his head. "Nothing at all, sir. And my name is Guyiser, Guyiser Blackman."

Mr. Bagwell extended his hand. "Well, Guyiser, thanks for everything. You saved my life. I sure hope I see you again."

"Good luck to you, sir. Have a Merry Christmas." Loaner barked as Guyiser got into his truck. "Yes, we can go now. We did our good deed for the day."

The Factory

Part 4

Make me this; Make me that.
I have an idea; I have a plan.
I can do it; I know I can.

Guyiser had just reached for Mr. Gibson's door handle when a man and woman walked through the door. He heard, "Ya'll come back now," as he entered. "Guyiser, my boy. Come in, come in. Sit down and stay a while."

Guyiser and Mr. Gibson sat in rocking chairs. "You look in good spirits today, Mr. Gibson."

"Oh, I couldn't be better." Mr. Gibson rocked in his chair looking at Guyiser. Finally he spoke. "Guyiser, how would you like to be rich?"

Guyiser looked at him puzzled. "Well, someday, I hope to be."

Mr. Gibson continued. "Well, someday may be sooner than you think. You're a creative, smart, honest, young man. Moreover, my instincts tell me you're going places. Now, I want to get to the point. I'm an old man. I've done it all, and I want to do it again! I want to live through you. I want to give you my wisdom and experience. I have plenty of money and have had good fun all my life. You are the son I never had." Mr. Gibson rocked some more. "I have a long-time friend of some sixty years. He has a factory in Kentucky. It's a bicycle factory. I've been buying from him for more than fifty years. Now, he's sick. He and his wife, God love her, can't run the factory anymore. We started out together with a small bicycle shop years ago, like you. Now, his factory is worth a million, maybe more. However, it's going downhill since Jessie's health got poor. Last week Margaret called me, and we talked a long time. They want to put the factory up for sale;

they gave me first choice at it. I told her I'd think about it. This is where you come in. I'm too old to take it on by myself. But, you're young with young ideas, and you could make this factory grow again. What I would like to do is for us to go up there and see the plant to see what you think."

Guyiser could not believe his ears. "A million dollars! That's a lot of money. Do you have a million dollars?"

Mr. Gibson began to laugh and laugh.

"No, son, no, no, no. If I buy it, it's all on paper, just paper. Besides, Margaret will keep a percent of the stock in the company. All I want is for you to think about it. Besides, you have nothing to lose and everything to gain." Mr. Gibson laughed and rocked some more. "Think about it. President of you own company."

Guyiser sat in his truck. His plan was to come to Nashville, pay Mr. Gibson some money, pick up some old bicycle frames and parts, and do some shopping for presents. Now, Mr. Gibson had hit him with something he could not conceive. *A million dollar factory.* Guyiser and his father were thrilled when they made a hundred dollars at the swap meet. *This was a lot more than a hundred dollars.*

The snow fell all the way back to the house. It was a very long, slow ride as he passed tow-trucks helping people. He kept thinking about the word 'factory'. He had never even had a job. *What did Mr. Gibson expect him to do? Sure, I have many ideas, but…. So what? Pa would know what to do. What does a factory do? I guess they make things or build things, but what then? I don't understand. Are Mr. Gibson, this woman Margaret, and I doing all the work? I hope I don't have to read a lot of stuff or do the inventory.* Then out of the blue, he heard Cindy's voice, 'When you're a big shot, you'll have someone do this for you.' *That's it. I'll talk it over with Cindy.* She's smart about things. Guyiser turned and petted Loaner's head.

"What do you think?" Loaner began to bark. "Okay, we'll do it your way." Guyiser smiled and laughed.

As the red truck pulled up to the barn, Guyiser saw a truck and a car parked. Inside the barn, Mr. Blackman moved his chair by the warm stove. Cindy was showing someone a tricycle. "Yes sir, this is the last one." She waved at Guyiser. "Guyiser, could you put this tricycle in Mr. Wayne's car?" Cindy wrote in the sales book while Guyiser loaded the tricycle in the car.

"And have a Merry Christmas and a Happy New Year," he said as he waved goodbye. Guyiser came to Cindy and hugged and kissed her. "Where are all the bicycles?"

Cindy smiled and kissed his cheek. "Santa and I have sold seven bikes and one tricycle." She jumped up and down. "It's the Christmas rush."

They walked over to Mr. Blackman. "Pa, you did good today. You and Cindy have put us over the top. I never thought we would sell so many bicycles, especially in this weather. And, speaking of weather, it's really coming down out there. Let's close up and go in the house. I have news that I want to talk to you two about."

The house was warm and there was the smell of good food cooking as they sat around the kitchen table. Guyiser leaned back in his chair. "And, that's all I know right now. What do you think?" He looked at Cindy and then at his father.

Mr. Blackman spoke first. "Well, it sounds like a pretty big thing to me. I think I would go up there and see the factory and see what I was getting myself into first. What does Mr. Gibson want you to do?"

Guyiser stood up and went to the window, looking out. "I don't really know, Dad."

Cindy got up and went to Guyiser. "This may be your big chance in life. My dad would say that this was opportunity knocking. And like Mr. Gibson said, 'You have nothing to lose and everything to gain.' I know that you can do anything you set your mind to." Cindy smiled and held Guyiser's hands. "This could be your penthouse office you want."

Guyiser looked into Cindy's eyes. "You may be right."

Cindy sat in Guyiser's lap at his desk. The snow had stopped that morning, but it had left almost two feet of the white stuff. Guyiser marked off the days that had passed on his calendar. "Only two more days till Christmas, Cindy. All the people who bought on lay-a-way have paid for and picked up their bikes." He smiled. "According to this inventory list, I only have six bikes left and two, I hope, to repair." He kissed her, "Cindy, how can I ever, ever thank you?"

She got up and walked to the stove. "Oh, I'll think of something. You can start by you and your dad being on time for Christmas dinner. Maybe Daddy can give you some advice about the factory."

Guyiser smiled and motioned to Cindy. "Come here, you." Cindy sat on his lap. Guyiser reached for her skirt and shook the little bells. He smiled at her and put his hand under her sweater. "Pink?"

She smiled back, "Yes, pink."

He touched her bra. "Let's see." They wrestled playfully as Cindy giggled and tried to get away. Their kisses became more passionate as Guyiser's hand went under her bra. Her warm, firm breast felt good in his hand as he raised her sweater and kissed her nipples.

Cindy became very excited as she felt his excitement growing. Her hand roamed over his chest and into his lap.

As they kissed and kissed, "Oh, Guyiser," she whispered, "I want to, but not now."

Guyiser kissed her lips and squeezed her breasts. "I want you so bad. I think about you every day and night."

She put her hand over Guyiser's, "I know. I think about you, too."

He moved his hands away and held her tight. "When you're ready, when you're ready," he whispered.

"Dad, pass me the scotch tape, please." Mr. Blackman handed the tape to Guyiser. "You wrap a pretty present. What's in the box?"

The kitchen table was full of rolls of paper, bows, and ribbon. Guyiser wrote on a card. "It's a little elephant for Mrs. Taylor. She collects them. He cut some red paper and placed a small box on it for size. Then he opened the box and looked inside. He closed it and carefully folded the paper around it.

"Who's that for?" Guyiser put a white bow on the box and held it up, looking at it.

"It's for Cindy."

Mr. Blackman poured another cup of coffee and watched Guyiser wrap his last two presents. "Let's go in the living room and see what Santa brought last night." Guyiser followed his father to the living room. The tree lights blinked, saying 'Merry Christmas' as Mr. Blackman picked up two colorful boxes. "Merry Christmas, Guyiser."

Guyiser picked up a large green and white box with a big red bow on it. "Merry Christmas to you, Dad."

They sat by the fireplace and opened their gifts. Mr. Blackman was like a little kid. He tore the paper off first. "Oh, man," he said as he held up a tan, leather suede coat with fur around the collar. He quickly stood up and put it on. "Look at me," he said as he went to the mirror. Admiring himself, "It's a perfect fit, Guyiser."

Guyiser went to the tree and picked up another box. "Check this out."

Again, Mr. Blackman tore the box open. "Wow, this is sharp." It was a tan western style hat. He quickly put it on and went back to the mirror. "I'm pretty handsome, don't you think?" He smiled to himself as he modeled, "Thanks, son." He gave Guyiser a big hug. "Open yours, open yours." Guyiser opened one of his boxes. He took out two dress shirts, one white and one a light blue.

There were two neckties and two pairs of dress pants.

"Man, this is just what I need!"

"Open the other one," Mr. Blackman said.

Guyiser put the box to his ear and shook it. He smiled and opened the box. He took out a pair of beautiful black wing-tipped dress shoes. He held them up looking at their shine. "Pa, I never had a pair of dress shoes. They're beautiful."

Mr. Blackman smiled, "All business men wear wing-tip shoes." He walked to the kitchen door. "Come watch this." Guyiser stood in the doorway. Mr. Blackman got a can of dog food from the cabinet and called to Loaner. Loaner came in and stood looking at them. Mr. Blackman held up the can. Loaner went over to him. Mr. Blackman looked at Loaner and spoke, "Tail."

Loaner sat down. Mr. Blackman looked at Guyiser as he opened the can and put the food in a bowl. Loaner sat licking his lips. Mr. Blackman put the food down beside Loaner, walked over to Guyiser, and smiled. Loaner looked at the food and then at

Mr. Blackman. The two men stood watching Loaner for about three minutes. Loaner did not move. Mr. Blackman finally spoke, "Time." Loaner gobbled up the food. Mr. Blackman laughed, "We've been working on that a week. He's a really smart dog. One day I told him it was time to eat, and he caught on fast. I love your dog. Well, we better get ready to go. Don't want to miss Mrs. Taylor's cooking." They laughed.

"You're right about that. I'm getting tired of your rabbit stew. Merry Christmas, to you."

"Merry Christmas, Guyiser."

Ham, turkey, fried chicken, green beans, mashed potatoes, gravy, cornbread, cranberry sauce, and all the trimmings kept Mrs. Taylor busy. She was in 'heaven' as she scurried around the kitchen. Cindy was setting the table with their best chinaware. She called out to her mother, "Mother, I forgot. Which side do the spoons go on?"

Mrs. Taylor came into the dining room. "Every year I have to tell you; they go on this side," she said as she placed a spoon down. "Big spoon here, little spoon here. Now, go get ready. Wear that blue dress, you know, I like it on you."

Cindy rolled her eyes. "Yes, Mother."

"And, no boots. Wear your heels."

"Yes, Mother."

"And tell your father to bring in some more fire wood."

"Yes, Mother. Anything else?"

"No, my daughter. Just go, go, go." Mrs. Taylor went back to the kitchen shaking her head. "I have to do everything around here."

Cindy stood in front of her full-length mirror adjusting her blue dress. She picked up her hairbrush and walked to the window, brushing her long, blond hair. As she looked out, she saw her father picking up firewood. Guyiser picked up several logs as Mr. Blackman stood watching them. The two dogs ran around chasing each other in the snow. She stood smiling to herself.

The men came in and put the wood by the fireplace. "You could of helped, Dad." Mr. Blackman took off his coat and hung it on the coat rack.

"Oh, no. Don't want to get my new coat dirty. Mind if I keep my hat on a while, Mr. Taylor? Gotta break it in." They all laughed and sat down.

"Cindy told me about the factory. It sounds good. What do you think?"

Guyiser looked at his father. "I don't know, Mr. Taylor. All this is so sudden. But, everybody seems to think I should look into it."

Mr. Taylor lit his pipe, "It sounds like Mr. Gibson has a lot of confidence in you. With your ideas, it just might be profitable for you."

Guyiser leaned forward. "What would you suggest?" He sat back, eager for the answer.

"Well, like you dad said, I'd go up there and check it out and see if your ideas fit in."

Guyiser listened, "Then what?"

"Well, let me start by telling you that ideas are worth a lot of money. Ideas are what make a company grow. Take your bike shop, you started with ideas and followed through with them. Look what you have accomplished. If you find you can take your ideas and run with them, things will take their course. At that time, and this is important, Guyiser, get a contract with the company and Mr. Gibson. I'm sure Mr. Gibson is an honest man, but sometimes in business, people steal other's ideas and work. They make all the money and pay the owner of the ideas peanuts. You have to look out for yourself. That's the story is a nutshell. What do you think, Mr. Blackman?"

Mr. Blackman took off his hat, "I agree with you, especially about the contract. But, to get a contract, you have to make a commitment to the work, to the factory, to Mr. Gibson, to the backers, and to yourself. It's not going to happen overnight. It may take a year or two, maybe more. Isn't that right, Mr. Taylor?" Mr. Taylor shook his head in agreement. Mr. Blackman continued. "I've watched you commit to things all your life. You always finished the job. I've taught you to tell the truth. When you give your word, it's solid. But you, and only you, should decide what to do. Not me, or Mr. Gibson, or Mr. Taylor, or anybody should tell you what to do with your life. You're young, Guyiser, with many, many years ahead of you."

Mr. Taylor lit his pipe again. "Guyiser, if I had a son, I'd tell him just what you have heard. You're a good young man, and I'm sure you will always make the right decisions. Your father raised you that way. Now, to change the subject, how did your bicycle sale end up?"

They sat talking about this, that, and the other thing the rest of the day. Mrs. Taylor came in to the joined them. Cindy floated down the stairs and sat beside Guyiser. She kissed him on the cheek with, "Hi, boyfriend."

He kissed her back with a, "Hi, girlfriend."

Mrs. Taylor stood up, "Is everybody hungry yet? It'll be about ten more minutes. Cindy, come help me."

"Yes, Mother."

With the top button of their pants undone and a glass of Scotch, a glass of Jack Daniels, and a glass of eggnog, the three men stretched out in the living room watching a football game on a big screen T.V.

Mr. Blackman patted his big belly. "I won't have to eat for a week."

They all laughed. Cindy and her mother finished in the kitchen and came into the living room.

Mrs. Taylor stopped and looked at the men stretched out. "If you get hungry later, we left the food on the table. Help yourself."

Cindy went over to Guyiser. "You look like a pet pig." She laughed. "Let's go outside and walk it off." Guyiser slowly got up as Cindy put on her coat and boots. They walked down the driveway holding hands.

Soon they stopped and Cindy leaned against the wooden fence. "Did you get enough to eat?"

Guyiser leaned against the fence and looked to the sky. "I'm about to pop."

Cindy laughed, "Me, too." She looked to the sky. "Did you talk to Daddy?"

"Yes, we talked. Your father is a pretty smart man. He gave me a good insight into the business world. I think I know, now, what I have to do."

She stepped over and hugged Guyiser. "I'm glad he helped. He's always helped me." They kissed.

Mrs. Taylor came out of the house and rang the bell on the porch. She called out, waving, "Come in, come in." Cindy and Guyiser started walking back to the house, holding each other.

Inside, everybody sat around talking. Mrs. Taylor stood by the Christmas tree. "Your attention, please." She nudged Mr. Taylor, "Sit up straight, honey. First of all, we are happy to have such good neighbors and friends. We have little presents for both of you."

She bent down, picked up a present, and read the card. "Guyiser, for you. And this one is for Mr. Blackman."

Guyiser went to the tree and picked up two boxes. "Mrs. Taylor, to you from us. Mr. Taylor, Merry Christmas from us." Guyiser looked at Cindy. "Cindy, you have been a bad girl." They all laughed. "But, this is for you from me. Merry Christmas."

Mrs. Taylor said, "On the count of three, everybody open their presents."

Together, they counted, "One, two, and three." They all started opening their gifts. Mr. Taylor's eyes smiled big as he saw the black and white ivory onyx chest set. Mrs. Taylor held up the shiny elephant with its nose in the air. Mr. Blackman saw a gold pocket watch and a gold chain wrapped in a long dark blue neck scarf.

Guyiser quickly stood up and put on a dark blue blazer with gold buttons. He also held up for all to see a light blue dress shirt and a silk necktie. He sat by Cindy as she opened her present.

Guyiser watched her face as the box opened. Cindy took a big breath as her eyes went wide open. "Guyiser, it's beautiful," she said as she held up the charm bracelet. With her other hand she held up a gold necklace with a gold ring in it. "Oh, Guyiser, I love it."

Guyiser took the bracelet. "This is a bicycle, when we met. This is a little reindeer, our first kiss. This is my heart. This is a tower, like T.V. stations have. This is a little dream weaver, for your hopes and dreams. And this is a little house, for your future." He put the bracelet on her wrist. She held up her arm, looking at all the gold charms.

"Oh, Guyiser, it's beautiful." Tears of joy came to her eyes and ran down her cheeks.

"And, this," he took the necklace and held it up, "they say it's a friendship ring." He looked at Cindy. "But, to me, it's much more than that. May I?" He put the chain around her neck and fastened it. "You look beautiful."

Cindy ran to the mirror and looked at the necklace and ring around her neck. She held her arm up to see the bracelet and necklace together. Guyiser stood behind her, hugging her and looking at her in the mirror. Cindy began to cry, "I'll always remember this." Mr. and Mrs. Taylor, Mr. Blackman, and Cindy and Guyiser stood in a circle holding hands and saying a prayer together.

It had been a perfect Christmas card day.

Everybody hugged each other as Mr. Blackman and Guyiser prepared to leave. Cindy and Guyiser stood on the porch hugging. "I'll never forget this day, boyfriend."

They stood holding each other as Mr. Blackman tooted the truck's horn. "Cindy, girlfriend, I gotta go into Nashville and take care of a few things tomorrow, so I'll see you later, okay? Thanks for today. I'll dream about you tonight." Guyiser touched the ring around her neck. "Goodnight, sweetheart." He called for Loaner as he got in the truck. Loaner came running from the barn barking.

Mr. Blackman stood by the fireplace looking at his new watch. "You know, they are really good people. Here we live this close and never really met. Say you're going to Nashville tomorrow?"

Guyiser was in the kitchen with Loaner.

"That's right. Going to see Mr. Gibson and pay him, and go to the bank, and to have the oil changed in my truck. Anything you need?" He took a big ham bone from a paper bag and looked at Loaner. "Tail." Loaner sat down.

"Maybe you could pick up some feed and some more salt for the deer."

Guyiser put the bone on the floor and walked to the living room door. "Okay, I can do that." He looked at Loaner staring at the bone. "Time." Loaner attacked the bone. Guyiser smiled and walked into the living room.

"Maybe you could pick me up a couple bottles of wine."

Guyiser passed him and stopped as he went to his bedroom. "Nope, I can't feed your habit."

Mr. Blackman looked at him.

"You don't like my drinking, do you?"

"No, I don't, Dad, that stuff will kill you, and I don't want to see anything happen to you. I love you."

Snowplows were busy and were doing a good job on the roads as Guyiser and Loaner rolled into Nashville. The 'Merry Christmas' banners hung across the streets had been replaced with 'Happy New Year' banners. Guyiser petted Loaner. "Happy New Year, Loaner." Loaner just smiled and looked out the window. "Well, boy, let's go see Mr. Gibson first." He pulled into the alley and parked. "Let's go, boy." Guyiser knocked on the back door. He heard Mr. Gibson unlock the door and open it.

"Well, well. My two favorite people. Come on in, Guyiser and you too, Loaner."

They sat talking. "And I got all kinds of dress shirts, pants, ties, a real pretty blazer, and a pair of wing-tipped shoes. The food at the Taylor's was unreal."

Mr. Gibson rocked and smiled, "Sounds like a great day. Did you have time to think about what we talked about?"

"I sure did. Gave it a lot of thought. Do you think we could go up there sometime after the first of the year? Maybe before January 14th? I feel real good about the factory."

Mr. Gibson kept rocking. "You made a good decision, Guyiser. You make me happy. I'll make plans with Margaret for us to pay her a visit." They stood up and shook hands.

"Well, I had better get going'. I have things to do. Come on Loaner. I'll be back sometime next week to see you again. Are we all square with what I owed you?"

"Everything is 'A' okay, Guyiser. Drive carefully."

The bank was only a block away, so Guyiser and Loaner started walking down the alley. Guyiser put the small tin box of money inside his jacket. Loaner started a low growl as they walked. "What is it, boy?" Guyiser petted his head and then looked up to see two men standing in front of him. They were dressed in long black coats and had on black western hats. They both had beards and one man wore small glasses. Loaner's growl grew as they came closer. "Easy, boy." The taller of the two stepped in front of Guyiser. Loaner began to growl and to show his teeth. "Hold on, boy. Do I know you?" Guyiser saw that Loaner was very upset. "Me. Tail. Tail!" Loaner sat down.

"You're Blackman's boy, ain't you? How did your sale go? Make a lot of money?"

Guyiser crossed his arms. "You know my pa?"

The second man stepped up. "Oh, we know your pa all right. He owes us money. A lot of money."

The man with glasses took a step to Guyiser. Loaner growled and showed his teeth again. The man looked at Loaner and stepped back, pointing his finger at Guyiser. "You tell your pa we're gonna collect. You hear me? One way or another, we'll collect!" The men walked away. Guyiser stood shaking as he watched them disappear.

The wind and snow had torn the tarp off the chicken pen's roof. Mr. Blackman was on a ladder, nailing it back on. Guyiser got out of his truck and heard the hammering. "Dad? where are you?"

"I'm over here, Guyiser. Give me a hand."

Guyiser and Loaner walked around the house to the pen.

"Hand me that edge." Guyiser stretched the tarp and handed the edge to his father.

"Dad." Guyiser started to shake.

Mr. Blackman looked at him. "Boy, you're as white as a sheet. What's wrong?"

"I met two men in town. They scared me. Said you owed them money. And they were gonna get you."

Mr. Blackman climbed down the ladder. "Nothing to worry about. Just a friendly bet I lost." He walked past Guyiser.

Guyiser reached out and grabbed his arm. "These are real mean men. Said it was a lot of money. And one way or another they would collect it. They scared me real bad. It's more than a bet. What's going on?"

Mr. Blackman jerked his arm away from Guyiser. "I'll handle it, boy. Leave me alone." Guyiser had never seen his father this way. His eyes were mean and as cold as steel. Loaner playfully barked at Mr. Blackman. He picked up a board and threw it at Loaner. "Shut up, dog," he yelled as he walked to the house.

Guyiser was amazed at his father's reaction and started to shake again. "Me." Loaner came and sat by Guyiser.

As the evening became late and dark, coldness set in. Mr. Blackman put a log on the fire and sat drinking from his wine bottle. The reporter on T.V. was describing a robbery at a liquor store. "The owner said it happened very quickly. All he could tell us was that one of the two men hit him, while the other man took money out of the register. Luckily, the owner is all right, and he only lost forty-two dollars. Thanks for joining us. This has been the Eleven O'clock News." Mr. Blackman clicked off the T.V. and took another drink.

Guyiser came in drying his hands. He sat down on the couch looking at his father. "Dad, I think you owe it to me to tell me what's going on."

Mr. Blackman, staring at the fireplace, took another drink. "Guyiser, I love you, boy. I'm sorry I yelled at you today. But, my business is my business. And, I really don't want to talk about it." He sat in silence for a moment. A smile and laughter finally came. "You know, being Santa Claus was the best time of my life. All those kids laughing, my red suit, and the snow in my beard." He turned to Guyiser. "Can I be Santa Claus next year?"

Guyiser sat looking at this tough, kind, and loving man. Only good thoughts came to his mind. Guyiser went to his father's chair and knelt down. Looking at his father.

"Sure, Dad. Sure, anything you want."

Guyiser sat on the edge of his bed talking to Loaner. "He didn't mean to yell and throw that board at you. He really loves you. He's just got stuff on his mind. So, if I can let it go, you should too." Loaner was looking at his master as if he understood everything Guyiser was saying. "What do you say?" Loaner barked a few times. "Good boy, now let's get some sleep."

The kitchen in the Taylor house was a busy place. Mrs. Taylor and Cindy were putting foil around bowls of food. Mrs. Taylor was counting the bowls. "Beans, corn, potatoes, hand me that ham and cornbread.

And don't forget that jug of tea. And, Guyiser likes my banana pudding."

Cindy stood looking at the food. "Mother, this would feed an army."

Mrs. Taylor stood proudly looking at all the food. "This will make a good dinner for them."

Cindy smiled, "Yes, and tomorrow night, too."

Mrs. Taylor put her arm around Cindy. "You look so pretty today. Go comb your hair again." They hugged and laughed as Cindy walked away. "And, wash your hands."

Another cold, gray day had pushed the night away. Guyiser was sweeping the barn floor. Loaner lay in the hay watching his master. The bike shop looked different than it did last week. Only a few bicycles stood on their kickstands. Only one basket was on the wall. Guyiser finished up and sat at his desk. The two men he had met in town were still on his mind. Guyiser set up his worktable again and put a bike upside down on the tabletop. He started putting a chain on the back axle. Then, he rolled the wheel, and the chain locked in place. He sat looking at the bike and began thinking about the bicycle factory. *What can I do to make the factory grow?* He thought about what Mr. Taylor had said, 'New ideas are what make companies grow.' He kept looking at the bike on the table. *A new type of bicycle. Take an old bicycle and make it better, safer, and faster. Well, with Mr. Gibson's help, I think I can come up with something. Something big, maybe something that would change the bike industry. Maybe I could find out from kids what they like and dislike.*

I feel like there is something missing about the style of today's bikes. Bicycles have been around for hundreds of years and there has never been much of a change in them. In Japan, Europe, and England they ride bicycles more than we do here. I bet they would like a better bike. Guyiser looked at his watch. "Time flies, Loaner. It's twelve o'clock. Let's go pick up Cindy."

Guyiser sat in his truck outside the Taylor's house. He tooted his horn. Cindy came to the door and motioned for him to come in. Their house always smelled good. Guyiser stood in the kitchen looking at all the bowls of food. "Wow! What's all this?"

Cindy handed him two bowls.

"Be careful, and don't spill it. This is for your dinner tonight. Put these in your truck and come back for more, okay?" Guyiser made a couple of trips to his truck. He entered the house with an envelope in his hands.

Mrs. Taylor and Cindy were talking in the kitchen when Guyiser came in. Mrs. Taylor picked up a bowl and handed it to him. "Don't forget your banana pudding."

"Banana pudding. Oh, Mrs. Taylor, you're a sweetheart. Thanks. Oh, Cindy," he handed her the envelope.

She opened it and took out two tickets. "Mother, look! Two tickets to the Grand Ole Opry for New Year's Eve. Guyiser, how did you get these?"

He just stood there with a smile on his face. "Do you wanta go?"

Cindy grabbed Guyiser and hugged him. "Of course I do. This is the biggest event of the year."

Guyiser hugged her back. "Dinner is included, and we'll see all the country stars on stage at the show. Also, they have a fireworks show at midnight."

Mrs. Taylor joined in. "Mr. Taylor and I went a few years ago, and we had the best time ever! I heard it's even bigger now. You two will have a blast. I'm jealous."

Cindy was very excited and kissed Guyiser. "I've always wanted to go there. And this is for New Year's Eve! Oh, thank you, boyfriend. Thank you, thank you."

It was just a short ride back to Guyiser's place. He tooted his horn, and Mr. Blackman came out. "Help me, Pa. We have a lot of food." They carried all the food into the kitchen.

Mr. Blackman dipped his finger in the banana pudding. "Umm, umm, that's good."

"Hey, Pa. That's for me."

"Oh, I forgot, Mrs. Taylor likes you best."

They laughed together.

The fireplace threw off its warm heat. Mr. Blackman sat in his big chair watching T.V. Cindy and Guyiser were playing checkers on the floor. Guyiser got very excited. "Cindy, I forgot. I have something to show you!" He hopped up and ran to his bedroom. He returned quickly and sat back down on the floor. "Look at these!" Guyiser handed her a handful of pictures. "Remember the pictures we took last week?"

Cindy spread the pictures on the floor.

They started laughing. "Mr. Blackman, you made a great Santa. Oh, look. We're kissing. Look at Loaner by the snowman. The kids look happy with you, Mr. Blackman." Mr. Blackman just smiled. "Oh, Guyiser, I want this one of us. It's precious."

Guyiser looked at the picture. "Yeah, that's my favorite one."

Mr. Blackman stretched in his chair. "I'm getting hungry. How about you two?"

Cindy got up. "I'll go set the table. Do you want to help me, Guyiser?"

They sat at the table eating and talking. "Pass me the potatoes, Guyiser"

"And then we agreed to see the factory after the first of the year. Margaret is sending a car to pick us up.

How about that!"

Cindy clapped her hands. "Good for you! How far is it from Nashville?"

"Oh, I'd say it's about a two hour drive, maybe a little more."

Cindy turned to Mr. Blackman. "Did Guyiser tell you about New Years?"

"Yep, I saw the tickets. You two are going' to have a good time." He laughed. "A good time. You tell your mother thanks for everything. Her cooking is the best.

I'm going back to my chair and watch some T.V. Get him to help you clean up."

Cindy smiled. "Yes, sir. He will." They cleaned up and put away everything. Cindy pushed Guyiser into the sink and kissed him. "Did you get enough to eat?"

He kissed her back. "Plenty. I'll eat some banana puddin' later."

"What time do you want to pick me up tomorrow?"

"Well, the tickets say dinner is from six to seven and from eight until eleven is the all-star show. The fireworks are from eleven thirty until twelve thirty. I guess that we should leave here about five o'clock. That should give us time enough. Is that good for you?"

Cindy kissed him again. "I love the way you think. Pick me up at four forty-five. I'll be ready." She kissed him and said, "I have to go. We're having company over tonight. Take me home, lover."

A light snow was falling as Guyiser sat at his desk in the barn. He marked a circle around December 31st. Next to the date, he wrote 'Cindy and me at the Grand Ole Opry'. He leaned back, saw Cindy's happy face and felt her excitement when she saw the tickets. The New Year looked very promising. There was a new venture ahead of him. He looked around the barn and saw himself picking out bicycle frames from Mr. Gibson's back lot. He saw himself laughing with his father as they hauled things to the swap meets. He remembered the day he met Cindy and Mrs. Taylor. Guyiser looked at Loaner and remembered Cindy saying, 'Why don't you call him Loaner?' And then he thought of his big red truck, the Christmas lights, his tree house, and Mr. Gibson. So many things went through his mind. Now it was time for him to start thinking about his future with the factory. There would be new people and new plans to make. This was going to be a new year and a new life.

A knock on the door brought him back. Mr. Blackman opened the door and went in. "Howdy. What's you doing'?" He sat by the stove and propped his feet up.

"Nothing much, Just thinking away."

Mr. Blackman took a bit of his tobacco plug. "News says the sun might come out today. What time you going into Nashville?"

Guyiser stood up and went to the window. "We're going' to leave here before five. That will give us plenty of time. I'm still concerned about this factory. I want to make a good impression. You know what I mean?" Guyiser walked over and sat by the stove. "I kinda wish you would be there with me."

Mr. Blackman laughed. "Don't worry, Guyiser. Those people think you know something they don't.

You have the advantage."

Guyiser rocked in his chair. "Maybe I could get Mr. Gibson to let you be my advisor. You know--a job for you."

Mr. Blackman looked at his son. "You know, I'd like that. Your advisor. How much does that job pay?" The thought made them laugh.

"I'm serious, we have always worked together. Would you do it?"

Mr. Blackman stood up and stretched. "I believe I would. I'm a little tired of swap meets. But, we'll see. I'm going' to feed the animals. See you later."

The sun did come out. Guyiser was hosing down his truck to get the mud and snow off. He stood back looking at it. "Looks good, Loaner. Good as new. "Let's go in and have some lunch."

In the kitchen, Guyiser was warming up the leftovers. He set the table and went to the door to call his dad. Loaner was already eating from his bowl as Mr. Blackman came in. As they ate, Mr. Blackman said, "That sun sure feels good out there. It'll melt some snow. You drive careful. It's still slick."

Guyiser scooped some pudding on to his plate. "I will, don't worry about me."

The bathtub full of warm water felt good as Guyiser stepped in. He lay there in the soapy water, thinking about Cindy and him at the Grand Ole Opry. He was excited because he had never been there. After his bath, he lay out his clothes. He wanted to look good for Cindy and the days ahead. A dress shirt and tie, his blazer and gray pants, and his winged-tip shoes.

Now that looks good together. He looked at his pocket watch.

"It's three o'clock, Loaner. Think I'll get dressed and see what I look like." He dressed fast and stood in front of the mirror smiling.

Guyiser adjusted his tie and put on his blazer. He looked down at his gray pants and black shoes. He stood looking in the mirror at his hair. It was long and at his shoulders. "Pa," he walked in the kitchen, "Pa, could you cut my hair? I want it shorter."

Guyiser sat in a chair with an apron around his neck. Mr. Blackman was cutting Guyiser's hair. "More?"

He held up the mirror. "Looks good, but maybe a little more."

Mr. Blackman clipped a little more and stepped back to look. "Makes you look older. Long hair is for kids. I like it."

Guyiser looked again. "You're right. I like it, too." He put his blazer back on and went to the mirror. "Yes, that's what I want—to look older." Guyiser went in the living room. "Pa, how do I look?"

Mr. Blackman looked him over. "You look like a young man going places. I know Cindy will like your new look."

"Thanks, Dad. I gotta go. Don't want to be late. Love ya."

Mr. Blackman stood on the porch waving as Guyiser drove away. "Love you, too."

Guyiser knocked on the Taylor's door. Mr. Taylor opened it and looked at Guyiser. "Guyiser? Come on in." Mr. Taylor kept looking at him. "You look different. You clean up real good."

Mrs. Taylor came in and saw Guyiser. "Oh, Guyiser, you look so handsome. Look at you. Turn around. Wait until Cindy sees you. Cindy!" Cindy came down the stairs with her mother's fur coat on her arm. Guyiser took a deep breath. She had on a beautiful black dress and high heels. Her hair was up with a silver tiara in it.

Guyiser walked to her, his eyes wide open. "Cindy, you're gorgeous. Wow! You're gorgeous!" He took her arm, still staring at her.

Mrs. Taylor came with a camera. "Picture, picture. This I have to have."

They stood by the banister as Mrs. Taylor snapped away.

Cindy looked at Guyiser in awe. "Guyiser, I've never seen you this way. You're a beautiful man."

"And you make a beautiful couple. Look this way." Mrs. Taylor snapped more pictures.

Guyiser looked at his watch. "We better get going." They walked to the door.

Mrs. Taylor said, "Just one more."

Her husband stood beside her, "Let them go. They'll be late. Bye, you two. Drive carefully."

Mrs. Taylor kissed them both. "Have a good time." Cindy and Guyiser waved as they got in the truck. "They make such a lovely couple."

Mr. Taylor kissed Mrs. Taylor. "They sure do."

The bright sunshine was a welcome relief from the gray days. It seemed to make everything larger. The blue sky was even brighter. Birds were flying again. Snowplows had cleared old highway 70 of snow as Guyiser and Cindy drove along singing and talking. "You know, I miss the Christmas music already."

Cindy looked at Guyiser. "Me, too." She ran her fingers through Guyiser's hair. "I can't believe that a haircut and a suit could change a person so much. You look like a person in charge, maybe 21 or 22. I really like what I see."

Guyiser smiled and looked in the mirror. "Yeah, I feel different, too. I've been wearing overalls and jeans all my life." He looked at Cindy and then back to the road. "But you, with that black dress and fur coat and your hair put up. Can I have your autograph?" They burst out laughing.

Fifth Avenue was blocked off between Broadway and Church Streets. A long line of people had already formed leading to the Grand Ole Opry steps.

Guyiser and Cindy sat at the red light. A traffic guard came up to the truck and looked at Guyiser and Cindy. "Move it!" Guyiser rolled down the window. The guard took another look at them. "Oh, I'm sorry, sir. Can I help you?"

Cindy leaned over to the window. "Yes, we have tickets to the Opry. Can you give us directions?"

The guard pointed up 5th Avenue. "Yes ma'am. I'll move the barrier for you, sir. Just drive up the street and the valet will park your vehicle for you. And, thank you, sir—ma'am. Have a good evening."

Guyiser rolled up the window and turned the corner. "What was that all about?"

Cindy was startled, too. "I think he thought we were VIP's" The valet ran up to the truck, opened the door for Cindy, and helped her out. Next, he ran around and opened the door for Guyiser.

"Good evening, sir. Here is your program for the evening. Just go over there and a shuttle will take you folks to the restaurant. It will also bring you back later for the show. Here are your tickets, sir. Thank you and enjoy."

Guyiser walked around the truck and stood next to Cindy. Another attendant ran up to them. "Your name, sir?"

Guyiser looked at Cindy and back to the young man. "Blackman."

"Thank you, sir. I'll take you to the shuttle so you can avoid the line. Follow me, please." They followed him to the front of the line. "The shuttle will be right here. Would there be anything else, sir?" The attendant stood there.

Cindy nudged Guyiser and whispered to him, "Give him some money."

Guyiser reached in his pocket and pulled out his money. He whispered back to Cindy, "How much?" She reached for the money, pulled out a twenty-dollar bill, and handed it to the young man.

"Thank you, thank you for your good service." The young man bowed and ran off.

Guyiser turned to Cindy. "So, that's the way you do it!"

She kissed his cheek and said, "You're learning, boyfriend. Oh look, here comes the shuttle."

The restaurant sat on the banks of the Cumberland River. As they entered, they could feel the festive atmosphere with colorful streamers and party hats. They saw the pictures of all the country and western singers on the walls.

A hostess greeted them. "By a window, sir?" Cindy nodded. "Follow me, please."

A waiter stood by their table and pulled out a chair for Cindy. "Thank you."

The hostess started to leave. "Oh, miss," Guyiser pulled out his money. "For you."

"Thank you, sir."

Guyiser sat down looking at Cindy. "Was that good?"

She laughed, "You are a silly boy." They sat talking and looking around the room.

Guyiser pointed to a picture high on the wall. "Look, Cindy. There's my favorite person, Minnie Pearl. See the tag on her hat?"

Cindy broke in, "And look at Elvis's guitar over there!"

Dinner was a dining feast. Cindy and Guyiser sat looking out the picture window. A large showboat all lit up and filled with waving people passed by. "I think that's a gambling boat. I've heard about them." Guyiser looked at his watch. "It's seven seventeen. Maybe we should go. We don't want to miss that show."

The shuttle pulled up to the doors of the Grand Ole Opry. An attendant helped Cindy and Guyiser out. Guyiser reached in his pocket for his money. "Your ticket, please." Cindy hand the tickets to him and nodded to Guyiser. "Not everybody, put that back."

Guyiser looked at her, "But."

The attendant punched holes in their tickets and handed them back. "Straight ahead, sir."

Cindy took Guyiser's arm as they walked up the steps. "Oh, Guyiser. I'm so excited."

They sat in the balcony to the right of the stage. There they could see everything. The auditorium was huge. Guyiser looked around at the monstrous room. "There must be a million people here."

Cindy squeezed his hand, "Well, maybe not a million. By the way, how did you get these tickets?"

Guyiser sat trying to count people. "1001, 1002. Oh, I lost my count. Tickets?" He leaned back and put his arm around Cindy. "Mr. Gibson. Funny, this was sold out months ago. But, he know everybody that is important from the mayor on down. He's quite a guy, you know."

The large velvet curtains began to slowly open. Excitement filled the large auditorium. Everyone stood up shouting and applauding as the host of the show, country singer, "J.D. HATFIELD" walked out waving to everybody. He took the mike and waved his hat. "Happy New Year," he shouted, "Happy New Year."

People all over Tennessee can be heard shouting and applauding as they watch us on T.V." Finally, the crowd sat down. "Country music means just that—all over the country, from New York to L.A. Tonight, we have hundreds of country and western performers to celebrate this New Year's party." Everyone applauded again. "This is a three-hour show with two intermissions. We also have the biggest fireworks display ever. They will be shot off down on the Cumberland River so everyone can see them.

So, let's start the show with your favorite group from ALABAMA!" The crowd went wild, throwing streamers into the air. Cindy and Guyiser stood up with the crowd and threw their streamers off the balcony.

"This is so exciting. I'm so happy, Guyiser."

The show had been spectacular so far. Guyiser and Cindy walked outside during the first intermission. They stood on the steps watching the crowd of people. Reporters, photographers, and the television media were everywhere. Guyiser stood with his long black and white scarf next to Cindy in her sexy black dress and fur coat. She was holding his arm, "Look at all this. It's amazing."

Guyiser looked at Cindy, "And so are you." She squeezed his arm.

A reporter and photographer came up to them. "May we take your picture and conduct a quick interview?"

Guyiser looked at Cindy, "Sure."

The reporter started writing, "Your names, please."

"I'm Guyiser Blackman, and this is Cynthia Taylor."

"And, Mr. Blackman, what are your plans for the next year?"

Guyiser looked at Cindy, "Well, I'm putting together a million dollar bicycle factory."

"Thank you, and you, Miss Taylor?"

"Well, I will be going to American Broadcasting School to be a reporter for television."

"Thank you, thank you both. Did you get enough pictures?" The photographer gave her a 'thumbs up'. "Thank you again. Happy New Year." With that, the reporter and her photographer disappeared into the crowd.

Guyiser and Cindy just looked at each other and laughed. "Let's go in before we say something silly."

The show had surpassed all of their expectations. Watching the Grand Ole Opry on T.V. was nothing compared to seeing it live. They had seen all the stars they knew and many they didn't. They sat on the outside patio of the restaurant talking about the amazing show. The night sky was full of stars and a big moon. A waitress came over to their table. "Can I get you anything?"

Guyiser looked at Cindy, "Yes, please. A small bottle of champagne."

The waitress looked a little surprised, "We only have one size, sir."

"We'll take it."

The waitress walked away shaking her head. Cindy grabbed Guyiser's arm and squeezed it, "You handled that just right."

Guyiser squeezed her hands, "Yep, I'm learning."

They both laughed. The champagne was cold with lots of bubbles.

Cindy held up her glass, "A toast," Guyiser held up his glass, "to Guyiser. "May he make millions of dollars next year."

"To Cindy. May she always be the person she is right now. And, lookout T.V." They laughed together, clicked glasses, and drank.

"Picture, picture, sir." It was a man with a Polaroid camera.

Guyiser looked at Cindy, "Sure."

The man focused his camera. "Smile and hold up your glasses." 'Flash.' "One moment, sir." The man looked at the picture and put it in a white frame.

"Oh, this is a good one." He handed it to Cindy. The man stood there waiting.

Cindy and Guyiser looked at the picture. "This is great, Cindy." The man smiled as he continued to stand and wait.

Cindy nudged Guyiser, "Money."

"Oh, yeah. Here's twenty. Happy New Year."

"Thank you, sir."

They sat looking at the picture. Fireworks began to fill the night sky. They came from the park across the river. The reflection of the fireworks on the river made a double image, which was beautiful. Oo's and ah's went up from the crowd. The fireworks went higher and higher in the sky. All the colors mixed. Guyiser and Cindy leaned back in their chairs. "I wish Pa could see this.

He loves fireworks." The fireworks slowed down. Guyiser poured more champagne in their glasses. The fireworks started up again after a few minutes. It seemed like there were even more. The fireworks came more often and were higher than before. The River Show Boat stopped in the middle of the river. People everywhere started to stand and to count.

The count grew louder and louder. The top of the River Show Boat lit up. Guyiser and Cindy stood up as the countdown continued. They counted with the crowd. '5, 4, 3, 2, 1,...' The sky exploded with color. Everybody was hugging and kissing. It seemed like Guyiser and Cindy could not stop hugging and kissing. The couple next to them hugged, kissed, and then shook hands with Guyiser and Cindy. Guyiser picked up the champagne bottle and took a big drink yelling, "Happy New Year!" They watched the fireworks slowly end as the smoke in the sky drifted away.

It took quite a while for the attendant to bring the truck. Cindy stood leaning against Guyiser with her head against his chest. "I don't feel so good."

"It's okay. I got you."

The valet opened the door and Guyiser helped her in. He got in and Cindy moved over close to Guyiser. "I'm sorry. That's the first time I drank champagne." She put her head on his shoulder and closed her eyes.

"That's all right, sweetheart. Just close your eyes. We'll be home before you know it."

The highway was clear all the way back to Centerville. Guyiser pulled into the Taylor drive and stopped. The house was dark except for a living room light. He looked at his watch. It was three fifteen in the morning. He carried Cindy to the house. She was out like a light. The Taylor's were sleeping as Guyiser carried Cindy up the stairs and into her room. He took her coat off and unzipped her dress. He lay Cindy down and took off her shoes. Guyiser stood back looking at this beautiful girl. He pulled the covers up around her. He sat on her bed looking at her. *She's such an angel.* "I love you, I love you, my girlfriend."

Inside his house, Mr. Blackman was asleep in his chair with the T.V. on. Guyiser put a blanket over him and turned off the T.V. He went to his room. Sitting on his bed, he looked at the picture of them smiling and holding up their champagne glasses. He had had many good times in the past year, but this one topped them all. He kissed the picture, put it on the night table, and lay on the bed. A smile was on his face as he went to sleep.

Mrs. Taylor opened Cindy's door. Looking in, she could see that Cindy was still asleep. She went in and sat on the bed. She bent and kissed Cindy and stroked her hair. Cindy stirred and opened her eyes. "Good morning, sweetheart. Must have been quite a night. You still have your dress on. Come on. Wake up. It's nine o'clock." Mrs. Taylor went to the door. "I'll go make you some breakfast. Come on. Get up."

Cindy lay there looking out the window. Her mind instantly saw the fireworks. She lay gathering her thoughts. It had been a night to remember. All the events went through her mind. Then, she remembered the champagne. She sat up in bed and held her head. She stood in front of her mirror. Her hair looked like it had been hit by a windstorm. Her dress was half off. She had a headache as big as all outdoors. "I'm a wreck."

Cindy walked into the kitchen wearing her bathrobe. "Good morning, Mother." She looked at the breakfast on the table. "Nothing for me. Could you get me some aspirin and tea? I'll be in the living room."

Mrs. Taylor came in the living room with the tea and aspirin. "Here, honey. Did you drink anything last night?"

Cindy took the aspirin and drank the tea. "Yes, ma'am. I had some champagne."

Mrs. Taylor sat down and leaned back. "Oh, yes. I remember my first champagne. It was on my graduation night. Your father and I were in the back seat of his car." She quickly stopped and leaned forward. "Did anything happen? I mean did you...?"

Cindy smiled and looked at her mother. "No, Mother. At least I don't think so."

"Drink your tea, dear, and tell me everything."

Cindy sipped her tea and leaned back on the couch. "Well, it started off good and got better and better. For some reason, they thought we were VIP's and,..."

Loaner barked as Guyiser appeared at the kitchen door rubbing his eyes. Mr. Blackman was at the table drinking his coffee. "Good morning, my boy. Have some coffee." Guyiser sat down as his father poured him a cup of coffee. "So, how did it go last night?"

Guyiser stretched and yawned. "It was great. I never knew that there were so many country singers. We had the best time." He slid the picture over to him.

Mr. Blackman looked it over, and a big smile came to his face. "Oh, yeah, champagne. I remember my first champagne." He laughed aloud. "Your mother and me parked on a hill watching fireworks on the 4th of July." He laughed again. "She passed out and I had to carry her home." He sat there looking at the picture in silence. "So, tell me your story, everything."

Guyiser leaned back and put his hands on his head. "Well, Pa. It started out good and got better and better."

The sun was out in Nashville as people and cars were busy on the streets. It was the beginning of a new year. Mr. Gibson sat rocking in his chair as he read the Nashville paper. He started laughing and adjusted his little round glasses. He continued reading and laughing. "That boy. He's going places. I just knew it."

The snow was melting off the Taylor's house. Chunks of ice fell off the roof. Mrs. Taylor was sitting watching the news on T.V. The weatherman was pointing to their area of the big map. "So, enjoy the sun while you can because we have a big cold front moving down from the northwest. It will bring us more guess what, snow."

Mr. Taylor drove up to the house and ran in. "Look, look!" He handed the newspaper to Mrs. Taylor. "Where's Cindy?"

Mrs. Taylor turned down the T.V. "She's up stairs resting. What's all the excitement?"

Mr. Taylor ran to the stairs and shouted to Cindy. "Cindy, Cindy, come down here, quick!" He turned to his wife, "Page twelve, page twelve." She opened the paper. Her eyes opened wide as she read.

Cindy came down and sat down next to her mother. "What's going on?"

Mrs. Taylor handed her the paper. "It's you and Guyiser. Read." Cindy took the paper. There was a picture of them smiling and standing on the Opry steps. She started to read, 'Millionaire, Guyiser Blackman and Miss Cynthia Taylor, television star reporter were among the many of the celebrities attending the New Year's Eve party at the Opry last night. They wished for everybody to have a safe and happy new year.'

Mr. Taylor pointed to the paper. "Now, that's a great picture of you."

"A star reporter." Cindy kept looking at the paper. "But, we didn't say anything like this."

Mr. Taylor patted her head, "Well, that's what a reporter does—embellish the truth a little."

Cindy leaned back looking at the paper, "I do like the picture, but millionaire, star reporter, that's really stretching it, don't you think?" A smile came to her. She threw the paper in the air and yelled, "I like it!"

Loaner barked and tugged on Guyiser's pant leg. "What is it, boy? You want to go out? I'm Going' over to the Taylor's. I want to check on Cindy. So, I'll see you later."

Mr. Taylor met Guyiser at the door.

"Well, come on in, Mr. Celebrity, come in, come in." Cindy was on the couch still in her robe.

Guyiser went to her, "You all right?"

Cindy hugged his neck, "I'm great. How are you?"

Mrs. Taylor came in with more tea. "Guyiser, I'm so proud of you two. Did Cindy show you the paper?"

"No, ma'am. I just got here."

"Cindy, show him."

Mr. Taylor handed him a newspaper. "I got ten of them."

Cindy turned to page twelve and handed it to Guyiser. He started to laugh. "That's us." He looked at Cindy. "That's us."

She started to read, 'Millionaire, Guyiser Blackman,' "That's you" 'and Miss Cynthia Taylor,' "That's me." 'Television star reporter were among many of the celebrities at the New Year's Eve party at the Opry last night.'

Guyiser kept reading, 'They wished for everyone to have a safe and happy New Year.' "But, I'm not a millionaire; what does this mean?"

Cindy kissed his cheek. "Well, if you remember, you said something about a million dollar factory, and I said something about going to school to be a reporter. This is the way it came out. Don't you just love it?" Cindy laughed.

Guyiser turned to Mr. Taylor, "I'm a millionaire, sir. Mrs. Taylor, I'm a millionaire."

"Do you want some more tea, son?" Mrs. Taylor got up shaking her head as she walked to the kitchen.

She stopped at the door, "Do you want to stay for supper?"

"No, ma'am, thank you. I just wanted to check on Cindy."

"Well, would you like some food to take home with you?

"No thanks, ma'am. We're having breakfast for supper."

Cindy stood up. "They do that a lot, Mother." Mrs. Taylor mumbled something and went to the kitchen.

"Come on, I'll walk you out." They stood on the porch holding each other. "It's going to snow some more. Well, boyfriend, what's your plan now?"

Guyiser picked her up and swung her around. "You." Cindy laughed. "No, I should spend some time with Pa and get ready to go see that factory. And, then there is you.

I want to spend time with you before you go away. You want to go see a movie next week? Remember, I'm a millionaire."

They laughed. "And, I'm a reporter. I'll report you if you don't spend time with me. I can't begin to tell you how much I enjoyed last night."

Guyiser kissed her. "It was my pleasure. Get some rest, and I'll see you later, okay?"

"Okay."

"Bye."

Mr. Blackman was putting anti-freeze in his truck as Guyiser and Loaner drove up. "Having problems?"

"Oh, no. Truck's fine. You need any of this?

It's gonna snow again."

Guyiser picked up a stick and threw it. Loaner took off chasing it. "Yeah, I can smell it in the air. You want to go into Centerville and have a good steak supper?"

Mr. Blackman put the hood down. "You know, that sounds like a good idea." He laughed and looked at Guyiser, "You mean just the two of us?" Guyiser nodded. "Well, let me know when you're ready. I'm gonna go feed Hay some hay." He laughed and walked away.

It was four o'clock and all the chores were done at the Blackman house. Guyiser, his father, and Loaner rode down the road to Centerville. As they passed the Taylor's house, Guyiser tooted his horn. Centerville was a farm town. People raised corn, beans, tomatoes, some tobacco, and most anything they could sell to make a living. The big events in the community were taking their crops to the large farmers' market where they met each other to find out the latest gossip. They talked about who lives where, who did what, new babies that were born, and this, that, and the other thing.

The hardware and feed store was a place where men would sit around and play checkers and talk about their tractors and crops. The coffee and donut shop next to the courthouse was a place where the men from the small police department hung out. But, the restaurant was the best place to eat. Mr. Blackman and Guyiser had been coming here for years. A cute young girl came to their table. "Can I take your order?"

Mr. Blackman looked up from the menu, "Where is Mrs. Jackson?"

"I'm sorry, sir. She died two weeks ago."

Mr. Blackman dropped his head. He had known her for fifteen years. "I'm sorry, too."

Guyiser reached across the table and touched his father's hand. "I'll be back in a few minutes, sir."

Mr. Blackman looked up at Guyiser. "Well, that's life. You live and then you die. But, life goes on." Mr. Blackman looked out the window. "You know, Guyiser. I have not done much with my life. I guess you are the best thing I ever did. And, I'm proud of you. There is a whole big world out there I've never seen, and I never will. But, I hope you do."

"May I take your order now, sir?"

Guyiser looked at the food on the table. He had tea and his father had coffee. "No beer or wine?"

Mr. Blackman smiled, "I quit. That's my new year's resolution. No more booze. You're right. It's not good for me."

"I'm proud of you, man. I'm, I'm proud of you!" Guyiser got up and walked around the table. He hugged his father. "I'm glad and happy for you. You make me happy!"

The two stood on the sidewalk outside the restaurant. "Guyiser, this was a good idea of yours." Mr. Blackman stood looking up to the sky. "Well, it's back. Snow clouds and cold air. Let's get back and start a fire. The house is cold by now. This coat you got me feels mighty good. Let's go, son."

The house was cold. They stood by the fireplace getting warm. "Oh, Dad, I got something to show you." Guyiser got the newspaper, turned to page twelve, and handed it to his father.

Mr. Blackman smiled and started laughing. "Good picture, but don't let this go to your head, young man. You two make a fine looking couple though. She's such a pretty girl. You're not so bad yourself."

The television was on as the two men sat watching a program. "What are you going to do tomorrow, Guyiser?"

Guyiser lay on the couch rubbing Loaner's back. "Oh, I have a couple of bikes I want to put together, and there is a leak in the back of the barn that I want to fix. How about you?"

Mr. Blackman stood up and stretched. "Me, I'm driving in to Nashville to pay the bank on the house. Tax time, you know. But, for now I'm Going' to bed."

"Dad, could you do me a favor and drop by Mr. Gibson's place and give him this? It's his favorite pipe tobacco and a new pipe in a glass box. Tell him I'll see him later, okay?"

Mr. Blackman took the box and put it on the table by the door. "Sure will. Good night, son."

"Good night, my main man, I love you."

Mr. Blackman stopped by the door and turned back to Guyiser. "I love you, too, son."

The light white snowflakes began to fall as Guyiser and Loaner stood looking out of the living room window. "Isn't that pretty, Loaner?" Guyiser walked to the fireplace and put a log on the fire. "Let's turn in."

Death

Part 5

When I die, bury me deep and
Let me watch from above
All the people that I loved.
Let them know that I tried
To guide my son
Till the day I died.

A beautiful white blanket was on the ground. The snow was still falling that morning as Guyiser got dressed and went to the kitchen. Hot water was on the stove, and a cup and a note were on the table. Guyiser sat down and read the note. 'Have some coffee. I wanted to get a jump on the day, so I've gone. I'll see you later. Feed the chickens.' Guyiser made himself a cup of coffee and started his day.

Mr. Gibson and Mr. Blackman sat rocking, talking, and laughing as they looked at the newspaper. "Yep, that's my boy."

Mr. Gibson lit his pipe, "And a fine young man he is. Tell him thanks for the new pipe and tobacco. This glass box will keep my tobacco nice and fresh."

Mr. Blackman got up. "I will, and I want to thank you for getting him those tickets. He will never forget that night. Well, I got to go. Wanna go down to the feed store and teach the boys how to play checkers."

They laughed as Mr. Gibson stood up.

"Okay, I'll see you later. Be careful."

Mr. Blackman pulled his fur collar around his neck and headed for the feed store. The bank was on his way, so he went in to take care of his business. Soon he was finished. "Thank you, Mr. Blackman. It's always good to see you."

Mr. Blackman went out into the snow and headed for the feed store. As he walked, he saw two men standing in the alley. The taller man with glasses was whittling a piece of wood with his knife. The smaller man was leaning against the alley wall. The taller man put his knife away as Mr. Blackman came closer. "Hey, Blackman saw you coming out of the bank. You got our money?" Mr. Blackman stopped. "Did your boy give you the message?" They laughed.

"You had your last chance, Blackman. Where is it?"

The shorter man opened his long coat showing a sawed-off shotgun. "So?"

Mr. Blackman walked right up to his face. "You ain't gettin' nothing', and if you talk to my boy again, I'll kill ya. You understand? I told you that you were stupid about what happened to your pot. And I ain't giving' you nothing'."

The man looked at his partner and spit on the ground. "That's a shame, Blackman. I guess we both lose, but you lose the most."

Mr. Blackman grabbed the man's coat and pulled him close to him. "You threatening me?"

The man grabbed his hands. "No, Blackman, I'm through threatening you." He jerked Mr. Blackman's hands away. "Let's go." The two men walked down the alley and disappeared.

Mr. Blackman was not afraid of them, but he was afraid for Guyiser. He walked to the feed store and went in. There were a half dozen men sitting around talking and laughing as he heard a man call out to him. "Come on over and sit down. How about a game?" After a while, he was relaxed and enjoyed playing with the men. A couple of hours had passed. Mr. Blackman looked at his watch and then out the window. Streetlights were on and the snow was falling from the dark clouds.

"Well, that's it for me. Gotta get back. Thank for the game. I'll let you win next time." He laughed, put on his coat and hat, and left the store. He walked down the alley to where he had parked his truck behind Mr. Gibson's Bike Shop. He got in and reached for his gun. He sat there looking at the gun and looking around for the two men.

He saw nothing, so he started the truck and drove off.

He was just outside of Nashville going up the two-mile hill. Traffic was light on Highway 70 as he topped the hill. He knew this hill, so he put the truck in second gear to slow down the truck. The truck started to pick up speed going faster and faster. He put his foot on the brake pedal—it went clear to the floorboard. As he pumped the brakes, the truck picked up speed. He began to slide from side to side. He was fighting the steering wheel as the truck started to slide sideways then went into a spin down the hill. Faster and faster, the truck went round and round. There was nothing he could do. He was coming closer and closer to the bridge. He knew he was going to hit it. At seventy miles per hour, the truck struck the bridge. The truck bounced off the bridge and rolled over and over down the hill to the water below. People saw what had happened and ran to help. Someone called 911. They dispatched the sheriff to the accident. When the sheriff arrived, Mr. Blackman was dead.

It was nine o'clock. Guyiser stood looking at his watch. The snow was falling as he stood at the window. He was going from room to room, for some reason. He went back to the window looking out. Through the snow, he saw headlights coming up the driveway. He then felt relaxed. As the headlights got closer, he saw that it was a sheriff's car. The car stopped and two officers got out. Guyiser knew something was wrong. He opened the door. Loaner started to bark. "Me, Loaner." Guyiser went out to the porch as the men came to the house.

"Hello, I'm Officer Burns, and this is Officer Adams. Is Mrs. Blackman here?"

Guyiser started to shake. "My mother is dead. It's just me and my father. I'm Guyiser Blackman. Could I help you?"

"Mr. Blackman, could we come in? We need to talk to you."

Guyiser opened the door. "Sure. Come on in."

Inside, Officer Burns spoke first. "Let's sit down, okay?" Guyiser and officers sat down in the living room. "I'm afraid I have bad news. Your father was killed in an accident."

Guyiser stood up, "What?"

The officer took a picture from an envelope.

"Is this your father?" Guyiser took the picture. "Dad! my Dad." He broke down crying. "No, No, it can't be." He screamed, "No, No, No!" He fell to his knees, looking at the picture.

"We're sorry, Mr. Blackman. His truck hit some black ice on the highway going down the hill. There was nothing he could do." The officer went to Guyiser and lifted him to a chair. Next, he took the picture away from Guyiser as Guyiser kept screaming and crying. "I am really sorry for you, Mr. Blackman. Is there anybody we can call for you?"

The other officer went to the kitchen and returned with a glass of water. "Your father's body is in Nashville, but we can have it moved anywhere you would like.

We're here to help you anyway we can." The officers stayed with Guyiser for a long time. Guyiser sat staring into the fireplace. Loaner came and lay at his feet. "How can we help you, Guyiser?" He kept staring at the fire.

"Can he be moved to the Holy Cross Funeral Home in Centerville? That's where my mother is buried."

Officer Burns patted and rubbed Guyiser's back. "We can do that for you. Can we do anything else? Call anybody?"

Guyiser took another drink of water. "A friend of mine in Nashville, a Mr. Gibson at Gibson's Bike Shop on Broadway. Could you let him know for me?"

Officer Burns wrote it down in his book. "I'll do that right away."

Officer Adams knelt down by Guyiser.

"One last thing, did your father have any enemies? Someone who might have wanted to hurt your father?"

Guyiser turned quickly to him, "Why do you ask a thing like that? He had nothing but friends."

Officer Adams spoke softly to Guyiser. "We have to ask. There was a problem with the brake line. We don't know if it was cut or damaged in the accident. Forgive me for asking. And, I'm sorry about your dad." The two officers went to the door. "We'll have your father moved early morning. We'll contact your friend the first thing. Again, we're sorry."

Guyiser sat looking at the fire and heard the car drive away. He walked to his father's room and fell on the bed crying, "Why, God? Why? Why?"

Shock set in. Guyiser walked the house looking at everything and seeing nothing. He left the house and staggered in the snow to his truck.

He truck drove itself and stopped at the Taylor's house. Guyiser fell on the steering wheel. The truck's horn sounded for a long time.

Mrs. Taylor got out of bed and went to the window. Looking out, she saw the truck with its lights on. She woke Mr. Taylor, "Wake up, Guyiser's truck is down in the driveway. Go see if he's all right." Mr. Taylor looked at the clock. It was almost one in the morning. He got out of bed and went downstairs to the door.

As he opened it, he saw the truck's headlights. He looked around the porch for Guyiser, but he was not there. The snow was falling as he put his coat on and walked to the truck. Guyiser sat slumped over the steering wheel. Mr. Taylor opened the door. "Guyiser? Guyiser?"

He sat Guyiser back and saw his eyes half closed and his face wet with tears. "Guyiser, son, what is it?" Guyiser did not answer. Mr. Taylor helped him out of the truck and into the house.

Inside, he sat Guyiser on the couch and called for Mrs. Taylor. She came down in her robe and went to Guyiser. She sat down and put her arm around him. Mr. Taylor put a blanket around Guyiser. He sat shaking with his head down. Mrs. Taylor kept rubbing his back. "Guyiser, son, what's wrong?"

Guyiser kept shaking and raised his head. "He's dead. My dad is dead."

Mr. Taylor sat down beside him. "What do you mean, son? What happened?"

Guyiser stared into the fireplace, "The sheriff said it was an accident."

Mr. Taylor looked at Mrs. Taylor. "Go get Cindy." He put his arm around Guyiser. "We're here for you, son. You hear me? We're here for you."

Cindy and her mother came down. Cindy ran to Guyiser and sat down in front of him. She saw in his eyes that something bad had happened. "Guyiser, it's me." He just stared at the fire.

Cindy looked at her father. "It's Mr. Blackman. He was in an accident. He was killed."

Cindy grabbed Guyiser and started to cry. "No, No, Guyiser, No." Mrs. Taylor, in shock, started to cry.

Mr. Taylor, with tears in his eyes, raised his head, "Dear God, hear this prayer. Put your hand on Guyiser and this family. Help us with this sorrow. Feel our pain.

Be with us in our time of need. Give Guyiser your strength and help him, dear Lord. Help him now. Guide him through this time. Touch his good heart. Amen."

Cindy touched Guyiser's face, "Guyiser, I'm so, so very sorry." She started to cry again. Mr. Blackman had been like a second father to her. She had only good thoughts and good times with him. Many of those thoughts went through her mind as she looked at Guyiser. The four of them sat in a silent state of their own. Each one had their own thoughts of their time with Mr. Blackman.

"Is there anything we can do?" They all sat at the dining room table. Two hours had passed.

"I don't know. I really don't know what to do. The sheriff said they would send his body to the funeral home in Centerville."

There was a knock at the door. Mr. Taylor went to answer it. "I'm a friend of Guyiser. I'm looking for him."

Mr. Taylor invited him in. "Come on in. He's here." They walked to the dining room.

Mr. Gibson walked quickly to Guyiser and hugged him and then started to cry. "Are you all right? I came as soon as I heard. I'm so sorry, son. I learned to love that man. I'm so sorry."

Guyiser stood and hugged Mr. Gibson. Guyiser felt he had cried himself out. With a small smile, he looked at Mr. Gibson. "I'm glad you're here." Some tears came to Guyiser's eyes. "He really liked you, too."

Mrs. Taylor poured more coffee for everyone. They sat talking and remembering Mr. Blackman.

Cindy sat next to Guyiser, holding his hand. Guyiser looked at her and squeezed her hand. "I guess I had better go into Centerville and take care of things."

Cindy got up. "I'll go with you. I'll go change."

Mr. Gibson spoke up, "I'll go too, if that's all right with you." Guyiser nodded.

Mr. Taylor spoke, "And we'll be in later."

Because Centerville was a small town, most everyone had heard about the accident. Guyiser, Cindy, and Mr. Gibson sat in the office of the Holy Cross Funeral Home. Mr. Thomas, the director, was talking with them. "Everything will be taken care of, Guyiser, I promise you that. I knew your mother and father for years and years. Your father was a good friend. Let me show you something." He and Guyiser went to the window.

"You see that backhoe out there? When I started out, your father gave that to me. He was a friend when I needed one. Therefore, you don't have to worry about a thing. Why don't you go now and come back later? I'll take care of everything."

Mr. Gibson, Guyiser, and Cindy sat at the kitchen table at the Blackman house. "Oh, Guyiser, I've got something for you." Mr. Gibson handed him a phone.

"This is a wireless cell phone. I think you need one." Guyiser took it and looked it over. "You can call anywhere in the world on this phone. Here are the instructions. I put my phone number in it already. All you do is push this button and that button, and my phone will ring. This is your phone number."

Guyiser showed the phone to Cindy. "And I will put my phone number in it, too. This is just what you have needed." Cindy smiled at Mr. Gibson. "Now, we can keep track of him." They laughed.

Guyiser took the phone, looking at it. Mr. Gibson saw his puzzled expression. "Let me show you. Press this button and listen."

Guyiser pressed the button and put it to his ear. "It's ringing." 'This is Gibson's Bike Shop. I am closed for today, but leave a message at the sound of the tone. Goodbye.' Guyiser looked at Mr. Gibson. "That's you."

Mr. Gibson said, "Now, say something like, 'Hi, this is Guyiser. How are you?' The tone sounded. Guyiser repeated what Mr. Gibson had said. "Now, push this button, the Send button."

Guyiser looked at Cindy. "Do you know about these phones?" She nodded.

"Yes, Daddy is getting me one for school so I can call them every day."

About then, Mr. Gibson's phone rang. He took it out of his pocket. "That's your message. Want to hear?" He pressed a button and handed the phone to Guyiser. Guyiser listened and heard his voice, 'Hi, this is Guyiser.'

He looked again at the phone. "This is amazing."

Mr. Gibson took back his phone. "Now, you're part of the world."

Cindy took Guyiser's phone. "I'll put my number in here, too. Now, you can call me anytime. And, what is your number?" She wrote it down on a paper and looked at it. She started laughing. "Look, Mr. Gibson, Look, Guyiser. The number spells out 555-SNOW."

Guyiser laughed. "555-SNOW, that's funny." Cindy and Mr. Gibson looked at each other.

They were glad to see Guyiser laugh.

Mr. Gibson stood up, "Guyiser, I've got to go back to take care of a few things, but I'll be back later"

Cindy stood up, too. "Me too. Mother and Daddy will want to know what's going on. But, I'll see you in a little bit."

Guyiser walked them to the door. They all stood hugging. "I want to thank you both for being here for me. I've never been alone. Thank you both." He stood on the porch as they drove down the driveway. Guyiser suddenly realized that Loaner was not by his side and started looking for him. He walked through the house calling for him. Then he saw Loaner lying on Mr. Blackman's bed. Guyiser went in and sat on the bed. "You know, don't you? You know that he loved you." Loaner moved over and put his head in Guyiser's lap. Guyiser started to cry again. "It's just you and me, boy."

Guyiser and Loaner sat in the church in front of his father's casket. *This man was not only my father, but also my friend and comrade. He was the only man in my whole life. He might have been a little rough around the edges, but his heart had always beat with kindness.*

Several people that Guyiser did not know came to pay their respects. They would come to Guyiser, shake hands, hug, and tell stories about Mr. Blackman. Guyiser sat there, as more people would walk to the casket and say their goodbyes. It made Guyiser feel good to see people that cared about his father. He thought about how fast things happen. *One day you die, the next day you lie in a casket, and the next day you are put in the ground.*

And, like his father said, 'You live, you die, but life goes on.'

Cindy came and sat down beside Guyiser. "Hi, how do you feel?"

Guyiser took her hand. "I feel fine, now that you're here. Are your parents here?"

Cindy nodded. "They're talking with Mr. Thomas to see if there is anything they could do. Oh, Mr. Gibson is here, too. Guyiser, Mother, Daddy, and I think you should stay with us tonight."

Guyiser sat looking at the casket. *Alone, alone. He and Loaner were alone. Then he heard his father's voice saying,*

'But life goes on.' He squeezed Cindy's hand. "I would like that."

The burial service was small and quick.

Everyone had left. Guyiser and Loaner sat looking at the pile of dirt covered with flowers. He looked over at his mother's grave and back to his father's. He said a short prayer and stood for a while. Cindy and her parents along with Mr. Gibson stood by their cars as Guyiser walked to them. "I want to thank all of you for helping me through this. And I thank you for being my friend."

Cindy came to him and took his hands, "Will you stay with us for a while?"

Guyiser looked up to the sky and back at Cindy, "No, I would like to be alone for a while. Tell everyone I'm going home now. I'll be all right. Thanks, Cindy." With that, Guyiser went to his truck and drove away.

Days had passed. Guyiser had taken down the Christmas tree. He had cried the whole day he went through his father's room and boxed his father's things. He had learned to make adjustments in his new life. He had found his strength again, and Loaner had started to play in the house with him. Guyiser was sitting in his father's chair watching T.V. when he glanced down at his phone on the table. He picked it up and looked at it. *Push this button and phone numbers will appear. Push this button to call that number.* He started pushing buttons. He listened as a phone rang in his ear. "Hello, hello."

"Mrs. Taylor?"

"Yes."

"This is Guyiser."

"Oh, Guyiser, it's so good to hear your voice. How are you?"

"I'm doing pretty good. How are you?"

"Oh, I'm fine. Just doing some housework. When are you coming over? I made banana pudding."

"That sounds mighty good, ma'am. Maybe soon. Is Cindy there?"

"No, honey, she and her father went to Centerville this morning."

"Oh, well. I'm just trying out my new phone and thought I'd call. Would you tell her I called?"

"I sure will. Would you like to have supper with us tonight?"

"Thank you, ma'am. Not tonight, but maybe tomorrow."

"I hope so, honey. I miss seeing you."

"Thanks for talking with me, Mrs. Taylor."

"Anytime, Guyiser, anytime."

"Well, goodbye, ma'am."

"Goodbye, sweetheart. I'll tell Cindy you called. Bye."

Guyiser pushed the off button and looked at the phone and smiled. He pressed a button again and the name, Gibson, appeared. He pushed the other button and heard a phone ring. "Hello, Gibson's Bike Shop."

"Hello, Mr. Gibson?"

"Yes, it is."

"Hi, sir. This is Guyiser."

"Guyiser, my boy. How are you? I was just thinking about you."

"I'm fine, Mr. Gibson. Just trying out this new phone. I really like it. How are you, sir?"

"I'm doing fine."

"Good."

"How is Loaner doing?"

"Oh, he's fine. He's full of play."

"Well, you sound good, Guyiser. When am I going to see you?"

"Well, I thought I would drive in to town in a day or two. I want to thank you for all your help and support."

"Guyiser, I'm always here for you."

"I know that, Mr. Gibson. You're a true friend, and I'll never forget it. I'll let you go, sir, and I'll see you soon."

"I hope so, son. You take care."

"I will, sir. You too."

"Goodbye, Guyiser."

"Goodbye, Mr. Gibson." Guyiser pushed the off button. He sat there thinking. *Life goes on.*

Guyiser had fed the cow and chickens. He stood in front of the barn looking at the Christmas lights. He could not help but think of his father playing Santa. He started to take the lights down. The gray sky was cold as he sat in the barn at his desk. He circled the date, January 3, and wrote the words "MY DAD." and then crossed off the 4th, 5th, and 6th. Loaner started barking and ran to the barn door. A car pulled up, and a man got out carrying a briefcase. Guyiser went to the door. "Can I help you, sir?"

"Yes, are you Guyiser Blackman?"

Loaner barked again. "Me," Loaner stood by Guyiser's legs. "Yes, I am."

They shook hands. "Can I talk with you?"

"Sure. Let's go in the house. It's warmer."

They sat in the kitchen having coffee. "My name is Brown." He put his briefcase on the table and opened it. "First, I would like to tell you that I am sorry about your father's accident. I am with American Life Insurance Company. Your father had a policy with us. Life insurance." Mr. Brown took some papers out and slid them over to Guyiser.

"I didn't know that." Guyiser picked the papers up and looked at them.

Mr. Brown continued. "I have a check for you. The policy names you as the benefactor. All I need is your signature here and here." Guyiser took the pen and signed the papers. Mr. Brown handed the check to Guyiser. "Do you have any questions?" Guyiser looked at the check. 'Payable to Guyiser Blackman, Beneficiary, in the amount of $20,000.00 Dollars' "Well, if there are no questions, I'll be leaving now." Mr. Brown put his papers in his briefcase and stood up. "Again, I'm sorry for your loss."

After Mr. Brown left, Guyiser sat at the kitchen table looking at the check. He started to cry.

"Oh, Pa. I had rather have you back."

The on again, off again snow had stopped. Guyiser was chopping wood. Loaner was trying to catch a little field mouse. Guyiser's phone began to ring. It surprised him, and he missed the log. His ax sunk into the ground. He started pushing buttons. Finally, he hit the right one. "Hello, who is this?"

"It's me, boyfriend. What are you doing?"

"Cindy, it's you. You're the first one to call me. I'm chopping some wood. What are you doing?"

"We just got back. Guess what? Daddy got me a cell phone. Now we can talk all the time. Mother said you had called."

"Yeah, just trying out this phone. Do you have a new number?"

"Yes, the number is 708…."

"Don't tell me now. Maybe you could put it in my phone for me. I don't know how."

"Okay, I will. It's good to hear your voice. I've missed seeing you. It's been too long. Are you all right?"

"Yes, and I've missed you, too. Do you want to get together?"

"Yes, I do, but not tonight. How about tomorrow?"

"That sounds good to me."

"Okay. I'll call you or you call me."

"Sounds good. You have a good night."

"You, too. Good night, sweetheart."

"Good night, girlfriend."

The house was too quiet. Guyiser went to the T.V. and flipped through channels. Cartoons caught his eye. He stood watching the figures run around in fast motion.

He stood there smiling. He turned the sound up high. Anything to break the silence in the house. To hear a voice and music made him more relaxed. He did not have much to do. His father had always taken care of everything. He and Loaner went outside. Guyiser fed the cow and the chickens. He gathered the eggs from the pen. Then, he sat in the living room putting pictures in a photo album. With every picture, there was a memory. Smiles came as he looked at a picture of Santa, Cindy, and Loaner. Another smile came as he put a picture in the album. It was of him and Cindy kissing. His last picture was of him and Cindy at New Year's holding up glasses of champagne with big smiles. *And life goes on.* Loaner lay by the fireplace watching Guyiser.

"Hey, boy. What you want to do today?"

Guyiser closed the photo album. There lay the insurance check on the coffee table. He got up and went to a dresser by the kitchen door. He pulled out the bottom drawer. There was his father's small tin box. This is where his father kept his money. He picked it up and went back to the couch. Setting it on the coffee table, he opened it. The small box had a lot of bills in it. He began to count the money. He could not believe how much money his father had saved. There was $1,200 in loose bills. *This must have been money from the swap meet sales.* At the bottom was a stack of bills with a rubber band around them. It was mostly hundred dollar bills with fifties sprinkled in here and there. He started counting, "...8, 9, 10." He made another stack.

"...7, 8, 9, 10." When he had finished, he sat back looking at all the stacks of bills. "...7, 8, 9."

There was $9,500.00 in cash. *Where did he get all this money?* He quickly put the money back in the small tin box. He put the check in also and closed the box. *Wow! what's this all about?* Guyiser put the box back in the drawer and closed it. He stood looking at the drawer. A voice came to him. 'And one way or another we're gonna get him.' *Was this money the bet that his father told him about?*

The phone started to ring. The sound jarred his thoughts. He went to answer it. "Hello."

"Hi, boyfriend. What are you doing?"

"Oh, hi, Cindy. I'm, ah, just sitting here putting pictures in my album. What are you doing?"

"Oh, just helping Mother around the house.

You want to get together? We got the pictures of us back. They're great."

"Sure. I'll come over and pick you up."

"That's okay. I've got the wagon today. I'll drive over. I'll be over in about an hour, okay?"

"Okay. See you when you get here."

"Okay. Bye."

"Bye."

The old teapot whistled. Guyiser made himself a cup of coffee and opened a can of food for Loaner. The station wagon pulled up to the house, and Cindy tooted her horn. Guyiser went to meet her. "Hi, baby. Help me unload. Mother sent over some food for you." Guyiser kissed her and held out his hands as she handed him the bowls of food. She picked up a couple of bowls, and they went in.

The kitchen table was full. "Boy, your mother sure does love to cook. Look at all this."

Cindy hugged Guyiser, "I'm a good cook too, you know."

Guyiser kissed her. "You are so pretty today. Is that a new blouse?"

"No, I'm just tired of wearing sweaters."

He looked at her neck. "I see you're wearing the necklace. It looks good on you."

Cindy kissed him. "It's a gift from my boyfriend. Let's go sit down. I want to show you the pictures." The fireplace popped and crackled as they sat looking at the pictures. "There are two sets, so you can have one. I like them all."

Guyiser lined them up on the coffee table.

"You know, we do look like a million bucks." He opened the photo album and started putting pictures in it.

"Start at the beginning and look at them."

He handed the album to Cindy and went to the fireplace to add another log. "Oh, Cindy, can you help me with this phone? Some things I don't understand."

They sat on the couch. Cindy explained the different buttons and menus. She put in her new cell phone number. "Now, this number is my home number, and this number is my cell phone. I carry my cell phone with me always, okay?"

Guyiser took the phone. "Oh, I get it! It's pretty simple after all. Thanks, Cindy." Guyiser was silent for a while. "Cindy, can I show you something that's just between you and me? It's been on my mind."

She looked at him concerned, "Of course you can—just between you and me." Guyiser went to the drawer and returned with the tin box. He put it on the table and opened it. He handed her the check. "Oh, Guyiser!"

He pointed to the box, "And, there is almost $10,000.00 in cash in there. I just found it this morning. What do you think?"

Cindy was speechless. She looked at the box and then the check. "Guyiser, I think this is a gift to you from your father. I think it's his way of telling you that he loves you. He was a good man, and this is his way of taking care of you."

Guyiser sat looking at the box and listening to Cindy. "I never thought of it that way. I guess you're right. The way you explained it to me makes me feel better.

I never thought of it that way." He put the check back in the box and put it away. He sat down and hugged and kissed Cindy. "Thank you, Cindy, for helping me understand."

They sat in the kitchen eating. They were enjoying themselves talking and laughing about nothing and everything. "Anyway, tell your mother the food was great, and I thank her, okay?"

Cindy stood up and began to clean up the dishes and to put away the food. "Why don't you go in the living room and relax? I'll finish up here and be right in." Guyiser kissed her and went to the living room. He sat on the couch with his feet up on the coffee table. Cindy came in, "All done." She crawled up beside him. "What are you thinking?"

"Oh, I was just thinking how awesome you are and how indebted I am to you. I don't know how I could do things without you."

Cindy kissed him long and tenderly. "You're sweet. Turn around, I'll rub your neck." Guyiser turned around.

"Oh, yeah, that feels good." Cindy massaged his neck and shoulders.

"Shhh, let me do my magic." She kept rubbing and massaging his neck. "So that feels good, does it? I know, go get a blanket and a couple of pillows." Guyiser looked at her and went to his bedroom. Cindy got up and put a log on the fire. He came back. "Spread it out here on the floor and put the pillows here. Now, take off your shirt and lie down. I'm going to give you a good back rub and massage."

Guyiser did as she said. "Ohh, that sounds good."

Cindy straddled him and began to rub his neck and back. "You feel tense. Does this feel better?" She rubbed a little harder.

"Oh, yes, right there."

Cindy got up and turned the lights out and came back to Guyiser. She continued to massage his back. The fireplace threw off warm heat as she rubbed. She bent and kissed his back in several places. As she massaged his back, she spoke softly to him. "You feel good to me. Turn over." She got off him, and he turned over on his back. She straddled him again and continued to rub his chest. "I love your body. You're in great shape." She looked into Guyiser's eyes, leaned forward, and kissed him. Guyiser put his arms around her and passionately kissed her back. Cindy sat back and looked at him.

"Have you ever made love before?"

Guyiser took her hands and kissed them.

"No, have you?"

Cindy stood up and unbuttoned her jeans and stepped out of them. Again, she straddled him. "No." Guyiser watched her as she unbuttoned her blouse and took it off. Guyiser's heart beat fast as she reached around and unsnapped her pink bra. The straps fell off her shoulders as she took the bra off. They kept looking at each other. Guyiser looked at her body. Her firm young breasts were beautiful. She leaned down and kissed his chest over and over, as she moved to his lips. She kissed him tenderly and whispered to him, "I want to be your first."

Guyiser kissed her intensely. He looked deeply into her eyes. "And, I want to be your first."

They explored each other's bodies for a long time as they kissed and kissed. Guyiser kissed all of her body, her breasts, her neck, her thighs, her body.

Cindy reached for him and pulled him to her. "I want you, so get inside of me." Guyiser lay on her moving slowly. "Oh, Guyiser, Oh, Oh."

He whispered to her, "Are you all right?"

With passion Cindy said, "Yes, Guyiser, yes, oh, yes."

Guyiser continued to move slowly. He became tense. "Cindy, Cindy, something is happening, oh, Cindy." He moved faster, "Oh, Cindy." His movements slowed down. He fell on her with his head in the pillow. "Oh, Cindy." He kissed her neck and then her lips. He started to move off of her.

She grabbed his waist. "Stay inside of me."

She began to move under him. "Oh, Guyiser, you feel so good. Don't move." She moved faster and hugged him tightly.

"Oh, Guyiser, Oh, Guyiser, Oh, Oh," and then it happened for her. "Oh, Oh, Oh, Guyiser."

They lay there holding each other. They kissed each other over and over, as they looked into each other's eyes. They were no longer a young boy and a young girl. They had become a young man and a young woman. The fire's glow on her body was radiant. Guyiser sat with a smile looking at her. Cindy lay there smiling back at him. "Are you all right? I think I see some blood."

She smiled bigger. "That's natural. I am no longer a virgin, thanks to my boyfriend. It was wonderful." Cindy rose up and kissed him. "I'm going to clean up."

Guyiser looked into the fireplace as she left.

A big smile came to his face. *Yes, it was wonderful.*

The two sat on the couch looked at each other. It was a while before Cindy spoke, "You want some banana pudding?"

Guyiser sat there with a smile on his face, "No, I've had dessert. Thank you." They both started laughing.

Cindy's cell phone rang. "Hello. Yes, Mother, Yes, Mother, No, Mother. We just finished dessert." She looked at Guyiser smiling. "I know, Mother, I will, Mother, Okay, I'll be right there. I love you, too. Bye." Cindy clicked off and turned to Guyiser. "I don't know if having a cell phone was a good idea or not. Mother has called me eight times in the last three days." She laughed. "One time I was upstairs in my room." They laughed again. "Sweetheart, I have to go."

Guyiser made a pouting face. "I know, I wish I could stay, too, but.." She kissed him and got up and put on her coat. He followed her to the door. Outside, they stood holding each other. The sky was dark gray, and it had started to snow again.

"Cindy, I, I don't know what to say. I feel like a new person."

She kissed him, "I know what you mean. Guyiser, I think I love you. You're everything to me." They stood there holding each other. "I know that I love you. I've said it a thousand times."

"I know, Cindy. It's been only a short time, but I hope we are always together."

"I hope so, too, Guyiser."

Guyiser stood on the porch watching the snow fall as Cindy drove away. Loaner came walking out and stood by Guyiser. "Hey, where you been?" Loaner yawned.

"Oh, you been asleep; are you hungry? Come on, let's go in."

The snow fell all night long. Guyiser sat having coffee and watching the nine o'clock news. The pretty blond weather woman was giving the forecast. "But the snowplows have been working all night, and the roads look pretty good this morning. But, buckle up and drive carefully."

The phone rang. "Hello."

"Hi, sweetheart, how are you?"

"How am I? I feel great."

"I just wanted to call and hear your voice."

"I'm glad you called. I was just thinking about you. What are you doing today?"

"Mother is taking me shopping. She wants to buy me some new clothes for school. The new shopping center is open now. What are you doing today?"

"Oh, the usual things. Gonna feed the cow and the chickens, and have to fix a fence that's down."

"Okay, Mother. I got to go. Call me tonight, okay?"

"Okay, I sure will. Bye."

"Bye."

Guyiser and Loaner hopped in the truck. They drove along the property line checking the fence. They ended up at the west end of the property and there it was. A tree had fallen and had broken the fence down. The west end of the property was an area that his father had said not to go into. A small creek ran in this area, and his father had said there was a snake bed there and to stay away. There were a lot of trees with a clearing area in the center of the trees. Guyiser and Loaner walked around the clearing.

He noticed some tools by the tree line. There was a shovel, a hoe, a rake, some fence poles, and a water bottle. He picked them up and put them in the truck. Next, he backed the truck to the fallen tree and tied a long rope to it and pulled the tree away from the fence. "Hey, Loaner, this will make a lot of firewood." Guyiser repaired the fence and pulled the tree back to the house.

As night fell, Guyiser fed the cow and chickens. He and Loaner were now in the kitchen eating supper. Thoughts of the clearing and of the tools he had found went through his mind. *Oh well, I guess Pa had planted tomatoes there or something.*

Guyiser lay in his bed. He had talked with Cindy and everything was all right. He had fixed the fence, fed the animals, locked up the barn, and everything was in order. *Let's see, I'll go into Nashville tomorrow and have lunch, buy some more feed, see Mr. Gibson, go to the bank, and come home.*

It was about three o'clock. Guyiser and Loaner had had lunch, picked up the feed, and were on their way to visit with Mr. Gibson. The sky was gray, and snow was falling. It was a quiet day on the streets of Nashville.

Guyiser and Mr. Gibson sat in the bike shop talking. "Guyiser, that's a good sum of money. And, I agree with Cindy. It is a gift from your father. You should get it in the bank as soon as possible. I wouldn't carry it around with me."

Guyiser closed the box. "Yes sir, that's what I'm going to do right away. Thanks for your advice and for talking with me. Come on, Loaner. Let's go. Bye, Mr. Gibson, and thanks again."

"Bye, Guyiser. We'll see you later."

The Murder

Part 6

Revenge is mine, said the Lord,
He who lives by the sword will die
By the sword. But, a little help
Will make things sweeter. Forgive
Me, Lord, but I want to help.
Stay with me, Lord, step by step.

Loaner and Guyiser stood outside of Mr. Gibson's store. "Okay, boy. Let's put this on." Guyiser attached a leather leash to Loaner's collar. He tucked the tin box under his arm, and they headed for the bank.

Halfway there, Loaner started to growl. As they walked on, the growl grew stronger. Guyiser stopped and looked around. "Easy, boy." At a passageway between the buildings, a cat jumped out of a garbage can and ran away. Guyiser laughed and kept walking. Loaner's ears were back, and his tail was straight out. His growl became louder. As they came to the passageway, two men stepped out in front of them. The taller man with glasses grabbed Guyiser's coat. Loaner showed his teeth and growled. Guyiser pulled back on the leash. "Me, me, Loaner." The man pulled Guyiser into the passageway and Guyiser dropped the leash. The two men pushed Guyiser against a wall. Loaner stood ready to attack as he growled. "What do you want?"

The two men laughed. "What you go in the box? Some money for us?" They laughed again. "Give me that box, boy!"

Guyiser hugged the box tighter. "I ain't giving' you nothing'."

With that, the taller man hit Guyiser's face. Guyiser's mouth started to bleed. "Give me the box, boy!" The man tried to pull the box from Guyiser, but he would not let go. The man hit him again and again. Guyiser fell to the ground holding the box. Loaner pranced around and growled, wanting to attack. The man knelt down and pulled out a long hunting knife. He put it to Guyiser's neck. "You're as stubborn as your old man, and you know what happened to him." He laughed. "Now, let go of the box, or I'll cut your throat."

Guyiser looked at Loaner. He was ready to attack. His teeth were showing, and his eyes were piercing.

His large body was tense and his growl furious. Guyiser looked at the man and smiled, "You want it when?"

The man put the knife tighter to Guyiser's neck. "I want it now, boy!"

Guyiser looked at Loaner, "Now, Loaner, Now!" Loaner was waiting for this command. He lunged at the man with all of his weight. The man fell backward as Loaner attacked. He went for the man's neck. His long teeth sank in deep as he shook his head, growling. The man tried to stab Loaner but cut his leg. He let out a yell as Loaner mauled him. Blood gushed from his neck as Loaner shook his head violently. The man stopped moving. He was dead.

The other man opened his long coat, pulled out his sawed-off shotgun, and aimed it at Guyiser and Loaner. Guyiser yelled loudly and kicked the shotgun as hard as he could. The gun fell to the ground. Guyiser quickly scrambled for the gun. Picking it up, he pointed it at the man. "Get against the wall! Quick!" Guyiser stood up and called to Loaner. "Me, Loaner, me!" With blood dropping from his mouth, Loaner slowly released the man. He stood by Guyiser, growling at the other man.

Guyiser walked to the man and shoved the shotgun under the man's neck. "You killed my Father, didn't you?" He shoved the gun in the man's neck, again.

"Please, don't kill me. It was him. He did it. He cut the brake line." The man started to cry. "Please don't shoot me mister."

Guyiser took the gun away from his neck and shoved it in his stomach. "Why? Why did you kill him?"

The man stopped crying. "The money. He owed us money for a drug deal."

Guyiser stared at the man. "That's a lie. You're lying."

"It's the truth. He sold us pot, and we gave him money. Then he told the police the pot was in a warehouse."

"You are lying to me!"

"Please, mister, don't shoot me. I'll do anything you say. I'll go away. You'll never see me again."

Guyiser cocked the hammer back on the gun, "Well, you're right about one thing. I'll never see you again." He pulled the trigger. The shot echoed in the passageway. Guyiser watched the man slide down the bloody wall. He dropped the shotgun and sat down looking at the two dead men. Loaner lay beside him, licking his leg.

Two sheriff officers were going in the restaurant across the street and heard the loud shot. They drew their guns and ran to the passageway. They saw Guyiser sitting with Loaner. One of the officers went to check the two dead men. The other officer stood pointing his gun at Guyiser. "They are both dead." The officer stood Guyiser up. "What happened here?"

Guyiser pointed to the tin box. "They tried to rob me."

The officer opened the box and saw all the money. "We're taking you downtown. You can tell your story there. Let's go." The officers put Guyiser and Loaner in their car and called for an ambulance.

Guyiser sat in the office of the police station. "Can I call a friend?"

"Not just yet. We have to read you your rights." Guyiser sat listening to the officer. "Now, could you tell us what happened?"

"Well, they beat me and were trying to rob me. Could I please call my friend?"

The officer put down his pen and looked at Guyiser, "Yes, you have that right."

Guyiser made his call, "Mr. Gibson, this is Guyiser. There has been a problem. I'm at the police station in trouble."

"Guyiser, are you all right?"

"Yes, sir, but two men are dead."

"Guyiser, do not say a word to them. I'll be right there with my lawyer."

Guyiser hung up and turned to the officer.

"I've never been in trouble before. My friend and a lawyer are on their way. He said to talk to you when they get here."

Minutes later Mr. Gibson and his lawyer arrived. Mr. Gibson came to Guyiser and hugged him. "Are you all right, son?" He looked at Guyiser's swollen face and cut lips. "This is Mr. Levine." Mr. Levine shook hands and asked the officer for a moment with Guyiser.

Mr. Levine, Guyiser, and Mr. Gibson sat talking. "And, if I shake my head, do not answer their questions, okay?"

Again, they all sat in the sheriff's office. The officer pressed a button on a tape recorder. "This is the statement of Mr. Guyiser Blackman in the presence of his lawyer, Mr. Levine.

Okay, Mr. Blackman, from the very beginning tell exactly what happened."

Guyiser looked at Mr. Gibson. "Well, I had just left Mr. Gibson's bike shop with Loaner, my dog. We were headed to the bank." Guyiser continued to explain about the two men dragging him into the passageway and beating him. He talked about the struggle over the box and the man with his knife to Guyiser's neck. He told how Loaner protected him. He also told about the second man with the shotgun. "And I kicked the shotgun out of his hand, and the gun fell to the ground." He thought for a moment and looked at Mr. Gibson. "We fought for the gun. It went off, and that's all I remember."

Mr. Levine interrupted. "It seems to me it was self-defense. Mr. Blackman fought for his life and property." The sheriff turned off the tape recorder and sat back.

Mr. Levine continued. "I ask that you release Mr. Blackman on his own recognizance. He has never been in trouble. As his attorney, I will take full responsibility for him."

The sheriff leaned forward, "I see no reason to hold you, Mr. Blackman. However, we will hold the money as evidence until the hearing. Mr. Levine, do you agree?"

Mr. Levine stood up and shook his hand. "Yes, I do, Sheriff. I thank you."

The sheriff looked at Guyiser. "You should let a doctor look at you, and I would take your dog to a vet right away. He needs to have his cuts taken care of, and he needs to be cleaned up real good."

Guyiser stood and shook his hand.

"Thank you, sir. I'll do that right away."

The three of them and Loaner stood on the sidewalk in front of the police station. Mr. Levine was talking to Guyiser, "I'm just glad you are okay. They could have killed you. Your dog saved your life. There will be an investigation, and if anyone comes to see you about this, you call me right then. Don't worry about a thing, okay? Now, here is my card and number. Again, do not talk to anyone about this and do not sign anything without me being present. Mr. Gibson, it's always good to see you. Guyiser, you have a good friend here. I've known him a very long time. Well, good night to you both."

Guyiser shook his hand, "Thank you, Mr. Levine, for everything. Good night. Mr. Gibson, how can I ever thank you? I was really scared this time. All this has gotten to me. I'm sure glad that you were there for me."

"Guyiser, son, I'll always be there, anytime you need me. We're partners, remember. Now, you go take care of Loaner. There's a vet on the edge of town. I'll call you tomorrow. Are you sure you're all right driving?"

Guyiser shook his hand and hugged him. "I'll be all right, sir. I have friends." He petted Loaner, "Let's go see a doctor, Loaner. Good night, sir."

The snow had stopped. Loaner lay on the couch beside Guyiser. Guyiser rubbed his dog's long shiny coat as he looked at the white bandage the vet had put around his leg. He could not help but think of how Loaner had come to his aid. His mind became cloudy with thoughts of the shotgun and the man pleading for his life. He could hear the words, 'drug deal'. Guyiser could feel his finger squeezing the trigger. He looked at his father's chair. "Pa, did you? If you did, Pa, no one will ever know. I promise." Guyiser closed his eyes. It had been a long day. Sleep came.

"Look outside, folks. The sun is here," the weatherman was saying. "And, it's going to be here for a few more days." Guyiser walked into the living room drinking his coffee. He went to the window and looked out. The sky was clear and bright.

His phone rang. "Hello."

"...Good morning, sir."

"...Much better. He'll be all right. Vet said a few more days."

"...Yes, sir. He seems like a good man."

"...Oh, I will. Well, if we could put it off a day or two."

"...Yes, sir. I will. Thanks for calling, Mr. Gibson."

"...You too. Bye now."

Loaner jumped up on the couch beside Guyiser and barked. "How you doin', boy? You want to go out?" Loaner licked Guyiser's face. "Yes, I love you, too." He went to the door to let Loaner out. Cindy rode up the drive on her bicycle. Guyiser waved and ran to meet her. "Hi, baby. You're looking good this morning." The two walked to the house. They sat in the kitchen talking.

"I tried to call several times. Where were you?"

Guyiser got up and poured more coffee for them. "I think the batteries are dead in the phone, but I got some more."

Cindy stood up and walked over to Guyiser. "What happened to your face?"

"Oh, that. I uh, had a flat tire and bumped my head.

I didn't get home till late. The tow truck took a long time to get to me and change the tire. But, everything is all right, now."

Cindy touched his face. "Oh, poor baby. Why don't we go in your room, and I'll make you feel better." She smiled and kissed him.

"Well, it does still hurt a little." He picked her up and headed for his bedroom. "Are you sure?"

"Yes, sweetheart, I want to."

Their lovemaking made the sun shine even brighter. Cindy sat on the bed rubbing Guyiser's chest. "You know, I will be leaving tomorrow night. So, you better get plenty of batteries for that phone. I'll be calling you all the time."

Guyiser pulled her to him. "Or, I'll be calling you. I'm really going to miss you, Cindy."

She kissed him several times. "And, I'll miss you. I love you, Guyiser Blackman." She got up and dressed. "Mother and Daddy are taking me to the airport. Will you be seeing me off?"

Guyiser lay there watching Cindy dress. "You are so beautiful. Of course I will."

Cindy called for Guyiser. "Come in here. I have something for you." Guyiser got dressed and went into the living room. "Here, this is for you, so you don't forget me." She handed him a beautiful black briefcase. "Now you can look official. I want my boyfriend looking good."

Guyiser hugged and kissed her. "I love it. Thank you, sweetheart. Believe me, I'll never forget you."

Guyiser put the bike shop on hold. So many things had happened to change his life. He sat in the barn at his desk looking out of the opened doors. The warm sun was melting the snow. He missed all the excitement of his sale. Loaner came limping in and lay on the hay. Guyiser went to him, "You been running too much. You're staying in for a while." He was petting Loaner when his phone rang. "Hello."

"...Yes, it is."

"…Oh, hi, Mr. Levine."

"…Oh, fine, sir."

"…On the 15th. That's fine for me."

"…Yes, sir, I'll meet you there."

"…Thanks for calling."

"…Goodbye."

Guyiser sat at his desk and marked on his calendar the 15th, Hearing, 10am.

It was late evening. Guyiser and Loaner sat watching a movie on T.V. The sky was clear and the moon was shining on the snow. They sat by the bright warm fireplace eating popcorn. Guyiser laughed as he threw popcorn at Loaner. The phone rang. Guyiser looked at his pocket watch. It was nine thirty. He answered the phone. "Hello."

"…Mrs. Taylor, is everything all right?"

"…Oh, good."

"…Yes, ma'am."

"…Yes, ma'am. I'd like that very much. Thanks for asking."

"…Yes, ma'am, about six o'clock. I'll see you then."

"…You, too. Good night."

Centerville was a pretty town. The sun was out, the stores were open, and people were walking around. Guyiser and Loaner walked around town shopping. As the day passed,

Guyiser found himself standing at his father and mother's graves. He placed flowers over their graves and stood thinking about the past. *If you only knew, Pa, if you only knew.* He kissed their headstones and walked away.

The Taylor house was a busy place. Cindy was packing her third suitcase. Mrs. Taylor kept coming in her room with something else to pack. "You will need this."

"No, Mother, I don't need a toaster."

"Well, you never know, take it anyway."

Mr. Taylor came up the stairs with two more suitcases. "Do you think this is enough?"

Cindy laughed, "Well, that depends on Mother."

Mr. Taylor laughed with her, "I know what you mean. You should see all the sandwiches she made for you." He picked up two of the packed suitcases, carried them downstairs, and put them by the door. Just then, Guyiser knocked on the door. "Guyiser, my boy. Come in, come in. How are you doing?"

"I'm doin' good, Mr. Taylor. Good to see you, sir."

"Sit down, son."

Cindy came down carrying a suitcase. "There's one more, Daddy."

Guyiser went to her and took the suitcase. "This is heavy. What's in here, the kitchen sink?"

Cindy laughed, "No, just a toaster. I'm glad you came. Mother said you would be here.

How are you doing, good looking?"

Guyiser put the suitcase down and hugged her. "I'm a little sad you're leaving."

Mr. Taylor came down with the last suitcase. "Now, I'll go help your mother. Supper is almost ready."

Cindy and Guyiser sat on the couch. Guyiser pulled out a small blue box and handed it to Cindy. "Something to remember me by." Cindy excitedly opened the box. She held up a small gold charm. It had a little heart with 'I love you' on it. She hugged Guyiser's neck. "There's one more." Cindy looked and held up a small gold charm. It was a number one with the letters F-I-R-S-T on it.

Cindy looked at Guyiser. "I love it, and I'll always remember our first."

Supper was always a pleasure at the Taylor's house. "Mrs. Taylor, you did it again. That was the best supper ever."

They were sitting in the living room. "I'm glad you enjoyed it, Guyiser. And, I want to tell you something else. Cindy may be gone, but Mr. Taylor and I are not. We expect to see you twice a week for supper, do you understand me, young man?"

Guyiser smiled. "Yes, ma'am. I understand. And, I thank you."

Mr. Taylor stood up, "Well, I guess I'll load your luggage in the wagon."

Guyiser got up, "I'll help you, sir."

Everything was loaded and ready to go. Mrs. Taylor looked at the grandfather clock. "I guess we had better go. Are you all ready?"

Guyiser looked at Cindy, "Let's go outside." They stood on the porch hugging.

Mr. and Mrs. Taylor came out and went to the car. "You two coming?"

Guyiser looked at Cindy, "No, ma'am. I'll just say my goodbye here."

They stood holding each other. "In your briefcase I put paper, pens, and envelopes with stamps, so you had better write to me." Cindy kissed him.

"I promise I will." They stood kissing as the station wagon horn tooted. They walked to the car and Guyiser opened the door. They stood looking at each other. As they hugged, Guyiser whispered to Cindy, "I love you."

She whispered back, "I love you."

Guyiser stood waving as the car drove off.

Tears were in his eyes as he again said, "I love you."

Loaner sat watching Guyiser as he stood in front of the mirror tying his tie. "Want to look good for the hearing." He put on his blazer and looked at Loaner, "What do you think?" Loaner barked. Guyiser smiled, "Well, let's go."

The ride to Nashville didn't take too long. As he drove, Guyiser kept thinking of the story he had told the sheriff. *We fought for the gun, and it went off.*

Mr. Levine and Mr. Gibson were talking as Guyiser and Loaner came in the shop. "Good morning, Guyiser. We were just talking about you."

They all sat as Mr. Levine told Guyiser what was going to happen. "And, then it will all be over."

Mr. Levine looked at Mr. Gibson and Guyiser, "And put the leash on Loaner. They may ask about that. Any questions? Good, let's go. Don't want to be late. Judges hate that."

Guyiser was nervous as they sat in the judge's chamber. The judge and an attorney came in and sat down. "Good morning, gentlemen. This is Mr. Bond, the investigating attorney. Shall we get started?"

Mr. Bond stood up. "Mr. Levine, Mr. Blackman, good morning. There are a few questions I have. Mr. Blackman, did you know the two men who attacked you?"

Guyiser looked at Mr. Levine. "No, sir. I did not know them. I had seen them at the bank when I made a deposit."

"Mr. Blackman, is your dog trained to attack?"

"No, sir. Not trained, but he's very protective of me."

"Has he ever bit or attacked anyone before?"

"No, sir. Never." Mr. Bond went to Guyiser and pretended to hit him. Loaner sat there and did not move.

Mr. Levine stood up, "I object, Your Honor. He is trying to make the dog attack. Loaner knows the difference between hitting and danger."

Mr. Bond turned, went to a table, and picked up a long knife. He walked to Guyiser again. Loaner growled. Mr. Bond raised the knife to Guyiser's head. Loaner stood up growling. Guyiser spoke up, "I wouldn't do that, sir."

Mr. Levine stood up again, "You Honor."

The judge spoke, "Mr. Bond that will be enough. The dog can obviously sense danger."

Mr. Bond put the knife away. "Yes, you're Honor."

Guyiser looked at Mr. Levine, "What did that mean?"

Mr. Levine smiled, "Everything is fine."

Mr. Bond continued, "Mr. Blackman, I would like to ask you about the man with the shotgun. It bothers me how he was shot. Your statement to the sheriff says you don't remember."

Mr. Levine stood up again, "Your Honor, the statement says and I quote, 'We fought for the gun, and it went off. That's all I remember.'"

Mr. Bond continued, "'We fought for the gun.' Can you tell me who and how the gun was being held? Can you show me?" He handed the gun to Guyiser.

Again, Mr. Levine stood up, "You're Honor."

The judge looked at him, "For the record, I would like to see how the gun went off."

Guyiser looked at Mr. Levine. He nodded. Guyiser asked for Mr. Bond's help. Guyiser lay down on the floor. "The man opened his coat and pulled out the shotgun. He aimed it at Loaner and me. I kicked the gun out of his hands like this" Mr. Bond released the gun. "It fell about here. I grabbed the stock, here. He grabbed the barrel here." Mr. Bond held the barrel.

He was pulling and I was holding on here. He bent over me and tried to get my hands off the stock. I held on tight. The gun went off."

Mr. Bond was bending over Guyiser, "But, who pulled the trigger?"

Mr. Levine stood up and went to them. "Your Honor, Mr. Blackman was holding on to the stock, as you see here and not on the trigger. It is easy to see that the man bending over and pulling could have easily pulled the trigger by accident, which would cause him to shoot himself."

Mr. Bond was still bending over Guyiser. "Mr. Blackman, do this for me. Reach for the trigger and pull it."

Mr. Levine shouted out, "I object, Your Honor. Mr. Bond is trying to make something happen that did not happen. Even if Mr. Blackman released his grip, the man would have pulled the gun out of his hand." Mr. Levine turned to Guyiser. "Release the gun with one hand." Guyiser released one of his hands. "Mr. Bond, pull the gun out of Guyiser's hand." Mr. Bond pulled the gun out of his hand. "Now, who has the gun? Your Honor, if Mr. Blackman had released the gun with one hand, the man would have pulled it out of his grip. Mr. Blackman was holding the gun's stock with both hands." Mr. Levine turned to Guyiser, "When the gun went off, what happened next?"

Guyiser still lay on the floor, "Well, I was holding the gun stock here when it went off. The man fell back against the wall, and I dropped the gun about here. I remember getting up, falling against the other wall, and sitting down. I don't remember anything else until the two sheriff officers came." Mr. Bond took the shotgun, went to his table, and sat down. Mr. Levine helped Guyiser up, and they went to sit down.

"Mr. Blackman, Mr. Levine, and Mr. Bond, I want to thank you for this enactment of the event. As I watched it and heard Mr. Blackman's statement, I am ruling that the shooting was an accidental shooting, and or a case of self-defense. I rule that the charges, if any, be dropped against Mr. Blackman and that his property be returned to him.

It is in my power, by the state of Tennessee, that I dismiss this case. This hearing is over. Thank you, gentlemen." The judge stood up, gathered his papers, and left the room.

Mr. Gibson ran to Guyiser. He hugged him. "I knew it would be all right."

Mr. Levine shook Guyiser's hand. "You did well."

Guyiser hugged him. "You are the best. I'll never forget the way you handled this. Thank you."

Mr. Levine smiled, "The court will release your money in about a week. Loaner, you did a good job, too. He's a very smart dog."

They stood outside talking. Guyiser looked up at the blue sky. "Now, I can breathe better. Thanks, Mr. Levine. Thanks, Mr. Gibson. Can I buy you lunch?"

Mr. Levine was petting Loaner. "Not for me. I have to get back to the office. Good luck, Guyiser. Call me sometime. See you later. Bye."

Mr. Gibson and Guyiser sat in a restaurant having lunch. They talked about Mr. Levine and the hearing. "Well, Guyiser, I see you're happy again. Now you can get on with your life. When do you want to go see the factory?"

Guyiser leaned back and smiled.

"As soon as possible. I'm ready and looking forward to it."

Mr. Gibson looked at his watch. "How about the day after tomorrow? I'll call Margaret and tell her. So, plan on it, and meet me at the shop about eight o'clock."

Guyiser put money down for the bill, "I'll be there."

Guyiser sat in the swing on the front porch swinging. The day was about over. The sun had felt warm all day. A pretty white cloud floated by. He watched Loaner run around and play with a rubber ball. He closed his eyes listening to the squeak of the swing. Then he heard his phone ring. "Hello."

"...Cindy, baby. How are you?"

"...Oh, I'm fine. How's Florida?"

"...That's great."

"...Here, well, I'm on the front porch swinging. The sky is blue, and the sun has been out all day."

"...I miss you. How is school so far?"

"...What kind of assignment?"

"...Well, I'm glad you're happy."

"...You have a roommate? What's her name?"

"...Sandra, that's a pretty name."

"…She wants to be a camera operator." Guyiser laughed, "You can practice on each other."

"…Me, oh, same old thing. I went to Nashville this morning. Mr. Gibson and I are going to Kentucky to see the factory."

"…No, not tomorrow, the day after."

"…Who was that?"

"…Supper, I wish somebody would call me for supper."

"…I love you, too."

"…I will. Love you. Bye."

Guyiser lay in bed looking out the window. The sun was pushing the night fog away. The hills had patches of snow on them. It looked like another good day. Loaner ran in and jumped on the bed. He tugged at the blanket. Guyiser pulled back. They continued their play for a while. Guyiser got up and started to get dressed. The phone rang. "Hello."

"…Mr. Taylor, good morning, sir."

"…Busy? No, sir."

"…I'd be glad to. See you in ten minutes. Bye."

Guyiser finished getting dressed and went to his truck. Mr. Taylor was sweeping off the melting snow from the porch as Guyiser drove up. "Good morning, sir."

"Good morning, Guyiser. I hope you don't mind me calling so early."

"No problem, sir. You say it broke last night?"

"Yes, the pump has been making noise for two days, and it finally died." Mr. Taylor laughed. "No water." Mrs. Taylor woke me yelling. 'Get up, get up.' "I can't get anyone out here to fix it for two days."

"Well, don't worry, sir. I know a little about water pumps. What do you want to do first?"

"Well, I have a pump at the store. We'll go in and get it. With your help, we'll have water by noon."

"Sounds like a good plan, sir. Let's go."

The two men worked all morning replacing the pump. It was a big job. Mrs. Taylor walked out to the well where they were working. "Hi, Guyiser. I'm glad you could help. How's it going?"

Mr. Taylor looked at Guyiser and winked. "We'll know as soon as I flip this switch. Guyiser, you do the honors."

Guyiser reached for the switch on the post. "1, 2, 3," he flipped it. The pump started running smoothly and water started flowing.

Mrs. Taylor clapped her hands. Mr. Taylor and Guyiser shook hands. "A job well done, Guyiser."

Mrs. Taylor hugged Guyiser. "Now you two come on in. I made some good beef stew for lunch. Come on."

Mr. Taylor gathered up his tools. "We'll be right there, dear."

The Taylor house always smelled good. They sat at the table talking and eating. "More milk, Guyiser?"

"Yes, ma'am. This sure is good stew."

"I'm glad you like it. The roast beef makes it good. I have a big jar for you to take home with you."

Mr. Taylor asked for more stew. "Oh, Guyiser, have you talked to Cindy yet?"

"Yes, sir. She sounded real good. Says she really likes school and has a roommate."

Mrs. Taylor handed a bowl of stew to Mr. Taylor. "Yes, we talked to her, too. I'm glad she's happy. You know, you two are pretty serious about each other." She smiled, "Anything we should know about?"

Mr. Taylor spoke up, "Now, hon. If they have something to say, I'm sure they will tell us, right Guyiser?"

Guyiser took a drink of his milk, "Yes, sir. I'm glad we got that pump fixed. I should be going. Thanks for the stew. It'll taste good tonight." Guyiser went to the door. "Ya'll have a good day. Bye now."

Mrs. Taylor looked at her husband, "I hope we didn't say something wrong."

"What do you mean 'we', dear?"

It was a very exciting day as Guyiser and Loaner drove into Nashville. A beautiful morning had opened its eyes. Guyiser pulled into a parking space and looked at his watch. Seven forty-five. He couldn't help but see a big, long, black car parked in front of Gibson's Bike Shop. He adjusted his tie, buttoned his blazer, took a big breath, and went into the shop with his briefcase in hand. Mr. Gibson greeted him with a big smile. "My, my. You look sharp, Guyiser."

Guyiser looked at Mr. Gibson, "So do you, sir. I never saw you in a suit before."

"Oh, Guyiser, this is James, our driver."

"Nice to meet you, sir."

"Nice to meet you, Mr. Blackman."

Mr. Gibson looked at his watch, "We should be leaving now. It's a long drive."

James stood by the opened car door. Mr. Gibson, Guyiser, and Loaner go in. "Wow! What a car. Look at all this stuff. Wow!"

Mr. Gibson laughed, "You might have to get used to all this stuff. I kind of like it myself."

Highway sixty-five was a wide highway. The ride was smooth. Mr. Gibson took off his coat.

Guyiser took off his coat. "It's over a two-hour ride to Bowling Green, so relax and enjoy the ride."

Guyiser put his briefcase on his lap. "I thought about this trip all night long, but this car is something else."

Mr. Gibson enjoyed Guyiser's excitement. "It's called a limousine."

Guyiser repeated the word, "Limousine." They talked as the limousine sped down the highway. "You know, Mr. Gibson, I've always thought of being successful at something, but I never thought of bicycles. I've learned to love them—putting them together, taking them apart, and even sitting looking at them."

"You're right, Guyiser. You should love what you do. However, remember, there's a business part of it, too.

Being happy, having fun, and making money; that's what success is all about."

Guyiser sat listening, "Well, I'm good at two of those things, and money is my goal. I want to be rich at what I do." He looked the limousine over and at James. "Yes, sir. That's what I want."

Bowling Green, Kentucky, was a beautiful city. They drove over a long, high bridge as they entered the city. "Well, we're almost there."

Guyiser looked from one window to another. "This looks bigger than Nashville." Mr. Gibson was enjoying watching Guyiser.

It was twenty minutes later when James opened the sliding glass. "We're here, sir."

Mr. Gibson opened his window and pointed.

"Yes, there it is."

Guyiser looked out the window, "Wow! It looks like an airport. Look at all those big buildings."

"Yes, Guyiser. It is a big place, and you're right, there is an airplane here. Do you see all those buildings there?"

"Yes, sir."

"In their day, they were all production buildings. Now, they just sit there."

Guyiser looked at the buildings, "But, why?"

Mr. Gibson laughed, "That's a part of business you'll learn. You can make bicycles all day, but if they don't move, you lose money. But, you'll see." They pulled through the gates and up to the main building. James opened the doors for them. Loaner jumped out, barked, and ran to a tree. James told Guyiser that he would watch Loaner while they were inside.

"You are expected at the office to check in. I'll show you, sir." Guyiser was amazed. As they walked in, they saw several bicycles on display. They walked to the reception desk.

"May I help you, gentlemen?"

Mr. Gibson spoke, "Yes, please. We have an appointment with Mrs. Spellman."

"Your names, please."

"Gibson and Blackman."

"Oh, yes, sir. She is expecting you. Here are your badges." Mr. Gibson took them and handed Guyiser his. Guyiser looked at the badge. 'Mr. G. Blackman, V.I.P.' Mr. Gibson put his badge on and smiled at Guyiser as he fastened the badge to his lapel.

"Mrs. Spellman, your guests are here in the lobby." She came out and went to Mr. Gibson.

"Oh, Earl. It's so good to see you. You look wonderful."

Mr. Gibson hugged and kissed her. "Margaret, you're as pretty as ever. Oh, Margaret, I would like you to meet Guyiser Blackman. He's the young man I told you about."

"And, a handsome young man you are. Earl has told me all about you, Guyiser. Welcome." Guyiser liked her right away. She was well dressed, soft-spoken, and must have been a beautiful girl in her day. For now, at her age, she was still a very charming and a pretty lady. "Come in and visit for a while. After, I'll have my assistant show you two around the plant, okay?" Mrs. Spellman had a very large and beautiful office. "I'm sorry Mr. Spellman could not be here. I'm afraid he's been very sick for over a year and doesn't come to the plant anymore. In fact, to be truthful with you, that is why the factory isn't doing well. Earl, you know the business. I hope you can do something."

Mr. Gibson stood up, "Well, that is what we are here hoping to do. I'm sorry about Jessie. He has always been a good friend. Did you say someone could show us around?"

Mrs. Spellman touched her intercom. "Have Brooks come in my office, please." She turned back to Guyiser and Mr. Gibson, "Brooks has been with us for years and can answer most of your questions."

Brooks led them to the parking structure, "We'll take this golf cart, gentlemen. We have a lot to cover."

He showed them the four large buildings. "Building #1 is our shipping and receiving area." They rode through the building. Guyiser was all eyes. He was taking notes on everything. "Building #2 houses our production offices. This is where the design and art departments are. Building #3 is our largest building. This is where we put the bikes together along with assembling all the parts. From here, we send them to Building #4 where we box and store the bikes until they are shipped. Accounting, payroll, sales, and general offices are where we started. Now, we will go to the hangar where we store our airplane."

They drove into the hangar. There sat a beauty. It was a twin-engine Learjet. It had room for twelve people, had a kitchen, and restrooms. Guyiser was amazed. He walked around it in awe. "What is this used for?"

Brooks laughed, "Well, the board members say it's used for clients to promote the company, but I think it's used for their own personal use. And, it costs the company a lot of money to maintain and to fly this bad boy."

Guyiser was writing down everything. Building #4 bothered him. Something did not set right. Building #3 had opened his eyes to a lot of possibilities. Building #2 was a dead place with old and dead ideas. Building #1 was a money building and should be watched closely. He looked at the parking areas of the different buildings. "How many people work here?"

Brooks laughed again, "It's hard to say right now. Would you believe there used to be three shifts here? Those were great times. People were everywhere. The place was as busy as a beehive. Now look at it!"

"What happened?"

"I don't know for sure. Maybe it was bad management, lack of sales, poor backers, no cash flow, I don't know. When Mr. Spellman was here, he controlled things and made things happen. Then, over a year ago, when cancer hit him, the plant started going downhill. Mrs. Spellman tries hard, but she is not Mr.

Spellman." Brooks turned to Mr. Gibson, "I hope you take it over. I've heard a lot of talk about you, sir."

The day had been very productive. James stood by the limo with Loaner as Guyiser and Mr. Gibson came out of the office building. They had said their goodbyes to Mrs. Spellman. They were ready to head back to Nashville. Guyiser put down his window as they rode past the factory. He wanted one more look at all the buildings.

Mr. Gibson was smiling as he wrote notes in his notebook. "It sure has changed since I was last here. Well, what do you think?"

That was a big question for Guyiser. He opened his briefcase and looked at his notes. "I think we could make it work, but I also see a lot of changes to be made. That plant has a lot of potential. Everything is there, except it needs to be expanded in different directions. There also has to be a way to move product. But, you know, Mr. Gibson. I am very excited about it. I see things, maybe as Mr. Spellman did. I see all kinds of things happening."

Guyiser looked out the window thinking. Mr. Gibson sat there listening and watching Guyiser. "And, Guyiser, I believe you could make those things happen. I'm glad to see your mind working and your excitement. You give me what I need to hear and see, 'Partner'. Tell me a little more about what you would do—some of your thoughts about making money."

Guyiser looked at his notes. "Money? Making money? Well, Mr. Gibson, first, we're going into the 21st century. People change. They want new things in their lives. In the 40's, 50's, and 60's that factory gave people just what they wanted. A bicycle was used as cheap transportation and for fun, you know? Bicycles will always be a part of our lives, and I'm glad about that, but that factory can do so many other things. It can turn out products that people will buy and that distributors would want to sell. I could go on and on."

Mr. Gibson's eyes were smiling. "You know, you're right. I knew there was something, but I just couldn't put my finger on it. You are right."

Guyiser was thinking about what he himself had said. He reached for his billfold. He searched through it and found what he was looking for. He pulled out a business card and studied it. He handed it to Mr. Gibson. Mr. Gibson looked at the card and then at Guyiser. "You know this man?"

Guyiser smiled. "Yes, sir. We spent some time together. He said I saved his life. Why? Do you know him?"

"Well, I know of him. He is the biggest distributor of toys in the South. He's a very powerful man, too. I hate to use the word 'Mafia', but he and his friends control almost everything that moves. I know they have the United States divided into territories."

Guyiser laughed. "You must be thinking of someone else. Mr. Bagwell is a very nice man with a family. He invited me to Alabama to visit him anytime."

"Guyiser, he may be a nice family man, but his company and his associates buy distribution companies or put them out of business. They are very big and powerful. However, on the other hand, since you know him, maybe. Well, who knows?"

James opened the sliding glass. "We are in Nashville, sir. Is there any place you would like to go?"

"Yes, James, 300 East Broadway." Mr. Gibson turned to Guyiser. "That's Mr. Levine's office. "I'll tell him to get started on the factory and draw up a contract between you and me. I don't want to lose you to someone else." Mr. Gibson laughed. "Mr. President. Oh, James, take Mr. Blackman back to the bike shop. Guyiser, you convinced me. The factory will be our big play ground." He laughed again and leaned back. "Yes, my boy, we're going to make a lot of money and have fun doing it."

Guyiser stood some place in the middle of his thirty-five acre farm. He stood and looked to the north, the south, the east, and the west. The open fields were always a place he could clear his mind and think his thoughts. He closed his eyes and put himself in the center of the factory. He could see it all. He saw large trucks at the loading docks being loaded with products. There were men on forklifts hauling boxes. There were men and women working on the assembly lines putting things together.

Engineers were working with the design and art department developing new ideas. He could hear the

230 | Robert Cory Phillips

sounds of the machine shop turning out parts for different types of products. He saw the parking lots full of cars. There were employees everywhere. Then he heard the loud speaker in Building #2, 'Mr. Blackman, could you come to your office, please?' He saw himself giving approval to a design submitted by the engineers. 'Yes, I like that. Get started on it.' Guyiser opened his eyes and looked to the sky. He heard his father's voice. 'Guyiser, if you can dream it, you can do it.' He fell to his knees, "I can see it, Dad, I can do it."

It was the next morning. Guyiser sat at the kitchen table. His briefcase was open and his notes were spread out. He made more notes as new thoughts came to him. He put his pen down and picked up his phone.

He looked for 'Gibson' and pressed the button. "Hello, Mr. Gibson, sir. How are you?

"Yes, sir. I can't get it out of my mind."

"Oh, no, sir. More than ever."

"Yes, sir. I spent all yesterday thinking about the whole thing. That's what why I'm calling. I would like to go up there and spend a few days or a week going over things."

"No, I want to. I saw a motel close by and I can …"

Mr. Gibson interrupted him. "You don't have to do that. There is a two-bedroom apartment in the hangar. It's upstairs overlooking the whole hangar. You have an office with a large window, a kitchen, a T.V., and everything you need. You should stay there. Mr. Spellman had it specially built."

Guyiser did not hesitate, "Wow! I didn't see that. That would be perfect. You think it would be all right?"

"Guyiser, my boy, we are the new owners." Mr. Gibson laughed. "You can do anything you want to do." Guyiser's mind went wild with thoughts. "Hello, Guyiser, are you there?"

"Yes, sir. Yes, sir. I was just thinking. I'll be going there sometime this week. I'll call you."

"Well, you go enjoy yourself, Guyiser. I'll stay here and get some work done with Mr. Levine. You take care now. Bye."

Guyiser started to pack his clothes. Why wait? He would ask Mr. Taylor to watch the house and feed the cow and chickens. Everything else would take care of itself. Everything was packed and put in the truck. He walked with Loaner around the house and barn.

Everything was okay. The lights were out, the doors were locked, and the animals had been fed. Guyiser put the keys over the front door ledge where Mr. Taylor could find them. He went to the truck with a big bag of Loaner's food. He stood looking at the house. "Well, that's everything, Loaner. Let's ride, boy."

"News At Eleven" New Home

Part 7

I can hang my hat on any nail,
Some places home; some places hell.
But any place I make my nest,
I'll do my best to stay and rest.

It was a good long drive to Bowling Green. The sun had begun to sink into the west as they passed Nashville and turned onto Highway 65. It was about an hour later when Guyiser stopped for gas. Loaner was glad for the stop. He ran around and did his business. Guyiser came out of the store with chips, candy, coke, cookies, milk, a loaf of bread, lunchmeat, and cans of dog food. "Let's go."

When they finished their drive, it was almost dark. Guyiser stopped the truck. He sat looking at all the buildings. He started the truck again and drove up to the gates. There was a man standing on the front steps. He held up his hand as he came to the truck. "Can I help you?"

Guyiser saw that he was a security guard. "Yes, I am Guyiser Blackman. This is my pass card. I will be staying at the hangar. Can you help me?"

The guard looked at the pass and at Guyiser. "Oh yes, sir, Mr. Blackman. I'll show you the way." The guard got in his golf cart and waved to Guyiser. Guyiser followed him around the complex to the hangar. The guard got out and unlocked the large sliding door. He came to Guyiser, "You can drive your truck inside, sir. I will unlock the apartment for you." Guyiser drove in and parked as the guard closed the big door and locked it. He then unlocked the walk-in door. "If you want to take the truck out, I'll unlock the door for you. We keep this hangar locked at all times. This way, sir." The guard took Guyiser upstairs, unlocked the door, went in, turned on the lights, looked around the apartment, and came back to Guyiser, "Everything is all right, sir. Can I help you with your bags, sir?"

Guyiser walked around the apartment. "No, thank you. I can handle everything now."

The guard started to leave. "Oh, my name is Jim. Here is a key for the walk-in door. If you need anything, just press the intercom. I will answer it right away. Enjoy your stay, sir. Good night."

Guyiser stood in the large living room. The front side was floor-to-ceiling glass, which overlooked the entire hangar. He stood looking down at the jet plane. The office was large with a wet bar, a sitting area, and a big desk. It too was all glass and overlooked the hangar. The two large bedrooms each had their own bathroom.

The master bedroom had its own patio with a waterfall and a view of several buildings. Guyiser sat on the king sized bed looking around the room. Loaner ran from room to room-checking things out.

Next, Guyiser unloaded his things. He stood in the kitchen putting food in the refrigerator. He pressed a button and ice fell out. "Wow!" He walked back to the living room. He was very amazed. The apartment was quite impressive. It was easy to tell that Mr. Spellman had great taste and was a very creative man. Guyiser went in the office and sat behind the desk. He could feel the power. He swiveled the chair to look out over the hangar. He pretended to press a button, "Miss Smith, send them to the hangar. I'm in my office." He leaned back in the big chair and began to laugh. He and Loaner took a walk in the night air. The stars were out winking at the moon. Lights from the town a few miles away flickered in the darkness. He and Loaner went back to the hangar. There sat the big jet. Guyiser walked around the plane in a state of amazement. At the front of the jet was painted, 'Margaret I'. He could see Mr. and Mrs. Spellman boarding the plane and flying away. He could feel their happiness the day they bought this plane. *What a life they must have had.*

Guyiser woke up in the big brass bed. Loaner jumped up on the bed with his bowl in his mouth. He dropped it and barked. Guyiser threw it down the hallway. Loaner barked and ran after it. Guyiser got dressed and walked out on the patio. It was the beginning of a beautiful day.

It was eight ten in the morning as the two walked to the office building. The receptionist greeted him. "Good morning, Mr. Blackman. It's good to see you again. The guard said you arrived last night."

"Good morning to you. Is Mrs. Spellman in?"

"No, sir. She will be in later. Can I help you or get you some coffee?"

"You know, that sounds good."

"I will bring it to you, Mr. Blackman, in your office, okay?"

"Oh, no. I'll take it with me. It's a long walk for you."

The lady laughed, "I mean in your office here in this building. I'll show you." She led Guyiser down the hallway and opened the double doors. "This is your office. We call it the East Wing. This was Mr.

Spellman's office. He liked to see the sun come up. I will be right back."

Guyiser walked around looking at all the built-in books shelves filled with books. A large bay window was behind the huge desk. "Wow! Look at all this." He walked to a sitting area and stood looking at a gold leafed couch and two chairs. The coffee table was inlayed with pictures of bicycles and a plane, a map, some money, and gold coins all under a glass top. He went to the desk and sat down. The warm sun came in the bay window.

The receptionist came in carrying a silver tray with coffee. "Sugar, cream? I don't know how you like it." She set the tray on a table beside the desk.

"Would there be anything else, sir?"

Guyiser looked at her, "Yes, please. What is your name?"

"Oh, I am sorry, sir. My name is Kate."

"Ah, Kate, how long have you been here?"

"I have been here six years. Two years as Mr. Spellman's assistant."

"Well, Kate. I guess you know everything that goes on around here. Is that right?"

"Pretty much, sir. Some good, some not so good."

"Kate, I'd like to talk with you later, okay? Oh, by the way, this is Loaner. He's with me always. Don't be afraid of him." Loaner barked and ran out of the office.

"He is beautiful, Mr. Blackman. Oh, by the way, you have your own golf cart so you don't have to walk around. This is a big place. If you need anything else, just buzz me. Oh, yes, you also have a two-way radio to call me if you are out in the plant."

"Thank you, Kate. It's good to have you around. We'll talk later, okay?" Guyiser sat drinking his coffee and looking at pictures on the wall. The office was plush, but it overpowered him. Mr. Spellman was all over the office. This was his office and Guyiser could feel it. Anyway, he liked the hangar better. It was more open, and the apartment was great. He also felt comfortable in the upper office. The apartment would be his nest.

Guyiser and Loaner sat in the golf cart. "Let's ride." With that, they started. As they rode around, Guyiser became more comfortable with the grounds and the buildings. He would drive in a building through one door, ride around making notes, and drive out another door. Building #3 was his interest. As he drove in the building, he saw a man sweeping around some big machinery. He drove to him, "Good morning." The man stopped and waved. "Hi, my name is Blackman. I'm a new, uh, partner here. Can I talk with you a minute?"

"Sure, how can I help you?" They walked around talking for a while.

"What about this machine?"

"Well, sir, most all of the machines are set up to turn out frames. Those make handlebars. The paint machine and dryer are over there."

Guyiser kept making notes. "Can these machines make other things like a different frame or handlebars?"

"Sure, with a few alterations and a new design they can do anything."

Guyiser's mind was full of ideas. "How about a kid's wagon or a skateboard or something like that?"

"Mr. Blackman, you give me a blueprint and the size you want and with a few changes, these machines can cut, fold, and bend most any kind of tin or metal. In fact, Mr. Blackman, between you and me, that's what this factory needs—something new. We've been turning out bicycles too long, in my opinion." The man laughed.

"What about the wheels?"

"No, Mr. Blackman, we don't do any rubber work here. That's a different world. It's cheaper to buy wheels and tires from outside like from Japan, China, or Mexico—outside."

Guyiser shook his hand and got in the golf cart.

"It's been good talking to you. You've been very helpful to me. What's your name?"

"Just call me Buck. Nice talking to you, Mr. Blackman." Guyiser waved as he and Loaner drove off.

Guyiser sat at his desk in the hangar. He was going over his notes. He found that the inventory of bicycles was very large. The factory was producing only two kinds of bicycles—boys and girls. They were only different in size and color. He opened his briefcase and took out drawings of his four bikes, the Mountain Man, Faster, Lady Thriller, and Speed Man. There were drawings of other ideas he had thought of while sitting in the barn. Now, he could make them come to life. He became very excited about the conversation he had had with Buck.

He would take his drawings and ideas to the design and art department to get their feedback. *Make a plan, work a plan.* He would get cost together, have blueprints made, and have pictures and drawings made. He had even thought of a logo for all these products. He would call them 'Blackie's'—Blackie Bikes, Blackie Wagons, Blackie Sport Products, and Blackie Safety Equipment. Guyiser sat looking out over the hangar and the jet. *I'll get everything together and approach Mr. Gibson with it all. I want to show him that I'm serious and that I know something about business and making money. If only Cindy could see me now.*

Then it dawned on him. *Cindy, I haven't talked to her in days.* He picked up his phone and dialed her number. The phone rang a few times.

"Hello."

"Hello, Cindy?"

"No, she's not here. Who's this?"

"I'm Guyiser Blackman, who's this?"

"I'm Sandy, her roommate. Hi, Guyiser. Cindy told me all about you. You're all she talks about."

"Where is she?"

"She and a film crew went to Daytona to cover an auto race. She should be back in a couple of days."

"Oh, well. Tell her I called and uh, that I miss her, okay?"

"I sure will. How are things in Centerville?"

"Good, I guess. I'm in Bowling Green, Kentucky, at the bike factory."

"Well, I'll let her know you called."

"Thanks, Sandy. You do that. Bye."

"Bye, Guyiser."

Guyiser was disappointed he had not talked to Cindy. Then he thought, *Well, I'm busy too, so I understand.* The intercom buzzed on the desk. Guyiser pressed the button. "Yes?"

"Mr. Blackman, this is Kate. It is four thirty, and I will be leaving for the day. Is there anything you need or that I can do for you?"

"Yes, Kate. Will you set up a meeting with the design and art department for me?"

"Yes, sir. There are only two people there now, but I'm sure they want to meet you."

"Thanks, Kate. Say nine o'clock in the morning?"

"No problem, sir. They will meet you in Building #2 at nine o'clock. Good night to you."

"Good night."

Soon after, the intercom buzzed again. "Yes?"

"Mr. Blackman, this is security. I just came on duty and wanted to check in with you. If there is anything you need, just call me."

"Oh hi, Jim. Yes, there is. Would you unlock the hangar doors? I want to take the truck out."

"Yes, sir. I will be right there." It was two minutes later when the big door slid open. Guyiser and Loaner drove out and stopped.

"Where can I get a good steak around here?"

"Go out the gate and turn right. About four or five miles on the left is a very good steak house with a bar."

"Thanks, Jim. Can I bring back something for you?"

"Oh, no thank you, sir. I am fine."

Guyiser drove to the main gate and stopped. He turned and looked at the big office building. He began to feel this was his place. He began to feel the power he had. People were responding to his requests. They called him 'Mr. Blackman' and 'Sir.' He felt in control. This was a long way from the barn where he had started.

The steak house was a very large wooden building. Inside there was a great atmosphere of soft lights, plush carpet, a fireplace, and lots of windows. Green plants and candlelight graced the restaurant. A pretty girl with long dark hair greeted him. "Are you alone, sir?"

"Yes, just my dog and me."

"I'm sorry, sir. No dogs are allowed."

Guyiser looked at Loaner, "Do you mind?" Loaner looked at Guyiser and barked. "I'll take him back to the truck."

Guyiser returned as the waitress opened the door. "He's a beautiful dog. You two must be very close."

He smiled, "Yes, we are." She took Guyiser to a booth and handed him a menu.

"I haven't seen you here before. Are you new in the area?"

"Yes, this is my second day here." Guyiser looked at the menu and back at her.

She stood smiling. "Well, I hope you come back to see me. My name is Carla. And yours?"

"Ah, hi. I'm Guyiser."

"Well, Guyiser, what would you like tonight?"

He felt she might be flirting with him. He smiled at her, "A big juicy steak, charred rare with blue cheese dressing."

"And Guyiser, a drink from the bar?"

"You know, I think I will. Jack Daniels on the rocks." They smiled at each other.

"Yes, sir." He watched her walk away.

The steak was delicious. Guyiser sat sipping his drink. Carla came back to him. "May I offer you dessert or anything else?"

Guyiser smiled. "No, not tonight. Maybe some other time."

Carla smiled back. "I hope so. Here's your check and here's my number if you want to make a reservation or something." She smiled. "Oh, this is a doggy bag with steak and ribs for your dog. What is his name?"

"Loaner, his name is Loaner."

"That's a great name. Thank you, Guyiser. I hope to see you again."

As Guyiser drove back, he thought about Carla. She was very attractive, friendly, and very aggressive. But, she was no Cindy. Cindy was a total package for him. But, Carla could be nice to talk to. Guyiser turned in the gates and looked for Jim. He continued to drive to the hangar. Jim was standing there and opened the big door. "Did you find it okay, sir?"

"Yes, Jim. It was great."

"Glad you liked it. Good night, sir."

"Good night, Jim. Thank you." The guard locked the door and went away.

Guyiser sat at his desk putting his notes together for his meeting with the art department. He went in the kitchen. Loaner followed him. "Look what I have for you.

Steak and ribs!" Loaner stood wagging his tail and smiling. Guyiser went to the bedroom. He stood looking at the big brass bed. Someone had made it up. He looked around the room. His suitcase had been put in the closet. Someone had hung up his jeans and shirts. Guyiser was a private person like his father. He did not like what he saw. "Loaner," he yelled again, "Loaner." Loaner came running in. "Loaner, this is our hangar. This is our place. This is my bedroom. That is my office. I don't want anyone, you hear me, anyone coming in this hangar unless I'm here. You understand? Protect, Loaner, protect!" Guyiser went to the door. Loaner understood the command—protect. He barked at his master and ran out.

The morning sun came through the patio doors as Guyiser put on his jeans and sweatshirt. He stood at the top of the stairs overlooking the hangar.

He threw a tennis ball at the jet. Loaner ran down the stairs after it. Guyiser stood laughing at Loaner chasing the ball. He walked down the stairs with his briefcase ready for the day. "Loaner, you stay here, okay. I'll be back soon."

Building #2 was a short ride away. It was eight fifty-five as Guyiser walked into the building. He walked down a hallway passing a few empty offices. He came to a door with a sign on it, 'Art Department'. He knew what he wanted to do. He took a big breath and opened the door. Two men sat at a drafting table having coffee. "Good morning, guys."

An hour had passed. Guyiser and the two men had made a good connection. "Yes, sir. We can do that." He put down his pencil and showed one of his plans.

"What do you think, Scott?"

"I like the idea. I have a few suggestions. I would make this a little wider and make the seat more of an oval shape, like this." Scott drew his idea.

Tim was sketching out a logo. "How about this, sir?" It was a long oval shape with the word 'Blackie' written from the top of the oval to the bottom. "I see it with a silver background and with black letters. It would look good on the front of the bicycles and make great looking promotion tags. It would even look good on your letterhead. What do you think, boss?"

Guyiser held up the drawing. "I like it, Tim. It's simple and eye-catching. Can you make me a computer printout in color?"

"No problem, sir."

Guyiser turned to Scott. "Scott, this is a new project.

I want to get started on it ASAP. It's a stationary bike for exercising." He handed the drawing to Scott. "My drawing is a little rough, but you can get the idea. See, it has only one wheel. The chain goes from here to here." Guyiser explained the entire idea. Scott began to sketch a plan. He became excited with the idea. "How about putting blinking red lights on the handlebars in a small box here? It would be battery operated. The cable would connect to the wheel here. When the person reaches their set speed by paddling, the lights will blink and they can maintain that speed. I would put a better seat on the bike, too."

Guyiser watched as Scott continued to draw. "Wow! What an idea. That would make it fun, too. Scott, you're a genius. Make me a detailed drawing of all the parts. That's hot!"

The day had been a very productive one. Scott and Tim were excited about all the new projects. The three of them sat talking about getting the plant back to work. Scott and Tim were telling Guyiser about the good days and how these new projects would be a real shot in the arm for the factory.

Guyiser explained how important it was to get everything down on paper and to get about twenty copies of everything made right away. "Guys, I need all these plans, now. Buck has already started making machine changes. I want a prototype of everything made as soon as possible, okay? Get me everything on paper, now, even if you have to work overtime. Thanks, Guys. You help me, and I'll help you."

Guyiser left the building feeling great. He sat in his golf cart thinking about the meeting. He rode around the plant gathering ideas. Soon, he was at the office building. Kate was on the phone as he came in. Guyiser waved and walked to the office. He stood looking at his name on a gold plaque on the door. He looked out the bay window. Kate came in. "Good morning. How was your meeting? Would you like some coffee?"

Guyiser sat at the desk. "No, thanks. We drank coffee all morning. The meeting with Scott and Tim was a giant step forward. Sit down. Kate, can I talk to you about my feelings?"

"Of course, sir. Anything you say will never leave this room."

He smiled. "Well, it may sound silly, but I don't care for this office. It was Mr. Spellman's place and he and Mr. Gibson were close friends. I had rather Mr. Gibson's name be on the door and this be his office. After all, he is the CEO and boss, my boss."

Kate smiled, "I understand. It will be changed."

"And, Kate, I am a private person. My father taught me to clean up after myself and to make my own bed. So the hangar and apartment feel good to me. That's where I want to stay. If you could tell the person who hung up my clothes and made my bed."

Kate interrupted him with a smile, "I agree with you, sir. I am private, too. I do not want someone knowing what color of panties I wear. I'll take care of that."

Guyiser smiled, "I'm glad you understand. One more thing. I would like to meet the accountant or bookkeeper. I'm interested in the cash flow system."

"Well, Mr. Blackman, you are in luck. She is here today. I will take you to her office and introduce you. She and Mr. Spellman were very close. I am sure you will like her. Anything else?"

Guyiser stood up, "Speaking of the Spellman's, I didn't see Mrs. Spellman's car outside."

Kate stood up. "She called in and said Mr. Spellman was very ill. I think she may not be coming back."

Guyiser walked to the door. "I'm sorry to hear that. Would you send them flowers from Mr. Gibson and me?"

Kate walked to the door. "They would like that. I will do that today. Now, let's go down to accounting."

Mrs. Watson was an older woman who had worked for the Spellman's since the beginning. She knew where every penny was. She knew all the accounts by their first names. Guyiser sat beside her as she pulled book after book of accounts out of the desk. There was a picture on her desk of the Spellman's and her standing by the jet. "Yes, Mr. Blackman, those were good times." She looked over her glasses at him. "Where do you want to start?"

Guyiser looked at all the ledgers. "Mrs. Watson, to be honest with you, I'm not good with figures."

She opened a ledger and smiled. "Neither was Mr. Spellman. I would explain something to him, but he would just sit like a bump on a log. Then, he would pick up the phone and make a call. I can hear him now, 'Hello, Joe. How are things? My accountant said you forgot about me.' She smiled, "And in a few days, I would get a check and another order."

Guyiser leaned back, "He must have been quite a man. Tell me, Mrs. Watson, does this company have any money to work with?"

Mrs. Watson took off her glasses and leaned toward Guyiser, "Just between you and me, there would be a lot more if the backers wouldn't dip into the till. It is not my place to stop it. They are backers, you know. Let me show you something. Look here at this credit card expense list. This backer took the jet for four days to entertain his family and his cousin. Did you know it cost $200.00 just to roll the jet out of the hangar—just to roll it out? Now, look here. 'Crew of three, service maintenance, gasoline, new tires, limo service, hotel rooms, food, entertainment, tips.' "Now, this is from here to Ohio, to New York, and back here.

For six people and the crew the bill came to a total of $9,700.00. And, this does not include insurance. This is the funny part. Yes, his cousin does have a toy store in Ohio, and he does buy from us. But, look at this. Last year, he bought 320 bicycles at $61.00 each for a total of $1,952.00. It does not make sense. It does not add up. We lost $7,000.00. Mr. Spellman would not have put up with this. And, Mr. Blackman, there have been three trips in the jet since Mr. Spellman left over a year ago. I hope you and Mr. Gibson can do something about this. To answer your question, yes, there is money to work with and ways to get more. But, there has to be more control over what we have."

Guyiser could not believe that backers would take advantage of the company. "Mrs. Watson, would you please make copies of all these things for me? There will be a stop to this, I promise you that!"

Guyiser left the office and walked past Kate shaking his head. "Mr. Blackman, I see you are finding out about this place."

He stopped and looked at her, "Yes, and there are going to be changes."

Guyiser sat on the patio watching the dark clouds. The sun was peaking over the east mountains. He sat drinking coffee and thinking about the day before. He had people busy making things happen. He could not wait to get back to Nashville to tell Mr. Gibson of his plans and of what Mrs. Watson had told him. He also missed the farm and his barn.

The sun began to lighten the sky. There were a few more things he wanted to do before he headed back home. Visiting Shipping and Receiving was one of those things. He went to the bedroom, made the bed, and got dressed. In the living room, he sat watching T.V. A commercial came on. It was about a horse race in Bowling Green. Then it hit him. *How about a bike race!* His mind started working. *This would be good for the factory. The racetrack would be around all the buildings.* He saw kids and their bikes all over the place. He saw a tour of the factory for kids, their parents, and friends. *We would award prizes and trophies. We would get television coverage and radio advertising. We could let the public know about the plant and stir up interest. We would show our new products and safety features for kids. This is a great promotional idea. I'll present it to Mr. Gibson.*

The sky had cleared, and the sun was bright as Guyiser and Loaner drove up to the loading dock. There were two freight trucks backed up to the doors. He watched a man on a forklift pull up to a truck and drop his load. A man walked down the steps and over to Guyiser, "Good morning. You must be Mr. Blackman. My name is Tom Maker. I'm in charge of shipping and receiving." They shook hands. "Buck said you would be coming around. Come on in. I'll show you around." They walked around the large building as Mr. Maker pointed out the layout. "We get orders from the front office most every day. Some days are busier than others. We have an inventory to pull from over there. The freight company comes and takes the bikes away. That's about it."

Guyiser looked at all the racks of bicycles.

He read a label on a box. 'Spellman-Girls-Blue-22 No. 27841.' "How many bikes do you ship per day?"

"Well, that varies from day to day. I'd say now, it would be about two to 250 a day. It used to be sometimes maybe 1,000 a day or more." He laughed. "Mr. Spellman and his sales people had orders piled up this high. Somebody has to stay on top of this; you know what I mean?"

Guyiser nodded his head. "Can you get a new bike out of a box and put it together for me? I want to ride around on it."

Mr. Maker called out, "Frank, pull me a 26-incher and put it together for me. Boys,…"

Guyiser's phone rang. "Hello."

"… Oh, good morning, Kate."

"… That's great. I'll pick them up later. Tell her thanks for me."

Guyiser dialed the art department. "Hello, Scott. How's it going?"

"… Good man. Say about four o'clock?"

"… Great, that's great. Thanks a lot, Scott."

Mr. Maker rolled the bike up to Guyiser. "Here you go, sir. Fresh out of the box."

Guyiser looked the bike over thoroughly. "What's this?"

"It's a flaw in the paint. Sometimes the sprayer spits out air. I've seen it before."

Guyiser looked at him, "This is unacceptable. Doesn't anyone inspect these things?"

"Well, sir, we used to have a Q.C. Department, but since the layoff, no one watches."

Guyiser gave him a look. He got on the bike, "Come on, Loaner." He rode away. He had repaired many bikes and knew if they felt right. As he stopped, the wheel felt off. He got off to check it. The spokes were loose, and the chain slipped. "I can't believe this." He walked the bike over to Building #3 and over to Buck. "Hi, Buck."

"Good morning, Mr. Blackman. What you got there?"

"I've got a problem, Buck. Will you check this bike out for me?"

"Sure will."

"Thanks, Buck. It's straight out of a box. I'll be back later, okay?" Guyiser and Loaner walked back to his golf cart. "Get in, boy. You like to ride."

Guyiser opened the office door, and Loaner ran in. "Well, good morning, sir. Hi, Loaner. Here are your copies from accounting that you requested."

He looked them over and smiled, "Thanks, Kate. Just what I wanted. Could you get me the phone number of whoever we buy wheels and tires from?"

"I can do better than that; I can call them now if you would like."

"That would be great, Kate. I have a problem with them."

"You can take the call in your, uh, Mr. Gibson's office. I will call for you now." Guyiser sat at the desk. The intercom came on, "Oh, Mr. Blackman, your call is on line two."

Guyiser picked up the phone, "Hello. Who is this, please?"

"... Yes, I have a problem with your company. I am Blackman, Guyiser Blackman. I have taken over the Spellman's business here in Bowling Green, Kentucky. And, yes, that's exactly what I'm calling about."

"... No, I have not received your memo."

"...Recall?"

"...For the last six months? You must be kidding me. Do you know what that would cost me to do that?

"...Well, I would hope so."

"...No, I just discovered the problem."

"...Well, fax me the memo again with the recall numbers. We'll get started today."

"...Of course, I need replacements, today!"

"...Then, I'll look for them tomorrow."

"...Yes, me, too."

"...Yes, I'll look for the fax in ten minutes."

"...I'm sorry, too."

"...I will. Bye." Guyiser was hot. This was a setback. He went to Kate. "They are sending a fax with recall numbers on all the bad wheels. Let shipping know not to ship any more bicycles until the replacement wheels get here. Let Buck know to start replacing wheels. Let him hire extra help. We don't want to lose many shipping days. Let accounting know to start keeping track of payroll so we can bill them for all this stuff. What a mess."

Kate heard the fax machine. "There's a fax coming in now." She handed it to Guyiser.

"Make copies and get them to everybody. And, I need a copy for myself. Oh, Kate, I'll be leaving tonight. I'm going back to Nashville, but I'll keep in touch. You have been great, Kate. Thanks for everything."

Guyiser went back to see Buck. Buck had finished with the bicycle. "Well, sir, there it is. I checked everything. The chain slips because it is one link too long. We can correct that. The paint—it's our sprayer, but it should have been caught. The wheel is a problem. Twenty-two spokes out of thirty-eight were loose or damaged. That's why the wheel rode funny and is potentially dangerous, you know?"

Guyiser nodded, "Yes, I know. There was a memo sent out six months ago telling us about a recall on the wheels. A computer error, they said. They are sending replacement wheels tomorrow. Buck, we need to get started now. Hire as many people as it takes. Open boxes, replace the wheels, and reseal the boxes. Thank God, it was only the front wheel. And the paint, have a couple of people touch up these spots and get someone to repair the spray machine. I don't want this to happen again, okay?"

"Yes, sir, Mr. Blackman. I'll take care of all the chains. And, I'll work with Maker to start unpacking the bikes. You know, there are about two to three thousand boxes in inventory. It's going to take a long time."

Guyiser looked at the shipping orders, "I know, but have Maker try to keep up with his orders. I think we can replace and ship, replace and ship, and lose only a few days of shipping." Guyiser shook hands with Buck. "I'm depending on you, Buck. You're a good man. I won't forget you. I'm going back to Nashville for a few days, but I'll be back to help, so do your best."

Next, Guyiser went to shipping and explained everything to Mr. Maker. The art department had done a good job on all the drawings and the new logo.

Guyiser sat at his desk going over all the paperwork that had been generated in the last few days. He looked out over the big hangar. It was quiet and peaceful. The large jet sat there all shiny. Loaner ran around chasing his tennis ball. Guyiser went in his bedroom and lay across the brass bed. He closed his eyes and thought, *Going home, going home.*

"News At Eleven" Retreat

Part 8

Two steps forward, one step back.
Look it over and you can see
Where to go and what to be.
A fresh start down life's road
Can open your eyes and lighten
The load.

Guyiser woke up at four thirty in the afternoon. He knew it was a long drive to Nashville and then on to Centerville. He and Loaner loaded in the truck and headed home. Jim was standing at the gate. Guyiser pulled up to him and stopped. "How's it going, Jim?"

"It's going well, Mr. Blackman. Going for a steak?"

"No, Jim. I wish, but I'm headed home for a couple of days. I just wanted to let you know that there will be some new employees coming in to work, so keep an eye on things, okay?"

Jim patted the truck, "Glad to hear that, sir. Everything will be okay here. You have a good trip. Bye."

Guyiser turned on to Highway 65 and took a deep breath. "You ready, Loaner. We're going home." Loaner started to bark. Guyiser petted his head and smiled. "Going home."

A good night's sleep was what Guyiser needed. He had not realized that the past week had drained his body and mind. Even Loaner slept all night. The morning sun streamed through Guyiser's bedroom window. He lay awake looking out and thinking about everything. It was a good feeling to wake up in his own bed. It was not the big brass bed, but it was his. He was slowly getting dressed when Loaner started barking. There was a knock on the door. Guyiser went to the living room window and saw Mr. Taylor. "Hey, Mr. Taylor. Good to see you, sir. Come on in."

Mr. Taylor shook Guyiser's hand and gave him a hug. "My boy, it's good to see you. I saw your truck outside. How are you?" They sat in the kitchen having coffee and talking.

"Oh, it's a big place. I guess it's about twenty acres." Guyiser was excited as he told Mr. Taylor all about the factory and the people. They talked about Mrs. Taylor and Cindy. "No, sir. That was the sad part. Her roommate said she was busy in school and was in Daytona working. I really miss talking to her."

Mr. Taylor nodded, "We do, too. She has only called us two times, but we did get a letter from her."

Guyiser looked out the kitchen window, "Oh, uh, Mr. Taylor, I'll be going back to Kentucky in a few days. I was wondering if I could give you all the chickens and my cow. The chickens are good layers, and the cow gives good milk."

Mr. Taylor smiled, "Yes, I know. I milked her and gathered eggs last week. Sure, I'll take them."

"Good, sir. That would take a lot off my mind, thanks. I'll take them over to you tomorrow."

Mr. Taylor stood up and hugged Guyiser, "Glad to have you back, son. You're coming to dinner tonight, you hear me? Mrs. Taylor will be glad to see you. Well, son, I've got to get into town, so we'll see you later."

Guyiser walked him out. "It's good to be home, sir, even for a little while. Tell Mrs. Taylor I want some of her banana pudding." They laughed and Mr. Taylor drove off.

Nashville looked great as Guyiser and Loaner topped the hill and headed into town. It was to be an exciting day. Guyiser's ideas and papers were all in order for Mr. Gibson. Mr. Gibson met him with a big hug. They sat and talked and talked about this, that, and the other thing for a while. Then, Guyiser proudly opened his briefcase and took out his papers. He spread them out on the table as Mr. Gibson watched. "So, Guyiser, looks like you have been pretty busy. What do you have there?"

Guyiser smiled and looked at all the papers, "Well, sir. I don't know where to start. I guess I'll start with the problem I found. This memo got lost somewhere about six months ago. It's a recall on bad wheels from this company." Guyiser handed the memo to Mr. Gibson. "As soon as I found out about the problem, I stopped shipping product. The good part is everything is under control now." Guyiser explained all the bikes' problems and how he had handled everything. Mr. Gibson rocked, smiled, and listened. "Now, Buck has made some adjustments on the machinery so we can start production of my four types of bikes. This will give the company more products to manufacture and to sell. Here are the drawings from the art department." Mr. Gibson rocked, smiled, and nodded. "Now, sir. Here are drawings of a brand new line of products we can very easily manufacture. I call it 'Blackie Sports Equipment'. It is a stationary bike for exercising with a new twist. I want to get a patent on it."

Guyiser explained about the blinking lights. "This could be the biggest money-making idea we could have for the company."

Mr. Gibson's rocking became faster, and his smile got larger. He sat looking at the stationary bike drawing. Next, Guyiser showed him drawings of the new logo. He was very excited as he told of promotional ideas he had for the future. As he came down from his high, he handed Mr. Gibson his last papers. "Mr. Gibson, Mrs. Watson and I spent several hours going over these accounting records. You may not like what you're reading. In the past year and a half, the backers have been ripping off the company.

You are the only one who can put a stop to it."

Mr. Gibson had been an accountant. His chair stopped rocking, and his smile disappeared. He read the report and calmly put it down. "What would you do, Guyiser, about this?"

Guyiser took out his own report, "Well, first, I would ground the jet. Then I would cut all the expense accounts for everybody. That should make everybody mad. I would next have a meeting and let everyone know that the company is under new management." Guyiser smiled. "I would tell them that it would be five to eight years before the company would hopefully be back on its feet. The backers would have the option of selling their stock to us or wait it out. This might scare someone into selling. Besides, I would offer to buy their shares. Mr. Olsen is the problem backer. Maybe we could buy him out. You know, use a little pressure. The record shows that the Spellman's have 52%, Olsen has 20%, Anderson has 14%, and Goldman has 14%. Now you are the new owner."

Mr. Gibson interrupted, "I'm buying 40% of the Spellman's stock. They are keeping 12%. That way we can still control the company. Guyiser, I'm very impressed with you and the way you're handling things. I like the way you think. I like the direction you are taking. This is going to be a fun ride for me!" Mr. Gibson's chair began to rock again. He smiled at Guyiser, "And Mr. Levine and I have a contract for you that I think will please you. It gives you a very nice six-figure income with an 8% bonus, per year, of the profits from the factory's income. And, the contract states that all your expenses will be paid—all."

All he was hearing stunned Guyiser, but it sounded good. Mr. Gibson got up and went to his desk. He returned with some papers. "These are from Mr. Levine. Your money was released from the court and is now in your bank account. You just need to go to the bank and endorse the insurance check. That should make you happy. In addition, here is your contract with the company and me. Just read and sign. It will be about three weeks before I take over the factory officially. But, for now, you are in charge of everything, Mr. President. You have the power to do anything, and I'm behind you 100% and so is Mr. Levine. Now, my boy, get to work and make us rich."

Guyiser was in heaven when he left the shop. He was now the president of a factory worth a million plus. His grin spread all over his body. His confidence had been assured. Now, he could make a plan to make all his dreams come true. He would always remember this as a special day in history. All the way back to Centerville, he was making plans.

Guyiser and Loaner sat on the couch. The T.V. was on, but the volume was turned down. Guyiser looked at his father's chair. He heard his father's voice, 'Guyiser, son, when I come to work for you, things will be great.' *If only you were here now, Pa. I'll do my best to make you proud of me.* Guyiser started to cry. "Come on, Loaner, let's walk." Guyiser loved to walk in the open fields. He could lose himself in the wind, kick dirt, and watch birds flying high in the sky. He stood on a hill looking down. As a young boy, he used to roll down this hill laughing and having fun. That was a long time ago, and now he was a young man." He walked down the hill to the bottom and looked up. His father stood on top laughing and waving. He heard his father saying, 'Life goes on.'

The sun was sinking as Guyiser and Loaner walked back to the house. The Taylor's would be expecting him, so he cleaned up and headed that way. As he and Loaner drove up, the Taylor's were swinging on the front porch. Loaner headed for the barn as Guyiser walked up the steps. Mrs. Taylor got out of the swing and walked to him. She gave him a big hug and a kiss, "Oh, Guyiser, how I have missed you. You could have called, you know."

"I know, ma'am. I've just been so busy, but I did think about you."

"Well, thinking is not good enough. We want to hear from you. Are you hungry, son?"

Guyiser smiled a big smile, "Yes, ma'am, I am."

Mrs. Taylor opened the door, "Well, come on, Taylor. Guyiser is hungry. We're having fried chicken tonight."

As usual, supper was a special event. After the meal was over, they sat in the living room. Mrs. Taylor was sewing pieces of material together for her patchwork quilt. Mr. Taylor was showing Guyiser how to play chess. "This piece can only move this way, and this piece can move in any direction; she's your queen."

Guyiser liked this game and caught on quickly. "Speaking of queens, has Cindy called? I really miss your daughter."

Just then, the phone rang. Mrs. Taylor answered it. "Hello."

"...Well, speak of the devil; it is Cindy. Why haven't you called? We've been worried about you."

"...Busy, my foot. Guess who is here? Guyiser."

"...Okay, but your father and I want to talk to you when you are finished." Mrs. Taylor handed the phone to Guyiser.

"...Hello, Cindy. Gosh, it's good to hear your voice."

"...Yes, sweetheart, I miss you, too. How are things?"

"...And you got to meet him? Wow! So what's next?"

"...How many in a class?"

"...Then what?"

"…That sounds great. Have fun."

"…Me? Right now I'm playing chess with your father and eating your mother's banana pudding."

"…We had fried chicken."

"…I will. I'll write you a letter and tell you everything. I miss you, girlfriend."

"…Me, too."

"…I will. Okay. Bye." Guyiser handed the phone to Mr. Taylor and went out on the porch. He sat on the steps watching the dogs chase each other.

Soon, the Taylor's came out. "Well, she sounds pretty good. She's happy meeting people. We are glad she's still getting good grades. What are you going to do now, Guyiser?"

He stood up and stretched, "Well, I'm going home now and get a good night's sleep. I'll head back to Kentucky tomorrow night. I've got a lot to do there." Guyiser hugged Mrs. Taylor, "Thanks for having me over, and I will call you. Mr. Taylor, I'll get the animals over tomorrow sometime. I'd better be going now. Thanks for everything. Ya'll be good. Bye." Guyiser called for Loaner. "Good night."

Guyiser lay in bed thinking about Cindy. He looked at their picture on the night table. He picked it up and kissed it. "Good night, sweetheart."

Cindy sat on her bed reading notes she had made in Daytona. She looked over on her night table at the picture of her and Guyiser. She held the picture thinking of Guyiser and their lovemaking. She kissed the picture and put it back on the table. She had two classes the next day. One class was Communications. The other class was in a studio where she would give a news report in front of the cameras.

The morning Florida sun filled the classroom. Cindy and ten others sat at their desks listening to the instructor. "You have to believe you're talking to someone. You have to talk to the camera as if it were your friend. In fact, it is your only friend. The camera can tell if you are serious, afraid, or truthful. It reads your smile, your eyes, and your thoughts. If you like the camera, it will like you. Remember that. Love the camera. Forget the director. Forget the sound person. Just report the truth to the camera. Miss Taylor, I see you're taking notes. That's good. I have another one for you. Go into the bathroom and stand in front of your mirror. Look at yourself; really look at yourself. Now, turn away and think of what you want to say. Think like this, 'Good evening. I am Cynthia Taylor, and this is today's news.' Now, slowly turn to the mirror and talk. Practice different tones of your voice. This goes for all of you. Relax, think, and talk. Some of you have a studio session later today, so work on the camera and know what it does and sees. Everybody go have a good day. I'll see you tomorrow. Class dismissed."

Cindy was excited about the class. The instructor had given her some insights on what to do and what to expect. She walked across the grounds to the large studio building and went in. No one was there yet. She walked around looking at the soundproofed walls.

She saw the long sound boom hanging over a desk. There were two large cameras on wheels. She went to a camera and looked it over. She touched it. Then, she touched some of the buttons and walked in front of the long zoom lens. She spoke to it. "Hi, my friend. I want to be friends." She looked into the large round lens and saw herself. *This is my mirror.* She brushed her hair back and smiled, "I like you." Then, she went to the desk and sat down. She closed her eyes, and then looked at the lens, "Hi, I am Cynthia Taylor and this is the morning news. Today here in Florida, the Governor has announced…." Someone clapped their hands and walked up to her. "Not bad, not bad. But, I wouldn't say 'Hi'. I suggest 'Good Morning', or 'Good Afternoon', or 'Good Evening'. It makes it more personal. Hi, my name is Jeff, Jeff Fisher. I'm one of the staff directors here."

Cindy stood up and extended her hand, "Hi, Jeff Fisher. I'm Cynthia Taylor. I hope you don't mind me being here. I just wanted to get the feel of the studio."

Jeff shook her hand, "Oh, I like it. You have a good grip. And, no, Miss Taylor, I don't mind. In fact, I'm glad to see your interest." A few people started coming in the studio. The lighting man turned on the stage lights. The sound woman put on her headset. A young girl came over to Cindy. "Are you first?"

Cindy nodded, "I think so."

"Well, come with me. I'll fix your hair and makeup."

Cindy sat in a tall chair while the makeup girl touched her up and brushed her hair. A script girl came to Cindy. "Are you Miss Taylor?" Cindy nodded. "Well, here is your script. Try to memorize the first part. The last part will be on the teleprompter for you to read. Good luck."

Cindy read the script while the girl finished her lips. "There you go. You look great. Someone will come to get you. See ya." Cindy sat looking around. She looked in the makeup mirror and closed her eyes. She thought, *I can do this.*

"Miss Taylor, we're ready for you." Cindy opened her eyes. A young man was standing in front of her. "This way, Miss Taylor." She followed him over to where the crew was working.

Jeff came over to her. "You look great. Come over to the desk, and we'll get started." Cindy sat behind the desk. Jeff continued, "Tell you how this works. See the red light beside the camera lens? Well, when it's on, the camera is on, and you speak to that camera. You say the first part of the script, okay? Always make eye contact with the camera. Now, we are using a two-camera setup. The other camera is over there. My assistant will point to it after you finish with your first part of the script that you have memorized. You turn to it, the camera. See that box beside the camera? That is a teleprompter with words on it for you to read. It's that simple. Don't get nervous. This is not live. It is just a test. If you make a mistake or screw up, don't worry about it. Everyone does their first few times, okay? I'll be in the booth watching you on a monitor. I might ask you to do this several times. So, take your time and do the best you can. Good luck." Jeff winked at Cindy and left.

The assistant came over to Cindy. "When we're ready, he will call, 'Action'. That's when you start talking. At the end, he will say, 'Cut', which means its over." He ran to the camera and sat down. "Quiet on the set."

Cindy turned around in her chair and closed her eyes. She heard someone call out, "Rolling, we have speed." She slowly turned around and looked at the camera.

"Action."

Cindy spoke, "Good morning, America. Thanks for joining us. This morning there is a lot to talk about." The assistant pointed to the other camera. The red light came on. Cindy looked at the box and started reading the news. Jeff looked at the monitor. *She's amazing, she's beautiful, the camera loves her, and she's perfect.*

Cindy finished reading the news. She heard someone yell, "Cut." Jeff came running out of the booth. "Cynthia, that was outstanding. You handled it perfectly. Would you like to see the playback? Come on, come on." They sat in the booth. The engineer played the tape back. Cindy watched herself. Jeff was excited. "What do you think?"

Cindy looked at the monitor. "Well, I could have done it better, I think, and I don't like my hair."

Jeff looked at her and began to laugh. "You want to brush your hair the way you like it, and we'll do it again?"

Cindy stood up, "Yes, I would, if you don't mind."

Jeff stood up and smiled, "Anything for Miss Taylor."

Cindy became more and more comfortable with the camera and the flow of what to do. After the third take, she no longer looked at the assistant's pointing. She could see him out of the corner of her eye. Her movements became more comfortable and automatic. Each take was better than the last. Jeff's voice came over the speaker, "Cynthia, just for fun, try it one more time. Try it in a fun, sexy kind of way. Don't be serious, okay?"

Cindy heard sound calling out, "Rolling, we have speed." She thought of when she and Guyiser would playfully play after their lovemaking. She heard them laughing and rolling around on the bed.

"And action."

She looked into the camera lens. A warm smile came on her face. She was talking to Guyiser. "Good morning, America. Thanks for joining us this morning." Jeff was leaning into the monitor. Her smile, her eyes, and her softness hypnotized him. She was warm and tender. She had a play in her voice. At the end of the report, Jeff kept looking at the monitor. The crew looked at the booth. Cindy continued to look into the camera. She then looked at the recording booth. The studio was quiet.

All of a sudden the speaker came on, "Cut, cut. I'm sorry, cut." Jeff walked out of the booth. "Okay, next setup, everybody." He walked over to Cindy.

He leaned down on the desk, looking at her. "Cynthia, that was perfect. I would like to schedule you for more studio work. I believe you have what it takes to be a television reporter. I'll talk to the Dean of the school about your schedule. You go have a good day, okay?"

Cindy smiled, gathered her papers, and stood up. "Thank you, Jeff. It's been fun." Jeff watched her walk away out the studio door.

It was afternoon. Guyiser had taken Hay and the chickens to the Taylor's house. He was packing some things he wanted to take back with him to the factory. He sat looking through his photo album. He kept looking at a picture of Cindy. He put the album in his briefcase and continued gathering a few more things. Loaner was standing by the truck as Guyiser came out of the house and locked the door. "Hey, fella. You want to go back up there? Well, let's go." Loaner jumped around barking and then jumped in the truck.

They rolled into Bowling Green at six that evening. The ride had been a good one. The sun was beginning to go down, and the city lights lit up the sky. It wasn't long before Guyiser saw the buildings of the factory on his left. "We're here, boy."

Jim came to meet the truck as Guyiser drove through the gates. "Mr. Blackman, good to see you, sir. How was your trip?"

Guyiser handed him a flashlight. "It was good, Jim. I relaxed on my farm and saw some friends. It was good. Is that what you wanted?"

Jim turned on the flashlight and aimed it at the office building. "Yes, sir. It sure is strong. Thank you, sir. I'll open the hangar for you."

"That's okay, Jim. I'll use the walk-in door. I want to go get something to eat. I'll see you later." The hangar looked good to Guyiser. He unloaded his things and turned to Loaner, "You stay here and protect. I'll bring you something back."

Guyiser could smell the charcoal smoke as he entered the steak house. A waiter came to him. "Table for one, sir?"

Guyiser looked around. "Is Carla here tonight?"

"Yes, sir. She's on a break. Would you like to sit in her station?"

"Yes, please." Guyiser sat looking at the menu.

"Well, hello, stranger." Carla stood smiling.

"I missed seeing you."

He smiled back, "It's good to see you. How's it going?"

"Same thing. Nothing changes. Where is Lonesome?"

Guyiser laughed. "It's Loaner." They laughed. "I'm hungry. How about a good steak and a Jack Daniels?"

"You got it. I'll be right back." Soft music came from the dimly lit bar area. Guyiser finished his steak and motioned to Carla.

"Now, that was a good steak. Is the bar crowded, Carla?"

"Not right now. The band starts about nine. You should check it out." She smiled. "Here's your check, sir, and something for Loaner."

"Thank you, Carla. I think I will have a drink at the bar. I'll see you again." Guyiser left his money with the check on the table and went to the bar. There was a couple sitting by the fireplace. He sat at the bar looking around the cozy room.

"Yes, sir. What can I get for you tonight?"

Guyiser looked at all the bottles behind the bar. "Oh, I'll stay with a Jack Daniels on the rocks."

The bartender put a napkin on the bar, "You got it." Guyiser sat sipping his drink. He started thinking about the factory and hoping things were going well with the bikes. He wanted to get things started with production, but he knew that a board meeting should be called soon. Mr. Gibson should be there for that. He looked at his pocket watch. It was eight o'clock.

"You mind if I sit here?"

Guyiser looked up to see Carla.

"No, not at all. Would you like a drink?"

"Not now. I'm just taking a break. So, how do you like the bar?"

"It's nice. Could use a fish tank, but it's nice."

"You know, that would add a little life in here. Do you work around here?"

"Yes, down at the bike factory."

"That's a nice place. I used to work there."

"Oh, what did you do?"

"I worked in the public relations department before the big layoff. Now, I'm a working girl, if you know what I mean."

"What's your last name, Carla?"

"Comings, Carla Comings. What's yours?"

Guyiser took a drink and motioned to the bartender, "One more. Carla, where is the restroom?"

"It's down that way, second door on the right. Say, uh, I have to get back. I see some people in my station. Come back and see me soon, Mr. Guyiser, okay?"

"You can count on it. Good night." Guyiser watched her walk away. He finished his drink and headed back to the factory.

Guyiser opened the hangar walk-in door and went in. There sat the big jet. Loaner came running to him and jumped around. "See, I told you I would bring back something for you." Upstairs he sat at his desk and opened his briefcase. He took out his photo album and put pictures in the frames he had brought. He put a picture of Cindy on his desk. He hung pictures of his father on the wall. Then, he hung a picture of Cindy and him. He went to the bedroom and put a picture of Cindy and him on the night table. They were smiling and holding champagne glasses. Guyiser sat on the brass bed looking at what he had done. The apartment was beginning to feel like home. He went to the living room and hung his shotgun over the large fireplace. When everything was hung, he stood in the living room looking out the large windows at the jet below. *I want to keep this place just for me!*

The apartment patio had become a favorite place for Guyiser to sit in the mornings. It was almost like his tree house. He could sit up high and look out over the buildings and watch the sun come up. It was almost seven o'clock. He saw several cars pull into the parking area.

They belonged to the new hired people that Buck had needed. Guyiser finished breakfast and put on a clean pair of jean and a sweatshirt. Loaner jumped around barking. "You want to ride, boy? Well, let's go."

The first thing Guyiser wanted to see was how shipping was doing. His golf cart pulled up to the building. There was a large freight truck at the dock. As he went in, he saw eight men working. Some were opening boxes. Some were replacing wheels on bicycles. Mr. Maker came up to him. "Good morning, boss."

"Hello, Mr. Maker. What's going on?"

"Things are looking good, sir. The replacement wheels came in, and we got started replacing them right away. Only missed a day and a half in shipping."

"How many men are working?"

"Well, we have a total of ten, plus me."

Guyiser looked around, "2, 4, 6, 7, 8. I only see eight."

Mr. Maker looked around, "They're here somewhere."

"Okay, I'll see you later." Guyiser left the building. He drove to Buck's building. There were several men and women working at varying jobs. "Good morning, Buck. I see you have everything under control."

"Good morning, Mr. Blackman. Yes, but it wasn't easy. I hired some people who used to work here. So, they know what they're doing. That helps. How was your trip?"

"It was wonderful, thank you. Did you get the specifications on the new line of bikes from the art department?"

"Yes, sir. I was just waiting for you to give me the okay. I made adjustments for cutting the tubes and putting the frames together. Check out these blueprints and make sure that's what you want."

Guyiser looked at all the blueprints. There were girls and boys bikes in different styles and shapes. There were different sizes and four different colors for each design. "Looks good to me, Buck. What about the paint sprayer?"

"I'm working on that now. I have a man who knows everything about that machine."

"Buck, you're a good man. I'll let you know later about everything, so just stand by, okay?"

"Oh, Mr. Blackman, the exercise bike is going to make this company work. It's going to be a real shot in the arm for us."

"I hope so, Buck. We are going to have a complete sports line. I'll check with you later."

Guyiser and Loaner headed for the office.

Kate was on the phone as he came in. She waved to him. "Yes, I will. Right now. Thank you. Bye. Good morning, Mr. Blackman. How was everything in Nashville?"

"Kate, you wouldn't believe it. Mr. Gibson and I had a great meeting and everything is going ahead as planned. How are things with you?"

"My son is sick at school. I have to take off today. Oh, I have two messages for you. This is from the wheel company wanting to know if you received the replacements. And, this is from Mr. Simson, the buyer of a big chain store. They want to order bikes."

Guyiser looked at the message. "Wow! This is great. I'll call him right away. You go ahead and take care of your son. Let me know if you need anything."

Guyiser sat in his office in the apartment. He looked around at the pictures he had hung on the walls. He looked at two large doors at the end of the room. He had not really noticed them before. He got up and went to the doors. There was a panel on the wall with a button on it. He pressed the button and the doors opened. It was an elevator. He pressed the button again and the doors closed. "Look what I found, Loaner. No more stairs to climb for me!" He went back to his desk and noticed a large picture of a lighthouse on the shore of the ocean at sunset. He went to it and tried to straighten it. It swung open. There in front of him was a wall safe. He turned the handle, but it was locked.

He stood looking at it and then closed the picture back over it. Things like this made him curious.

Guyiser went back to his desk and sat looking at the picture. Then, he looked at the messages. *A buyer from a big chain store calling. Well, let's see what he wants.* Guyiser dialed the number. "Hello, Mr. Simson, please."

"...Thank you."

"...Hello, Mr. Simson. This is Guyiser Blackman, returning your call."

"...That's right, Spellman Bicycles. How are you?"

"...Fine. How can I help you?" The two talked for quite a while. Guyiser laughed, "You're right about that."

"...Okay, our fax number is on our letterhead. You'll get it tomorrow. Thanks for your order. We'll have to get together soon."

"...I will. Right now. Thanks again. Bye."

Guyiser leaned back in his chair and laughed out loud. "My first big account!" He called accounting. "Mrs. Watson, this is Guyiser. Hi. I've got some good news."

"...Yes, a new account. They have eight stores. They'll be sending orders next week."

"...Good idea."

"...Check them out."

"...Yes, I'll follow up."

"...Okay, Bye."

A super day was shaping up. Guyiser hopped in his golf cart and headed to shipping. As he rounded the back of the building, he saw two men sitting by the door. He parked and walked over to them. "Hi, guys. What's going on?"

The two men were laughing and talking loudly. One of the men was smoking. "Hey, dude. Everything's cool." He handed Guyiser the cigarette.

Guyiser took it and looked at it. It was marijuana. He looked at the smiling men. "You're fired. Get your stuff and get off the property." The two men started laughing. Guyiser went to the golf cart and got his radio. "Tom, come in, Tom."

"This is Tom."

"Tom, this is Blackman. Come to the back of the building outside the back door, now!" Mr. Maker came within a minute. Guyiser handed him the joint. "Get them out of here, now. They're fired." Guyiser was as mad as a bull. He looked at the two men. "You got something to say to me?" He was hoping they would say anything. He wanted to fight them both.

Mr. Maker stepped in, "You heard him. Get out of here, now!" He turned to Guyiser, "I'll take them out the gate, Mr. Blackman." Guyiser sat in the cart shaking. Soon he settled down.

The excitement of the day had disappeared. Guyiser needed to clear his mind of the incident with the two men. He headed back to the hangar. As he walked in, he stood looking at the big jet. He walked around it, touching the cold metal. He went to the door of the mid-section. His hand reached for the handle, and he pulled open the large door. A stepladder came down.

Guyiser walked up the steps and stood looking in. As he walked in, he felt the plush carpet and the clean cool air. He stood looking at the double seats facing each other. He saw a kitchen area with a wet bar and stools. He walked forward to the cockpit and went in, looking at all the buttons and controls.

He sat in the pilot's seat. This was his first time in a plane. He was in awe of everything. The feeling of the power of the plane was the strongest feeling he had ever felt. He could feel himself high in the sky like a bird. He looked out the window and saw the ground way down below him. A smile finally came to him. He was the pilot. He was in charge. Loaner barked and ran up the steps and into the plane looking for his master. Guyiser took the mike and called into it, "All aboard, or sit down please, or something like that." He laughed at Loaner standing there. "I need a captain's hat. What do you think?"

Guyiser got up and walked to the back of the plane. He sat in a big double seat and looked out the window. He turned to the seats in front of him, "Now gentlemen, my company can fill all your orders." He started laughing and laughing. Then, Guyiser climbed out of the jet and closed the door. He walked over to the double paneled doors. He had found the elevator. The door quickly opened when he pushed the button. The two went in. The doors opened again, and they were in his office. "How do you like that, Loaner? No more stairs." Loaner barked and headed for the kitchen. Guyiser sat at his desk looking at the large jet. He turned to Cindy's picture on his desk. "How I wish you were here!"

Jeff Fisher sat in the Dean's office talking. "Was I surprised? Just look at this tape." Jeff put the tape in the VCR and pressed 'play'. He and Dean Winters sat looking at the monitor. The camera opened on Cindy's face as she spoke. 'Good morning. Thanks for joining us.'

Jeff looked at Dean Winters, 'We have a lot to talk about.' Jeff said, "Now, watch her transition." Cindy turned to camera #2. 'Early this morning, the senator gave this statement.' The short two minutes ended. Jeff turned to the Dean, "This is take two." The tape continued. "Look at her eyes. The public will love her." The tape continued to roll showing takes three and four. "Now, this is take five. Cynthia wanted to do it a different way, her way. She changed her hair and her whole mood. Watch this!" 'Good morning, America. Thanks for joining us. We have a lot to talk about.' Jeff looked at the Dean for his reaction. 'Early this morning, the senator gave this statement.'

Dean Winters leaned in close to the monitor as Cindy continued her report. As the tape ended, he leaned back in his chair. "Tell me about her."

Jeff took our Cindy's profile. "She was president of her debate team. She worked on the school newspaper for three years. She and three others were arrested or detained for standing up for animals' rights. She wrote and reported a story of a black student and a white teacher. Her report was in complete contrast to what the school had said. Her report brought changes in the school's policies. She graduated highest in her class of 500.

Dean Winters interrupted, "That's enough."

"But, Dean, there's more, here."

Dean Winters took Cindy's profile. "I like her. She has a special quality about her. I am glad you brought her to my attention. But, she has only been here three weeks. What do you suggest, Jeff?"

"Well, sir, I think she should work in a studio.

With her talent, I don't see her as an outside reporter, unless it's something big. She's not afraid to ask questions to any politician or even the President. She would be great for a sit-down interview. That's what I would like to tape—a one-on-one interview with the mayor or someone important."

Dean Winters thought for a minute. "Why don't you work with her on that? Set up a subject for her and let her make up several questions to ask. See how she does. Give her a week and set up a taping. I want to be there to watch her."

Jeff stood up, picked up the tape, and shook Dean Winters' hand. "Yes, sir. And, thank you, sir." Jeff was excited about the project. He had found a diamond in the rough. He wanted to make her shine. He also knew it would be a big feather in his hat if he found the next 'America's Sweetheart.'

Music filled the apartment. Guyiser was having his favorite breakfast of eggs, bacon, toast, and jelly.

He finished eating and with coffee in hand headed for the patio. A few clouds were blocking the sun. Guyiser stood smelling the clean air. He could tell that rain was on the way. He sat at his desk making a schedule of things to be done. He knew he was now on a time schedule for putting things together. Buck was doing his part. Shipping was now back on line. Accounting had orders to fill. He was ready for Mr. Gibson to give the okay to start production. The picture of the lighthouse and ocean loomed in front of him. He sat looking at it. Then, he reached for the intercom and buzzed Kate. "Kate here."

"Hi, Kate. This is Guyiser. How is your son?"

"…That's good, but if you need to take off again, just do it. Kate, could you give me the Spellman's home phone number? Just want to check in with Mrs. Spellman."

Guyiser wrote down the number, "…9801. Got it. Thanks, Kate."

"…Are you all right?"

"…Great. Okay. I'll talk to you later." Guyiser looked at the picture and dialed the number. "Good morning. This is Guyiser Blackman. Is Mrs. Spellman there, please?"

"…Yes, I'll wait." Guyiser put the phone on speaker and walked to the picture. He swung it open and stood looking at the safe.

Mrs. Spellman came on the line, "Hello."

"…Hi, Mrs. Spellman. This is Guyiser. How are you?"

"...Glad to hear that. We miss seeing you around here."

"...Yes, ma'am. I am sorry about that. I was wondering if you had some time today when I could drop by and see you." Guyiser went back to the desk.

"...That would be fine. Thank you, ma'am. I'll see you then." He sat looking at the safe. His intercom buzzed, "Blackman here."

...Oh, good morning, Buck."

"...So, it will be working by this afternoon?"

"...Great. Keep him on stand-by, will you? Say, how much trouble would it be to make up one of each of the new bikes and the exercise bike? I need to get some promo material made up."

"...No, just one each, painted. We can change colors on the computer in the art department."

"...Good man. Do it."

"...Okay. Bye."

It was noon when Guyiser drove up the Spellman's tree-lined driveway. A small mansion stood on this ten-acre property. As he drove up, he saw a guesthouse with a limo parked in front. The driveway took him to the brick mansion with stained glass windows. A small woman in a black and white maid's uniform greeted him, "Good morning, sir. You can wait in the living room. I will let Mrs. Spellman know you are here, sir." She smiled and walked away. Guyiser stood looking at everything. *Boy, they sure know how to live.*

"Good afternoon, Guyiser." Mrs. Spellman came to him with a big hug.

"Good afternoon, Mrs. Spellman. You look great."

She laughed, "Thank you, Guyiser. Sit down, sit down." They talked for a while about the house, James, and the factory. It was a very pleasant meeting as their conversation continued, "I'm afraid his health is getting worse. His mind started going about two years ago." Mrs. Spellman wiped her eyes. "He doesn't even know me most of the time."

Guyiser held her hands. "I'm so sorry, Mrs. Spellman. It must be very hard on you. Mrs. Spellman, I found a safe in the apartment in the hangar."

She looked at him, "A safe? In the hangar? I had forgotten about that old thing. It's been there forever. I don't know if it even works."

Guyiser squeezed her hands, "I know. It's a little rusty. But, I have some important papers and things that I need to put away. I thought I could use the safe so they would be in a safe place. Do you know the combination? It would really help me."

"Maybe. Mr. Spellman has a metal box in his desk over there. Let me look." She got up and crossed the room to the desk. The box was locked in a drawer. She unlocked the drawer and took out the box. Then, she spread the papers out on the desk looking through them. Guyiser stood watching her. She opened an envelope and took out a paper. "This looks like it. Yes, it is. See the 'M' here. That stands for me, Margaret. 17-28-34-M. But, it's actually empty. Mr. Spellman used the safe in his office, so you're welcome to it."

Guyiser took the paper, "Thank you, Mrs. Spellman.

If there is anything in it, I'll get it to you." She put everything back in the box.

"Don't worry about it, Guyiser. If you find anything, just throw it away." She hugged Guyiser again.

"Mrs. Spellman, if there is anything I can do for you, please call me. I should get back to the factory. We have some things going on today."

Mrs. Spellman walked him to the door, "I talked to Mr. Gibson. He's very impressed with you."

Guyiser kissed her cheek, "And, I'm very impressed with you, Mrs. Spellman. You have a good day, ma'am. Bye."

Guyiser sat in his truck. He could not wait to get back. He drove to the factory gates and stopped. He looked at the gates and the office building beyond them. He drove in and to the hangar. As he went in, Loaner came running to him with his tennis ball in his mouth. "Want to play, boy?" Loaner dropped the ball and barked. "We will later. Come on. Do you want to ride?" The elevator doors opened and Guyiser walked into his office. He sat at his desk looking at the picture on the wall. Then, the phone rang. "Hello."

"…Cindy!"

"…I'm fine. How are you? Gosh, I miss you."

"…I know. I love you, too."

"…Oh, things are moving right along. I have a good group of people to work with. How about you?"

Cindy picked up the picture of them from the night table. "I'm looking at you right now."

"...I miss you, too."

"...Oh, me? Everything is great here. Classes are going well. I had a taping the other day. Our crew is going on location again. I wish you were here."

"...About three days. It's a lot of work."

"...I know. I'm looking at my charms now. Number one, first." Cindy laughed.

"...Yes, I thought about that the other day."

"...Well, sweetheart, I just wanted to hear your voice. I'll let you go back to work."

"...I love you, too."

"...I will. Okay, boyfriend. Bye Bye."

Cindy missed everybody. She missed her home; her dog, her mother's cooking, and even her bedroom. She had phoned her parents, but it was not the same as being there. She sat on her bed looking at the picture, and a smile came to her face. Sandy came in bursting with excitement. Cindy looked at her.

"Hey you, what's happening?"

Sandy smiled and handed her an envelope. "I just got an assignment to shoot a music video of rock stars! Oh, here. This is for you."

Cindy took the envelope and opened it. "Rock stars, can I come?" She laughed and read the letter. "Hey, listen to this, 'Miss Taylor, Dean Winters and I have evaluated your taping and are setting up a special interview session. Please contact me ASAP to discuss the session. Respectfully, Jess Fisher' Wow! I wonder what this is all about."

Sandy looked at the letter. "Well, it must be important if the Dean is involved. I've got to go. Rock stars, right on!"

Cindy sat looking at the letter. She jumped off the bed and put herself together. She stood in front of her full-length mirror with briefcase in hand. "I look good."

Jeff Fisher's office was in the studio building. Cindy knocked on the door. "Come in. Well, good afternoon, Miss Taylor. Have a seat. You look great." Cindy sat looking around the office. There were pictures on the walls of Jeff with famous people and a few trophies sitting around. "How's it going? You got my message, I see."

"Ah, yes I did. What does it mean, special interview?"

"Well, uh, Cynthia, the Dean and I talked, and we want you to interview a special person one-on-one. This will be a sit-down interview. The person is a wealthy attorney, a banker, and an entrepreneur of many things. He is one of those 'Good Ole Boys' from the South. He's visiting from our neighboring state and has agreed to the interview."

Cindy became excited. She opened her briefcase and took out her pad and pen. "Who is he? I mean his name."

Jeff went on to explain all the details. Cindy took notes on everything he said. "Now, he's a mean tempered old man. You have only four minutes to interview him, so your questions should be straight to the point. They can be on any subject you want. You can use our library and our computer for your research. This is big time, Cynthia. Don't hold back on your questions. Make them tough, okay?"

Cindy smiled and kept writing. "Any subject and four minutes. Got it."

"One more thing, he's given many interviews, and he stretches his answers out. You know, to eat up time.

So, cut him off if you need to; you know what I mean? But always be respectful, kind of." Jeff smiled. "Okay. Now, you have only one week to prepare. Do your best." Jeff stood up and extended his hand. "Good luck."

Cindy left the office and sat under a tree. She had made many notes. She decided to make a list of subjects and questions for each subject. Next, she went to the library and started her research.

The automatic lights came on at the factory. The sun had set for the day. Guyiser sat looking at Cindy's picture. He got up and went to the wet bar and made himself a drink. He pulled the picture of the lighthouse open and looked at the safe. After getting the paper with the combination from his desk, he started dialing the numbers. He then pressed the letter 'M' and turned the handle. The safe door opened and a light came on. He stared at all the things in the safe.

There was a large, heavy, sealed envelope and a newspaper. He put the things on his desk. He looked again in the safe and his eyes widened. There were two stacks of money. He put all the money on the desk. His heart was beating fast. There were some papers, letters, and pictures. He put them all on the desk. There was also a handgun. The safe was now empty. He sat in his chair looking at everything. The money was first. He started counting. He had stacked the money in to thousand dollar stacks. Thirty-eight thousand and still counting. He took a big breath and continued his count. Finally, he leaned back in his chair, took a big drink, and sat looking at all the money. He couldn't believe his eyes. There was fifty thousand five hundred dollars in cash.

Where did Spellman get all this? Why was it in the safe? What was Spellman going to do with all this money? Guyiser's mind went crazy with questions. One thing he knew was Mrs. Spellman did not know about the money. He picked up the gun. It was loaded. He put it down and picked up the papers. They had dates from years ago. There were invoices, memos, and letters to different accounts but nothing seemed special. He picked up the folded newspaper and a package of pictures fell out. He looked at the strange pictures. There was a man in bondage being whipped, a man in a dress, a man tied to a bed, and a woman giving the man oral sex. All of the pictures involved sex of all positions. All of the pictures were different, except the man in each picture was the same. Guyiser had never seen anything like this before.

He put the pictures down and picked up the newspaper. It also had a date from many years ago.

Then, a picture in the paper hit his eye. It was the same man who was in all the pictures. He started to read. 'James Olsen resigns his city post after a murder of a call girl in his home. Olsen says a burglary was taking place as they entered the house. The woman had been shot and killed. Olsen was also shot in the shoulder. The burglar escaped. Police have no clues at this time.'

Guyiser leaned back in his chair. *Olsen, Olsen, could that be the same Olsen who is a backer? Why did Spellman keep this newspaper? Why the pictures?* He reached for the sealed package. He opened it and dumped out its contents. A .45 caliber handgun fell out. It was sealed in a plastic bag. Guyiser sat looking at the sealed bag. He looked at the newspaper. He looked at all the strange pictures. He looked at all the money. *What was the connection? Did Spellman have anything to do with this?* Guyiser went to the bar and made another drink. *There must have been a reason all of this was in this safe.* He gathered everything and put it all back in the safe. He locked it and put the picture back.

Guyiser did not sleep well that night. Guns, a newspaper, pictures, and money went through his mind. *What have I found? Mr. Spellman must have had some reason to keep all these things.* Guyiser lay in bed trying to put all the pieces together. *If Mrs. Spellman did not know about the safe, then this was Mr. Spellman's secret. But why? And Olsen and the pictures of him and the newspaper story. A woman killed. A gun in a sealed bag.* Things were trying to come together but Guyiser could not make sense of it all. Sleep finally put his mind to rest.

Blowing rain against the patio door woke Guyiser the next morning. He lay watching the rain fall. His mind started to work. *Was last night a dream?* He got up and went to the safe. As he opened it, he saw it was not a dream. Everything was there. Guyiser dressed and sat at his desk drinking coffee. *Mrs. Watson had been working at the factory the longest of anyone here. She knows about everything. Maybe she could help put things together.* Guyiser pressed the intercom, "Kate here."

"Good morning, Kate. This is Guyiser. How are you today?"

"Oh, good morning. I'm fine but a little wet. The rain caught me by surprise."

"Yes, I know. It woke me up. Is Mrs. Watson in today?"

"Not now, but she will be in later."

"Good, I'll see her then. Oh, Kate. There used to be a girl who worked here. Her name is Carla Comings. Do you know her?"

"Yes, sir. I remember her."

"Well, would you pull her file for me?"

"Sure will."

"Thanks, Kate. I'll see you later."

Guyiser sat at his desk going over some notes he had made. The rain was coming down heavy. He could hear it beating down on the tin rooftop. It sounded good. He thought about the farm. He remembered when he would walk in the fields and when it rained. Those were the good ole days. Loaner came running in the office and sat looking at Guyiser. "You hear that rain, boy? You want to go out in it?" Loaner barked and ran to the door. The intercom buzzed, "Hello."

"Good morning, Mr. Blackman. This is Buck."

"Hi, Buck, how's it going?"

"It's wet but good. Say, I cut the frames and put them together. The paint sprayer is working just fine now. What color would you like to try out first?"

Guyiser thought for a minute. His father always sprayed everything gold or silver. He used to watch his father spray the paint and then step back admiring his work. He would turn to Guyiser and say, 'What do you think?' Guyiser smiled, "Gold, Buck. Spray everything gold."

"Yes, sir. You can take a look about three o'clock."

"Thanks, Buck. I'll see you later."

Guyiser found his yellow raincoat in the bedroom closet. He stood at the patio doors watching it rain. Loaner barked. "Okay, okay. Let's go." As they walked in the rain, Guyiser laughed watching Loaner run around in the rain. Soon, they came to the office building. Kate was standing at the door watching the rain come down. Guyiser and Loaner went in.

"Where is your cart?"

"Oh, it's at the hangar. I like to walk in the rain." Loaner shook his fur coat and rainwater went everywhere.

Kate laughed, "I'll take care of that. Mrs. Watson is here now, and I have Miss Comings' file for you."

"Great. Thanks, Kate. How's your son?"

"Oh, he's fine now, thanks."

Guyiser knocked on Mrs. Watson's door and went in. They sat talking about the rain and other small talk. Then, Mrs. Watson said, "The Wall-Burg Department Stores checked out just fine. I didn't know they were so big. They have eight large stores here in Kentucky and are expanding into Tennessee." Mrs. Watson handed Guyiser some papers. "They will be a big account for us."

Guyiser looked the report over, "This is great. I want to have copies to show Mr. Gibson. This should make him happy." Guyiser put the report on the desk. "Mrs. Watson, you have been here since day one. What can you tell me about Mr. Olsen?"

Mrs. Watson took off her glasses and looked at Guyiser. "Mr. Olsen? Well, let's see. In the beginning, he and Mr. Spellman were friends of a sort. Mr. Spellman had put a lot of money into the factory and needed more. That's when Mr. Olsen bought in. He bought 20% of Mr. Spellman's stock. Everything was fine for a long time. Then, they started fighting over things. Mr. Olsen wanted this, and Mr. Spellman wanted that."

Guyiser interrupted, "But, Mr. Spellman had control, didn't he?"

"Oh, yes, but Mr. Olsen wanted more control. They fought over everything. Then, all of a sudden, it all ended. No more fighting. Why, I do not know. Mr. Olsen stopped coming around here. I was glad. I don't care for him too much anyway. Business picked up.

Mr. Spellman was happier. Then, after a few years, Mr. Spellman's health got bad. And, here we are today."

"Mrs. Watson, do you know anything about the murder Mr. Olsen was involved in at his home?"

"No, only what I read in the papers. But, it's strange. That's when the fighting between them stopped. Things around here changed. That's all I know."

Guyiser stood up, "And, it's going to change again. Thanks for your help. You're doing a good job here. And I know that I need you. Can I have a hug?"

Mrs. Watson smiled and stood up, "You sure can, son."

It was still raining as Guyiser and Loaner went to see Buck. Rain pounded on the rooftop of the warehouse. Guyiser and Buck stood looking at the four gold bicycles. Guyiser walked around them with a smile on his face. "I like them, Buck. What about the tricycles?"

"They're next. Now, look at this, sir." Buck went to a blue tarp and pulled it off. There stood the stationary exercise bike for the sports line.

Guyiser was stunned. "Wow!" He walked around it touching all the parts. "Wow, Buck!" He got on and started to pedal. "It's so smooth." He held the handlebars and pedaled faster and faster. Then, he got off and stood again looking at the bike. "Now, that's a workout."

Buck stood with his hands in his apron. He was smiling at Guyiser's pleasure. "Yes, sir. That's my favorite."

Guyiser shook his hand. His eyes were still big and smiling. "We're in business, Buck. I'll let the art department know so we can get started putting a catalog together. The others look perfect, too. Thanks, Buck. We're on our way."

Guyiser sat at his desk. He had talked to Scott about setting up a photo shoot of all the bikes. They had an idea for several different catalogs. They would call one 'Blackie's Gold Series'. This was for his father. He knew this would make him happy. The stationary exercise bike would be a special series called 'Blackie's Workout.' It would feature the bike and safety products. His blinking lights would come later to increase sales.

He now had a full line of bicycles he loved. Four were his own bikes and two were Spellman products. There were two different tricycles and a sports workout line. That was nine different products. His love for bicycles was helping his dreams come true. And to think, it all started with scrap bicycle frames and parts he had found in Mr. Gibson's alley. Making money was now his goal. His mind started thinking of sales, orders, distribution, advertising, and new accounts. *Where to start? Where to start?*

Guyiser looked at the folder on his desk. He opened it and started to read. It was Carla Comings' folder. She had worked in public relations for the factory. She was twenty, single, and had been a secretary at a large bank. She had experience dealing with people. Carla had also worked for a law firm. She also spoke two languages.

Guyiser liked her and sat thinking about how she could help him and the factory. His eyes drifted to the lighthouse picture. He thought of all the things in the safe. Mrs. Watson's conversation was fresh in his mind. Some things started to come together. But, there was still a mystery with unanswered questions.

Guyiser stood looking out the patio doors.

The rain had stopped. Night had fallen. He was excited about the bikes and catalogs coming together. He wanted to talk to Mr. Gibson and Mr. Levine. Mr. Gibson was the one who could give the okay to start production and to let Guyiser do his thing. Guyiser had things ready. He could start production, hire people, and make things happen. But for now, he was hungry.

The steak house was busy. The chatter of people was loud as he walked in. The band was playing, and the room smelled good. He saw Carla at a table taking an order. She waved to him. He walked to the bar and looked in. The band was good. Carla came up behind him. "Hi, mister, want a date?"

"Maybe, what's your name?"

"Just call me Carla." They laughed. "Are you ready?"

"Lead the way, Carla." Guyiser sat down at a booth.

Carla stood looking at him, "I'm glad to see you. How have you been?"

"Oh, I'm great. Busy, busy. You look nice tonight. I like your hair down. It's sexy looking."

Carla smiled. "Thanks for noticing. A good steak and Jack Daniels tonight?"

Guyiser handed her the menu and smiled, "Yes, ma'am and a little conversation later?"

She smiled, "Well, that may cost you. Maybe. I'll be right back." Carla had a way about her that Guyiser liked. She was fun and sexy. She made him feel good. But, she was also business and to the point. He liked that.

Guyiser finished his dinner and looked around the restaurant. The crowd had thinned out. Carla came back to his booth and sat down. "Do you mind?"

Guyiser was surprised, "Not at all. Sit down, sit down."

Carla leaned back in the booth, "This was a busy night. So, how have you been?"

"Oh, I'm good. A little bored. Tell me, what is there to do around here for entertainment?"

"Well, the usual—movies, dancing, and I like horse racing. Have you ever been?"

"No, but I hear races are fun."

"Well, I'll take you sometime."

Guyiser took a drink and looked at her. "When?"

She was surprised but just smiled, "Anytime you want."

Guyiser thought for a moment, "Carla, when you worked at the bike factory, did you ever know a man named Olsen?"

It didn't take her long to answer, "I sure did. He was a freak. He asked me if I liked to beat up men. Can you imagine that? Why do you ask?"

"Oh, no reason, except I think he's strange, too. So, when are you taking me to the races?"

Carla counted on her fingers, "How about this weekend?"

Guyiser took out a small notebook. "That's good for me. I'll pick you up."

She looked at him, "About five o'clock on Saturday? My address is."

Guyiser interrupted, "7902 Erwin Boulevard."

"How did you know that?"

He smiled, "I know a lot about you. You're twenty. You've worked for a bank and a law firm. You're single. You speak two languages. What languages do you speak?"

Carla sat staring at Guyiser. "French and German. But, how did you know?"

Guyiser smiled, "The horse race sounds fun. Saturday at five o'clock, right? I have to go, Carla. Loaner is waiting for me." He stood up. "I'll see you then. Good night."

"Wait, wait. Remember your doggie bag. Good night."

Guyiser lay on the couch watching T.V. He felt relaxed. Loaner lay on the floor looking up at his master. Guyiser flipped through the channels and stopped at the news. The weatherman was just finishing his report. "So, for the next few days, the rain is going to be on again off again. Keep your raincoat handy. Back to Jane."

"Thanks, Dan. The school board voted today." Guyiser's mind saw Cindy. He closed his eyes and saw the farm. He saw the barn with the sign over the doors, 'Guyiser's Bike Shop'. He saw Cindy sitting on his lap as they playfully played. He smelled the hay. He missed Mr. and Mrs. Taylor. He missed the great table of food and banana pudding. He remembered Mr. Gibson who had always been there for him. He missed the jolly old man. He heard Mr. Gibson say, 'Guyiser, I'm an old man. I've done it all, and I want to do it again through you.' Guyiser looked at the phone and his watch. It was too late to call, but that would be the first thing he'd do in the morning. He'd call everybody.

Even though Guyiser was a little homesick, Mr. Gibson had given him a responsibility, and he had accepted it. He was no longer a farm boy. Now, he gave orders to people. Each day he grew older and wiser. His mind worked differently now. Bicycles looked like a future instead of just something to play with. He had turned a corner in his life without even knowing it.

The Kentucky sky was gray with clouds as Guyiser and Loaner walked down the jet's long runway. Guyiser looked back at all the buildings. Cars began to pull into the parking lot. The day had begun. "Let's go back, Loaner. I've got things to do."

Guyiser sat at his desk holding his picture of Cindy. The intercom buzzed. "Hello, Mr. Blackman. This is Scott. Good morning, sir."

"Oh, hi, Scott. What's going on?"

"We have the photo shoot set up for this morning at nine o'clock. Thought you might want to be there."

"Sure do, Scott. Thanks. I'll see you there."

Guyiser looked at his watch. He wanted to talk to Mr. Gibson. He picked up the phone and dialed.

"Hello, Mr. Gibson. How are you, sir?"

"…I'm fine, thank you. Everything is going well. When are you coming up here? I miss seeing you."

"…Great. By then I'll have a lot to show you. We have nine different bikes to start production on and a lot of orders to fill."

"…Yes, sir. Nine."

"…That's why I'm calling. I'm at a point that I need help. Maybe four or five people fulltime."

"…Good."

"…Yes, sir. We are shooting a catalog layout this morning."

"I will. So, in about a week?"

"Great. I'll see you then."

"…You have a good day, too, sir. Bye now." Guyiser now had the okay he had been waiting for. Now he could really start things moving.

The office building was quiet as Guyiser walked in. Kate was having coffee and reading the newspaper. "Hi, Kate, how are you doing?"

"I'm fine. You're in a good mood this morning."

"Yes, I am, Kate. I talked to Mr. Gibson and got the okay I had been waiting for. Kate, would you take over the personal department? We need to hire some fulltime people."

Kate was excited, "Yes, sir. I need something to do around here. You just tell me what you need."

"Well, Kate, Buck has a man for the spray paint and dryer department. Hire him. We need four assembly people. Let the extra people go since we're caught up on the bike replacements. In about two weeks, we'll need a good sales person to head sales and to follow up on the old accounts. In two weeks, we're having a board meeting. Notify the members--Olsen, Anderson, and Goldman. Mr. Gibson will be here. Let Mrs. Spellman know, too."

Kate took notes on everything. "Oh, Guyiser, I'm so happy for you. It's been a long time since there has been life around here. I'll get started right away."

Scott and Tim were giving directions to the photographer as Guyiser and Loaner walked in. Scott walked up to Guyiser. "What do you think? Oh, let me show you the layouts we want to shoot." Guyiser looked on as Scott pointed out different angles of the bikes to be photographed. "These should make exciting catalogs, both the gold series and the all color series. Oh, yes, Buck finished the tricycles. We'll put them on this page. What do you think?"

Guyiser looked at all the drawings and layouts and then at Scott, "I say let's get started. I like it all, Scott."

The photo shoot was very professionally done. The photographer even had a director's chair for Guyiser. The photographer's assistant would roll in a bike and change angles of the bike while the photographer snapped away. It took about three hours to photograph all nine products. Scott was happy with the session. He had more pictures than he needed for the catalog. Guyiser watched the photographer break down all his equipment. "He's good. Did a good job. Okay, Scott, how long will it take to see something?"

Scott handed him the schedule. "I get the film back tomorrow. I'll scan everything into the computer and then lay everything out. Next, we put copy on all the pages. I should have a printout for your approval by tomorrow night or first thing the next morning. After that, we send it to the printers. That takes three days to a week."

Guyiser was taking notes. "That will be good, Scott. We can start sending our catalogs out to all our customers. That should generate a lot of business." He smiled, "Good job, Scott.

You and Tim did great. Thanks, buddy." He left the building in a great mood. His plan was coming together. In a few days, he would be able to see his plan in print.

The gold bicycles were beautiful. They would be classics in his line. The metallic finish was bright, shiny, and reflective. Guyiser wanted to display the entire line in the lobby of the office building. They would be the first thing people would see when they entered the building. They would set a standard for the company.

Guyiser was not used to down time. He had talked to Tom Maker about the orders and the inventory. Product stock was going down while orders were coming in. Production had stopped. This was not good.

Mr. Gibson had taught Guyiser that you can't make money if you don't have anything to sell. Production had to start, and soon. Guyiser knew that Buck had the answers.

It was three o'clock when Guyiser drove into the warehouse. Buck was doing some maintenance on the large machines. Guyiser sat watching him work.

What would happen if Buck were sick or injured? Worse yet, if he died? Who would run the machines and the factory? Guyiser walked over to him. "Hey, boss. Hand me that oil can, will ya?" Buck finished and wiped his hands on his overalls. "That's my baby."

Guyiser sat down on the golf cart. "Yes, it is, Buck. Take a break. I want to talk to you. I have four people for you to work on the assembly line. And, I think you need help. You know, someone to be your assistant. Someone to learn all about these machines."

Buck laughed. "You're getting rid of me?"

"No, no, nothing like that. You're too valuable! Buck, what do we need to start production in a big way?"

Buck laughed again. "People. Four new people is a good start. Maybe even six. You know, years ago, we had eighteen here. And that was busy times. You now have nine different bikes to build. You figure it out."

Guyiser sat and thought. "I see your point. We need to get back into production next week. What do you need?"

"Well, I could use a helper."

Guyiser smiled, "You got it. And four new people to start. Kate is hiring people now. Check with her. Get people you need, okay?"

It was Friday morning as Guyiser walked into the office building. Tom Maker and his men were setting up the bikes in the lobby. The stationary bike was up on a pedestal with the other bikes all around it. It looked like a Christmas tree of bikes. Guyiser stood looking at them. They told the story of what the company was all about.

He walked to where Kate and Buck were. "Good morning, good morning. I like it," he said pointing to the bikes. "So, what's going on?"

"Well, we have good news. We hired some people who used to work here."

Buck stood up, "And, I found me a good helper."

Kate handed Guyiser some applications. "These people can start Monday."

"That's great, Kate. Do you need anything?"

"No, sir. I'm fine."

"Okay, Buck, you know what to do. Put them to work."

It was also Friday morning in Florida. The only difference was the sun was shining in the blue sky. Cindy and Sandy sat on their beds talking. Cindy had done a lot of research for her interview. She had notes spread out all over the bed. Jeff had told her not to hold back on her questions to the lawyer. "What about this one?" Cindy cleared her throat, "Sir, you said you were against black people in politics. Do you still feel that way?"

Sandy put her hands over her mouth, "Oooh, that's a rough one. Did he really say that?"

Cindy nodded and picked up a note. "Right here in a Alabama newspaper. How about this one? You spoke against women's abortion rights. Why?"

"Oh, Cindy, I like that one."

Cindy looked at all her notes. "I have so many things I want to ask him, and I only have four minutes. Maybe Jeff will give me more time. Look at all this stuff. Health care, Social Security, Human Rights, Border Crossing, and the list goes on and on."

Sandy laughed, "Well, look at it this way, you can ask someone else about those things. Let's go to lunch. I'm buying."

"But, Sandy, the interview is Monday."

"I know, but you have all weekend to work on it. Let's go. Come on."

Guyiser sat at his desk eating an egg and bacon sandwich. He looked at his calendar and saw Saturday circled. Carla, the races. He had almost forgotten. He thought about their meeting. It wasn't really a date— just two people meeting at five o'clock. Guyiser pressed the intercom button. "Kate here."

"Hi, Kate. I'm going into town tomorrow. Would you get me a limo? I don't know my way around very well."

"...You could? That would be great. Maybe a big black one."

"…Yes, for the evening."

"…Yes, have him pick me up here about four fifteen."

"…No, that's all. Thanks, Kate. You have a good weekend."

"…Oh, I will. Bye."

Guyiser looked at the picture on the wall. He swung it open and dialed the safe combination. The door opened and the light came on. He stood looking at everything, reached in, and took out a stack of money. He took out five hundred dollars and put the rest back. He smiled as he locked the safe and swung the picture back over it. As he looked down at the jet, he saw Loaner running around in the hangar. He knocked on the window. Loaner looked up at him and ran up the stairs. "Hey, boy. Are you hungry?" They played all the way to the kitchen.

Stars were out in the Kentucky sky. The rain had passed. Guyiser and Loaner played on the living room floor. "You're too strong for me, Loaner. Let's quit." Loaner smiled and barked. Guyiser lay on the couch watching his favorite movie. He finished his popcorn and was waiting for his favorite line in the movie. Then he heard it. Guyiser and Clark Gable said it at the same time, "Frankly, my dear, I don't give a damn." Guyiser laughed and clapped his hands. "That's my favorite part, Loaner." He went in his room and lay down on his big brass bed. It had been a good, long week. Now, he had a whole weekend to relax, and he wanted to enjoy it.

Saturday morning. The plant was quiet. No one was there. Guyiser woke to a bright sunny day. He had seen a little coffee shop down the road. It was time for a good breakfast. He and Loaner got into the truck and headed that way. After breakfast, they went to a shopping center that he had seen close to town. There were many shops in the center. A men's shop caught his eye. "Let's check it out, Loaner." Guyiser stood looking at the display window. The store had suits, shirts, ties, and shoes.

A salesman came up to him as he entered the store. "May I help you, sir?"

"Yes, that suit in the window, can I see it?" Guyiser liked the dark blue pin striped suit as he stood in front of the mirror. "I'll take it and these two ties and these shirts."

Guyiser stood on the sidewalk looking around. It felt good to shop and spend money. This was all new to him. He and Loaner bought ice cream cones. Guyiser laughed as he watched Loaner lapping at the ice cream. Next, he saw a beautiful gold watch. "I'll take it." The flower shop smelled so good. "I'll take those and some of those."

Guyiser sat in his truck looking at his new gold watch. "You like this?" Loaner barked. Guyiser drove in the gates of the factory and stopped. The office building looked so plain. He thought about it and drove to the hangar.

"News At Eleven"
The Date

Part 9

Love is as fickle as life itself.
Can you help me find my way?
Can you help me from day to day?
I have needs. I have a past.
Will my love grow? Will my love last?

The day had been perfect so far and had gone by fast. Guyiser stood in front of his full-length mirror looking at himself. The suit, the shirt and tie, his wing-tipped shoes, and his watch all made him feel and look great. In fact, he felt like a millionaire as he looked down at the big jet sitting in the hangar. The intercom buzzed. "Hello."

"Hi, uh, Mr. Blackman. This is Jim at security. There's a limo at the gate for you."

"Thanks, Jim. Bring him to the hangar, okay?" Guyiser stood outside the hangar doors as the big black shiny limo drove up. The driver got out and opened the back door. "Hi, Jim. Haven't seen you lately. Is everything all right?"

"Yes, sir. Couldn't be better."

"Good man. I should be back about midnight, so I'll see you later."

"You have a good evening, Mr. Blackman."

The driver greeted Guyiser, "Good afternoon, sir. My name is Robert. If there is anything I can do for you, please ask." He was a well-dressed man in a black suit and black hat.

Guyiser looked over Robert and the limo. "Thank you, Robert. I will. This is the address where we will pick up my lady friend for the evening. We're going to the races. Do they have a VIP entrance?"

"Yes, sir. I'll take care of everything."

Guyiser looked at his watch. "Good, let's go."

It was three minutes until five as the limo stopped at the address. "Robert, would you mind going to the house and getting Miss Comings for me?"

Carla looked out the window and saw the limousine. She got her coat and opened the door. "Miss Comings?

I am here to pick you up."

Guyiser stood by the limo as Carla came up to him. "My, my. Look at you and this limo."

He stood smiling, "You look wonderful. These are for you." Guyiser handed her a box of yellow roses. "Shall we go?" He sat looking at her as they rode along. She did look beautiful. Her low-cut black dress, long dark hair, and jewelry made her sparkle. She had blue eyes and a sexy smile.

"Guyiser, you went all out for this. I'm impressed."

Guyiser opened a bottle of wine and poured their glasses. "Well, I don't know my way around, and I thought this would give us a chance to talk. Cheers." The ride was long and smooth as they talked and laughed.

There were several limousines parked along the entrance as Robert drove to the VIP area. The usual media and reporters were there to see who was arriving. Robert parked and opened the door in front of the red-carpeted walkway. Guyiser got out as flashes went off. He helped Carla out, and the flashes continued. They started to walk to the doors of the stadium.

A reporter called out, "Mr. Blackman, Mr. Blackman, please." Guyiser and Carla stopped.

More flashes went off. A young woman waved. "Mr. Blackman, remember me? At the Grand Old Opry?" The cameras kept flashing. "Who is your date tonight?"

Guyiser smiled at Carla, "She's not really a date. This is Miss Carla Comings. She is in public relations."

"How is the bicycle business?"

"It's doing great. Growing larger every day, thank you. We have to go now. Thank you."

Carla and Guyiser went in. She pulled on Guyiser's arm, "What was that all about?"

Guyiser laughed, "It's a game we play. I say one thing, and they print something different. Look at tomorrow's paper. You'll see."

The general manager was watching everyone who arrived at the stadium. As Guyiser and Carla went in, the manager went to the reporter. "Who was that couple that just went in?"

The reporter looked at her notes. "Oh, that was Guyiser Blackman. He is a millionaire from Nashville. I interviewed him on New Year's Eve."

The manager ran to catch up with Guyiser and Carla. "Excuse me, sir. May I show you to our VIP lounge and box seating?" Guyiser looked at Carla. "Will you be having dinner, sir?" Guyiser looked again at Carla.

"Yes, please." The manager bowed to Carla.

"Please follow me, sir." They looked at each other and followed him to the dining room. They were seated at a table that overlooked the racetrack. "If there is anything I can help you with, please ask. Enjoy your evening." The manager left the room.

Carla reached for Guyiser's hand. "Who are you? I've been here hundreds of times, but I've never been treated like this."

He took her hand and smiled, "I'm a nobody, but I like all this treatment. Are you hungry?" It was a beautiful room. Guyiser looked around at all the people. He saw ladies with fur coats, men in very expensive suits, and waiters in full dress. This was very exciting to him. The waiter came to take their order. They sat talking and enjoying the food and atmosphere of the room. "Carla, I, uh, understand you worked in public relations. What is that about? What did you do?"

"Well, I did many things. I worked with Customer Relations. I was kind of a go-between; you know what I mean? I made sure the customers were happy. I handled problems. I worked with Advertising. My duties were working on new products and traveling sometimes. I just did what I was told to do. Why do you ask?"

Guyiser sat listening to her, "How would you like to do that job again?"

"Are you kidding? I love that kind of work. I'm only a waitress to pay my rent."

"Would you work at the factory again?"

"In a split second. Mr. Spellman was great to work for."

"Well, he's not there anymore. Do you know Kate?"

"Yes, she was there when I was there. Why?"

"Go see her on Wednesday. I think she has a job for you. Tell her I sent you."

Carla laughed, "And just who are you?"

"Well, I work there."

The evening was great. Guyiser and Carla sat in their VIP box seats yelling at their horses. There were seven different races and they bet on everything. Win, place, and show. In the fifth race, Carla grabbed Guyiser, hugged, and kissed him. "We won. We won!"

In the sixth race, Guyiser grabbed and hugged Carla, "We won again!" Guyiser was having a great time.

Before they knew it, they were standing on the red carpet waiting for their limousine. Cameras were still flashing.

Robert arrived and opened the door for them. "Where to, sir?"

Guyiser looked at Carla and stood thinking. "Back to the lady's house, Robert." As they rode through the city lights, Carla moved closer to Guyiser. He put his arm around her. They kissed for a long time. As they stopped at Carla's house, they kissed and kissed.

"I've had a great time, Guyiser. Do you want to come in? I'll take you home in the morning."

Guyiser sat looking at her. She looked beautiful. He touched her breasts as he kissed her again. He looked into her eyes as he touched her. "Carla, I can't tonight." Guyiser called to Robert. "Robert, do you mind? I'll look for you Wednesday, okay?" He kissed her again.

Robert opened the door and walked Carla to her door. She stood watching the limo drive away.

Guyiser lay in bed thinking about Carla. He wanted to spend the night with her. His mind wandered to Cindy. He wished Carla had been Cindy. That would have been perfect. He missed their lovemaking. Carla would have been good for him tonight, but then he thought about mixing business with pleasure. Maybe he had done the right thing.

Monday morning. The television studio was busy with people setting lights, adjusting mikes, putting furniture in place, and getting ready for the taping. The cameraman zoomed in and out setting his marks. Jeff and Cindy were talking off to the side. The attorney was in the makeup chair getting a touch up. "That's Mr. Montgomery over there. Now remember, be respectful, but firm." Cindy looked him over. He looked like a kind, older, Southern gentleman. She began to relax and lose some of her nervousness. Cindy had worked for a week on her research for her questions. She had practiced on Sandy and felt good about her preparation. She looked over her notes. Jeff put his arm around her, "Are you ready?" Cindy smiled and nodded. "You look great. Let's go." Jeff walked with her to the stage. "You sit here. We are using three cameras today. There will be one on you, one on him, and the other is for you for the beginning and ending of your interview. Okay?" Cindy nodded again. "Now, don't be nervous. He's just a man, okay? Good luck."

Jeff walked to the control booth. The Dean sat watching the monitor. "How is she?"

Jeff sat at the controls looking at the monitors. "She's going to be okay. She's cool, calm, and collected. Look at her." The camera was focusing on Cindy, zooming back and forth.

The Dean leaned into the monitor. "If this interview is good, we may use it as a fill-in." Cindy sat looking at her notes. She looked like a star reporter. She was wearing a blue-gray suit with a pink silk blouse and a lady's tie. The back lighting on her blond hair gave the appearance of a glowing crown.

The assistant brought the attorney over to the set. Cindy stood and extended her hand. "Good morning, sir. I'm Cynthia Taylor."

Mr. Montgomery shook her hand and looked her over. "Well, good morning, little darling. You're a pretty little thing." Cindy's attitude quickly changed.

"I'm not a little thing, sir." She knew at that point that she had lost respect for this man, but she would try to be nice to him. She had been born in Tennessee and was as Southern as he was, but she did not like being called, 'Little darling' or 'little thing.'

They sat down in their chairs. Cindy looked at her notes as the camera zoomed in on her face and then pulled back to a medium shot. Everything was ready. Jeff's voice came on the speaker, "Miss Taylor, are you ready? Everybody set? Quiet and cue the music."

The assistant pointed to Cindy. She smiled into the camera, "Today, we are here with a visiting attorney,

Mr. Montgomery." Cindy turned to him, "How are you, sir?"

The attorney leaned back and smiled.

"Oh, I'm fine, little lady."

Cindy's eyes went cold, "I have a few questions for you, sir. You recently said that black women should have abortions, but white women should no. What did you mean by that?"

The attorney shifted in his chair, "Well, I meant that black women have more babies than white women and are more subject to welfare from the state."

Cindy cut him off, "You also said that black people should not hold high positions in politics. Why not?"

The attorney shifted again, "Did I say that, little lady? What I meant was it would be a long time before we have a black president. If ever. Let me tell you a little story about that."

Cindy cut him off again, "Maybe later, sir. In 1992, you made a statement regarding human rights that I do not understand. You said, and I quote, 'Mexican handicapped people should not come to the United States for treatment.' End of quote. Could you explain that statement to me?"

"Well, that was taken out of context. I also said that Mexican hospitals could take better care of Mexicans, you know what I mean?"

Cindy looked at the camera and back at her notes, "No, sir. I do not know what you mean, but moving on…"

Jeff laughed and clapped his hands, "She's great. I love her." The Dean sat with his arms folded and a smile on his face.

Cindy caught the assistant giving her the 'cut' sign. The music came on low in the background. "Oh, the sound of music tells me we are out of time, sir. But I want to thank you for letting us know what kind of a man you are." She caught herself being rude. "And when you run for office, I am sure we will all vote for you. This is Cynthia Taylor reporting live." The music came up louder and the camera faded.

"Cut!"

Cindy got up and walked off the set. The attorney ran after her, "Wait a minute." Cindy turned around. "You made me look like a fool. All those Negro questions. You made me look prejudice. I like Negroes. They vote, you know. Moreover, black women do go on welfare and handicapped people, what kind of question was that? Young lady, you have a lot to learn about interviewing, but you will never interview me again."

Cindy just smiled at him, "I hope you are right, sir. You have a good day." She walked away.

Jeff ran out of the booth, "Cynthia, wait, wait. Cynthia, that was a wonderful interview. The Dean is still laughing at the attorney's answers. And, that last part; his mike was still on. We got everything he said to you. Wow! What a day!"

Cindy held his hand, "You mean that part about me having a lot to learn?"

"Yes, that was so stupid. He's an idiot. You were sinful! I loved it when you cut him off. How about me taking you to lunch? We'll talk some more. I've got some ideas." Jeff made Cindy happy with his excitement. "I'll meet you at the cafeteria. I want to talk to Dean Winters to see what he says about the interview." Jeff ran back to the booth.

Cindy smiled to herself. She had done her job. She had also experienced some emotions that she had not felt before. Cindy stood outside the building. She looked up to see the sign over the large doors. A big smile came to her. 'Studio-I'. This is what she had dreamed of—working as a reporter at a studio. (Her first interview was to be the first of many.) Cindy walked slowly to the cafeteria. She could not stop thinking of the attorney's anger with her. This made her feel good. Her questions and research made him say foolish things.

Jeff came bursting into the cafeteria doors, "A star is born, everybody!" He ran to Cindy and sat down very excited. "Listen to this." He grabbed Cindy's hands. "Dean Winters has a job for you! It's at a small cable T.V. network. He wants you to finish school and do more interviews just to polish you up. The cable station will give you experience for the major stations. What do you think?"

Cindy took a deep breath and sat back in her chair. "Wow! Are you serious?"

"Yes, I am. And, another thing. I will be your director. This will be wonderful for me to work with you. Cynthia, will you do me a favor? Will you have dinner with my wife and me? I want her to meet you. What do you say?"

Cindy was still thinking about the job offer. She never expected this. Out of all the people in the school, Dean Winters was giving her a chance to work at a television station. Cindy looked at Jeff. He had seen something in her that had made all of this happen. "Of course I will. I'd love to meet her."

Jeff looked at his watch and stood up, "Cynthia, I am sorry about lunch. Time is flying. I have another taping in ten minutes, and I have to get back. You were great today. I'll see you later, okay?"

Cindy sat there still stunned. Finally, she came around and reached for her phone. "Hello, Mother?"

Guyiser sat at his desk laughing and laughing. The sports section of the newspaper had a picture of Carla and him with an article about them. 'Millionaire playboy, Guyiser Blackman goes to the races. Kentucky horse races bring out the best. Mr. Blackman, king of bicycles, says his factory is growing by leaps and bounds. On his arm was the lovely Miss Carla Comings, head of public relations for his firm. It is easy to see that she could spark sales for the company.' "This is great—millionaire playboy, ha, ha, ha.

I wish." Guyiser put the paper down, still laughing. The intercom buzzed. "Hello."

"Mr. Blackman, this is Scott. Good morning, sir.

I saw you in the newspaper. Good picture. Did you win at the track?"

"Yes, we won about ninety dollars."

Scott laughed, "Now you have a million and ninety dollars. Mr. Blackman, we have the catalog ready for your approval."

"Good, Scott. I'll be right over."

Guyiser, Scott, and Tim sat at the drawing table looking over the computer printouts. Guyiser pointed to one of the bikes. "How about putting something about the safety of the children's bike here, you know? Something like 'Blackie's Bikes Give Your Child Safety Starting with Their First Ride.' And I like this, 'Comes in all colors listed: red, blue, silver, gold, yellow, and black.' And, this is Mountain Man, not Mountain Men, okay?"

Guyiser carefully looked over the four-color catalog. "This is ready to go." Then, he looked over the gold series catalog. "This I really like. I like what you did here."

Scott patted Tim on his back. "That was Tim's idea."

"Good job, Tim. This is perfect. Let it go." Finally, he looked at the stationary bike flyer. "Wow!" The flyer was a full page of the gold bike with inserts. "This will get their attention. I'm going to handle this bike myself. Put at the bottom here, 'Address Guyiser Blackman for details'." Guyiser turned to Scott and Tim. "You two surprise me. I didn't know you were this good." He stood up and shook their hands. "You deserve a bonus. Now, my next question is when?"

Scott spoke up, "We'll make the changes now and get everything to the printers today. We should have everything printed and back by Friday. So, Monday morning, you can start sending them out."

Guyiser smiled, "Now that's a good plan. Have about twenty-five hundred of each printed, okay? I'll get a list of accounts from Mrs. Watson. Have a good day, gentlemen."

Guyiser drove into the factory building and stopped. People were working everywhere. Buck was showing his helper about the large cutting machines. Tubes were coming out one end. Sparks were flying as two men were welding and putting the frames together. A man at the paint sprayer was adjusting controls. Another man was at the dryer taking frames out as they dried. Two men were putting wheels and chains on the bicycles. There were two women putting the bikes into boxes, which included a package of handlebars and foot pedals. They would close the boxes and put labels on each box. Someone would then pick up a load of boxes and carry them to shipping to be stored. Guyiser had never seen an assembly like this.

He walked over to Buck, "Buck, this is amazing."

Buck stopped working, "Good morning, Mr. Blackman. This is my helper, John."

"Hi, John."

"We saw your picture in the paper. I showed it to my wife and told her that you were my boss!"

Buck and Guyiser laughed. "So, how is it going, Buck?"

"Well, sir, I think we might use a couple more people. Putting the bikes together takes time. The seats, the front wheels, the back wheels and chain, the chain guard, and we still don't have an inspector. I've been doing that."

Guyiser looked at the men putting the bikes together. "I'll take care of all that. Anything else?"

"No, sir, not for now."

"Okay, Buck. I'll get right on it. See you later."

Running a factory was not an easy job. There were so many things to do. Guyiser sat at his desk going over his notes in front of him. He had talked to Mrs. Watson about a list of accounts both old and new. He had all their addresses ready for mailing. Kate was getting a few more workers for Buck. Shipping was ordering the supplies they needed. It was good to see the factory getting back into production. Guyiser sat thinking about what had to be done. *Hire Carla, the Board meeting, get more business, generate interest in bicycles, call Mr. Gibson, and call Mr. Levine. Call Cindy!* Guyiser looked at her picture. She was also part of his plans. He looked out at the jet. He could see them flying around the world. All this would come later.

Tuesday morning the phone rang. Guyiser and Loaner were having breakfast. He ran in the office to answer it. "Hello."

"...Hey, Mr. Gibson. I was just thinking about you."

"...Oh, I'm fine. And you, sir?"

Mr. Gibson sat in his rocking chair in his shop. "Couldn't be better. I got a big laugh out of the Sunday morning paper. Millionaire playboy. You know, son, that's good for the plant. Publicity like that spreads fast. Who's the girl?"

"...Well, I think she's good for business. Don't lose her. What else is new?"

"...That sounds good."

Guyiser looked through his notes. "And, I have a board meeting set up for next Tuesday like you asked."

"...Yes, sir, everybody. I have a few things to say."

"...Yes, sir. I'll be glad to. Oh, by the way, I picked up a new account for us. It's the Wall-burg chain."

"...I know it's big. You should see the orders."

"...Thank you, sir."

"...Yes, sir. I'll see you next Tuesday."

"...You, too. Take care. Bye, bye."

It was always good to talk with Mr. Gibson. He also had good news. The factory was now his. Everything was now final. Guyiser took a deep breath. Mr. Gibson was happy that Guyiser wanted to make him more a part of the factory. He took a piece of paper and started to draw. A nice design began to form. 'Gibson, Blackman Industry, Home of the American Bicycle.' He leaned back and looked at his drawing. Mr. Gibson would like this. A lot of people didn't know it, but Mr. Gibson had a big ego. But, he was not egoistical. He just liked attention and respect.

The rain clouds were back. There was no rain, just clouds. It was Wednesday morning as Guyiser stood on the patio looking at the gray sky. Loaner jumped up on the railing looking at everything. "What do you want to do today, Loaner?" Loaner jumped down and went to find his tennis ball. Guyiser went to his bedroom and made his bed. He sat at his desk drinking coffee and looking at the picture of the lighthouse. Every time he looked at it, Olsen came to his mind. He would think about the murder of the bondage call girl, the strange pictures, and the gun in a sealed bag. A few things started to come together. The intercom buzzed. "Hello."

"…Good morning, Kate."

"…Oh, good. I'll be right there." Guyiser combed his hair, put on his blazer, and headed for the office. Kate and Carla were laughing and talking as Guyiser walked in. "Hi, Carla. You look nice today. Hi, Kate. You do, too."

"Good morning, sir. We were just talking about you. I didn't know you were a playboy." They all started laughing.

Guyiser looked at Carla, "Well, everything you read is not always totally true. How are you, Carla?"

"Oh, I'm just fine, Mr. Blackman, sir." Carla looked at Kate and winked. "Would you like some coffee, sir?"

Guyiser laughed and waved it off. "Okay, okay, that's enough. Are you two finished talking?"

Kate handed a paper to Guyiser. "Yes, sir. Carla updated her application. Everything is fine."

"Good. Come on, Carla. I'll interview you," Guyiser said with a smile. "I'll show you around."

Carla picked up her coat. "Thanks, Kate. I'll see you later." Carla and Guyiser got in the golf cart and drove off.

He turned to Carla and said, "It's good to see you. I'll take you to my place first, and we can talk."

Carla's eyes were big as she looked at the jet.

She had never been in the hangar before.

"Man, oh man. Is this yours?"

Guyiser smiled, "Well, the newspapers would say 'yes', but it's really the company's plane. Come on, I'll show you around. They took the elevator up to the office. "After you." Carla looked around. "Come in to the living room. Over here is the kitchen. There's one bedroom with its own bathroom over there. My bedroom is in here."

Carla took it all in. "Look at this brass bed and the patio. You must love it here. You even have your own bathroom."

Guyiser slid open the patio door. "Come out here. I like it because I can see everything."

"Oh, this is nice, Guyiser."

"Come on in the office. I want to talk to you."

Carla took his hand. "And, I want to talk to you."

Guyiser sat at his desk while Carla stood looking through the large window down at the jet. "I can't get over all this. Why didn't you tell me about you?" Carla sat down as she looked all around.

Guyiser leaned back in his chair, "Well, there's not much to tell. I told you that I work here and I do. What did you think about the newspaper article?"

Carla laughed, "I thought it was a hilarious dream. I mean that picture of us and what they printed."

He laughed, "I told you. It's a big game. The media always takes things out of context. But, that's why I want to talk to you. How would you like to come to work for me? Like the paper said, in public relations."

Carla stood up and walked back to the window. "When do I start?"

"Right away, if you want the job."

Carla bent over and put her arms around Guyiser's neck. "And, do I get benefits?"

He turned around in his chair. "Yes, you do. But, there's a lot of work to do."

She sat down. "Okay, I'm yours. I'll start in the morning, if that is all right with you, sir."

Guyiser smiled and stood up. "Shake on it?"

Carla shook his hand. "I'll quit my job tonight."

"Thanks, Carla. You will be working out of my office until I can get you an office in the front, okay? Glad to have you aboard. Come on. I'll take you back."

"Guyiser, I want to thank you for this opportunity to work for you. I'll do my best. You can count on me."

He looked into her eyes, "Come on. Let's go." Carla went in the office building to say goodbye to Kate and to let her know that she was now an employee of the company. Soon she left the office and drove away. Guyiser drove around the plant and then back to the office building. He stood talking to Kate, "What do you think about her?"

"Well, she was a good employee for Mr. Spellman. She's more business than she lets on. I think you did the right thing in taking her on. She's a free-spirited person with good ideas. She will be fine." Guyiser was happy to hear this from Kate. He did not have doubts about her, but he did have feelings for her. He did not want to mix his feelings with business.

The gray clouds had moved east and the sun was trying to say hello. Guyiser and Loaner sat on the patio deck. It was a cool Thursday morning. The hot coffee was waking up Guyiser. He could hear noise from the factory machines. Music was playing in the living room. He went to his office and sat looking at all his notes. He looked at the picture of Cindy and the envelope next to it. He had written her a letter telling her about the factory and how much he missed her. Loaner started barking. He ran down the stairs and stood barking. Guyiser went down to check the door. Carla stood outside knocking. He opened the door. "Good morning, Mr. Blackman. My name is Carla. I'm here to work for you."

Guyiser smiled, "Well, good morning, Carla. My name is Blackman, but you can call me Guyiser." They laughed. "Come on in. Loaner, this is Carla. She will be working here, so you be nice to her." Loaner went to Carla and smelled her legs and dress. He sat down, smiled, and barked. Carla petted him.

"He is beautiful."

"Yes, he is and very protective of me, so don't ever hit me." Guyiser looked Carla over, "Come on. You sure do look nice today. I'm pretty casual, so if you want to wear jeans, it's okay with me. There is one thing I do like—a woman who smells good, you know, perfume, and fingernails, nice fingernails. That's the first thing I look for. You have great hands."

Carla looked at her hands, "Do you like this color?" They sat in the office talking. Carla opened her briefcase and took out a pad and pen. "Okay. I'm ready. What do I do?"

Guyiser stood and looked out the large window. "I have a lot of things I want to get done." He picked up a note and handed it to her. "I want this made. It's a stone wall with gold letters on it. It goes by the gates."

Carla looked at the drawing. "It's about ten feet long and eight feet high, right?"

"Right. I'll show you where I want it built."

Carla made notes. "When do you want this done?"

Guyiser smiled, "Yesterday. No, but I would like it finished by next Tuesday morning. We have an important board meeting, and I want it to be the first thing the board members see when they drive through the gates. Call a brick mason today and get this done. You pick out the letters, but make them big. Tell the workers to work all weekend if they have to. Next, our new catalogs come in tomorrow. Get a list of all the accounts and clients with their names and addresses from Mrs. Watson in Accounting. Have Kate hire two part-time people to stuff the envelopes. They can start

Monday morning. You can oversee this project." Carla kept writing. "Oh, next, make a list of phone numbers of accounts for yourself. You can call them and let them know about our Blackie Bicycles and our catalog that is on the way to them. This is PR work for you. Play up Blackman products and yourself. You are not a salesperson. You are head of Public Relations." Guyiser smiled, "Remember the newspaper? Do not take orders.

Have them send in their orders. Then you can follow up with a thank you card. This will be an on-going job for you. Take your time. Oh, Carla, get with the Art Department and have them put together new stationery and envelopes with the new logo, company name of Gibson and Blackman Industry, address, etc.

You approve this, okay? And last for today, I want to put an advertising campaign together for the company. I want something for the distributors. Maybe you and I could be seen together at some event that has press and reporters like we did at the races."

Carla laughed, "Oh, I know, I'll never get over that. Everybody in Bowling Green saw us."

Guyiser laughed, "That was fun, wasn't it? Even Mr. Gibson in Nashville saw it. He thought it was good publicity for the company. Wait until you meet him. He's the reason I'm here. He's a super man. You know, I just had an idea. Have a limo pick up him and Mr. Levine in Nashville and bring them here. They would like that. That's for next Tuesday." Carla wrote down all Guyiser was saying. "But, for now, the stone wall out front is first."

"Yes, sir, Mr. Blackman. I'll do that right now."

Guyiser watched as Carla crossed her legs. "Ah, let's go. I'll show you where the sign goes." They returned to the office. Carla sat behind the desk making phone calls. Guyiser was in the kitchen feeding Loaner.

The intercom buzzed. "Mr. Blackman's office."

"…Oh, hi, Kate. This is Carla. Yes, He has me busy."

"…Sure, hold on. Guyiser, Kate for you."

Guyiser put the intercom on speaker. "Hi, Kate. What's up?"

"Mr. Olsen called and wanted me to have the jet serviced for a trip. I told him he would have to clear it with you. He wants to meet with you tomorrow."

Guyiser turned and looked at the picture on the wall. "Tell him no, but I will meet with him Monday noon here in my office."

"Yes, sir."

"Thanks, Kate." Guyiser turned to Carla. "Would you pick up a good small tape recorder for me? I'm going out. Call me if you need anything."

Guyiser sat in his golf cart at the end of the runway. He watched Loaner run around, smell everything, and play with his ball. Guyiser was thinking about Olsen and their impending meeting. Images of the safe passed through his mind. The warm sun was clearing his mind. Pieces started to come together. *There wasn't a robbery that night. The woman was blackmailing Olsen with the pictures. Olsen had killed her and shot himself. The gun had Olsen's fingerprints on it. That's why it was in a sealed bag. But, why was it in Spellman's safe? What did Spellman have to do with it? And the money. Was Spellman blackmailing Olsen? It was possible.* Guyiser looked at his watch. He had been there for an hour. "Loaner, let's go." He drove back to his office.

Carla was writing on her pad as Guyiser sat in front of his desk. "Okay, Mr. Blackman, here is the way it stands. I have a brick mason who can do the job. I'm meeting with him early in the morning at the gates. He has a selection of heavy gold letters to choose from that work with the stone. He will give me an estimate tomorrow. If you approve, he can start digging tomorrow afternoon."

Guyiser sat listening. "Don't worry about the price. Just get it done. You approve everything."

"Yes, sir. Next, I had a good talk with Mrs. Watson. She remembered me from before. She's such a nice person. Anyway, she is putting together a list of all old customers and new accounts with names, addresses, and phone numbers. Oh, yes. She can make labels with everything on them. That will make mailing a lot faster. Kate has two temps coming in Monday morning."

Guyiser stood up and went to the window. "Call the Art Department and make sure the catalogs will be here tomorrow. And, let me know."

Carla stood and took his hand. "Is something wrong? You don't seem like yourself."

Guyiser squeezed her hand and smiled. "Oh, I'm all right. Just got things on my mind." He walked to his bedroom. "Carla, come here."

Carla stood by the door. "Yes, sir?"

"Did you make the bed?"

"Yes, you said to make myself at home. Would you like us to mess it up again?"

Guyiser looked at her. She looked pretty standing there. "What are you doing this weekend?"

Carla smiled, "Well, I have to see that your sign is built. I'll be around if you need me."

Guyiser walked to her. "Go home. I'll see you tomorrow."

Guyiser lay on the couch watching T.V. He flipped through the channels. An old black and white movie was just ending. It was *Casablanca*. Bogart was saying goodbye to the one he loved. 'Take care of yourself, sweetheart.' As the movie ended, Bogart tipped his hat and walked through the rain to his waiting airplane. Guyiser looked at his watch and went to his desk.

He sat staring at Cindy's picture.

He dialed her number.

"Hello."

"Hello, sweetheart."

"Guyiser! I was sitting here thinking about you, baby. I wanted to hear your voice." Cindy reached for their picture. "Oh, Guyiser, I miss you. Where are you?"

"I'm here at the factory."

"Are you alone?"

"Yes, I'm alone. Why?"

"I thought you would be with your Public Relations person?"

Guyiser laughed. "Oh, that. Well, don't worry about Carla. That was all publicity for the company.

Mr. Gibson thought it would help spread the word, you know?"

"It just looked like she was holding your arm pretty tight."

Guyiser laughed again. "I wish it had been you. I miss you so much. How are you?"

Cindy began to feel better.

"Things are great here. I got lucky. Listen to this. Dean Winters has a job ready for me at a cable station. It will start as soon as I finish school. It could even be sooner. I'm doing interviews now. I'm so excited about what's happening. Jeff Fisher, my director, made tapes of my work. I'll send you one. Oh, Guyiser, I miss you. When are we going to see each other?"

Guyiser thought of what to say. "I don't know, sweetheart. Things are just picking up. Every day there's something new. I love you."

"I love you, too. Mother and Daddy said to tell you hello and to call them."

"I will, sweetheart. Well, I'll let you go now. I just wanted to let you know I'm thinking about you."

"I'm always thinking about you, too, Guyiser. Thanks for calling. Sweet dreams."

"You too, honey. Good night."

"Good night, boyfriend."

Guyiser stood looking at the plane below. *How I wish we could just fly away together.* Then he thought of something he had read, 'The woods are lovely, dark, and deep. But I have promises to keep and miles to walk before I sleep.' Guyiser touched the window. The author of that verse must have been writing it just for him.

Guyiser and Loaner were out taking their morning walk. He felt great. The talk with Cindy, the clear blue sky, the shining sun all helped Guyiser feel like this was going to be a good day. Carla drove up and parked by the hangar. Guyiser saw her and called to Loaner, "Go get Carla, boy. Bring her to me." Loaner ran to the hangar barking.

Carla petted him. "Where is Guyiser?" Loaner barked and ran to Guyiser. Carla went to meet him.

"Boy, you look great."

Carla smiled. "You like this look?

Guyiser looked her over. She wore a pink silk blouse with jeans and high-heeled shoes. Her hair was pulled back in a ponytail. "I sure do."

Carla stepped close to him, "Smell."

"Boy, I like that." He took her hands and looked at her nails. "You are perfect. Come on, I want to show you off." They walked to the hangar and got in the golf cart. "You can use this cart anytime you need it."

Guyiser started to drive off. Tim pulled up and honked his horn. "Good morning, Mr. Blackman. I picked up the catalogs this morning. They are beautiful."

"Good job, Tim. Take them to the office. We'll follow you." Kate had Tim put the catalogs in an empty office. All four stood looking over the catalogs.

"Oh, uh, Miss Comings," Tim took some papers out of a folder, "if you will approve this, I'll take them to the printers now, or we can Xerox them here in the Art Department."

Carla looked over the letterhead. "Looks nice and clean to me. Is this what you wanted?"

She handed the copy to Guyiser. The logo was sharp. Everything was correct. He handed it back to Carla. "Yes, I'm happy with it."

Carla looked it over again. "I like the logo.

Let's make copies here, Tim. It will be faster. You can do the envelopes, too. Get me some copies right away so I can type a letter to our customers."

Tim took some of each catalog and the letterhead. "I'll bring you some finished copies as soon as I Xerox them."

"Thanks, Tim." Guyiser was looking and reading the different catalogs. "Well, Kate and Carla, what do you think?"

Kate was looking at a color catalog. "These are wonderful, all of them. The response should be awesome."

"Carla, what do you think?"

"I believe Kate is right about response. Orders should start pouring in. If I were a customer or distributor, I would carry this line. People won't forget the Blackie Series. And, this gold series is hot! It is a beautiful flyer. Just think, Guyiser. You could walk in a store and there would sit all your bicycles. That would be exciting to me."

Guyiser held up the catalogs and smiled. "They are just what I imagined. I agree with both of you. They are hot looking. Wait until Mr. Gibson sees them. I know I am proud to have my name on them, and I'm sure he will be, too. Let's go show Buck and Shipping. Kate, we may need more sales people in a couple of weeks. Keep that in mind. Oh, and please show these to Mrs. Watson."

Guyiser and Carla sat in the golf cart. "Oh, Guyiser, I met the brick mason this morning on my way in. They will start digging in about an hour and then pour the foundation. He said they would start building in the morning, and they would finish by Sunday. I'll be here to watch. Guyiser, I'm so excited about the catalogs and the wall."

He looked at the catalogs. "Me, too. Oh, one more thing. I would like to have two large flags mounted on the building. Get an American flag and a Kentucky state flag. Put one there and the other one over there. And, have gold lettering that says 'Office' and 'Lobby' put on the double doors."

"Yes, sir. That would look nice. Right now, the building looks a little plain."

They drove into the factory and parked. It was busy. People were going in all directions. Guyiser waved to Buck. "I sure like all this noise, Buck. Oh, this is Miss Carla Comings, our new Public Relations person."

"Glad to meet you, Buck. I've heard that you are the man around here."

"Nice to meet you, ma'am. Yes, ma'am. If you need anything around here, just see me. I saw your picture in the paper. Glad you're with us." Guyiser handed him the catalogs. Buck looked over them. "My, my, these are pretty." Buck laughed. "I guess I'd better put these machines on high speed, don't you think? I'll start ordering more supplies. These are going to sell real good."

"Glad to hear you say that, Buck. Show these catalogs around to everybody. Let them see what we're all doing here. We've got to go now. If you need anything, see Miss Comings or me."

"Nice to meet you, ma'am."

"Nice to meet you, Buck. Please call me Carla. We're all family. Bye."

They sat in the cart.

"You know, Carla, I never thought of it that way. We are a family. That makes me feel good. A family. A family."

Guyiser was sitting in his office looking at the lighthouse. Carla was at the gates watching the workers. Loaner sat in the cart with her. "You are so pretty, Loaner." The workers had finished pouring the foundation and were putting up 'wet' signs. A worker with a shovel walked to Carla. Loaner started to growl. As the worker came closer to Carla, Loaner jumped from the cart and stood by her growling and showing his teeth. Loaner took a step and growled louder. The man froze. Carla saw what was about to happen. "Drop the shovel."

The man dropped it. Loaner stepped back, still growling.

"I'm sorry, ma'am. I didn't mean anything. Wanted to let you know we're finished, and we'll be back in the morning."

Carla called to Loaner, "Loaner, come to me." Loaner hear the word 'me' and jumped back in the cart. Carla took a deep breath. "I'm sorry about that. I'll see you tomorrow." The man turned slowly and walked away, leaving the shovel.

Carla drove back to the hangar. She told Guyiser what had happened. Guyiser leaned back in his chair. "He's a very smart dog. I told him to protect you. That's what he was doing. How did you call him off?"

"Well, I said, 'Loaner, come to me.' And he did."

Guyiser smiled, "He responds to the word 'me'.

He will come to your side. However, NEVER! NEVER! say 'Now' or you will be sorry. NEVER say 'Now' to him, NEVER! Okay, now back to business. Tim brought the Xerox copies for you. What kind of letter are you going to write?"

"Oh, uh, something letting the customers know that the company is known as Gibson, Blackman instead of Spellman. I will talk about the new products and ideas you have. I will invite them to tour the factory."

Guyiser liked that idea, "That sounds good. Say something about bringing their children, too. Maybe we can get some ideas from the kids, you know? What about this? We will have a grand opening on a certain day and have the press here. Maybe we'll even have television coverage. What do you think, Miss Public Relations?"

"I like it. I really like it! Customers, distributors, and the general public all at the same time. I'll start working out the details and let you know what I come up with. But for now, I'll put a letter together to go with the catalogs."

Guyiser stood up. "The desk is yours."

Carla came to Guyiser, putting her arms around his neck. "Guyiser, this is fun working for you."

Guyiser hugged her as they kissed. "Would you like to celebrate tonight?"

She kissed him, "I thought you would never ask. Yes, I would. But now, leave me alone so I can get this letter typed."

Guyiser went to the patio. The warm sun felt like a summer day back on the farm. He stretched out on the lounge sofa and closed his eyes. Faint music came from the living room. Chatter of the typewriter came from the office. Loaner sat watching Carla type. Then, he went to check on Guyiser. Everything was all right. He lay down in the sun beside Guyiser. It was about an hour later when Carla came out on the patio. She pulled up a chair beside Guyiser. "Are you awake?"

Guyiser looked at her, "Kind of."

Carla cleared her throat, "Listen to this:

'Dear Customer,

Gibson, Blackman Industries are proud to announce their grand opening coming soon. Formally Spellman and Company, we offer the same great service that you expect. Now, with a larger staff, we can offer faster and better service. Your friendship is now our pleasure.

Our pledge to you is always an open door policy for comments and ideas. Enclosed is our newest line of bicycles for your consideration. The catalogs show the bicycles, which consist of the strongest frames and the best safety features that only Gibson, Blackman can bring to you. Allow us to fill your stores with the most colorful and fun boys' and girls' bikes. These bicycles are something that all customers will want to buy for their children. Adults also will find the Blackie trademark to be the best built bicycle for their riding pleasure. The bicycles are lightweight and offer miles of fun for all.

Waiting to hear from you,
Miss Carla Comings, Public Relation Department.

In care of Gibson, Blackman Industries,

Bowling Green, Kentucky, Home of the American Bicycle. P.S. See catalog for our address and phone number. Fax your comments and orders for service.' Well, what do you think?" Carla put down the paper.

Guyiser sat up and looked at her. "Miss Comings, I think you are a genius. That letter says it all. It's directed to people we want to reach and to their customers. I wouldn't change a word of it. Make sure that letter goes with every catalog we send out."

Carla sat back in her chair. "Thank you, Guyiser. You make me feel like I'm really helping you."

"You are, Carla. Just look at what you've done in just a few days. I'm really glad you're here. Now, how about dinner and drinks?"

Carla and Guyiser had finished dinner and were drinking and talking. "Well, Mr. Blackman, what's on your mind?"

"Well, let's see—a Monday noon meeting, getting the mailing out, and the board meeting on Tuesday."

Carla reached for his hands. "No, I meant for tonight."

He kissed her hands and looked at her. "You, me, my brass bed? Would you like that?"

"Yes, Mr. Blackman, I would like that."

Carla walked around the big brass bed lighting candles. She was wearing one of Guyiser's dress shirts and her panties. Guyiser was in the living room putting on some nice music. She sat on the bed unbuttoning the shirt as Guyiser stood in the doorway watching her. Guyiser walked to her and stood in front of her. Carla looked up at him and started to unbuckle his belt. Guyiser bent down and kissed her as she continued to unfasten his pants. Guyiser was very excited as Carla began to kiss his body. Her small noises and hands held Guyiser tight.

He reached and took the shirt off her body. His hands squeezed her breasts as she continued to use her hands on Guyiser. She lay back on the bed and held her hands to him. Guyiser stood looking at her. She was beautiful. Her long body moved slowly. Her breasts were large and firm. Her long black hair covered the white pillow. Her blue eyes and pink lips were calling him. Guyiser fell into her outstretched arms. Passionately they kissed. Carla became submissive as Guyiser explored her body. Her breathing became faster as his hand found her wetness. His hand moved faster as they kissed. She reached for him and felt his hard strong body. "Get inside of me, Guyiser, now." He was ready to make love to her. He lay on top of her, still kissing passionately. Her long legs were on his shoulders as he began to move deeper inside of her. Guyiser looked at her as she threw her head from side to side with her eyes closed. "Yes, Yes," was mixed with heavy breathing. "Yes, oh, yes. Faster." Guyiser began to breathe heavily. He could feel his body begin to tighten. Carla screamed out, "Oh, Guyiser, yes, baby. Oh, oh, oh, oh." Guyiser could not hold back any longer and exploded with sensations of his own. His movements began to slow down. He found himself not moving, but Carla was moving slowly. With her eyes still closed, her body finally stopped. Guyiser fell to her side, still breathing heavily.

Carla rolled over to him. "I knew that it would feel like this. You're a wonderful lover." She kissed his neck and cuddled up to him. Guyiser put his arm around her and held her tight. "You know, the first time I saw you, I thought about this. And, it was better than I had imagined." Carla turned his head to her, "I want to tell you something. I know about Cynthia. I know you care about her. Her picture is on your desk and on the walls. I don't want to come between you two. However, what we have is a special thing, and I want to keep it. I love to make love to you. It won't interfere with other things, all right?"

Guyiser looked into her eyes, "Well, I thought about that. Cindy has been a very special person in my life. I'm glad you understand. But, you and I—I want to keep what we have. I think we both want the same things. And making love, well, you make me feel good about what we have. So...."

Carla touched his lips, "So, let's keep it that way." Carla reached down and touched Guyiser.

"You feel good. Are you a morning person?"

Guyiser laughed, "I'm an anytime person."

She laughed, "Me, too." They lay in a spoon position and went to sleep.

Guyiser reached for Carla only to find a note on the pillow. 'Dear Guyiser, I hate to love and run, but I have a lot to do today. See you later, Carla.' Guyiser smiled and fell back on the bed.

Another day had started as Guyiser and Loaner walked the runway. This was Loaner's favorite time. He would chase the ball and bring it back only to chase it again. He would sit and look at Guyiser and learn a new command or trick. Guyiser would just look at Loaner and think about Cindy saying, 'Just call him Loaner.' He had saved Guyiser's life at one time. He still wore the black leather studded collar that Mr. Blackman had given him. As the two were playing, Guyiser saw Carla's car parked at the gates. "Come on, Loaner. Let's go this way."

Carla was talking to a worker as Guyiser walked up, "That would be great. Everything is in the boxes." She turned to Guyiser, "Well, good morning, Mr. Blackman. I had to run all over town to find these flags. Oh, here is the tape recorder you wanted."

Guyiser looked at it. "It's so small."

"Yes, but it's the best made."

"Boy, you have been busy."

"And, I'm not through yet. My girlfriend is having a baby shower tonight. I still have shopping to do."

Guyiser looked at the men working. "That's looking really good."

Carla put her arm around Guyiser's waist.

"I love those polished stones. After the mortar sets, the letters will go on. That's what I want to see." She looked at Guyiser, "I'm still thinking about last night."

Guyiser kissed her cheek. "Me, too. So, you're busy tonight?"

"Yes, she is a good friend, and I want to be there for her. Oh, the workman said they would put the flags up later today." Carla looked at her watch, "I've got so much to do. I've got to go." She smiled, "Is there anything you want?"

Guyiser smiled, "Well, we could, no; you go have a good day."

"Okay, we'll talk later. Bye."

"Bye."

Guyiser sat watching the workers at work.

The wall was bigger than he had thought it would be. It looked better than he had planned, too. Carla had picked out the polished stones in different colors. She had done a good job. A worker walked over to Guyiser. "You like?"

Guyiser nodded, "I like very much."

The man smiled, "The mortar will dry very fast in the sun. We put the flags up next."

Guyiser stood up. "You do good work."

"Thank you, senor. We do our best."

Guyiser walked back to the hangar. He sat at his desk and opened the tape recorder box. The instructions said the recorder could be used for clear, sharp, long-distance recording. It was a remote-controlled unit, and the mike could be placed anywhere. He sat looking around the room. The ceiling fan above the desk looked like a good place. He taped the mike to one of the blades so it could not be seen. Next, he inserted the small tape into the recorder and turned it on. He walked around the room talking. He sat at his desk and talked. He sat in front of his desk and talked. He wanted to be sure that every word would be recorded. Guyiser sat again at his desk and played back what he had said. "Perfect." Every word was clear. He sat looking at the lighthouse. He had a plan of exactly what he wanted to do. He went to the bookcase and took out a dictionary. He sat at the typewriter and slowly began to type.

It was evening as Guyiser leaned back in his chair reading what he had typed. He put the paper in the desk drawer. He lay on his brass bed thinking. A cool breeze came through the patio doors as he fell asleep.

Monday, Monday, be good to me. Guyiser had had a good weekend. He stood in the bathroom singing and shaving. Today several things would come together. The mailing of the catalogs was very important to him. Carla sat at the gates looking at the finished wall with the letters on it. The flags were up, and a slight breeze made them wave. A car drove up behind Carla's. She walked back to see Kate. "Good morning, Kate."

Kate got out and looked around, "Hi. Wow! Look at this. I always thought we should have a greeting sign, but this wall is the perfect thing."

Carla was happy with the finished work. "And, the flags really set off the building, don't you think?" Another car drove up with two girls in it. "We'd better go in."

The letter, catalogs, and envelopes were all set up for the two girls to start stuffing.

Guyiser sat in his cart at the gates. He was proud to see the building and the wall. *Well, let's see, a waterfall would look nice. I'd like some plants and more lighting, and we should blacktop the driveway.* He could see things he wanted to do for the future. He drove to the office and went in. "Good morning, ladies. It's a beautiful day."

Kate and Carla were at the reception desk having coffee. "Good morning, Guyiser."

"Good morning, sir. The girls have already started on the mailing. The wall is beautiful."

"Thanks, Kate. Carla did it. And, how is Miss Comings?"

Carla smiled and handed him a cup of coffee.

"Miss Comings is just fine. I'm going to help the girls, okay? If you need me, just call."

"Oh, Carla, did you order the limo for Mr. Gibson?"

"Yes, sir. I did that on Friday."

"Oh, Kate, is Mrs. Watson in today?"

"She will be in around nine o'clock."

"Good, I'll need you both later, okay? And, when Mr. 'Olsen gets here, let me know."

"Sure will."

Cindy was also busy in Florida. She and Jeff sat in his office. "Tell me more."

She handed her notebook to Jeff, "It is a weekly series. I call it 'The Weaker Sex.' Each week I have as guests three of the most important women in their field. I think this would be something everybody would enjoy. The women could tell how they made it in a man's world.

Up and coming women could see what is ahead for them. Housewives would watch and see themselves as the power they are."

"Cynthia, I love it. I can see it now. Yes, yes. It would work."

"Jeff, turn to page 32." He flipped through the pages. "The same format can apply to a men's series. We would have three up and coming men in business. They would tell what they have to go through to make it." Cindy handed Jeff a newspaper article. "Like this young man. He is trying to make it with his bicycle business. He, a banker, and a young stockbroker all-together on a show could really be exciting for the viewer. 'The beginning of a Man' is what I call this series."

"Yep, we know about the older men, but how the young man makes it could really take off. Cynthia, I had some ideas, but your ideas could be the best of them all for a series. Cable would pay a bundle for this! Besides, I know the major channels would jump on it. Please, please, keep this to yourself. People will steal these ideas. They're always looking for new programming. Let me find a buyer. This could put you in heaven, and me, too. However, it's our secret. I know people who know people. Let me handle this, okay? Trust me; we will go to the top."

Jeff left Cindy full of excitement. She had been working on this idea for a long time. She could see the interviews in her mind--the interviews with all kinds of categories for men and women. She also pictured Guyiser and how he had started in his barn. A big smile came to her face as she thought of him.

The Conflict And The Power

Part 10

I know what I want; I know what I need.
And, I will get it; I will succeed!
I will make a plan and carry it out,
Nothing can stop me, for I can see
I rule life, and life is for me.

Guyiser sat at his desk holding the picture of Cindy. *I sure miss you, girlfriend. I wonder if you ever think about me.* The intercom buzzed. "Hello."

"Mr. Blackman, your appointment is here."

"Thanks, Kate. Send him to the hangar. I'll meet him here."

"Yes, sir."

Guyiser stood at the hangar door as Mr. Olsen drove up and got out. "Mr. Olsen, I'm Guyiser Blackman. Come in."

Mr. Olsen touched the plane as they walked to the elevator. "Kate told me about what you're doing around here."

The elevator doors opened. "Come in and have a seat." Guyiser sat behind his desk. "It's interesting to meet a man like you, Mr. Olsen."

Olsen looked at Guyiser, "You're pretty young to be running this company, aren't you?"

Guyiser smiled, "Mr. Gibson doesn't think so."

"Blackman, I'll come to the point. I have been a backer here for a long time. When I ask for something, I get it. Now, what's with the plane?"

"Mr. Olsen, the plane is grounded by my orders."

"Blackman, I use that plane to get business for this company."

Guyiser laughed. "Yes, I know about your cousin in Ohio. The plane is still grounded. Mr. Olsen, you are here because I have business with you." Guyiser took a big breath and leaned back in his chair. "Let me tell you a story. It's about a rich man, a man that was high up in the city's government at one time. He had a good reputation. He had worked hard to get it. He also had a strange fetish of bondage, of cross-dressing, of being tied up and whipped, and of sex in bondage positions. Do you know what I mean?" Olsen's eyes were like steel. "Anyway, one night, his mistress showed him a lot of pictures of him, strange pictures. She wanted money—lots of money. Does this ring a bell? She said she would expose him to the world. You know, blackmail. Well, guess what he did? You guessed it. He shot her with a .45 caliber handgun. He killed her. That man said a burglar shot them. The police never found the burglar or the gun. What do you think about that? Never found the gun." Guyiser stood up looking at Olsen.

Olsen became very nervous. "What does this have to do with me?"

"You killed her! I have the gun with your fingerprints on it. I also have the strange pictures of you. I'm sure you have seen them. You panicked that night and called Mr. Spellman. He came over and you two made up the story of the burglar. Your bodyguard shot you to make the story look good. Isn't that right? You gave Mr. Spellman the gun, and you put it in a sealed bag. Mr. Spellman took the gun and the pictures and said he would get rid of everything. Am I right so far?"

"Yes, I killed her. She was blackmailing me. Spellman was to get rid of everything."

"Well, guess what? He kept everything. Now, I have everything."

Olsen put his head in his hands. "What do you want?"

Guyiser sat in his chair. "It's not so much what I want; it's what you want. Do you want to go to prison for the rest of your life? You're an old man. That's a long time." Guyiser leaned forward, "Tell you what. I'll give you the gun and all those dirty pictures for all your stock in the company. I think you have about twenty per cent, don't you?"

"That's a lot of money."

"Is it worth your life?" Guyiser reached into his desk and took out a paper. He slid the paper over to Olsen. "Now, this is an agreement signing over your stock and interest in the company to me for the amount of $95,000.00. What do you say?"

Olsen looked over the agreement.

"When do I get the gun and pictures?"

"You will get them as soon as my attorney and your lawyer make it legal, possibly tomorrow."

Olsen reached for his pen. "And the $95,000.00?"

Guyiser laughed, "You're not getting any money, Mr. Olsen, sir. You're getting your life." Guyiser reached for the intercom, "Hi, Kate. Would you and Mrs. Watson meet us in the lobby? We'll be right there."

They all stood in the lobby at the desk. Guyiser pointed, "Just sign there, Mr. Olsen." Olsen signed the paper. "Kate, would you sign here, and Mrs. Watson, would you sign here as witnesses to his signature. In so signing, he is giving me his stock in the company and he will be leaving us." Guyiser smiled, "Thank you, Mr. Olsen, Kate, and Mrs. Watson. Now I'll sign. Kate, make copies of this. Mr. Olsen should have a copy for his attorney." Kate went to make copies.

Olsen turned to Guyiser, "Well, farm boy, you got what you wanted."

"And, Mr. Olsen, you got what you have desired for a long time." Guyiser took out the tape recorder from his blazer. "You can pick up your things Wednesday morning. Kate will have them for you. And another thing, I don't ever want to see you around here again." Kate came back with the copies and handed them to Guyiser. "Thank you, Kate. One is for Mr. Olsen, one for Kate, one for Mrs. Watson, and one for me. File these, Kate." Guyiser turned and walked out the door.

Mr. Olsen folded the paper and looked at Kate. She smiled at him. He turned and walked out of the building. Before Guyiser could drive off, Olsen called to him. "Blackman, how do I know you have the gun? I want to see it."

Guyiser laughed, "Do you think this old farm boy would lie to you? No, sir. I had rather give it to you than the police. You killed a woman. I want this company. It's that simple. You'll get everything as soon as your lawyer makes everything legal. So, you had better call him right away, don't you think? Mr. Olsen, you're a rich man. Maybe you should retire and leave the country. That's what I would do."

"Blackman, I'll get you for this."

Guyiser laughed, "You can pick up your things as soon as I hear from my lawyer that the transfer has been made. So, enjoy your life in Mexico, France, or somewhere. I've got a company to run." Guyiser drove off.

Guyiser sat at his desk talking on the phone.

"...Yes, sir. Everything is all set up. I'm very excited about the meeting. It's going to be a family meeting."

"...Yes, sir, everybody. And, I have a surprise for you. No, not now. I'll tell you when I see you."

"...No, sir. It might rain tonight. I don't want you and Mr. Levine driving in it. The limo will pick you up at nine o'clock in the morning."

"...Yes, sir. I'm looking forward to seeing you, too."

"...Thank you, I will."

Guyiser jumped up and shouted as he hung up the phone. "Yes, yes, I did it!" He stood in front of the safe and opened it. There was all the money. *The money had not been a part of the Olsen situation after all. It was Mr. Spellman's rainy day money. Now it's mine!*

He closed and locked the safe.

Guyiser spent the rest of the day helping with the mailing of the catalog. Tomorrow was going to be a big day for him. Everything—food, flowers, and drinks had been ordered for the meeting. He sat looking at the piles of envelopes that were ready to be sent out. "Kate, let's wait until late tomorrow before we send these out. I want Mr. Gibson to see all this. Girls and ladies, you all have done a great job today. I want to thank you." He stood up and looked at his watch. "Let's quit for today. Oh, Carla, could I see you for a minute?"

Carla and Guyiser sat at the conference table as everyone left. "How are you doing?"

Carla smiled, "My fingers are sore and my back hurts."

Guyiser smiled, "Maybe a good massage is what you need. I give pretty good ones."

She looked at him, "That sounds good. Do you want to do it now?"

He stood and bowed, "My brass bed awaits you, my lady."

Their lovemaking was better than before. Carla lay in Guyiser's arms. "That felt so good. Guyiser, you wore me out."

He rolled her over and straddled her. He put lotion on his hands and started to rub her back. He rubbed her shoulders, arms, fingers, legs, and feet. He rubbed her buttocks as she moaned. She spread her legs as his fingers rubbed her inner thighs. Guyiser became very excited. He leaned down and kissed the cheeks of her buttocks. Carla did not move. She was sound asleep. Guyiser got off the bed and stood looking at her beautiful body. He pulled the sheet over her and kissed her lightly. "Sleep good, baby."

Guyiser went to the other bedroom and crawled in. Carla had worn him out, too. He soon was asleep. It was about midnight when Guyiser woke up. He went to check on Carla. There again, he found a note on the pillow. He lay on the bed reading it. 'Mr. Blackman, you gave me just what I needed. Thank you. Tomorrow is a big day for you, so you need your rest, too. I'll see you in the morning. You can rub me anytime. Carla.' Guyiser smiled, grabbed the pillow, and went back to sleep.

The sky was gray and cloudy that morning in Kentucky. Guyiser stood looking in the mirror. The pinstriped suit made him feel rich. His hair was slicked back, making him look older. He put a white handkerchief in his jacket pocket and smiled at himself. He wanted this day to be perfect. As he sat at his desk looking at his notes, he felt that some money in his pocket might feel good. He opened the safe and took out a bundle of money. *About five hundred would be enough.* As he put the rest back, an envelope fell to the floor. He opened it and began to read. He sat at his desk and finished the letter. It was from Mrs. Spellman to Mr. Spellman. As he read, he smiled big and then broke into laugher. Loaner was watching him. "Well, well, Loaner, I never saw this coming. I never thought of them this way. It's a whole new story. Well, well." Guyiser put the letter back in the safe and smiled as he closed the picture over the safe. "Well, well." He looked at his watch. He gathered his notes and put them in his briefcase. He looked once more at the picture of the lighthouse.

So, that's what happened.

Guyiser and Loaner left the hangar and drove to the gates. The big stone wall with the letters in gold was something that made him proud. The flags on the building stood out. As he walked into the lobby, he saw the impressive display of all the bicycles. A table by the doors had catalogs surrounded by flowers. He could tell that this was Carla's touch. He walked down the hallway looking at the empty offices. Then, he came to the main office, Mr. Gibson's office. He went in, turned on the lights, and sat behind the large beautiful desk. On the center shelf of the large bookcase was a big, pretty portrait of Mrs. Spellman. Guyiser got up and went to her picture. He looked behind it. *No, no safe.* The sound of the front doors made him put the picture back in place. Kate had arrived. Guyiser went to meet her.

"Good morning, Kate. My, you look nice."

"Hello, Mr. Blackman. Oh, so do you. I'm going to make some coffee. Do you want some?"

"No, thanks. Not now. I'll be back later."

Guyiser drove around the plant. The machines made their noises. People were working in the factory. A freight truck was at the loading dock. He drove to the end of the runway and stopped. He sat looking at the large buildings. This was a place he could reform and reflect on his thoughts. His ambition to succeed was now stronger than ever. The stocks from Olsen had given him a sense of power. In a few hours, he would show Mr. Gibson his power.

Carla and Kate were busy in the large conference room. A side table was set up with food. There was coffee, doughnuts, bagels, jelly, and juice. Flowers placed around the room filled the air with their aroma. Carla was putting paper and pencils at each of the seats of the long table as Guyiser walked in. "Ladies, ladies, good morning to all." He looked around the room.

"Everything looks wonderful."

Kate walked over to him. "Everyone should be here in about an hour. I have to go back out front."

Guyiser went to Carla, "You look gorgeous. If I didn't know you, I would want to."

Carla looked to the door and back at Guyiser, "And, I feel wonderful. Thank you, sir."

Kate came running into the room, "They're here."

Guyiser, Kate, and Carla stood outside the doors as the limo driver opened the door for the guests. Guyiser stepped down to meet them. Mr. Gibson gave Guyiser a big hug. "Guyiser, my boy, I love that wall. And, you. You look as handsome as ever."

Guyiser smiled. "And, it's so good to see you, Mr. Levine. I'm glad you could make it."

They shook hands. "Guyiser, it's good to see you again. How have you been?"

"Busy, Mr. Levine. Busy. Oh, let me introduce these ladies. This is Kate from Personnel and this is Carla Comings from Public Relations." Mr. Levine greeted them. "Come on, come in."

Carla opened the door. Mr. Gibson took her hand, "I've seen you in the papers and heard all kinds of good things about you." He kissed her cheek. "And, you, Kate. You're an angel." He kissed her hand. Mr. Gibson and Mr. Levine stood in the lobby looking at the display of gold bicycles. "Very, very impressive, Guyiser."

Kate led them to the main office. Mr. Gibson's name plate was on the door. He stood looking at it and looked at Guyiser. They all went in. Mr. Gibson sat at his large desk. Mr. Levine and Guyiser sat in front of him.

Carla stood beside Guyiser. Kate went to get coffee. Mr. Gibson sat smiling as he rubbed the desk top.

Guyiser smiled as he watched Mr. Gibson. "Well, so much has happened. I don't know where to start. Miss Comings and I have put together a large project for the company. In fact, the wall and sign out front were her ideas. But, the catalog has been something that will start generating business. Carla, would you mind?" Carla handed each of them catalogs and the flyer with the letter attached. Mr. Gibson sat smiling as he read the letter and looked at the catalogs.

Mr. Levine read the catalogs. "I'll take a dozen of everything."

Guyiser laughed, "Just fax your order in, sir."

Mr. Gibson looked at Guyiser.

"Do you really have all these products? These are beautiful catalogs."

"Yes, sir. I'll show you the plant later. We put a lot of time and thought into this project. The letter Carla wrote says it all. The mailing will go out today. I have great expectations for these catalogs. They will make things happen."

Mr. Levine turned to Mr. Gibson, "Well, Earl, from a business and legal point of view, this could be a deep gold mine." He next turned to Guyiser, "What's your follow up?"

Carla handed Guyiser his notes. "We have an advertising and promotional campaign set up. We plan to advertise in newspapers, magazines, and even on T.V. We want to reach both stores and distributors, especially distributors. That's where the money is. We have the product. Now, 'I have to sell it' as Mr. Gibson taught me."

Everyone was in the conference room. The two backers were there along with Buck, Tom Maker, Scott, Tim, Kate, and Mrs. Watson. Guyiser stood and got their attention. "I want to thank everyone for being here. Mr. Gibson has a few words for us."

"Good morning, everyone. I'll keep this short. We have a great factory here thanks to everyone here today. As you know, Mr. Spellman started with a couple of bicycles. Today, we have nine different types of bicycles and the number is growing under the management of the president of the company, Mr. Blackman. He will make us all prosper. I want to thank you all for your hard work. Thank you, and my office or Guyiser's is always open to you. Everyone enjoy your day." Mr. Gibson sat down.

Guyiser stood up, "We all have work ahead of us, and we will prevail. So, by the end of the year, we can share in good bonuses to reward our hard work.

But for now, to work and have a good day." Everyone applauded and went back to their jobs.

Guyiser stood at the end of the long table. "Mr. Anderson and Mr. Goldman, this is the first time I've had the pleasure of meeting with you. Thank you for being here today. You may be wondering about Mr. Olsen. Mr. Olsen has resigned from the company. He is no longer a backer with us." Guyiser looked at Mr. Levine and Mr. Gibson.

"I have bought his stock. As it stands, Mr. Gibson is CEO and the owner. Mrs. Spellman and Mr. Gibson control the company. Gentlemen, today is like the first day of a new business. We must be patient with our growth. The company is financially solid, and our growth can only go up. So, I just wanted to bring you up to date on everything. Are there any questions or comments?"

Mr. Anderson spoke, "I think I can speak for both of us, it is good to have you and Mr. Gibson in charge. The company has been idle for a long time. It is good to see it moving again."

"Thank you, Mr. Anderson and Mr. Goldman. Mr. Gibson, do you have anything to say?"

"No, Guyiser, I think you have said it all."

"Well, gentlemen, that's all. Thank you." Everyone shook hands, happy with the meeting.

Mr. Gibson, Mr. Levine, and Guyiser sat talking. "Guyiser, I can't tell you how much I'm impressed with you. You have really grown and matured into quite a young man. It seems like yesterday you were in my alley picking through old bicycles for parts. And, look at you now. But there's something about you getting the stock from Olsen. How? What's that all about?"

Guyiser smiled and handed a paper to Mr. Levine. "I'll tell you about that later. Mr. Levine, can you handle a stock transfer today? It's very important to me. I have an appointment set up for you to meet with Olsen's lawyer today at two o'clock."

Mr. Levine read the agreement. "Only $95,000.00? This is worth eight times that. Sure, Guyiser, I'll take care of this today. As your attorney, I'll handle everything."

Guyiser happily shook his hand. "I knew I could count on you, sir. I'm sure glad you're on my side. The limo can take you anytime."

Mr. Levine looked at his watch, "Well, it's one thirty now. I'll go now and take care of this. Earl, I should be back in a couple of hours. Then we can head back to Nashville. See you later."

Mr. Gibson sat behind the large desk that was now his. Guyiser sat in front of him. "Now, Guyiser, how did you get Olsen's stock?"

"Well, Mr. Gibson, I got lucky. I had something he wanted, and he had something I wanted. It's kind of like you and Mr. Spellman. I know about you and Mrs. Spellman. I know that you still love her. I know she still loves you. Sir, I always wondered why you and Mr. Spellman didn't stay in business together. I wondered what happened to your friendship and why you went your way and he went his. Then I found out about your affair with Mrs. Spellman. She is a wonderful woman.

She cared for both of you, but she had to let her love for you go. And, as a gentleman, you stepped aside. I respect you for that, sir. Now, Mr. Spellman is dying, and you are the one she turns to. That's why you bought this factory—to be together. You have waited a long time for her."

Mr. Gibson sat looking at the portrait of Mrs. Spellman. "Guyiser, my son. You are right about everything. We have been in love with each other over thirty some years. I've always been sorry about my friendship with Jessie but never about my love for her." Mr. Gibson went to her portrait and touched it. Guyiser stood beside him.

"She is a great lady."

Guyiser and Mr. Gibson rode around the plant. Guyiser wanted to show him everything. They rode slowly through the large buildings as Guyiser pointed out all the work going on. Freight trucks were at the loading dock. Stacks of inventory were building up again. Guyiser drove to the end of the runway and stopped. "This is where I like to come and think."

"You're doing a great job, Guyiser. I'm really proud of you, but you have changed so much. Don't lose your real self, you know?"

Guyiser smiled, "Sir, I am enjoying this so much. I love the attention I get. I love the ride, but I wish you were here to enjoy the ride with me."

"Son, it's a ride for me to see you grow. I want to see you go higher and higher. Let's head back, okay? I want to thank you for the limousine. That meant a lot to me. I am also very impressed with my name on the office door."

The limousine was waiting for them. Mr. Levine was talking to Guyiser as Mr. Gibson said goodbye to Mrs. Watson, Kate, and Carla. "Here are your copies of the transfer. The stock agreement was very simple. It's all yours now. Mr. Olsen had signed over everything to you yesterday. But, I still can't understand why he would do that. I would have paid him five times that amount."

Guyiser just smiled at him, "Just send me your bill."

Guyiser sat in his office reading all the papers Mr. Levine had given him. He leaned back in his chair. The stock was worth $500,000.00. That is what Olsen had given for his life. Guyiser wondered if he had done the right thing. *A woman's life for $500,000.00. Mr. Gibson was right.* He had changed. Power and control had taken over him.

There was a cloud over Guyiser's office, but in Florida, it was a beautiful sunny day. Cindy and Jeff sat talking at a hotdog stand on the beach. Jeff handed Cindy a tape. "Everybody is crazy about you and the kids. This could be your best tape ever."

Cindy laughed, "I loved those kids and the things they said. Wow! Maybe I should work with kids all the time."

Jeff shook his head, "No, no, no. That just shows how diverse you are. I think we should stick with your young men and young women series. Let's tape one of each to show the networks the format, you, and the direction of the show."

"I see, fifteen minutes on one and fifteen minutes on the other. That will give the network a thirty minute show."

"And, a weekly show. That's what they are looking for. Trust me, I know."

Cindy sat taking it all in. "Okay, where do we start?"

Jeff took a bite of his hotdog and thought, "You research who you want to start. Make a list of names. I'll have my staff contact your people and set up dates for the show. We'll do the ladies in the morning and the men in the afternoon. How's that sound to you? Keep your questions tight, you know what I mean? Your time frame is about six to seven minutes for each guest. Then I can edit a great show. Cynthia, this will be your most important show. It's your first, so make it fun and interesting."

Cindy finished her hotdog and drink. "You know, Jeff, I really enjoyed working with the kids. Maybe I...."

Jeff cut her off. "Forget about it. That's history. Let's move on, all right? I just want the best for you. Trust me, okay? Let's go."

Guyiser, Kate, and Carla sat in the break room having coffee. "So, what do you think, Kate?"

"Well, the mailing went out. I would say that in about a week or so you should start seeing some results from the catalogs."

Guyiser looked at his cup, "That's about what I thought. Carla, I want you to get started on some advertising. Write some newspaper ads and some magazine ads. I want to see 'Blackie Bicycles' everywhere. You have good ideas; put them to work. I'm going away for a while. I need a break. Kate, you and Carla work together. You two are in charge. Carla, get with the Art Department and have them help you, okay? And, Kate, there's a package for Olsen. He'll be picking it up soon." Guyiser left.

Kate turned to Carla, "Boy, is he uptight."

Carla finished her coffee, "It seems that way. I know he has had something on his mind all week. Maybe a few days off will do him good. I'm going to get busy. I'll see you later."

Guyiser packed a few things, and he and Loaner headed home. Carla met him at the gates. "Guyiser, I'll miss you. Are you all right?"

He looked at her and nodded. "I'm all right. I just haven't been myself lately. The factory, the catalogs, and the meeting have all been too much. I just need to clear my head, and my farm sounds good right now."

Carla leaned in the truck and kissed him.

"I understand. When you get back, I'll be here for you. Drive carefully. Bye."

"Thanks, Carla. Bye."

The farmhouse looked great to him as he unlocked the front gate. Loaner took off running like crazy. He, too, knew he was home. Guyiser stood looking at the weeds that had grown up. The door squeaked as he opened it. The house had a musty smell to it. He stood looking around. Everything was in place. It was far from the hangar with its big apartment and jet, but this was his home sweet home.

Next, Guyiser walked to the barn and pulled the big door open. There stood six bicycles. A small field mouse ran across the floor. Guyiser smiled and went to his desk. He sat looking around the room.

For some reason, it looked smaller. He took the small leather pouch off the nail and looked at it. He remembered putting money and checks in it and showing it to Mr. Gibson. *Is this enough, Mr. Gibson? Mr. Gibson smiled and said, 'Yes, Guyiser, that's enough.'*

Guyiser was hungry. He knew right where to go. "Come on, Loaner. Let's go." The Taylor house was a sight for sore eyes. Guyiser ran up the steps and knocked on the door.

Mrs. Taylor opened it and put her hands to her face. "Guyiser, you have come home!" With hugs and kisses, Guyiser went in. "My, my, let me look at you. You've lost weight. Come in the kitchen. I'll fix you something. It's so good to see you." He felt right at home, as he sat eating a ham sandwich while Mrs. Taylor poured more milk. "I'm so glad to see you, Guyiser. We have really missed you. Mr. Taylor will be so glad to see you. Have you talked to Cindy lately?"

"Yes, ma'am, but not often enough. Guess she's busy like me."

"Well, she sent us a tape of her. You'll have to see it later. Mr. Taylor should be home soon. Guyiser, would you spend the night with us tonight?"

He was surprised. "You know, Mrs. Taylor, I'd like that."

"Good, honey. You can sleep in Cindy's room. She would like that."

It was evening as Mr. Taylor and Guyiser sat in the living room having a game of chess. Mrs. Taylor sat sewing a button on Guyiser's shirt. Mr. Taylor studied his next move. He moved his queen. Guyiser moved his king. Mr. Taylor again studied his next move. He moved his queen again. Guyiser quickly moved a piece. His king was exposed. Mr. Taylor put Guyiser's piece back in place. "Guyiser, you can't do that. Guyiser, son, take your time.

You're moving too fast. You'll lose." Guyiser looked at Mr. Taylor. He heard Mr. Taylor's voice, 'You'll lose.'

It was though a ton of bricks had hit Guyiser. Mr. Taylor's voice echoed in his head. 'You're moving too fast. Take your time.' Guyiser reached for Mr. Taylor's hand. "You're right. That's my problem. I've been moving too fast." He leaned back in his chair. "And, I don't want to lose. Thank you, Mr. Taylor." Guyiser stood up. "Excuse me, please. I'm going to take a walk."

The night air was cool. The sky was clear, and the road was lit by the moon. *Mr. Taylor has opened my eyes. The factory has changed me. 'Moving too fast. You'll lose.'*

kept going through his head. He found himself walking fast and stopped. *Slow down, Guyiser, slow down.* He looked up to the sky, "Help me, Pa." He closed his eyes, "Help me, Pa." He looked down. There was a beer can. Guyiser kicked the can. He took a few steps and kicked it again. Again, he took a few steps and kicked it again. Again and again, this went on. Guyiser found himself enjoying kicking the can. It had slowed him down. As he kicked the can, he thought about his bike shop in the barn. His life there had been slow and comfortable. He kicked the can again. The factory should be the same way. He stopped and looked to the sky. "Thanks, Pa. I see now." One last kick and the can went in the ditch. He turned and walked slowly back to the house.

Mrs. Taylor knocked on the door. "Guyiser, Guyiser, breakfast is ready."

Guyiser turned over and looked at the clock. "Yes, ma'am. Be right there." He had slept for ten hours. Guyiser sat at the kitchen table. Mrs. Taylor kept putting food in front of him as he ate.

"You looked so tired last night. I thought you should sleep late this morning."

"Mrs. Taylor, I feel great this morning. Cindy's bed felt so good. You know, she looked so pretty on that tape."

"Yes, she did, Guyiser, and she's so happy."

Guyiser finished his breakfast, "Mrs. Taylor, that's a perfect way to start the day. Now, I'm going back to my place and work it off. Thank you, ma'am."

Guyiser walked up and down his driveway swinging the scythe and cutting down weeds. He went to the barn and cut the high weeds around the front and sides. He saw Loaner running in the tall grass in the field. He put the scythe down and rubbed his shoulders. He shouted for Loaner. Loaner came running to him. "Look at you. You've got stuff in your fur." Guyiser picked and brushed him off. "Let's go into town. What do you say?" Loaner barked and ran to the truck. Guyiser drove to the gate as a man drove by on his tractor. Guyiser tooted his horn. The man stopped. Guyiser ran to him. "Howdy, do you do grass cutting?"

"Yep."

"Well, I got work for you."

The man climbed down. "Your name Blackman?"

"Yes, it is."

Cindy sat on the beach under a tall palm tree. Her list of guests was ready. Her questions were ready. She made notes for Jeff. It was just a matter of time before all of her talent would be brought together. She looked at all of her notes and dialed her phone. "Hi, Jeff. Cynthia. What's going on?"

"...Wow! So soon? Well, I have it all together. When can we get together?"

"...Sounds great. I'll see you then. Bye bye." She dialed the phone again. "Sandy, Cindy. Meet me at Studio B in about an hour."

"...Yes, I just talked to him. Maybe he has news for me. Okay, see you there. Bye."

Jeff sat in his office talking on the phone and watching tapes on the monitor. "Okay, Jack. See you in an hour."

"Yes, she will be here."

"Okay. Bye."

Cindy was very excited about everything. The ocean air, the blue sky, and her outlook on life were as bright as the sun as she drove back to campus. Sandy sat on a bench outside the studio. Cindy parked and ran to her. "Hi, babe. How was the beach?"

Cindy sat down and handed her a notepad. "Wonderful. It really cleared my head. Look at my list."

Sandy looked at all the pages. She laughed and hugged Cindy. "You did it. You pulled it all together. Oh, Cindy, this is great!"

Cindy smiled and took the notepad. "Let's go in."

They knocked on the office door and went in.

"Hi, Jeff. This is my friend, Sandy. She's the one I told you about."

"Hi, Sandy. Heard good things about you. Have a seat, ladies."

Cindy took out her notepad and handed it to Jeff. "Well, here it is--my first show. Sandy and I worked out some camera angles you might like."

Jeff studied the notepad, turning pages. "Tell me about yourself, Sandy."

"Well, I have been behind the camera for about two years, working freelance with film and video. I came to this school to learn more about television."

Cindy patted her hand. "And, I would like Sandy to be my camera person. I would also like you to consider her for the show."

Jeff laughed at one of the notes, "This is sexy. I love it. Keep this for sure." Jeff turned to Sandy, "Sandy, I would love to work with you. Anything to make Miss Taylor happy. Cynthia, your list of women and men looks good. I'll get on this right away and get some dates set up. Okay, now for some news. Last week, I met a man named Jack Weber. He is in programming at a small cable network and liked your tape." A knock on the door interrupted Jeff. A young well-dressed man looked in.

"Jeff, hi. Am I late?"

"No, come on in. This is Miss Taylor and Sandy. Have a seat. I was just saying that you liked Cynthia's tape."

Jack sat looking at the two girls. He eyes scanned their bodies. "Yes, I did. Miss Taylor, I like what I see. And the series is nice, too."

He kept staring through Cindy.

"Jeff, I'm running a little late on everything today." He turned to Cindy, "However, if you would have lunch with me, we could talk about things."

Cindy looked at Jeff and Sandy, "Okay, we'll talk."

"Good. Jeff, I'll get back with you." Jack stood up. "Miss Taylor, shall we?"

Cindy looked at Sandy. "I'll be right out. Would you wait outside for me?"

Jeff stood up and went to the door. "I'll walk you out, Jack."

Sandy turned to Cindy, "I don't like him. Something about him doesn't sit right."

"I feel that way, too. But, I'll see what he says. I'll see you later."

Cindy and Jack sat in the studio cafeteria. She opened her briefcase, moved some papers, and closed it. "Cynthia, may I call you Cynthia?"

"Sure."

"Cynthia, I can really help you. My network will pay you very well for your series. You are a very attractive lady."

Cindy leaned back in her chair and put her arms behind her. Her breasts stood out large and firm. Jack's eyes went right to them. Cindy smiled, "Tell me more, Mr. Weber."

"Well, I think we should have dinner tonight and talk. We should spend some time together. Maybe drinks at my place. We could get to know each other, know what I mean? I can get your career started, you know? Especially if you're nice to me."

Cindy stood up and smiled, "Goodbye, Mr. Weber."

He sat and watched her walk away.

Cindy was in Jeff's office. Tears came to her eyes. "Listen to this." Cindy turned on her tape recorder. Jeff listened to the tape. At the end, he turned it off and went to Cindy. He put his arms around her as she cried.

"Oh, Cynthia, I'm so sorry. I didn't know. But, believe me. I'll get him for this. Someway, I'll get him."

Jeff patted her back. "And, I have an idea how. Don't worry about this. Just go home. Let it go, okay? I'll keep this tape." Jeff smiled at Cindy. "It will be okay, trust me." Cindy left the office. Jeff looked at the tape and smiled, "That bastard. He doesn't know what he's in for."

Guyiser spent the next few days working on the farm. He chopped wood, painted the house, and cleaned the barn. Mr. Jones had finished most of the fields. Guyiser felt rested and ready to go back to the factory. Both he and Loaner had gained weight and strength. They sat in the truck at the gate. Guyiser looked at the house, barn, and fields. "Well, Loaner, are you ready to go to Kentucky?" Loaner moaned and barked. Guyiser laughed, "We'll be back."

As Guyiser drove through Nashville, he thought of Mr. Gibson. The pressure was off from the Olsen situation, the catalogs, and the meeting, but now he had some more work to do.

The big buildings did not look as intimidating as he stopped at the big gates. In fact, they looked friendly. The large wall, the flying flags, and the cars parked in the parking lot all said 'Welcome back, Guyiser.' A big smile was on his face as he walked into the office building. Kate and Carla came to meet him. "Good morning, ladies." He hugged them both.

"Mr. Blackman, you look great. We missed you."

Carla touched his arms. "You have been working out."

Kate looked him over, "And, you have gained weight. You look taller."

"Kate, I feel like a new man. How are things around here?"

Carla took his hand. "Wait until you see. I've got ads ready for you. I know you'll just love them."

Kate was excited, too. "You will be pleased to know that already the mailing has brought in orders.

And, this is only the first week."

Guyiser raised his hands. "Thank you, God. Kate, let me know about all the new orders that come in, okay? Carla, follow them up with a thank you and a nice letter from the company. Carla, bring your ads. I want to see them."

Guyiser sat at his desk. Carla had left notes for him. He turned and looked out the window at the jet. Carla came in the hangar. Loaner ran to meet her. She and Loaner took the elevator and walked in to the office. "Guyiser, you look great." They hugged and kissed.

"Carla, I feel great. Let's see your ads." One by one, Carla handed him the copies.

"Scott and Tim were great to work with. They had lots of ideas. These are the ones I thought were the best."

Guyiser studied one that read; 'Feel like a million' It showed the Blackie 'Gold Series' with a picture of a man sitting on the gold exercise bike. Carla handed him another ad. It was a picture of an elephant standing up with one foot on a bicycle. It read, 'Strongest bike made. The Mountain Man by Blackie, on and off road comfort.' She handed him the last one. "This is my choice for the girls' bike." A beautiful girl wearing a tight body suit was standing by the bicycle. It read, 'Lady Thriller for her pleasure. Slim down, Look great, and enjoy the ride. By Blackie'

"Well, sir. What do you think?"

Guyiser stood up and spread them out on the desk. A big smile crossed his face. "The elephant, how did you get this?"

Carla laughed, "We had so much fun. Scott and I went to the circus. We took the Mountain Man bike and paid a man a hundred dollars to have his elephant stand on it. Scott took the picture. It was a fun day."

Guyiser laughed. "Wish I had been there. And the others?"

"We shot those pictures here at the factory."

Guyiser touched each of the ads. "These are the most creative ads I've ever seen. Get these in every catalog, full page, and let's start with magazines."

Carla handed him several magazine advertising quotes. "I've already started that. Here are their prices for the ads. These are national magazines. They are all over the USA."

Guyiser looked at the figures. "Excellent. Let's run a full page in all of these for four months and again about two months before Christmas. Carla, I know you're good at some things, but these are outstanding. Have Scott get these to the printers now. I love them."

She gathered all the artwork and papers. "Yes, sir. I'll do that right now. And, do you want me to come back?"

Guyiser smiled, "Let's have dinner tonight."

A simple dinner was all Guyiser and Carla needed. They sat in the truck at the hangar kissing and fondling each other in passion. Loaner was in the back of the truck watching them. "Oh, Guyiser, let's go to your brass bed. I want you so much." They stood by the truck kissing more. A shot rang out hitting the truck door. Guyiser grabbed Carla.

"Get down!" In the moonlight, Guyiser could see a car parked by the roadside. Another shot rang out hitting the fender of the truck where they lay. Guyiser called to Loaner and pointed to the car. "Now, Loaner, Now!" Loaner started running and barking. His speed increased as he came to the car.

The man was leaning on the hood of his car with a rifle. He saw Loaner getting closer as he ran and barked. The man got in his car but not soon enough. Loaner jumped in the car and attacked the man. The man threw his arm up as Loaner's big teeth closed down. The man screamed and yelled as Loaner bit him. Blood rushed from his arm as he tried to beat and hit Loaner. Loaner only bit in deeper. The man made a fist with his free hand and hit Loaner. Loaner released his arm and caught his fist with his big teeth. His strong jaws clamped down on the man's hand. Again, the man cried out in pain.

As Loaner bit the man's fist, he shook his head violently. Blood flowed from Loaner's mouth.

Guyiser and Carla reached the car and heard the man screaming for help. Guyiser ran to the car and opened the door. Loaner had pinned the man with his weight and was biting and growling. Guyiser called Loaner off. "Me, Loaner, me, me!" Loaner released the man's hand and stood growling at him. "Me, boy, me." Loaner turned and jumped off the man and stood by Guyiser. Guyiser pulled the man out of the car and to the ground. He took off his belt, wrapped it around the man's arm to stop the bleeding as Carla took the man's belt, and put it around his other arm. He was still screaming in pain. Guyiser grabbed the man's head. "Shut up! Shut up! Why did you try to kill us?"

The man cried, "Just you, senor, just you."

Guyiser shook his head, "Why?"

"Mr. Olsen, senor. He paid me." The man continued to cry as Guyiser looked at him.

"Can you drive the car?"

"Maybe, senor, sí."

Guyiser helped him up and into the car. He reached in and took the rifle. "You drive to the hospital now before you bleed to death. Get out of here, now!" They watched the car speed away. Guyiser knelt down to look at Loaner. "Are you all right, boy? Come on, I'll get you cleaned up."

They walked back to the hangar. Carla stopped at the door. "Guyiser, why? Why did Olsen want you dead?"

Guyiser looked at her, "Are you all right?"

Carla nodded, "Yes, but...."

Guyiser cut her off. "I think you should go home. We'll talk in the morning."

"But, Guyiser...."

"I said we'll talk in the morning!" Carla understood his tone of voice. She walked to her car and drove away.

It was early morning. Guyiser sat at his desk. Loaner was playing with his ball in the hangar below. Guyiser rolled his Rolodex and found the name Olsen. He dialed the number. A woman's voice answered. "Hello. This is Guyiser Blackman. Could I speak to Mr. Olsen, please?"

"I'm sorry, sir. Mr. Olsen has moved out of the country."

"Well, is there a number where I could reach him? It's very important."

"No, sir. In fact, today I am closing the office for good. But, sometime next week, he will be picking up his last messages. Would you like to leave a message?"

Guyiser looked at the picture over the safe. "Yes, please write this down: Guyiser Blackman says hello and I'm alive, healthy, and looking forward to seeing him. His man did a sloppy job. Would you read that back to me?" The woman read it word for word. "Thank you, he's concerned about my health. Please be sure he gets the message, okay? Thank you very much. Goodbye."

Guyiser went to the safe and took out the tape and recorder. He sat playing it repeatedly. He had a plan.

He leaned back and smiled, "I'll get you for this, you son of a bitch. I'll get you back; you should have just walked away. You strange son of a bitch."

Carla sat across from Guyiser in his office. "Well, tell me about last night. I could have been killed. You owe me an explanation."

Guyiser stood up looking at the jet below. "You're right, Carla. I do owe you an explanation. He walked around the office. "What I'm going to tell you must never leave this room. Did you know about Olsen being involved in a murder years ago? Well, I heard from someone that it was his bodyguard who shot his bondage mistress but it was Olsen. He did it because she was blackmailing him. I confronted Olsen with this and told him the police should know about what he had done. He became very angry with me and told me I had no proof but I do. He was wrong. I do. He is a very paranoiac type man and very dangerous. I think with me out of the way, he would feel safe. Carla, I'm sorry you were there last night. I'm just glad you were not hurt."

Carla went to Guyiser.

"Guyiser, next time you could be killed."

He kissed her, "I don't think there will be a next time. He knows I got his message and besides, he has moved out of the country. I'll be all right now. Now, how are those ads coming along?"

The day went by slowly. Rain clouds came again and covered the sky. Guyiser sat on the patio playing the tape. The intercom buzzed. He went in his office and answered it, "Yes?"

"Mr. Blackman, you have a call on line two."

"Thanks, Kate."

"Hello."

"Mr. Guyiser Blackman?"

"Yes."

"This is Lisa Blue. I work for the producer of the Cynthia Taylor Show. I am calling to see if you are interested in being interviewed on Miss Taylor's show."

Guyiser smiled and looked at Cindy's picture. "The Cynthia Taylor Show, I would be honored."

"Thank you, sir. We have a date set for you for the eighth at one in the afternoon. Is that good for you, sir?"

"That would be fine."

"Great. The address is 17240 A Street, Tampa, Florida. The studio is one block from the hotel where we will reserve a suite for you. Are there any questions, sir?"

"Miss Taylor will be there, right?"

"Oh yes, sir. She is looking forward to seeing you."

"Well, tell her I'm looking forward to seeing her, too."

"I will, sir. And, thank you. Have a good day, sir."

Guyiser leaned back in his chair holding the picture. "Well, well. The Cynthia Taylor Show. That's what you wanted, isn't it, girlfriend?" He circled the eighth on his calendar and counted the days. He put the picture back and picked up the tape recorder. He pressed the intercom to the Art Department. "Scott, how are the ads coming along?"

"...Great."

"...Yes, uh, do you know how to edit an audio tape?"

"...Good. Bring your recorder over to my office and show me."

"...Yes, now, if you don't mind."

Guyiser and Scott sat in the office. Scott put a blank tape in his recorder. "Okay, let's talk about something." Scott pressed the Record button. "Mr. Blackman, the ads are being printed now."

"That's great, Scott. You have done a great job and I owe you a lot of money. How did you do it so fast?"

"Well, I had help. Tim did some of the work, too. We worked all night on this job."

Guyiser laughed. "You mean you did it.

Tim only helped with the job?" He stopped the recorder. "That's enough. Now show me how you edit this tape."

Scott played the tape back and forth, pushing the buttons, and showing Guyiser as they went along. Soon he finished some of the tape. "Now, listen to this." Scott pressed Play, 'Mr. Blackman, how did you do it? The ads you have done so fast are being printed now. A lot of money helped you with this job. Mr. Blackman, that's great.' Scott pressed Stop and laughed. "See how easy that was. Play, Record, Stop, Rewind. Just use two recorders. It's easy. It may take some time to get what you want and to get the timing just right, but you can do it."

Guyiser leaned back, "Yes, I can, Scott.

Thanks for showing me."

Scott looked at his watch. "Well, I'm off. You keep my recorder for as long as you need it. And, here are some blank tapes. Have fun."

"Oh, I will, Scott. We'll see you later. Good night."

The intercom buzzed. "Yes?"

"Hi, Guyiser. Are you busy?"

"Oh hi, Carla. A little."

"Do you want to get together tonight?"

"No, sweetheart. I do have some things that might take me a while to do. Maybe tomorrow, if you want to."

"Okay, tomorrow. I'll see you then. Good night."

Guyiser woke up on the couch. Loaner stood licking Guyiser's hand. He had been working all night on the tape. "You hungry, boy? Okay, okay. I am, too." He opened a can of dog food and mixed it with some dry food in a large bowl. He watched Loaner enjoy his breakfast. The phone rang. Guyiser walked to his desk to answer it. "Hello."

"Guyiser"

"Good morning. Mr. Gibson. You're up early."

"Guyiser, I have some bad news. Mr. Spellman died last night."

Guyiser sat down. "Oh, Mr. Gibson, I'm so sorry. How is Mrs. Spellman?"

"She's taking it pretty hard. She knew it was coming, but now it has happened."

"How can I help, Mr. Gibson? I want to do something."

"Maybe later, Guyiser. James is coming to get me now. I will be there in a few hours."

"Well, how are you, sir?"

"I'm very sad, Guyiser. Can you meet me at the Spellman's place? I would like that."

"Yes, sir. I'll head over there right away."

"Thank you, Guyiser. I'll see you there. Bye."

Guyiser called the office and told Kate the news. "Kate, would you let everyone know that I'll be at the Spellman's house? I'll call you later, okay?" He put everything in the safe and got dressed.

Jesse Spellman had lived a rich and full life. His friends extended over some sixty years. His ambition had taken him from a small bicycle shop to a million-dollar business. He was very proud of this accomplishment. Now, it was time to give all of this up and take his last breath. Mrs. Spellman had been by his side through their thick and thin years. She was now surrounded by all their friends from the past. The funeral was a beautiful event. People, friends, employees, and the press and media were all there. A long line of cars followed the big black hearse to the gravesite. Mr. Gibson sat beside Mrs. Spellman as everyone watched the coffin being lowered into the ground. Tears were on everyone's face. This was the final farewell to Mr. Spellman.

Guyiser and Mr. Gibson helped Mrs. Spellman into the limo. The Spellman mansion was quiet that day. The three of them sat in the large living room talking. "Guyiser, thank you for all of your help. Mrs. Spellman and I both are grateful."

Guyiser reached for their hands. "I only wish I could have known him. When I ride around the plant, I feel his presence everywhere. His name will always be a part of the factory. I promise you that."

"Guyiser, Mrs. Spellman and I are going away for a while. She has been in this house too long. She needs to get away. You understand, don't you?"

"Yes, sir. I do. And, I agree."

"We have talked and would like you to stay here at the mansion, if you would like to."

"I'll do anything that you want me to do, sir." Guyiser stood and went to Mrs. Spellman, "Again, I am sorry, Mrs. Spellman. I'll be going now and leave you two to talk. Mr. Gibson, if you need anything, you know where I am." Guyiser left the house and went back to the factory.

It was two days later. Guyiser walked in the office building. Kate and Carla were busy on the phones. Guyiser listened to Carla giving out prices and taking orders. He looked at Kate. She was saying goodbye and thank you for your order. She hung up and looked at Guyiser.

The phone rang again. "Good morning, Gibson, Blackman, how can I help you?

"...Yes, sir."

"...Yes, I'll send it out today. Thank you for calling." Kate looked at Guyiser, "It's been this way all morning. Look at this." There was a stack of orders for bicycles and a stack of people wanting a catalog. Mr. Spellman's death had sparked a flood of interest and orders.

Guyiser walked over to Carla. She handed him a stack of papers. "Thank you for calling. Bye now." Carla turned to Guyiser. "We need help!"

Guyiser smiled and winked at her. "Send some of the calls to me. I'll be in Mr. Gibson's office."

The factory was very busy. Guyiser was talking to Buck. Buck pointed to a large machine. "We had to start up another machine. John is running it. I think we could use a few more fitters, boxers, a painter, and a dryer. We started up a machine we haven't used in a year. Mr. Blackman, I'm so happy, I could spit."

Guyiser laughed, "Well, go ahead. Spit. I will, too." They both spit and laughed. "So, you need about four, five, or more people."

"Yes, sir. If we want to keep up, we do."

"See Kate. Tell her what you need. We're on a roll. Let's keep it up."

Guyiser sat at his desk looking at his Rolodex.

Carla sat across from him taking notes. "The ads will come out next week. The new flyers will be here tomorrow. What else?"

Guyiser stood behind her, looking over her shoulder. "Carla, it's time we took a trip. We're going down to Alabama for a couple of days. Book us on a plane and get us a room at a hotel. We're going to see a friend of mine."

She looked up at him and smiled, "One room or two?"

Guyiser kissed her. "One. Are you busy tonight?"

Carla stood up, put her arms around him, and kissed him again. "Well, I'll check my book, but I think I'm free tonight."

It was a night of passion and lust. After a couple of hours of hot lovemaking and many different positions, Carla lay in Guyiser's arms. He was fondling her breasts. "You have the greatest boobs."

Carla put her hand under the sheet, "And, you, you have the hardest body."

Guyiser smiled looking at the beamed ceiling.

"Carla, take a note."

She looked at him, "Now?"

"Yes, now."

Carla got out of bed and got her notepad. She jumped back in bed and sat waiting. Guyiser laughed. "I love to see you walk around naked. You have a great butt."

Carla hit him with her pad. "Is that all you wanted? To see me walking around naked?"

Guyiser laughed again, "No, no. Write this down. For our trip, get us a limousine. I like that word, limousine. Don't you? Get a big black one and put this down, I want a sign over the plant building with gold letters, 'Spellman Building'. No, no. Put the sign on the hangar up high. That's where his jet is. He would like that."

Carla leaned and kissed Guyiser. "That's sweet. Now, do you know what I would like?" Carla threw the sheet off of Guyiser and straddled him. "I want to be on top this time." Guyiser pulled her to him, kissing passionately. His hand grabbed her butt cheeks as she began to move slowly and then faster.

"Yes, baby. Ride me." Carla did. She could feel Guyiser deep inside of her as she moved faster and faster. She threw her head back as she exploded violently and fell on his body.

"Wow! Oh, Guyiser, wow!"

Guyiser smiled, "Take another note. I like you on top."

The rain was pouring down in sheets. Guyiser stood looking out the patio doors. The weatherman had said rain, but this was a real storm. He went to his desk and sat looking at reports that Mrs. Watson had sent. He looked at 'Incoming', 'Outgoing', 'Paid', 'Received', and other reports. Nothing made sense to him. It just seemed like a bunch of numbers, but the papers did look impressive. In his mind, all he could see were people working, machines running, stock building up, orders coming in, and freight trucks taking bicycles away. To him, this made sense. As long as Gibson, Blackman was making money, he didn't care how much. That part of business was some other person's job. Seeing his ideas and work come to life and hearing about orders coming in was enough for him.

He sat looking at a business card. Bagwell Enterprises, Distributor of Toys. He dialed the number. "Bagwell Enterprises. How may I help you?"

"Hi, this is Guyiser Blackman. Is Mr. Bagwell in, please?"

"One moment, sir." Guyiser looked at the jet.

"Hello, Guyiser Blackman. How are you, young man?"

"Mr. Bagwell, I'm fine, sir. I didn't know if you would remember me."

"Well, there are not many people named Guyiser that I know of. Is it still snowing there in Tennessee?"

"No, sir. But, it's raining hard here in Kentucky."

"Say, was that you I saw in the sports page at the horse races not too long ago?"

"Oh, that. Yes, we had a good time there."

"Well, why didn't you tell me you were in the bicycle business? We could do some business together."

"Well, sir. That's what I'm calling about. I have a large factory here in Kentucky, and I wanted to invite you to come and visit me."

"Tell you what, Guyiser. Why don't you come down here first and see my warehouses. I'll take you to the dog races. What do you say?"

Guyiser smiled. This is what he wanted to hear. "Now that sounds fun, Mr. Bagwell. How about the twelfth of this month? That good for you?"

"That would be just fine, Guyiser."

Guyiser wanted to seal the deal on the phone.

"By the way, how's the weather there? Not two feet of snow, is it?"

"No, thank God. But, I'll never forget that day I almost died."

Guyiser laughed, "Oh, it wasn't that bad. Hey, it was good talking with you. We'll see you on the twelfth. You take care now."

"Looking forward to seeing you again, Guyiser. You take care, too. Bye now."

"Goodbye, Mr. Bagwell."

Guyiser had just been fishing and had caught a big one. Mr. Gibson had told him about how big Bagwell was and that his distribution was all over the South. He had stores in seven states. Guyiser leaned back in his chair and yelled. Loaner came running to see what was wrong. "Loaner, Loaner, Loaner. We're going to be rich!" Guyiser looked at the jet. "I hope."

It rained all day. Guyiser and Loaner went to the office building. Kate and Mrs. Watson stood watching the rain come down as Guyiser came in. "Good morning, ladies. It's a beautiful day, isn't it?"

Kate took his raincoat. "If you're a duck. Oh, Carla called. She said she was sick and sore and wouldn't be in today."

Guyiser smiled. "Mrs. Watson, you look lovely today. Guess what? Have you heard of Bagwell Distribution Company?"

Mrs. Watson looked at him, "Have I heard of him? Everyone has heard of him. He has the largest distribution company in the South."

"Well, Mrs. Watson and Kate, not to brag, but I saved his life one time. So I called him, and I have an appointment with him on the twelfth. He wants to do business with us!"

Mrs. Watson sat down. "Mr. Blackman, if you land that account, we would be set for life!"

Guyiser laughed. "I know, I know. Isn't it funny? What goes around comes around. Oh, Kate, I have to go to Tampa, Florida, for the seventh and eighth. I'll return on the ninth. Would you book me a flight?

It's a big interview for the company. And, as for the Bagwell trip, Carla will take care of that, okay?"

Kate wrote down everything. "You got it. I'll have you picked up on the morning of the seventh. That's great news, Guyiser. Oh, I talked with Buck. Everything is taken care of."

"Kate, I couldn't get along without you or you either, Mrs. Watson. Now, I'm going to walk in the rain. I feel great! Bye, ya'll."

Guyiser was energized. He had things to do. Cindy was first on his list. As he and Loaner played in the rain, he could see Cindy's smiling face and long, blond, curly hair.

Cindy could see Guyiser as she lay in bed holding their picture. She became excited about seeing him, which would be in just a few days. Jeff had everything set and ready for taping. She lay smiling and thinking about the barn and Guyiser saying, 'Maybe you could interview me on your show.' Now it was going to happen. *A few days, only a few days. Oh, Guyiser, what are you doing right now?*

Guyiser stood in the living room of the Spellman mansion. Mr. Gibson and Mrs. Spellman had left for Europe, and the house was empty. The servants and James were on leave. Guyiser and Loaner walked through the mansion looking at everything. The four large bedrooms all had patios. Mrs. Spellman had a beautiful collection of antiques. These items represented a great age. Guyiser stood at the patio doors of the master bedroom looking down at the large swimming pool. Rain was bouncing off the water. This was an awesome house. Even the guesthouse was a two-bedroom house with a large garage for the limousine. Guyiser went down stairs to the den. It was an office and library with tall-beamed ceilings. The furniture and the antique desk were worth thousands of dollars. Guyiser sat at the desk thinking about Cindy and him living in this house.

If she were only here now.

It was the morning of the seventh. Guyiser was in the office--saying goodbye to Kate and Carla. "Oh, ladies, have some good news for me when I get back. And, Loaner, you protect. I'll bring you something back." Loaner barked and stood between Kate and Carla.

"Mr. Blackman, have a good trip, and don't worry about anything here."

Carla walked Guyiser out and to the waiting car. "I know this is important to you. I'll be thinking about you. I don't know how to say this, but say hello to Cynthia for me." She kissed him. "Hurry back, Guyiser." The big black car drove off to the airport. It was at that moment that Carla knew it was more than just sex between them. She really cared for him. Tears came to her eyes.

It was some six hours later when Guyiser sat in his hotel room on the phone. "I'm sorry, sir. She is in the studio taping this evening. Would you like to leave a message? I'll try to get it to her."

"Yes, just tell her Guyiser is at the hotel. Tell her to call me if she gets a chance. I'll be here all night. Thank you."

Guyiser sat in the hotel restaurant having dinner. He motioned to the waiter. "Would you check the desk for me? I'm expecting a phone call. Thank you."

The waiter returned, "No, sir. No messages for you, sir."

Cindy sat on the set. "We are rolling. Speed." Jeff called action.

"Hello, America. I'm Cynthia Taylor. Important news coming up next. Stay tuned."

"Cut. Okay. Guys next setup."

Jeff came to Cindy, "That works fine. You all right? Good, go change and get a touch up. We'll start again soon."

"Cindy went to the assistant, "Any calls for me?"

He looked at his clipboard, "No, ma'am. Nothing."

It took the crew about an hour to set up, change the camera, and lights. Cindy stood on a kitchen set. "Everybody ready? Rolling, We have speed. Action, Cynthia."

"Hi, I'm Cynthia Taylor and I guess you're wondering what... I'm sorry; I can't see what the cue card says."

"Cut. Brian, get it together. Get the cards in order. Okay, everybody settle down. Rolling. Speed. Action, Cynthia."

"Hi, I'm Cynthia Taylor."

"Cut." Jeff came out of the booth and went to Cindy. "What's wrong? You okay?"

Cindy looked at her watch. "I'm all right. It's just, uh, can I have a break. I need to go to the restroom."

Jeff looked at her and could see she was not herself. "Sure, sure. Take your time. We'll start again when you're ready."

Cindy walked off the set. "I'll be right back. Thanks, Jeff." Soon Cindy came back. She went to the assistant. "Any calls yet?"

"No, Miss Taylor, no calls."

Jeff came up to her. "You look great. How do you feel?"

"I'm okay. Let's do it."

Jeff walked her to the set. "Okay, you ready? Energy, energy, okay." Cindy took a deep breath. "Rolling, Speed, Action."

"Hi, I'm Cynthia Taylor, and I guess you're wondering what we are cooking up for you. Well, tune in tomorrow and smile at me. See you tomorrow."

"Cut. Great. Great. Last setup. Move it. Move it." Jeff came to her smiling. "I knew you could do it.

That was perfect. And, I loved your timing. Last setup, okay. Make a change and we'll go when you're ready. And, remember, America loves you, baby."

Guyiser lay on the bed. The phone rang and a light blinked. He jumped up excited and called the desk. "Yes, this is room 1025. Do you have a message for me?"

"Yes, Mr. Blackman, the studio will pick you up at eleven o'clock in the morning and take you to the set."

Guyiser's heart dropped. "Is that all? I mean no more messages?"

"No, sir. That's all. Good night, sir."

The Interview

Part 11

Flowers are red; some are blue,
I have a dream, so do you.
It will take time for things to grow,
But I'll love you always,
I want you to know.

Jeff and Cindy sat in Jeff's office. "Okay, Cynthia. Today is your day. Let's make it your best. I have three of the largest cable network executives and producers with me in the booth. So, today all of your work comes together. Just keep that beautiful smile of yours working, okay? Relax, have fun, and enjoy the show."

Cindy took Jeff's hands. "Jeff, I want to thank you for believing in me. I've learned so very much from you. You have become my best friend. If all goes well today, and I'm sure it well, I want you with me always."

Jeff squeezed her hands. "Cynthia, the first time I saw you, I knew you had what it takes. Your dedication to your work, your personality, and your good instincts will take you a long, long way. I am honored to be a part of your career. I thank you. Now, as they say in show business, break a leg." They stood up and hugged.

Cindy sat in the makeup chair getting her final touch up. She looked around the studio. The lights were set. Sound was ready. The cameras were ready to roll. Sandy waved to her and gave her the okay sign. Cindy smiled and waved back. Jeff's voice came over the speaker, "Miss Taylor, are you ready?"

Cindy looked up at the booth. Guyiser was standing behind the large window. He waved to her. Cindy lit up like fireworks in the sky. She sat looking at him. Tears came to her eyes. It had been so long. She ran to the booth and went it. "Excuse me, gentlemen. Mr. Blackman, may I see you a moment?" She led him into the women's restroom and locked the door. They stood looking at each other. "Kiss me, Guyiser, kiss me." They embraced and kissed with passion. "Oh, Guyiser, how I have missed you."

Guyiser held her tightly. "My girlfriend. You just don't know. Let me look at you. Wow! You are so beautiful. Your hair is shorter, but you still smell like the Cindy I know.

I've missed you."

There was a knock at the door, "Miss Taylor, are you all right?"

Cindy looked at Guyiser, "I sure am. I'll be right there." She turned to Guyiser, I sure am, and tonight I'm going to show you how much I've missed you." Cindy was on the set. The music came up. Cindy looked at Guyiser in the booth. As the music faded out, Cindy was looking at her notepad. She heard Jeff call action. Cindy looked into the camera lens with a big warm smile, "America, how are you? I'm Cynthia Taylor, and I have an exciting, fun, and very interesting show for you today. We are going to explore the weaker sex and the beginning of a man.

Three women and three men will tell us about the hard way up. This is Patricia and Ann. Let's start with you, Pat. Your magazine, *Woman*, sounds fun. How did you get started?"

"Cynthia, it was hard." The interview was going well. Jeff sat flipping from one camera to the other.

"Now you, Ann. You were a police officer, a detective, and a district attorney. Now you have your own law firm. What's next, governor?"

"No thanks, Cynthia. But, as a woman, it has been rough. I started out in a high school as a patrol officer and..."

Jeff spoke to Sandy on her headset. "Get a close-up of Cynthia. Camera two, pull back into a two-shot."

Jeff cut back and forth during the interview.

"Thanks, Ann. I'm glad you're on our side. Good Luck." Cindy looked at the camera. "We'll be right back with the men. You don't want to miss this."

Jeff pulled up the music and faded out. He came out of the booth and went to the ladies. "Cynthia and I want to thank you for the interview and your time. Everything was great. Cynthia, may I see you for a minute?" They walked off the set and stood talking. "Now, Cynthia, do just what we did in rehearsal. When I ask you something, take your time, okay? Are you ready?"

Cindy took a deep breath, "Let's do it."

Jeff sat in one chair and Cindy sat next to him. He signaled the engineer in the booth and the assistant. "We're back. I am Jeff Fisher, and today we have a surprise for you. We are going to interview our hostess of the show, Miss Cynthia Taylor. Cynthia, why television? Why the media? Why did you choose this field of work?"

"Jeff, I love television. I love gathering news, covering events, talking with people, and bringing facts to the public. But, most of all, I want to be a part of history. This world changes every day. The growth of America is important to me. Television and the media give me the pleasure of telling millions of people what is going on around them."

"Cynthia, as a woman, has it been hard for you?"

"Yes and no, Jeff. Yes, my personal life has been put on hold, and there have been disappointing times and pitfalls along the way."

Jeff stopped her and looked into the camera, "We have one of those pitfalls on tape. I would like to play it for our viewers. This man thinks his power at a cable network can get him anything he wants. In this case, it's sex. Just listen to this." Jeff called for the tape to play. Cindy sat with her head down as the tape played. 'We should have dinner tonight and spend some time together—drinks at my place—get to know each other, you what I mean? I can get your career started, especially if you're nice to me.' Jeff looked into the camera. "This is what a young woman has to go through. It happens not only in television, but also in many types of jobs. Cynthia, I am sorry you went through this. This type of man should not be in this business or any business."

"You're right, Jeff. I never thought it would happen to me." Cindy turned to the camera. "If you think that sexual harassment has happened to you, write to me. I want to help."

"I do, too, Cynthia. Let's take a commercial break and we'll be back with Cynthia Taylor's The Beginning of a Man." The music came up and the picture faded. Jeff grabbed Cindy, "Wonderful, wonderful. When this airs, you'll get a ton of mail. Are you all right? Give me a hug."

Guyiser came to Cindy and hugged her, "Why didn't you tell me about this? I'll break his arms and legs."

Cindy kissed him, "That's why I didn't tell you. I'm all right. What do you think about the show so far?"

Guyiser stood still angry, "That bastard."

"Guyiser, let it go. You're here. I'm here. That's enough. Come on, I have a show to do."

Everyone was seated on the stage. Jeff started the music and talked to Sandy. "A wide shot and push in on Cynthia." Cindy was laughing as she winked at Guyiser.

"We're back with three gorgeous men. And, ladies, they are all single. We have Guyiser, Cory, and Robert. Guyiser is a bicycle millionaire. Cory is a stockbroker, and Robert is in high-rise real estate. Guyiser, how did you become a millionaire?"

"Well, I don't know for sure. I think the media made me one."

Cindy laughed, "And may I ask, how is your love life?"

Guyiser laughed, "Well, my girlfriend is here in Florida, and I'm in Kentucky. It's mostly phone sex."

Everyone laughed. "Cory, how did you get into stocks?"

"It was through my uncle. He took all my money when I was sixteen and bought stock in railroads. It grew and grew. Now, I buy and sell stocks and am doing great."

"Robert, what are big tickets?"

"Cynthia, that is a term we use in real estate. I buy and sell high-rise buildings and hotels."

"Guyiser, tell me how you got started."

"Me, well, I started out in an alley. I found a bunch of old bicycles and parts and fixed them up. And, with the help of my girlfriend, I sold them."

"Gentlemen, my last question. Where do you see yourself in the next two years? Not five or ten years, but two years from now? Robert?"

"I'm on my own island in the Keys with a big hotel."

"Cory?"

"I'm on Wall Street in a big New York penthouse."

"And, Guyiser, where are you in two years?"

"Well, Cynthia, I see me married, living on a farm—rich, happy, and living the American dream with a wife named Cindy. I'd have my dog-named Loaner and maybe a kid on the way. What about you?"

"Well, that's another show, Guyiser." Cindy laughed and turned to the camera. "That's it, America. Next week, a question for the ladies, do you wear panties all the time? And for the men, making love to older women. Now that should be fun and interesting. This is Cynthia Taylor saying be happy and smile at me. See you next time." The music came up and the picture faded. Cindy stood and shook hands with Cory and Robert. "I want to thank you both for being here today.

You were wonderful. Mr. Blackman, would you like to have dinner tonight?"

"It would be my pleasure, Miss Taylor."

Jeff came running to Cindy. He jumped up on the stage. "Cynthia, they all want the show! They're fighting over it now. They all want to put you under contract. We did it. You did it. But don't get too excited. I'll handle everything. Oh, I'm so excited. And you, Mr. Blackman. They thought you were so funny. Phone sex. They want you back again. Oh, I'm so excited. Cynthia, they want to meet with you. But, I'll handle everything, okay? Please excuse us, Mr. Blackman. It won't take long."

Guyiser stood watching them walk away. Cory came up to him. "Mr. Blackman, it was nice meeting you. Here's my card if you are ever interested in stocks."

"Well, thank you, Cory. As a matter of fact, I am. I'm at the hotel down the street. Maybe we can meet before I go back."

"I'm at that hotel, too. I'll call you later, Mr. Blackman."

Guyiser looked at his card. "Well, Cory, call me Guyiser. We're about the same age. Mr. Blackman sounds so old."

Cory shook Guyiser's hand, "Thanks, Guyiser. I'll call you this evening."

Guyiser shook his head and laughed, "No, no not tonight. Tomorrow about ten is okay."

"You got it. See you later."

Sandy came to Guyiser. "So, you're the famous Guyiser. When you said phone sex, I almost dropped the camera. Hi, I'm Sandy, Cynthia's roommate."

Guyiser looked her over. She wore tennis shoes, red socks, purple sweat pants, and a T-shirt with the words 'touch these' on it. "Well, hi, Sandy. You look just like you sound. I talked to you on the phone, remember?"

"Guyiser, are you really rich?"

"What?"

"Could you loan me some money, maybe a hundred thousand?"

Guyiser laughed, "Sure. No problem."

Cindy had finished her meeting and came to them. "So, you two have met."

Guyiser was writing out a check. "Oh, we met all right."

Cindy laughed and took Guyiser's arm, "Well, don't take her too seriously. Let's go."

Guyiser handed Sandy his check. He and Cindy walked away. "So, how was the meeting?"

Sandy waved the check. "Hey, hey, you didn't sign it!"

The hotel restaurant was busy. Guyiser sat holding Cindy's hands. "What did you say?"

"Well, I told them I had a good crew and Jeff, of course, and they all would be part of my contract."

"Contract?"

"Yes, and that's the hard part. It would be in New York or Texas for five years. I told them I would only sign for two years. They are considering it."

"Cindy, that's wonderful but New York? You're a Southern girl, Cindy. Not New York. That's Yankee territory."

Cindy laughed, "Guyiser, it's not about territory. It's about my work, about the public, and about being a part of something bigger than you or me. I don't want to sell out to some small network. It's like you, sweetheart. You don't want a small bike shop in Nashville. You want something bigger. I know you, Guyiser. Remember the barn? Now look at you—the president of a million dollar factory. We both have our dreams."

Guyiser leaned back in his chair, "Are we drifting apart, Cindy?"

"No, silly. See this necklace. I touch it all the time thinking about you. I love you, Guyiser Blackman."

Strong emotions from their passionate night had brought back moments and memories of a fireplace. Cindy sat stark naked straddling Guyiser. He caressed her breasts with love. Cindy touched her necklace. "Remember this charm? It was our first."

Guyiser pulled her close to him, "Yes, and it was just the beginning of wanting you more and more. Cindy, I want you to think about what I said at the interview. I meant that. You, me, a farm."

"I know, Guyiser, and I want that too, but let's give it two years. Then it will happen."

Guyiser held her tight, "That's a long time, sweetheart."

Cindy sat up and kissed him, "Guyiser, look at what we have accomplished in just a short time. We are in the middle of our dreams. Let's not wake up too early. Let's finish our dreams; then we can be together forever."

Guyiser looked into her eyes trying to find reasons to disagree with her. There were many things he wanted to complete, and his dream was not over. "You're right, girlfriend. You're right. I am just being selfish. I wasn't considering your feelings. I just love you so, so much."

Cindy kissed him deeply, "Thank you for understanding, but now I'm selfish too. Make love to me again, Guyiser. Make love to me like the first time."

Cindy left to meet with Jeff and to talk about the day before. Guyiser and Cory sat in the restaurant. "So, what's new and what's not?"

"Guyiser, I'm on top of something that is going to be the biggest money maker of the future. I've been watching this company from their beginning days. The company is called Horizon Communications. Their complex electronics have developed a system for worldwide data processing and electronic equipment, computers, and the Internet. No other company has this technology. It is so new that it can only go sky high. Six months ago, I bought ten thousand dollars' worth of stock. Today that stock is worth forty thousand. Guyiser, we're young. I would like to see us billionaires someday. This is the ground floor, man. I don't tell this to just anyone." Cory put down some figures on a paper. "Guyiser, look at this. If you buy stock today at $8.64 per share, okay, say you buy one hundred shares today, I want you to check your paper tomorrow. I bet you a hundred dollars right now that tomorrow the stock will be up at least to $8.90. In addition, next week it may be up to $12.00 and so on. Think about it. My money rolls over every day. I bought at $6.12 a share."

Guyiser took the paper, "I'll check this company out and call you tomorrow, Cory. This could be the beginning of a good friendship. But, now I have a plane to catch." They stood and shook hands. "It's been a pleasure meeting you, Cory. I'll call you tomorrow."

"Guyiser, I hope we can be friends. You take care now."

"No, Jeff. I'm getting off track. That's not what I want to do. I want to talk about women, not wearing panties or making love to older women. The United States may be on its way to war overseas. There are starving kids in this country. And..."

Jeff cut her off, "Cynthia, you'll get your chance for that and more. Let's talk about television. Stations have sponsors. Sponsors have customers. Customers buy what the sponsors sell. People watch your show to be entertained. They want to laugh. You give them joy. They want to see what you give them. Now, this is where the word 'ratings' comes in. The more people who tune in to your show, the more sponsors sell their products, the bigger the ratings are, the more money the station makes. The more the station makes, the more you make, and so on. Cynthia, this is your first television show. It's my job to make you popular and to generate a large audience that will want to watch you and your show."

Cindy sat tapping her foot. "Cynthia, you're young and beautiful. At your age, you appeal to a younger audience that will follow you for years to come. At that time, they will want to hear and see what you say about the war and about hungry kids. Then you will reach where you want to go. Please be patient. This is a ride that someday you'll look back on and laugh, trust me." Jeff stood up and went to Cindy, "Tell you what we'll do, once in a while; we'll sneak in a show about the war and whatever you want to talk about. How's that?"

Cindy stood up and hugged Jeff, "Okay, Jeff. I'll do these silly shows. I guess I've been thinking about me and television instead of television and me. And, ratings I never even thought about ratings. You have given me a completely new outlook on television. I'll be patient, Jeff. I will."

Jeff hugged her again, "Now, sit down. I'll tell you about an exciting offer for you, and us. How does $30,000.00 a show sound to you? And, to work in a studio in the Big Apple, New York, New York? They agreed to a two-year contract with an option!"

Cindy broke her pencil and sat with big eyes and an open mouth. "Are you serious?

My own show? For two years?"

Jeff clapped his hands, "Yes, sweetheart, for two years and with an option. And, I get to direct your shows. Cynthia, congratulations! But, I have to remind you that it's a lot of work and long hours."

Cindy walked around the office floating with each step. "I'm ready for that, Jeff. When do we start?"

"Well, first, I want you to go home for a while. Take a break and rest. I'll let you know. Cynthia, I'm so excited for you. Oh, one more thing. You don't have to worry about that Jack Weber type. This network is very professional. As a matter of fact, Mr. Jack Weber was fired and will never work in television again. Now, you and Sandy go to the beach or whatever you do. I'll see you later, okay?" Cindy ran out of the studio doors. She couldn't wait to tell Sandy the news.

Loaner burst out of the office door barking and barking. He ran to the gates jumping around and barking. The black car pulled up to the office building and stopped.

Loaner circled the car running and barking. Guyiser got out and instantly Loaner was on him. "Boy, am I glad to see you, Loaner. Yes, boy, I got you something." Loaner barked and circled him as Guyiser went in the office.

Kate came to meet him, "Mr. Blackman, welcome back. He really missed you, and so did we. How did it go?"

Guyiser hugged her, "It was amazing--the studio, and the people. I'll tell you all about it later. How are you? How are things here?"

"Guyiser, you won't believe it. We are flooded with orders. Even Mrs. Watson asked for help. The gold series has taken over. Everyone wants a gold bicycle. It's unreal."

Guyiser looked at all the gold bikes on display.

"Kate, I also want to know what is not selling. Can you come up with a list of what's not?"

"Well, sir, right now I would say the tricycles. And then the stationary bike."

Guyiser went and sat on the bike. "Well, I'm not worried about this one. When the ads break, orders will pick up."

Carla walked in. "Well, Mr. Blackman, working out? Glad you're back, sir. How did it go?"

"Carla, what happened to you; you're blond?"

Carla smiled, "You like it?"

Guyiser went to her.

"The truth—no. I like the way you were."

Carla took off the wig. "I don't either." She shook out her long black hair.

"Now that's the girl I like. Let's go down to my office."

Kate covered her computer, "Well, that is it for me for today. I'll see you two tomorrow. Bye."

Carla sat across from Guyiser shaking her leg. "So, how was she?"

Guyiser looked at Cindy's picture. "She's doing well. We had a good long talk. She has her life, and I have mine. Let's leave it at that, okay?"

Carla turned a page in her notepad. "Okay. Uh, the ad breaks in tomorrow's paper.

The new flyers will be here in the morning."

Guyiser stood behind her, "Carla, I like you just the way you are; don't change."

She went to the window. A small tear came to her eyes. "I know. I was just being foolish, thinking..."

"No, you were not thinking. Carla, think this way. You give me not only emotional and physical pleasure, but also support and the real thing I want and need. Carla, we're going to be together for a long time. It's you I need, not a blond wig. I'm so happy with you. Don't change. You and I have many things to do together. Now, sit down and take some notes." Guyiser sat at his desk. "Carla, we are going to have a party. Have you been to the Spellman's mansion? Well, that's where we're going to have it. As the head of Public Relations, I want you to put together an event like Bowling Green has never seen. I want newspaper and T.V. coverage. Make it the works with lots of country stars, customers, lawyers, everybody, even the mayor."

"Guyiser, that will cost a lot of money."

Guyiser laughed, "It's a business expense. In the end, it will come back. That's one thing I learned from Mr. Gibson. It takes money to make money. That's why our trip to Alabama will pay off. At the same time, we will have fun and enjoy life. Now, go home and put together a great plan. It's party time!"

"Mother, guess what. I'm coming home, and boy do I have news."

"…No, silly. I'm not pregnant! I have my own talk show."

"…Yes."

"…Yes."

"…No, Mother, not Nashville. It's in New York."

"…I know I'm a Southerner. Why does everyone bring that up?"

"…Yes, ma'am. In a few days."

"…Will you and Daddy pick me up?"

"…I will. Love you. Bye."

Sandy lay on her bed with her feet on the wall. "I want to go with you. I am your camera girl, you know. I'll be good, I promise."

Cindy laughed, "Well, I don't see why not. Yeah, we'll have fun!"

Sandy jumped off the bed. "Can I borrow some money?"

Guyiser stood at the end of the long runway. The sky was full of gray moving clouds. Loaner was running around chasing something.

Buck was busy as Guyiser talked to him. "Good morning, boss."

"Morning. How's it going?"

"Real good, real good."

"Buck, we're going to lay off on the tricycles for a while, but we do need more gold bikes. We need girls and boys of all sizes."

"Sir, I got a problem. One of the women has a problem with one of the men. He's been coming on to her, talking dirty, and she doesn't like it. It's a shame because he is a good worker. What should I do about it?"

Guyiser thought about Cindy. "Have her write me a statement today! I'll handle it."

Kate and Carla were opening boxes as Guyiser came in. "Hey, good morning, girls, or should I say ladies?"

Carla handed him the new flyers. "Hi. Look at these. And, the newspaper ad looks great, too. Here's the paper."

Guyiser took the flyers and the newspaper. "No, Kate and Carla. I'm serious. Is it good morning, girls; or is it good morning, ladies? I'm serious."

Kate and Carla looked at each other.

"Well, sir, I'm flattered to be called a girl, but I consider myself a lady. I don't know. What do you think, Carla?"

"Well, I'm a girl at heart, but to be called a young lady is kind of nice."

Guyiser looked at both of them, "Now, I'm really confused. Anyway, you two come with me. I want to pick out an office for Carla." There were two from which to choose. Carla went into the second office.

"This one, this one, Guyiser." She looked out the window and sat at the desk. "How do I look?"

Kate looked at Guyiser and smiled, "Girl, she's a girl."

Guyiser laughed, "Okay, Miss Comings, it's yours. Put 'Public Relations, Carla Comings' on a gold nameplate on the door."

Kate smiled, "I'll see you later. Oh, by the way, I have a corporate credit card for you. I'll get it."

Guyiser sat across from Carla. "You look terrific. I'll buy anything you are selling."

Carla came and sat in Guyiser's lap and kissed him. "Thank you, Guyiser. Thank you for my office. I love it."

Kate returned with the credit card. "Well, excuse me." Carla stood up. "Here you are, sir—all the money you want to spend." Kate winked at Carla. "I'll see you later, Miss Comings."

Guyiser spread the flyers out on the desk with the newspaper. "This will for sure let people know that Gibson, Blackman is in the race. Be sure to bring plenty of these on our trip."

"I will, Mr. Blackman. Everything is taken care of—the plane, the limo, and the hotel room."

Guyiser smiled and looked around the office. "You know, some flowers or plants would look good in here or maybe a big fish tank to look at. I like to look at my jet, myself. What's your extension number here?"

Carla sat and looked at the intercom. "My number is 2260. Call me anytime."

"Oh, I will. See ya." Guyiser left the office. Buck was talking to Kate. "Ah, Mr. Blackman. Here's the paper you wanted."

Guyiser looked it over. "Send him to the hangar."

"Yes, sir."

Guyiser sat at a small desk inside the hangar door. "Sit down, Pete. Is this true?" The man read the paper. "Well, tell me about it."

He looked at Guyiser, "Well, she is always teasing me. Sometimes I will hand her a box, and she will drop it and bend over, knowing I am looking at her butt. She doesn't wear a bra and her shirt is always open. I'll look at her boobs and she will just smile at me. What am I supposed to do?"

Guyiser leaned back. "Well, number one, stop looking at her butt. And, as far as her boobs, she is a woman. They all have boobs. Haven't you ever seen boobs before? Grow up, man! I'll have Buck talk to her about buttoning up her shirt. Now, I'm going to put you in Shipping and Receiving for a while. Don't see her. Don't talk to her. Leave her alone as well as all the other women who work here. And if you have a problem with that, get out of here now. Buck says you're a good man and a good worker. That's the only reason I'm not firing you. So, be cool, man. Just do your job, okay. Now, go see Mr. Maker. You're working for him now."

"Yes, sir. And, thank you, sir."

Guyiser took his newspaper and went to his office. He sat looking at the stock market section. There it was—Horizon Communications. He took his highlighter and drew through all the numbers. Numbers again. Something he was not good at. Cory had written a price of $8.64 per share. Nevertheless, Guyiser could not find that price. At the end of the article was another figure. Stocks for the small company were up to $8.84. Guyiser laughed and dialed Cory's phone number. "Brandon Investment."

"Hi, is this Cory?"

"Yes, it is."

"Cory, Guyiser Blackman here. You owe me a hundred dollars."

"Hi, Guyiser. What for?"

"Well, you said that Horizon would be up to $8.90. It's only $8.84."

Cory laughed, "Well, I was close. How are you doing?"

"I'm great. Say, I want to buy in to Horizon. What do I do?"

"Guyiser, you won't regret it. How much do you want to invest?"

"Well, you put in ten grand, so I'll start with $75,000.00 and see what happens. Do I send you a check or what?"

Cory laughed again, "No, your credit is good. I'll put you in today. Check the paper tomorrow. It will be up again, you'll see. Haven't you bought stock before?"

"No, Cory. I get my stocks another way.

Say, check your mailbox. I'm having a big party in a week or so. You gotta come." The intercom came on. "Hold on a minute. Hello."

"Guyiser, you have a call on line two."

"Thanks, Kate. Cory, I'll get back to you later. Bye. Hello, Guyiser Blackman here."

"Guyiser, this is Bill Simson with the Wall-Burg Stores. How are you?"

"Hi, Bill. It's been a long time. How are your stores doing?"

"Well, Guyiser, the stores are doing well, but I'm not with the stores anymore. I've been moved up in Wall-Burg. I am now the general buyer for the whole chain, which includes the European distribution as well as the U.S. distribution. I received your catalogs and flyers on your bicycles. I want to make you a deal. Your gold series is the talk of the town. Your stationary workout bike is something we need. Now, Guyiser, let me tell you about Wall-Burg. We have stores in thirty-six countries including Hong Kong, England, France, Germany, and Australia. We buy in bulk sizes and store the product in warehouses.

Then we send the product out to our stores all over the world. Now, we buy bicycles from several small companies and sometimes we can't get what we need. So, I need a deal from you on price. I'm looking at your invoice for a figure of $61.52 per bike. I need a better price. Remember, we're buying in bulk. What is your bottom price for us?"

Guyiser was caught by surprise. "Uh, Bill, what is bulk? I mean, about how many bikes are you talking about?"

"Well, a rough figure would be about 20,000 each. Your catalog has nine different types plus different sizes. I would say about 540,000 pieces to start. Can you handle that?"

Guyiser walked around in disbelief. "Uh, I'm sure I can. Bill, can I call you back? Give me about an hour, okay?"

"No problem, Guyiser. I know this must be a surprise for you, but I would like to do business with you. Sure, call me later. I'll be in all day."

"I will, Bill, I will. Bye now." Guyiser sat not believing what he had heard. This was big. He was used to orders of a hundred or more. *Where are you, Mr. Gibson, when I need you? What to do?* Bill had asked him two questions. 'Can you handle that?' and 'What is your price to us?' Being an optimist, Guyiser had said, 'Oh, sure.' Now he had to prove it. *Mrs. Watson would have some answers.*

Guyiser and Mrs. Watson sat in her office talking. Her fingers were working fast on her calculator. She wrote figures down and did some more calculations. After some time, she turned to Guyiser, "I think my calculator is broken. I can't believe these figures. Look at this:

I know you don't know about this stuff, but the bottom line is if we cut our cost of $61.52 down to $41.52, which is the very bottom, we still have a profit of two million, two hundred thousand dollars. Besides, that's just to start. Guyiser, you have $20,000.00 worth of wiggle room. Anything over $41.52 is a substantial profit, and I mean substantial!"

Guyiser walked around the room thinking out loud. "Can we do it? I mean that's a lot of product."

"Mr. Blackman, you can do it, but we will need more of everything. More equipment, supplies, space, and employees. Everything we have now but more of everything. That's up to you and Mr. Gibson."

"How about money? Can we afford to put money into this?"

"Well, sir, if you get a contract from Wall-burg, what we don't have, we can get."

"Mrs. Watson, that's all I needed to hear."

"Oh, Guyiser, this is an inventory of stock on hand situation. Find out what his initial order will be." Mrs. Watson looked at the catalog. "Now, the cost price is for bicycles and tricycles only. Your stationary bike is not included. It's separate. I'll have to do that figure later for you, but roughly, the cost is $94.80. You can tell him $87.50. I think he will go for that."

Guyiser left the office building and sat in his golf cart at the end of the runway. He looked at the five large buildings and at all the figures Mrs. Watson had given him. He was no longer in the comfort of his barn. He was now dealing with an emotional empire. He was faced with an enormous job. *Make a plan; work a plan* went through his mind. He looked at his watch. It was time to call Bill. Guyiser took a deep breath and drove to the hangar.

"Bill, hi. Guyiser. You busy?"

"I'm always busy, Guyiser. Thanks for calling back. Talk to me."

"Well, Bill, I have good news and bad news. Good news first. My factory can handle and supply you with what you need. Bad news, I'm looking at my inventory and I don't have 540,000 pieces in stock."

Bill laughed, "No one does. I don't want it all at one time. How about we start with about 50,000 pieces now, and say 20,000 pieces a month. How's that sound?"

"Now, that sounds like something I can handle, Bill. As for prices, I have a good figure for you. To give you a 35% discount, my account gave me a figure of $52.50 for bicycles and tricycles. With a 40% discount on the stationary bike, it would come to $88.50."

Bill did some quick figuring on his computer. "Guyiser, I want you to make a profit, too. $88.50 is good, and we will sell them at $159.95. That's good, but $52.50, let's move it up to $54.50 each. How is that for you?"

"Bill, you're the man! I'll take those two dollars anytime. Thanks."

"Guyiser, we have a deal. I'm comfortable with the prices, and I'll put a contract in the mail on Monday."

Guyiser did not take the elevator. He ran down the stairs yelling and shouting. "Come on, Loaner. I'm going to buy you a gold collar." He burst into the office building doors. "Where is Mrs. Watson?" He ran past Kate and into the accounting office.

"Mrs. Watson, look at these numbers!"

Mrs. Watson looked at the papers. "Oh my, Guyiser. Oh my." She reached for her inhaler and took in a big breath. "Guyiser, do you know that this means?"

"I know what this means, Mrs. Watson. We have a lot of work to do. That's what this means. The contract is in the mail! I have to go see Buck. I'll see you later."

"20,000 bikes a month? Mr. Blackman, you know what that would take?"

Guyiser laughed, "Yes, I know and you can do it. You have just received a promotion. I want you to put together a full crew for this account only! Order what you need—machines, painters, dryers, a new assembly line, people, and anything else you need. Just get it done. How long will this take?"

Buck looked at the machines and all the people working. "Well, sir, it took me a while to put this together. I'd say about two, maybe three months to have everything running smoothly."

Guyiser put his arm on Buck's shoulder, "Make it two months. This is a big job for you, Buck. I want you to have an office and an assistant manager. You just tell him what you want and when you want it. Let him do the work. You just oversee everything. You are the Plant Manager now. You will be paid very well. Just get it done, Buck. Just get it done."

"Well, sir. I see only one problem. That's space. There isn't enough room here."

Guyiser smiled. "I thought about that, Buck. We'll take the jet out of the hanger. The hangar will be just for the Wall-Burg account. But, keep this building working, too."

Guyiser sat in his office looking at the jet. He was happy and excited with his discussions with Buck and

Mrs. Watson. He was proud of the decision he had made. He pressed the intercom. "Hello, Carla."

"Carla, what are you doing?"

"Oh, hi. Just putting my office together. Come and see."

"Okay, I'll be there soon."

The bare office had really come together. Carla sat behind her desk. Guyiser walked around the room looking at everything. "You have quite an imagination. I'm impressed." Guyiser took a book from the bookcase, "*The Logical Woman.*"

Carla smiled, "I bought it at a garage sale."

Guyiser laughed and sat down. "Are you ready for tomorrow?"

"Pretty much. I have some packing to do. The limo will pick us up at eight o'clock. We'll be at the hotel in Montgomery at one thirty. Your meeting is at three. Here is our itinerary for there and back."

"Now, that's what I like--a woman who is organized."

Carla smiled, "Well, thank you, sir. I'm good at lots of things."

Guyiser smiled, "Boy, do I know that. Go home and pack. I'll see you in the morning. By the way, I like your office."

It was dawn, just before the sun came up in Florida. Cindy and Sandy were ready to go.

Sandy picked up two of her three suitcases.

"Can you carry that one for me? Please, please."

Cindy looked at her. "Good heavens, your shoes don't match. We're going to Tennessee, not New York. They will laugh at you back there." Cindy shook her head. "Well, let's go, girlfriend, or I'll go without you."

Sandy walked out the door. "Cindy, do boys pay for dinner back there?"

Cindy hit her butt with a suitcase, "Go, go."

Sandy sat by the window of the plane looking out.

"I love to fly way up there and look down. It makes me feel superb; you know what I mean? Cindy, don't they have T.V. stations in Nashville?"

Cindy put down her book, "Of course they do. They have radios, TV's, streets, lights, and even cars. Where do you think I'm taking you? Nashville is the capital of Tennessee, Dum-dum. And by the way, I get the window on the way back." They laughed as the airplane began to taxi down the runway.

Large gray clouds moved east as Guyiser and Carla stood in the airport looking at the planes coming and going. "I'm really excited, Guyiser. I've never been out of Kentucky before. I mean I've been to Nashville one time, but never to Alabama. Montgomery is the capital, right?"

"Yep, that's where we're going. Have you ever seen a dog race?"

"No, I didn't know they raced."

"Me, neither, but it sounds like fun."

Carla put her arm around Guyiser's arm.

"I know something else that sounds fun."

The speaker sounded, "Birmingham, Montgomery, now boarding at Gate 4."

Guyiser kissed her, "That's us. Let's go."

The sky began to clear the higher in the air the plane went. Carla and Guyiser sat in their first class seats drinking champagne. "What are you thinking about?"

Guyiser was looking at the bubbles in his glass. "Oh, nothing. Carla, did I tell you how beautiful you look today?"

"No, you didn't, and I miss hearing that."

Sandy was looking out the window, "Wow! Look at all the planes up here. One, two, three, and one over there makes four."

Cindy put her book down.

"Isn't love grand? You have to read this book!"

"Yeah, yeah, look!"

Cindy looked out the window, "Yes, they're pretty, Sandy." She went back to reading.

Carla and Guyiser lay in bed at the hotel. "More, I want more. Don't go to sleep." Carla put her hand under the sheet. "You can't go to sleep with that."

Guyiser smiled and squeezed her breasts. He put his hand between her legs. "You're right. Get on top."

Carla smiled, "After I kiss this for a while, boss man."

The two stood at the reception desk. "Mr. Blackman is here to see you, Mr. Bagwell."

Bill Bagwell came out of his office with his hands up. "My, my Guyiser, you look great. And, who is this pretty young lady?"

"Bill, this is my right hand, Miss Carla Comings, the head of Public Relations."

Bill shook her hand, "So, you're the one responsible for sending out that beautiful catalog. You know, I need someone like you to work for me. What do you say?"

"Mr. Bagwell, I would love to, but Guyiser has me under contract for ten years." They all laughed.

"Ya'll come on in and sit down. How was your trip?"

Everything was going well. Guyiser had been a little nervous about seeing Mr. Bagwell again. They talked for a while about this, that, and the other thing. Then, Mr. Bagwell turned to Carla, "Did you know that Guyiser saved my life one night? It's true. I was in the hospital for a week. Why didn't you tell me you had a bicycle company, Guyiser?"

"Well, sir, at the time, you were more important than telling you about my life."

Mr. Bagwell laughed, "I like this boy. Now, to some business. Tell me something."

Carla opened her briefcase and handed flyers and papers to Guyiser. Guyiser handed the flyers to Mr. Bagwell. "Well, to start, we have a big advertising program going on. This is directed at distributors like yourself."

Mr. Bagwell laughed, "Well, you ain't going to get many of them. I'm the biggest distributor of toys in the

South. I buy and sell distributors every day. You want something, you come to me."

Guyiser leaned back in his chair and looked at Carla, "Well, that's all fine and good, Bill, but I think the Wall-Burg chain may be bigger than you think."

Mr. Bagwell lit his cigar. "You got their account?"

"Yes, worldwide in thirty-six countries and the U.S.

"What do you need me for?"

"Bill, like you said, you're the biggest in the South. I want you to handle my bikes. You can reach where they can't."

"You're right about that. I got some 800 accounts. One of them is Toys-N-Kids. Ever heard of them?

They have some forty stores all over the seven states I cover. They are also in competition with Wall-Burg." Mr. Bagwell took a puff.

Carla saw her chance, "You know, Mr. Bagwell, competition is good for your business. I'm sure your accounts want to keep up with Wall-Burg, especially Toys-N-Kids. Don't you think so?"

Mr. Bagwell took another puff and looked at Carla, "Yep, yep. Guyiser, you got a smart young lady here. She knows when to talk and when not to. Okay, Guyiser, I'll handle your bicycles. I'll have my accounting department cut you an invoice. Now, let's talk about prices. What's your bottom dollar?"

Guyiser smiled. This was the fish he wanted to catch. Now to roll him in. "Bill, you're a friend. I'll give you the same price I gave Wall-Burg, $54.50 per piece if you buy in bulk. In addition, I will also give you about 200 new accounts. You can sell to them instead of me. This is a bonus for your business. How's that?"

Mr. Bagwell stood up and they shook hands. Mr. Bagwell kissed Carla's hand and looked at her. "You're beautiful. If I were not married and twenty years younger, my, oh my.

Guyiser, we got a deal! Now, are you two ready for the track tonight? Come on, I'll show you my warehouse."

Mrs. Taylor could not control herself. She burst out laughing. "She's the most unusual girl I have ever seen. A pink tennis shoe and a black one. And, Cindy, she should wear a bra with a tee shirt, don't you think? No, honey, the spoon goes on that side. What are you two going to do today?"

Cindy walked around the table changing the spoons. "We're going to Centerville for a while and Nashville tonight. Mother, be nice to her. She is a little different, but she's my friend."

Sandy came bouncing down the stairs and into the kitchen. "What's up? What are you laughing about?"

Cindy looked at her chest, "Sandy, Mother thinks you should wear a bra, and so do I."

Sandy walked over to Cindy and smiled at Mrs. Taylor. "I guess I have to wear panties, too." Cindy nodded. "Okay, okay."

They laughed and sang to the radio as they drove to Centerville. "That's where I went to school. See that tall water tower over there? You can climb on top and see the entire valley."

Sandy looked at the water tank. "Ooh, it must be exciting to see a cow in a field."

"Sandy, you promised to be nice. This is where I grew up."

"You're right, Cindy. I'm sorry."

Cindy drove around the courthouse and parked, "We're here."

Sandy got out of the car and looked around, "Girlfriend, I don't think so. This is not what I expected Nashville to look like."

Cindy laughed, "This is Centerville, dum-dum. We'll see Nashville tonight. Come on, I'll show you Daddy's hardware store."

Sandy clapped her hands, "Oh, boy. A hardware store. Let me write this down."

Mr. Taylor ran to the door and hugged Cindy. "My baby, you cut your hair. Your curls are gone."

"It's my new look, Daddy. You like it?"

"Cindy, I love you any way you are."

"Daddy, this is Sandy, my roommate."

"Mr. Taylor, I love all your tools."

"Sandy, it's nice to see you. How do you like it here?"

Sandy looked Cindy. Cindy smiled. "Sir, your house is heaven, and it is a pleasure to be in your town."

Cindy interrupted, "Daddy, this is her first time in the South. She's from up North."

"Oh, you're a Yankee. Well, that explains a lot of things. Welcome."

"Daddy, we're going to walk around town. We'll see you back at home." Cindy hugged him. "I love you."

Sandy extended her hand. Mr. Taylor looked at the fingerless glove on her hand. "Sandy, enjoy your stay here."

It had been a peaceful day as they sat on the front porch swinging. "You know, Cindy, it is kind of nice here. The smell of hay and all those bugs."

They started to laugh again.

"Well, you're right. It's not Florida, but it is my home. I didn't know how much I'd miss it." Cindy jumped out of the swing, "Let's get ready. Nashville, here we come."

Nashville did look good to Cindy and Sandy as they walked down the streets. The energy of the city was like a blanket, warm, friendly, and full of Southern hospitality. They stood on the corner of 4th and Church Street looking up at the tall buildings. "Look, Cindy, a television station—WLAC. Maybe we could get a job there. Oh, look, Printer's Alley. I've heard about this alley. Let's take a look."

Cindy had never been in Printer's Alley before and, of course, neither had Sandy. Printer's Alley was like a bottomless pit of bars and restaurants. Each neon light drew their attention. One stood out to them. 'Welcome, Studio People'. Country music poured out the door. Sandy grabbed Cindy's hand, "That's us. Let's go in." The bar was crowded. They sat looking at all the country stars' pictures on the walls. "Isn't this the most fun?" A few people were dancing. Sandy grabbed Cindy's hand, "You wanta dance?"

The music was good and so were the drinks. "Sure." They were having fun dancing and laughing.

Then, they heard a bunch of locals make comments, "Hey, hey, there's a gay bar down the street." The four guys laughed. "Sluts."

Sandy stopped dancing. "What did you say, dude?"

"You heard me. Go down the street."

Sandy walked over to the big guy. "Hey, mortal, you want a piece of me?"

The six-foot four-inch, two hundred eighty-pound man stood up and laughed. "Yeah, my truck is parked outside. Go wait for me, Lesbian."

Sandy let out a yell that shook the room. With all her might, she kicked him in the balls. He went down in pain like a building being demolished.

"That's the only piece of me you're getting.

Anybody else?"

Cindy came to her, "I think we'd better get out of here." They left the bar and stood outside.

"Cindy, I've never had so much fun."

Cindy took her hand, "That was incredible. Did you see his face when he fell? Teach me how to do that." They ran down the alley laughing.

Italy, an intellectual development of time. A country whose attention is devoted to the arts.

Cultured buildings. Developed lands for the finest grapes. The language of love. People stand and dance in the streets. Men could kiss each other in friendship, respect, and a true caring for humanity. Literary culture with classical scholars. A land in which Mrs. Spellman had grown as a child. Margaret and Mr. Gibson sat on the veranda overlooking the city. "Earl, I don't want to go back. This is where my heart belongs.

I want to live here. I want to die here. This is my true home." She held Mr. Gibson's hand. "Can you understand?"

Mr. Gibson kissed her hand. He looked out over the countryside. "Yes, I do. Any place that makes you happy makes me happy; as long as we are together."

"Oh, Earl, my heart and soul loves you so much."

Guyiser, Carla, Kate, and Mrs. Watson sat in Carla's office. "I don't want to get rid of all the accounts, just the ones that only order small amounts. Let's say the ones that only order $12,000.00 or less. What do you think, Mrs. Watson?"

"Well, that won't hurt us. With the Wall-Burg account and the Bagwell account along with our old accounts, we are now over $4,000,000.00 a year. You have brought the company a long way. Kate, Carla, what do you think?"

Kate answered, "What about new orders? They keep coming in every day."

"Kate, we'll keep all the new ones.

Carla, screen all of them. If they are going to expand, we'll keep them. If not, give them to Bagwell.

We sell him; he sells them. How does that sound to you, Mrs. Watson?"

"Well, it will eliminate a lot of dead wood for me. Then I'll be able to handle the large accounts much better."

"That's what we want, ladies, good public relations for our customers. I would like to see this company worth a billion dollars." Everyone laughed. "Okay, ladies, girls, let's keep the big wheel rolling." Guyiser left the office.

Buck and Guyiser sat on the floor of the hangar. Buck had blueprints spread out. "It's shaped like a big 'U'. Stock and supplies come in this hangar door and are stored here. Machines here, welding here, and then paint and dryers here. We'll put the assembly line beginning at the top of the 'U', inspection here, and boxed here. Then we'll separate the warehouse and store the product in this area until we ship them. I called Steinbeck and they have the machines we need. They will send a couple of engineers to set them up. The water supply is no problem, but we will need air conditioners and heaters. Kentucky gets cold in the winter." Buck laughed, "Thinking ahead. We could use a snowplow."

Guyiser laughed, "Yeah, I've been there. All in time, Buck. So what now?" They stood up.

"Well, sir, if we can get this plane out of here, we can start setting some things in place now."

Guyiser went to the plane and tapped on its side. He looked up to his office and thought about how excited he was to look down at the big plane. "Let's do it, but not today. Tomorrow."

"Yes, sir. We'll pull it out tomorrow."

The big wheel was in motion. The sun was breaking through the gray sky. Guyiser stood drinking his coffee while he looked down at the big jet. This plane had inspired him the first time he had seen it. Now, it was time to move on. He would now look down at machines, boxes, and workers. He would hear sounds of machines, smell paint, and hear voices of people talking. Loaner would not have a place to run and play. He felt sad about the change ahead of him. This was his hangar, his apartment, his office, and his private place. The thing he loved, bicycles, was now invading him. Loaner jumped up on the windowsill. "Well, boy, I guess we're going to have to learn to share."

The giant doors of the hangar began to open. There stood Buck and six men. Buck began to give orders, pointing in different directions. The large forklift backed up to the jet. The men surrounded the plane like soldiers at war. Buck stood outside the hangar with his arms in the air. He started waving his hands. The jet started to roll. This was what Guyiser had planned, but tears came to his eyes. He went to the patio and sat down. He didn't want to watch.

Carla stood at the hangar doors, watching as they pulled out the plane. The elevator doors opened and she looked for Guyiser. "Guyiser? Oh, Mr. Blackman." She walked through the bedroom to the patio and saw

Guyiser sitting and staring into space. She sat down beside him. "Guyiser, are you all right?"

"Yeah, I'm fine."

"Guyiser, look at me. This is a turning point for the company and for you. You're not losing anything. You're just making room for the future. You're making changes in your life right now—good changes. You, and only you, have taken this small company and turned it into a profit-making company worth, what did Mrs. Watson say, four million and growing.

Guyiser, everyone here is proud of you. Did you know that? I sat in Mr. Bagwell's office and watched you, listened to you, and felt so proud that I was working for you. I saw your eyes sparkle when Mr. Bagwell's rough voice said, 'Guyiser, we've got a deal.'"

Guyiser smiled and began to laugh, "You do a pretty good imitation. Carla, you're amazing. I guess I need a pep talk once in a while."

Carla stood up and smiled.

"I'm always here for you, Guyiser. Oh, here is your newspaper. Check it out. And, the sign company will be here tomorrow. Do you still want Mr. Spellman's name on the hangar?"

"No, no I don't. Put my name up there—'The Guyiser Building'. I need my ego built up."

Carla smiled and wrote in her pad, "How do you spell Guyiser? Oh, is the party still on?"

"Yep, and that reminds me. Let's take a ride over to the Spellman mansion. I want to check on the place."

"Okay, just let me know when. I'm going back to my office. Call me!"

Guyiser sat looking at the stock market section. All the figures and numbers stared back at him. His fingers went down the list of companies. *Horizon, Horizon, there it is.* He got out his paperwork and looked at the figures. His paper said $8.84. He took a highlighter and drew through the Horizon name and numbers. The amount was now $9.61. Guyiser had no idea what that meant, but to him the figure was going up. It was so easy in the barn. People would give him cash or checks, and he would put it in the bank. Now, he never saw money. Cory handled this; Mrs. Watson handled that. To Guyiser, money didn't matter anymore. As long as the company was growing and Horizon's figures were going up, everything was fine. His paychecks were being put in the bank for him. So, he didn't know how much money he had. Bills and debts were someone else's responsibility. Taxes—Mr. Gibson and Mr. Levine would handle that.

The phone rang on his desk. He went to answer it and looked out the window.

The plane was not there anymore. "Hello."

"Guyiser, you have a call on line two."

"Guyiser Blackman here."

"Mr. Blackman, sir. Good afternoon to you. My name is Yamamoto. I am what you call a brother of Bill Bagwell. He gave me your number."

"Well, Mr. Yamamoto, Mr. Bagwell is a good man. What can I do for you?"

"I am a distributor of toys in the West territory.

He suggested that I talk with you. I have seen your line of products and want to handle your bicycles."

"Well, sir, you have called the right person. I would be honored to help you."

"Thank you, Mr. Blackman. In the West, I also supply major stores, so I want to order from your company many bicycles."

"Mr. Yamamoto, I will be happy to supply you with your needs."

"Mr. Blackman, all your products will sell greatly in the Western stores. There is one series I find most valuable to me—your gold series. In the West, people do more exercising than any other place. I want to supply your stationary bike to every account I have."

"Mr. Yamamoto, I take great pride in my gold series. That is a very wise choice."

"Mr. Blackman, I also deal in Japan and Hong Kong, China. American products do very well there. When can I place an order with your company at the same price as Mr. Bagwell?"

"I will accept your order and ship to you upon your request, sir."

"Thank you, Mr. Blackman. I am honored to do business with you. You will be hearing from me soon. Thank you for your time."

"No, no, Mr. Yamamoto, thank you for your time. And thank Mr. Bagwell for me, also. Bye for now."

Mr. Yamamoto had brought Guyiser's attention to his stationary bike. Guyiser dialed his phone. "Hello, is Mr. Levine in, please?"

"...Yes, I'll hold. Mr. Levine, hi sir. This is Guyiser Blackman. How are you?"

"...I'm doing fine."

"...Oh, business is really good."

"...Well sir, I have an idea for a product for my bicycles, and I want to get a patent on it. Can you help me with this?"

"...Sure can. That's great. What do you need?"

"...Okay."

"...Okay."

"...I'll have all the plans and figures faxed to you right away. Thank you, sir. How are you doing?"

"...No, I haven't talked to him lately."

"...I will. I need to talk to him, too."

"...Okay, bye."

The jet, the hangar, and his apartment had all become secondary to him. He realized that Carla was right. This was a change for the future. He was now as excited as ever with the thought of the company expanding with his new idea of a new product. A loud machine drew his attention. He looked out the window to see Buck and a big forklift bringing things into the hangar. Buck had blueprints spread out on a table and pointing in different directions. Men were preparing to build walls. Guyiser smiled and went to see Buck. "What's going on, Buck?"

"Well, sir, the plane is tied down snuggling to the ground. We'll cover it later. You know, Mr. Blackman, it's going to be pretty noisy here for a while."

"Don't worry about it, Buck. You know what we need? Put on another shift of people; say from three p.m. to eleven p.m. The gold series is hot right now, so let's concentrate on gold bikes and stationary bikes. You were right. Gold is the answer. See Kate and tell her about another shift. She knows what to do. Gotta go. See you later. This is a really big hangar with the plane out, ain't it?"

Buck laughed, "Yes sir, it's as big as a barn."

Guyiser and Carla stood on the steps of the Spellman mansion. "Wow! What a place. What is that over there?"

It's a two-bedroom guesthouse with a big black limousine parked in the garage. Come on, I'll show you around." They stood in the formal dining room looking at the tall ceiling and the marble-topped table.

"Two, four, six, eight; this is the biggest table I've ever seen. Ten, Guyiser, there are fourteen chairs—and look at that big chandelier!"

Guyiser took her hand, "You haven't seen anything yet. Come on." The spiral staircase took them up to the bedrooms. "Three up here with a view for miles and one downstairs. Look at the pool and the garden." They stood on one of the large patios looking down.

"Well, what do you say? Can we have a good party here or what?"

"Guyiser, we can do a lot of things here." Carla smiled and he laughed.

"Come on, sexy. We got to get back."

"Mr. Blackman, Carla, here's your mail." Kate handed Guyiser a separate envelope, "Guyiser, you have got to read this one."

"Thanks, Kate."

Guyiser sat in Carla's office reading the letter. "Carla, this is your department. Put together nine boys' bicycles and six girls'. Call the mayor and let him know what we're doing for the orphanage. Ask him if he would like to be there when we give the kids their bicycles. I think he just might. Set a date and call the media."

"Guyiser, this is a wonderful idea. The press will eat this up. And, the party. I'll get started on a list of names for you and make up an invitation you'll like."

"Sounds good to me. I have to go to check on some things. See you later. Oh, yes. Have the kids invited. They should have fun."

Shipping and Receiving was very busy. Guyiser sat talking to Tom Maker. "Stock is beginning to run low, Mr. Blackman. In fact, we're going to have backorders soon."

"Well, don't worry about small orders. Wall-Burg is what we need to keep shipping...."

"Well, sir, that's what I mean. We went from a hundred bicycles up to a thousand bicycles a day. I don't want to run out of stock."

"Don't worry about that. We're putting on another shift. That should help until the hangar is producing. What about space?"

Mr. Maker laughed and pointed out his office window, "They don't stay on the floor that long. See those trucks; they're taking them out faster than Buck can make'em."

"Tom, my man, you're doing a good job. If you start running behind too much, let me know, all right? Just keep them moving. See you later."

Guyiser stood watching the men working in the hangar. Loaner was running around smelling everything and everybody. He did not quite know what was going on in his house. A large truck backed up to the hangar. It was loaded with lumber. The forklift started unloading the load of two by fours and plywood. Buck walked over to Guyiser, "Well, the walls are going up tomorrow. What about restrooms?"

Guyiser smiled, "Buck, I'm not worried about where people are going to pee. Put some Port-a-Potties out the back door for now."

Buck scratched his head, "Why didn't I think of that?"

"You would have as soon as you had to go." They laughed.

"You're right, boss."

It was one of those rare days in the Centerville area. The bright, beautiful, warm sun was pouring into Cindy's bedroom. She was writing in her notebook about Sandy's and her experience in Nashville at the bar. This was going to make a good T.V. show on how men think they see women. She looked at the picture of Guyiser and her. *I wonder how Guyiser sees me.* She held the frame and kissed Guyiser. Instinctively, she picked up the phone and dialed his number. "Hello, Guyiser here."

Cindy grinned and put a paper over the speaker, "Mr. Blackman, I'm a secret admirer, and I'm lying here naked thinking about you. Would you like to get together tonight?"

Guyiser smiled and looked at Cindy's picture, "Well, I can't tonight. How about a nooner?"

"Oh, Mr. Blackman, you're making me so hot. Tell me what you would do to me."

"Well, it's so dirty I can't say it over the phone. Why don't you come over here in about then minutes and I'll show you."

"Ten minutes! Guyiser, this is Cindy!"

Guyiser started laughing, "I know, baby. How are you?"

Cindy lay back on her bed, "Didn't I fool you at all?"

"Sure, girlfriend, I get these calls all the time."

"You'd better not. I miss you."

"Me, too."

"So, what's going on in Kentucky?"

"Cindy, things are going so fast here. I wish you were here to help me. How's things with you?"

"Guyiser, you won't believe it; I got my own T.V. show. We start taping in a month or so--in guess where.

New York. Isn't that wonderful? I'm so excited. It's only for two years, but then who knows."

Guyiser put the phone to his other ear, "Two years, and who knows."

"Guyiser, you don't sound happy for me."

"Oh, I am, Cindy. I really am, but I was kind of hoping."

"Guyiser, I love you. Two years will go by fast. We talked about this, remember?"

"I know, Cindy, I know. I'm making so much money that I thought we could..."

"Guyiser, it's not about money, sweetheart. It's about you and me doing what we have dreamed of."

"But Cindy, two years, and what about the who knows part?"

"The who knows part is about you and me getting that farm, Guyiser. Isn't that what you want?"

Guyiser took a deep breath. He knew that he was not going to win this conversation, "Yes Cindy, and in two years I hope that is what you want. So, how's the weather?" The big hangar doors opened, and a crew of men began to work.

"Oh, it's beautiful. Leaves are changing colors and...."

Guyiser cut her off, "Cindy honey, my crew just came in. I've got to go. I miss you and love you."

"Boyfriend, you're in my every dream. I love you, too. You take care of yourself. It's your turn to call me next. Bye, sweetheart."

Guyiser hung up the phone and sat looking out the window.

Loaner ran in the office barking. He jumped up on the windowsill and looked at the men making noise. "Easy, boy. What do you say you and I do something today? Want to go?" Loaner ran to the elevator, barked, and smiled. "You know that word, don't you?"

The Kentucky bluegrass was a perfect place to play. It was a beautiful, warm, sunny day as Guyiser and Loaner rolled around on the mansion's front lawn.

Loaner was a big and powerful German shepherd and smarter than most human beings. His sensitiveness was responsive to any of Guyiser's slightest changes. He would watch Guyiser sleep for hours, but when Guyiser moved, his head would go up to see his master's change. Even as a small puppy, he was sensitive. He mourned when Mr. Blackman died and felt Guyiser's pain. Tricks and commands were his favorite things to do for Guyiser. Guyiser was always challenging him with new thoughts and ideas. Guyiser stood with the ball, "Me, Loaner." Loaner stood by his side.

Guyiser threw the ball far away to his left side. Loaner waited for his command to get the ball. "No, Loaner, I want you to 'say' two times when I throw the ball to my left." They went and got the ball. Guyiser threw the ball again to his left. He looked at Loaner, "Say." Loaner looked at the ball and at Guyiser. He barked two times.

Guyiser smiled, "Get." Loaner ran to the ball and brought it back to Guyiser. "Good boy, good boy. Now,

Loaner, I'm going to throw it to my right. That way. When I say 'Say', you bark three times, bark, bark, bark." Loaner cocked his head and wagged his tail. Guyiser threw the ball far to his right. "Me, Loaner." Loaner moved close to his side. Guyiser pointed with his right hand and looked at Loaner, "Say." Loaner looked at Guyiser and barked three times. "Get." Loaner ran, got the ball, and returned. Guyiser got down on his knees and hugged Loaner.

"I knew you would understand. Let's do it again." Loaner was so happy. He had learned two new things—left and right. They ran, played, and rolled in the grass for an hour. Guyiser lay in the grass, "Let's quit, Loaner, I'm tired." Loaner jumped on top of Guyiser, "No, no, big lug. No more. We've got to get back."

They ran into the office building. Kate stood up and leaned on the counter, "Well, look at you two. You been playing football?"

Guyiser looked at Loaner, "No, but that's an idea, Kate."

Kate handed him some messages. "Guyiser, Mr. Gibson called. Wants you to call him back at this number."

"Is he all right?"

"Yes, he's fine and very excited about something."

"Thanks, Kate. I'll call him now." Guyiser went in Mr. Gibson's office and dialed the number.

Mr. Gibson sat on the veranda watching the sunset as the phone rang. "Chow, hello."

"Mr. Gibson, is that you?"

"Guyiser, my boy. Yes, it is. How are you?"

"Mr. Gibson, are you all right?"

"My son, I couldn't be better. This is the most beautiful country I have ever been in. I'm looking at pink and orange clouds as the sun sets. The air is so fresh and clean, and the wine is superb. Guyiser, Margaret and I have great news. We have decided to stay and live here in Italy. Guyiser, are you there?"

"Uh, yes sir. It's just a shock. What about all your plans—the factory, your shop, your home, and you and me? Mr. Gibson, have you thought this over good?"

"Yes, Guyiser, this is what I have waited for for a long time. Margaret is my life."

"But, but, you two could live here and be happy together."

"I know, my son, but Italy is Margaret's life. This is where she was born and raised. I love it here, too. If you could look in her eyes, you would understand. Yes, Guyiser, my plans have changed. As far as the factory, it's yours. Mrs. Watson, Kate, and even Mr. Levine has told me how you have single-handedly turned the factory into a giant multi-million dollar business. Guyiser, I'm not deserting you. I will always be a part of your life and the factory. I love you, son. Now, we are coming back. Margaret wants to gather her things. In fact, there is one thing that will make you very happy."

"Okay, Mr. Gibson, as long as you are happy. You know that I love you, too. You became my father when my dad died. You were there when I was in trouble. You gave me a life. It's just going to be different for me, you know? I'll just miss seeing you."

"Guyiser, all you have to do is close your eyes. I'll be there. Now, son, you think about all of this. Margaret and I will see you in about a week. We love you, Guyiser. You hear me?"

"Yes, sir, I understand."

Guyiser sat alone in the big office. He looked at the phone in his hand. Echoes of Mr. Gibson's voice ran through his head. *Guyiser, I'm not deserting you.* Nevertheless, the fact was, they would be thousands of miles apart. Mr. Gibson had always inspired him and had given him advice and direction since day one. He closed his eyes and saw Mr. Gibson rocking in his chair, *Put this on your flyer. You know Christmas can make your year. I'm sorry about your dad, but I'm here for you, Guyiser. Guyiser, I have a great deal for you. Guyiser, this is Mr. Levine.*

There was a knock on the door, and Carla came in very excitedly. Guyiser hung up the phone. "Oh, I'm sorry. Are you busy?"

Guyiser leaned back and looked at the phone, "No, but I'm about to be. What's going on?"

"Here is a list of names for the party—celebrities, the press, distributors, friends, kids, and the mayor. The mayor wants to be at the orphanage when you give the kids their bicycles. This is set for next week. Here is a sample of the invitation for your approval. What do you think? Most everyone likes the theme, Ride for Health. Guyiser, I want to put bicycles everywhere like around the pool, in front of the mansion, and at the gates. It will be very impressive."

Carla's excitement spilled over onto Guyiser. "Wow! This is pretty. I like these raised letters."

"They are called embossed lettering."

Guyiser smiled, "I know that. I just didn't know the word for it. Two weeks from now?"

"Yeah, that will give me enough time to put everything together. Oh, Guyiser, I'm so excited about all of this."

Guyiser looked at the list of guest. "Let all of our out-of-town guests know they can stay at the mansion. Carla, I approve of everything. Buy yourself the most beautiful gown you can find. I want you to be the most elegant, seductive, sensuous woman there."

Guyiser stood and walked to her. "You know, you're my woman. What do they say, 'The woman behind the man?'"

Carla kissed him passionately. "That's where I want to be, Guyiser. How about dinner tonight?"

Guyiser stood at Kate's desk, "Kate, Mr. Gibson and Mrs. Spellman are coming back next week. Would you please call James and the housekeeper back to work? The house is all dusty and someone needs to clean up the grounds. They know the routine. Oh, when you see the security guard, send him down to see me, okay?"

"I will sir, and it will be so good to see Mrs. Spellman again."

Guyiser nodded, "Yes, it will."

The hangar noise was almost quiet. Buck was waving at some men as Guyiser drove up. "Hello, boss. We got a lot done today."

"Looks good, Buck."

"Oh, I got me a good assistant. He knows a lot about factory work and about how to get things done. He's starting Monday. We have the second shift starting. That will help us catch up. I'll be training people for a few days. Oh, by the way, some of the machines are going to be shipped to us on Wednesday. That's sooner than I expected." Buck wiped his hands and laughed, "Yep, everything's gonna come together all right. Well, Mr. Blackman, it's been a long week. I'm going home and have some chicken and watch T.V. all weekend."

Guyiser looked around the hangar, "You deserve it, Buck. Go home. We'll see you Monday."

Guyiser watched the tired man walk to his car and drive away.

"Mr. Blackman, hi sir. Kate told me you wanted to see me."

"Oh, hi Jim. Yes, I do. I have a job for you. Do you know the Spellman place? I need you to work there for a week or so. What do you say?"

Jim put on his hat, "Don't mind at all. I worked there before for Mr. Spellman. What would you like me to do, sir?"

"Just patrol the house and the gates mostly. I want people to see you at the gates. Keep people out. Watch the house, you know? The house is empty, and I would feel better if you were there. I also need you to get me another security person, can you do that?"

"Yes, sir. No problem."

"Good man. Why don't you go to the house starting tonight? I'll check with you later."

"10-4, sir. I'm on my way."

Intuition was one of Guyiser's strongest points. His instincts about people and his foresight of things mixed with his imagination gave him the power to see the big picture. His new venture with the factory was a challenge for his mind. Every day his imagination was free to look at one thing and see many things to do with it. To find a different way to do something was stimulating and opened all kinds of avenues for Guyiser. He was left handed, but he would sometimes write with his right hand. He would walk in an out door. On an open road, he would drive on the wrong side just to feel what it was like. To challenge a challenge and to find a different way to do it was to him a fact of life. However, tonight, as he and Carla sat in the restaurant, his instincts were bothering him. "Carla, do you have any people who are enemies? I mean who really don't like you?"

Carla looked at him in surprise. "What? I don't think so. Maybe a girlfriend who's a little jealous of me, but not my enemy. That's a strange question, Guyiser, even for you. What brought this on?"

"I don't know. Things are going so well that I feel something bad might happen."

"Guyiser, that is paranoia. You know, like when you're driving and you see a police car behind you. You know you haven't done anything wrong. He probably just wants to go around you, so you didn't need to worry about it."

"Yeah, paranoia. I guess you're right."

Carla leaned over and kissed Guyiser. "How do you like your seafood linguini?"

"I like it. Is it from Italy?"

"Yes, it is, Guyiser."

Guyiser took another bite and a drink of his wine. "Good food."

Carla and Guyiser sat in the truck. Carla moved close to him and stroked his leg. "Are you going to take me to your apartment?"

Guyiser smiled as he started the truck, "No, not tonight."

Carla kissed his ear, "Here in the truck?"

"Nope, we're going to the big house."

Jim stood in full uniform at the gates of the mansion with his hand up, "Oh hi, Mr. Blackman."

"Hi, Jim. How's it going?"

"Everything is code 4, sir."

"Good. We're going up to the house for a few hours."

Carla leaned over to the window. "We have some work to do."

"Yes, ma'am. I'll open the gates, Mr. Blackman."

Guyiser stood by the bedroom door looking at Carla's beautiful nude body. Her long black hair spread out like a big black cloud on the white satin pillow. He slowly dimmed the lights and walked to her. He held her tight as he lay on top of her looking into her eyes. "Your eyes tell me a story. We are going to be together for a long time. I need you, Carla."

"I'll do anything for you, Guyiser, anything."

The heavens opened up an explosion as they made love. It was the nearest thing to saying, 'I love you.'

The weekend flew by. Guyiser and Loaner went shopping, took a short trip, and saw some of the bluegrass state of Kentucky. Now it was Monday, and it was back to work. Guyiser was right about all the good things happening. The factory was coming together faster each day. Orders were coming in. Bicycles were going out. His stock in Horizon had gone up and up. In fact, Cory had told him about an oil company in Juneau, Alaska, that was expanding. There was real estate in Hawaii with a large resort hotel being built. Guyiser trusted Cory's judgment and invested $50,000.00 in each one. He had also bought more stock in Horizon.

Guyiser liked to look in the newspaper and see the figures go up. He wasn't sure about the money. He just liked to see the numbers go up. Besides, Mrs. Watson told him, 'If you don't spend the money, you have to pay taxes on it, so spend some.'

Kate, Carla, Buck, and everyone was doing a great job. Kate had hired people for the second shift. She worked with Mrs. Watson on all the accounts. Carla was putting things together to make the company grow. Buck was running the production of the plant and overseeing the growth of the factory. Guyiser sat at his desk looking out the window. There was still something wrong. In the back of his mind, his instincts were still trying to tell him something. Suddenly, he spun around and looked at the picture of the lighthouse and the safe behind it.

His mind raced, *Olsen, that's it! Olsen.* He saw the man with the rifle shooting at him. He heard Olsen's voice saying, 'I'll get you, Blackman.' This was what had been hidden in his mind. Guyiser thought about what his father had told him as a small boy, 'Know you enemy; know your enemy, Guyiser.' Olsen was like a wounded bear that Guyiser had shot. Olsen was dangerous. This farm boy had hurt him financially and had made him leave the country. Guyiser knew this animal would strike again. 'Know your enemy, Guyiser.' This is what Guyiser had to do.

There were no clouds in Centerville; the sky was blue and the sun was warm. Sandy and Cindy sat on the edge of the bed. Sandy was excitedly watching Cindy on the phone with Jeff. "Okay, Cynthia, you and Sandy get it together. The station wants you in New York to start doing promotional shoots for your show."

Cindy grabbed Sandy's arm, "When?"

"They want you there Thursday."

"Jeff, that's great. Where do we stay?"

"You'll have to stay at a hotel until you find an apartment you like."

"You will be there, won't you?"

"Oh, yeah. Every step of the way."

"Jeff, say hello to Sandy."

Sandy grabbed the phone, "Hi, dude."

"Sandy, don't call me dude."

"Yes sir, Mr. Jeff." Cindy and Sandy burst out laughing.

"I'm sorry, Jeff. How are you doing?"

"Listen, Miss Clown, you take care of Cynthia. She's our bread and butter. You know what I mean?"

Sandy made a face, "Yes, sir. Have a good day, Jeff. Here's Cindy."

"Jeff, this is a dream come true."

"It's only the beginning for you, Cynthia. You'll have your own dressing room, a makeup and hair artist, wardrobe, and the works. If there is anything you want or need, just ask me, okay. We're going to make a great team, Cynthia, trust me. Now, I'll see you in New York. Take care. Bye."

Cindy looked at Sandy, "Can you believe this? It's really happening!"

Sandy broke out in song, "New York, New York, if I can make it there," Cindy joined in, "I can make it anywhere." They burst out laughing like kids watching monkeys at the zoo.

It was later that day. Cindy and Sandy were watching T.V. Cindy was throwing popcorn at Sandy's mouth. "You know, Sandy, I think we should live in a penthouse."

Sandy chewed on popcorn and flipped through the channels. "Yeah, with rich guys next door. Look! Look!" The program had been interrupted. Cindy leaned forward. Large letters were on the screen, 'Breaking News.'

A woman reporter came on, "Two FBI agents were shot this morning when they discovered a large truck loaded with cocaine. The driver was killed in the gun battle. The cocaine was valued at 1.5 million dollars. More on the agents' conditions on our later news broadcast."

Cindy was all eyes. "Wow! Now, that's news. That's what I would like to do, cover news events."

Sandy stood up, "You will, Cindy. You will, but they should have used two cameras. Let's go do something exciting like ride a cow or something." They ran out the door giggling like two little girls.

The elevator doors opened and Carla walked in. She went to Guyiser who was looking out the window. "Why so pensive?"

Guyiser kept looking out the window. "If you wanted to find someone in this big world, where would you start?"

Carla sat on the windowsill, "Well, that depends. A man is easier to find than a woman. I guess you start with their last address, maybe a phone number, friends, the Internet, or their social security number. It may take some time, but...."

Guyiser stood up looking out the window, "I don't have a lot of time."

Carla looked up to him, "Well then, I would hire a private investigator; that's their job."

"Find me one, Carla. Find me a good one."

Carla stood and touched his arm, "This sounds serious, Guyiser. You want to talk about it?"

"Not now, Carla. I just don't want anybody hurt, you, the factory, or me. I just want to know where this man is and what he's doing." Guyiser looked at her and smiled, "Now, where were we? What's going on?"

Carla was very concerned about all of this. She opened her notebook and sat down. "Instead of going to the orphanage, we will give the kids their bicycles here. The mayor, the press, and everyone will be here.

I thought it would be better publicity for the factory."

"Good thinking. I like it. What time?"

"It's set for one o'clock. You and the mayor can give the bikes at two o'clock, which will give time for the media to have a spot on T.V. on the six o'clock news."

"Wow! Now, that's what I call a plan. I'm amazed, Carla. You made a little thing into a city event."

Carla stood and went to Guyiser. She put her arms around him. "Just doing my job. That's what Public Relations is all about. I have to go back to my office. Call me."

"Call you? No, I'm going with you." They walked into the office building.

Buck was just leaving, "Hi, boss, Miss Comings. The new shift starts today. I just put in an order for more gold paint. Gotta get. See you later." Buck rushed past them.

Kate was faxing orders for supplies. "Guyiser, got a message for you. Mr. Gibson and Mrs. Spellman will be here tomorrow. They arrive at 11:10 a.m. James will pick them up at the airport."

"Thank God, Kate. He's just the one I need to see. Carla, will you take care of what we talked about?"

"Yes, sir. I'll do that right now. Oh, Kate, can you help me? I need chairs, tables, and some food and drinks for Wednesday."

"Sure, Carla."

"Guyiser, I'll see you later." Guyiser watched her walk away.

"She's quite a girl, isn't she?"

"Yes, she is, Kate. Yes, she is. You know, this is coming together perfectly with Mr. Gibson, the mayor, and the kids."

Kate handed him some papers. "Would you sign these orders? And, don't forget Mrs. Spellman."

Guyiser scribbled his name, "Yeah, and Mrs. Spellman. Gotta go. Loaner's hungry."

Guyiser stood with James as Loaner rolled in the grass. "He really likes it here, Mr. Blackman."

"Yes, he does, James. The grounds and the house look good. This is such a pretty place. How's the limo?"

"Perfect shape, sir."

Jim came over to them, "Hi sir, James. Oh, sir, I have another guard for you."

"Good, Jim. Let him work here. Train him on what to do. Show him the gates and the house. Have him watch Mrs. Spellman and Mr. Gibson. I want top security here. You come back to the factory. Wednesday we are having the mayor and a lot of kids here. Look sharp. Wear a tie, okay? We also have a second shift starting, so I need you at night. Is that all right with you?"

"Yes, sir. No problem."

"Good man. There will be a lot of overtime for you."

Jim grinned, "Thank you, sir. I can sure use the money."

Guyiser called for Loaner. "James, Jim, ya'll have a good day. I got to get back. You guys are doing a good job. If you need anything, call me."

Guyiser sat in his golf cart on the runway watching Loaner run around. The building cast a shadow as the sun started to hide. People were working. People were leaving. It was a good feeling for him to sit and see the jet, the people, the buildings, and to know that in his first year, he had accomplished so much.

Loaner began barking. He was jumping around and making circles around something. Guyiser went to see what he had found. It was a mother raccoon and several of her babies. They had walked out of the tree line and through the back gate at the end of the runway. Guyiser watched the mother stand up and snap at Loaner. The mother turned, and she and her coons went back out the gate and to the trees. Guyiser smiled and called Loaner, "Come on, boy. Leave them alone." Guyiser went to the gate and closed it, watching the raccoons waddle away. "Let's go, Loaner."

The intercom buzzed, "Yes."

"It's me. What are you doing?"

Guyiser leaned back and smiled, "Thinking about you."

"Oh, yeah? Well, Mr. Blackman, you want to get together?"

"Not tonight, hon. I got some things to do."

"Well, that's okay. I have some laundry to do and some house cleaning."

Guyiser laughed, "You do housework?"

"Of course, I do. I'm very domesticated." Carla laughed. "I'll see you tomorrow."

The Give-Away

Part 12

I give of my heart; I give of my soul,
I want you to share all of my gold.
The day is coming, for I can see,
Happiness for you; happiness for me.

Tuesday morning began a busy day for Kate and Carla. Mr. Maker had two of his men setting up a large white canopy tent with tables for food and drinks. There was a platform built beside the set. Chairs were placed in front of it. Bicycles of all colors were lined up beside the platform. Carla stood giving directions, "Put half the bikes on one side and half on the other side. Yeah, yeah, that's better. We'll put the gas balloons on them tomorrow. And, take the cover off the plane tomorrow, too."

Kate was on the phone as Carla walked in, "Yes, plenty of ice." Kate waved at Carla, "No, that's all. Just have everything here by noon, and don't be late! Thank you. Bye. You know, Carla, you have to tell people two or three times what to do."

Carla and Kate laughed. "Well, I have to go and make up cards with the kids' names on them. Have you seen Guyiser this morning?"

"No, but his cart is by the factory door."

"Good, that means he's busy. Maybe we can get something done. See ya'."

Buck wiped his nose on his shirtsleeve, "No, sir. They will be all right. They'll pick up speed in a day or so. It takes time to learn a new job. Oh, by the way, the new machines will be here in the morning, but it will take a week or so to put them together."

"That's okay, Buck, as long as we're on schedule. Going to make my rounds. See you later."

It was a beautiful day. Guyiser and Loaner had been to the Art Department for a visit with Scott and Tim.

They stood watching the forklift loading the bicycles on to a freight truck. It was good to see the bicycles going out the door. Mrs. Watson was glad to see checks coming in. Guyiser and Loaner hopped in his cart and headed for the office building. "Kate, it is a perfect day outside with the warm sun and fresh air."

"Well, I'm glad you're enjoying it, Guyiser. I've been trying to get a hold of you. You should carry your radio with you."

"Oh, that. Okay, I will; I will."

"Good news for you. Mr. Gibson called. He's at the big house and wants you to call him."

"Kate, I'll do that right now." Guyiser went to Mr. Gibson's office. On the way, he called for Carla to come to the office with him. "Mr. Gibson, afternoon, sir. Glad you are back."

"How are you?"

"Oh, I'm fine, sir. How's Mrs. Spellman?"

"Guyiser, she's busier than a bicycle sale at Christmas time." They laughed. "She has movers boxing and packing. She and the housekeeper are packing clothes. I just sit here and watch."

"What's the hurry, Mr. Gibson?"

"You know, Guyiser, that's one thing I love about her. When she makes up her mind about something, that's it."

"Well, sir, I hope she has time for tomorrow." Guyiser looked at Carla. She handed him a paper. "The mayor will be here."

"The mayor!"

"Yes, sir. We're giving bicycles away to kids from the orphanage. Miss Comings has the press coming. There will be food and drinks. You and Mrs. Spellman have to be there."

"Well, of course, we'll be there. What time?"

"Well, sir, Carla has it scheduled like this: The kids will be here at 1:00 so they will have some time to eat and play, the press will set up at 1:15, the mayor will be here at 1:30, and we will give away the bikes at 1:45 to 2:00. Then it will be over."

"I've got to meet Carla. Maybe she can organize my life." They laughed.

"Oh, you will meet her," Guyiser looked at Carla. "She makes my life a lot easier. She's dynamite. So, if you and Mrs. Spellman would come here around 12:30 that would be great."

"We will be there at 12:30, Guyiser. It will be good to see you. Bye now."

Guyiser turned to Carla, "This is great! And, you are dynamite. Everything is set, right?"

Carla looked over her notes, "Yes, sir. Just one little thing. Can the kids go in the jet? I think they would enjoy that."

Guyiser went to her and pulled her to himself. "They can do anything you want. You're the boss. It's your day. Carla, I can't tell you how important you are around here and especially to me."

"Well, thank you. You're pretty special to me."

"Carla, would you do something for me? I know you will be busy, but would you stay close to Mrs.

Spellman tomorrow? She's important. Just give her a lot of attention, that's all."

"Yes, I will. I met her once before a long time ago. She's a nice lady. So, let me go. I still have things to do, sir." Guyiser patted her butt. "Hey, that's sexual harassment."

Guyiser smile, "So, sue me."

Another gorgeous day was present.

Guyiser and Mr. Gibson sat in the golf cart outside the big hangar watching men at work. There were four huge cartons and several big boxes. The men were pulling boards off the large pieces of machines. "This is only for the Wall-Burg account. We needed the space. You know their account is about four or five million dollars a year, and that will double in a few years."

"Guyiser, this is amazing to see. I never in all my life thought this would happen, never. When I asked you to take on this factory, I never expected this."

Guyiser grinned, "Me neither. And there's more. We had to put on another shift just to keep up with all the orders."

Carla, Kate, Mrs. Spellman, and Mrs. Watson were sitting in Mr. Gibson's office laughing and talking as Guyiser and Mr. Gibson came in.

"Margaret, you should see what's going on around here."

"I know, Earl. We have been talking about it. Isn't it exciting? Guyiser, you're a genius."

"Mrs. Spellman, without Mrs. Watson, Kate, and Carla things would not have happened."

"Don't be so modest, Guyiser. I could see the change when we drove in. You have done a marvelous job."

"Well, thank you, ma'am. The press and kids are here. Would everyone like to go outside?"

Jim stood by the plane's door. Another guard stood by the platform. The camera crew had set up their cameras. Kids were eating and running around the jet, inside and out. Everyone stood under the tent watching the kids playing and chasing Loaner.

The mayor's car drove through the gates and to the plane. Guyiser went to meet him, "Mr. Mayor, thank you for coming today." They went to the tent. "Sir, I would like you to meet Mrs. Spellman and Mr. Gibson."

"It's my pleasure to meet you both. What you are doing for the community is wonderful. Miss Comings has told me all the wonderful things that the factory is doing by creating jobs and putting people to work. Mr. Blackman, I commend what you have done."

"Thank you, Mr. Mayor." Guyiser looked at his watch, "I know you're busy, sir. Should we get started?"

Reporters came to them, "Pictures, pictures please." Flashes from cameras captured everyone.

T.V. crews ran footage of everything. Guyiser called to a reporter, "Get pictures of Miss Carla Comings. She's the reason we are here today." Cameras flashed.

"Mr. Mayor, please sir, with Miss Comings." Flashes went off again.

Carla grabbed Guyiser, "Us, too." Cameras flashed.

It was a brilliant setting. The kids rode their bicycles up and down the runway. Camera crews packed up and drove away. Soon, the kids climbed in their bus and left with a truck loaded with their bikes behind them.

Mrs. Spellman and Mr. Gibson stood by the limousine talking to Guyiser and Carla. Mrs. Spellman held their hands. "This is a day we will never forget. You two have done a great and good thing for those kids. It is something they will never forget. When the mayor gave them their bicycles, I cried. Earl and I want you to have dinner with us. Would you?"

Guyiser kissed her cheek. "Oh course, we will. We would like that very much."

"Say about five?" James closed the car door and drove away.

"What a perfect day. Carla, you pulled it off perfectly." Guyiser looked into her eyes. He wanted to say more to her, but he didn't.

Mrs. Taylor came out on the porch with a frying pan in her hand. She looked for the girls and called out, "Cindy, Cindy."

Cindy came out of the barn with a shovel in her hand, "Yes, Mother, we're here."

Mrs. Taylor called out again, "Telephone. It's Jeff."

Sandy walked out carrying a rake and sneezed, "Cow shit, why do we have to do this? I'm a professional cameraperson."

Cindy laughed, "Come on, it's Jeff."

They ran to the house and into the living room. "Hello, Jeff." Sandy sneezed again. "What was that?" Cindy grinned, "That was Sandy. What's going on?"

"Cynthia, you got your wish. You know how you wanted to cover a war story? Well, guess what. We're going to Russia! It's not a war yet, but Russia is causing other problems. We are all going to cover a human interest story of the Russian people."

Cindy dropped the phone. Sandy picked it up, "What did you say to her?"

"Sandy, do you have a cold?"

"No, Jeff, I have straw up my nose."

"Put Cynthia back on."

"Here, Cindy, the genius wants to talk to you."

"I heard that, Sandy."

Cindy took the phone. "Jeff, what brought all this on?"

"News is a fast business, Cynthia. We have to stay on top of it."

"But, what about my show?"

Jeff laughed, "Cynthia, this is your show. We send the footage that we shoot back to the station. They air it every night. Isn't this great? Now, when you get to New York, I'll explain everything. Bring all your warm clothes. We will be there a month or so. Then we go to Alaska and back to New York. Now, get your butts here tomorrow. We have a lot to do before we leave. I'll see you tomorrow night. Bye."

Cindy sat in shock, "Sandy, we're going to Russia!"

Sandy sneezed again.

"Good, anyplace is better than that barn!"

The automatic lights came on, lighting up the mansion and its grounds. Mrs. Spellman was telling Carla about the sights of Italy. Guyiser and Loaner walked in with Mr. Gibson. They all sat in the living room. "Mrs. Spellman, did Carla tell you about her new project? She is starting a program called 'Books for Bikes.' She wants kids to collect books for the orphanage library."

Mrs. Spellman held Carla's hands, "Carla, what a wonderful idea. Education for children is so important."

Guyiser stood and went to the television set, "She even planned today's event so it would be on the six o'clock news." A commercial ended and the news came on. Guyiser sat down and held Carla's hand.

"Good evening. We start with a heartwarming story. Kids from a Bowling Green orphanage played on the grounds of the Gibson, Blackman Bicycle Factory today. The mayor gave bicycles to all the children and said, 'I am proud to be a part of this today. The Gibson, Blackman Company has not only reached into the community to give jobs to people, but has also remembered the children.'

Mr. Gibson turned to Guyiser, "Wonderful, wonderful."

The mayor went on to say, 'I would like to personally thank Mrs. Spellman, Mr. Gibson, Mr. Blackman, and Miss Carla Comings for letting these beautiful children know that they are not forgotten.' The reporter continued, "Here are some shots of today's events with the children. There will be more on this story on the News at Eleven. Now on to...." Guyiser turned off the sound. They all sat quietly.

Mr. Gibson finally stood and went to Carla. "That was a marvelous thing you have done." Mrs. Spellman sat wiping her eyes. Mr. Gibson went to her and sat with his arm around her. "Guyiser, I think this is a good time to tell you something. You have matured and have successfully taken on a big responsibility. We are very proud of you. Mrs. Spellman and I have talked about this, and we want to reward you. We want to give this mansion to you. It's yours."

Mrs. Spellman spoke up, "Guyiser, I will sign it over to you on one condition—that we can be your children's God-parents. We are family, Guyiser, and we love you."

Guyiser was shocked. He stood and walked around the couch. This was something he had never, never expected.

"I don't know what to say, Mrs. Spellman. This is your house."

Mrs. Spellman went to Guyiser, "This is my house, but it is not my life. My life is in Italy with Earl. That is what I want—not this house. Just enjoy it as much as I have." She kissed him on both cheeks. "God bless you, Guyiser."

Guyiser and Carla drove to the gates and stopped looking back at the mansion at the end of the long driveway. The light of a full moon lit up the big house.

"I still can't believe it. Me, a mansion. I never expected this. I never saw it coming."

"Guyiser, the gods are watching over you. You are a blessed child, a special person."

"But, Carla, it's so big."

Carla burst out laughing, "I've got an idea. Rent a room to me."

Guyiser laughed and hugged her, "You know, you have the best ideas. Let's go to my place and watch the eleven o'clock news."

The whole state of Kentucky was talking about the Gibson, Blackman's give-away. The phones were all lit up. Kate was writing messages, one after another. Carla walked in, "Oh, thank God. Carla, help me. This is all your fault."

"Where is Guyiser?"

Kate shook a handful of papers, "I don't know. His truck is gone. Look at these—the governor's office called, the mayor called, and calls are coming in from everywhere. Please hold, one moment, please hold."

Carla smiled, "I'll take calls in my office."

"Hurry!"

All day long, the calls came in. People sent flowers. Messages were delivered. It was late in the day when Carla buzzed Guyiser's office. "Yes."

"Guyiser, are you all right?"

"Yeah, I'm fine. Just busy all day. What's up?"

"Guyiser, the private investigator you wanted to talk to is here."

Guyiser stood up and looked out the window. His heart beat fast. "Send him down to the hangar. I'll meet him here."

Guyiser was nervous as he opened the safe. He stood looking at the tape and the recorder. The silver-handled gun lay on top of the newspaper. He took the paper and threw it on the desk. He looked at all the money and thought about Mr. Spellman and his part in all of this. That fact Guyiser had to protect. No one would ever know about Mr. Spellman's involvement. Guyiser would see to that to protect Mrs. Spellman.

Mr. Manning was a specialist in finding people. He used his muscle, knowledge, and size to get what he wanted. He and Guyiser talked about past people and things as Guyiser became more relaxed. Guyiser tapped a pencil on his desk. "I want to know about the legal parts."

"Mr. Blackman, any and everything we discuss is confidential. Even in a court of law, as an attorney, it is client, attorney entrustment."

Guyiser sat back in his chair, "That's what I wanted to hear." He slid the newspaper over to the investigator. "This is the man I want you to find."

Mr. Manning read the paper.

"This is an old murder case. James Olsen, that name rings a bell. The case was never solved. Do you have a personal interest in this?"

"Not the case, Mr. Manning, the man. I want to know where he is, what he's doing, who he talks to, his phone number and address, all his habits, everything.

I also want to know who investigated the case, police, detectives, names, and dates."

The investigator was writing in his notebook. "What about Olsen. You know anything about him?"

"I know he's dangerous. He's rich, was powerful, and I think he left the country, but I'm not sure."

"Well, Mr. Blackman, rich people can hide, but they can also be found." Mr. Manning slid the newspaper back to Guyiser. "My staff and I will get started on this today. I'll be in touch with you."

Guyiser walked in the office building with a renewed spirit. Instantly Kate waved memos at him. "Thank you, I'll let him know you called." Kate hung up the phone. She stood up with her hands full of messages. In her singsong voice, she smiled at Guyiser, "Oh, Mr. Blackman, you have a few messages." The phone rang again. "Please hold!"

Guyiser smiled and laughed, "Call Scott and Tim. Get them down here to help. Where's Carla?" Kate pointed.

"Scott, this is Kate. You and Tim get your butts down here now!" Kate smiled.

Carla handed Guyiser five newspapers, "Look at all this. Everyone wants in on what we've done. I've been returning calls all day."

Guyiser looked and read the papers. "Incredible. This is a million dollars' worth of publicity. Unreal. Look, this is a good picture of us."

Carla giggled, "Look at this one; we're all in it with the mayor."

"Wow! This will make Mr. Gibson and Mrs. Spellman happy."

"Guyiser, how was your meeting with Mr. Manning?"

"Carla, I feel so relieved. It is like looking at all these papers. I'm glad it's over."

"Good, now we can start thinking about the party. The invitations have been sent out, and I should start hearing from your guests any day now. Guyiser, I've got to return these calls, so..."

Guyiser kissed her. "You sure smell good. Okay, okay, I'll leave. Leaving now, leaving, bye."

One day ends; another day starts. Cindy and Sandy stood on the balcony of their room on the thirty-ninth floor overlooking the Big Apple in New York. "What a view. This isn't Tennessee, that's for sure." Sandy turned to the rental agent, "She'll take it."

The agent handed Cindy the agreement and a pen, "Just sign here, Miss Taylor, and it's yours."

Sandy took the papers and looked them over, "As her agent, I look at everything she signs. Looks good to me, Cindy, sign, sign!" Cindy laughed and signed.

"Thank you, Miss Taylor. There are other television people living here. Good luck with your show. Bye bye."

Sandy turned to Cindy, "Did you hear that? Other television people."

Cindy leaned on the balcony railing looking down at the city. Her dream was coming to life—a T.V. show, a penthouse apartment, and even traveling. She thought about Guyiser and heard her voice, 'Guyiser, you have your dream, and I have my dream.' Their worlds were now miles and miles apart. Sandy shook her arm, "Hey, hey, don't think. Let's go shopping. I want to buy some of those electric socks to keep my feet warm. It's cold where we're going."

Cindy kept staring out, "Yes it is, Sandy. It's cold."

One day ends; another day begins. The intercom buzzed and buzzed again. Guyiser put the bowl of dog food down on the floor for Loaner and went to his desk. "Hello."

"Guyiser, its Mr. Gibson on line one."

"Good morning, sir."

"Guyiser, my boy, have you seen the morning papers? We're in it again."

Guyiser laughed, "No, sir, not this morning. What does it say?"

Mr. Gibson laughed, "It says that millionaire Earl Gibson is to open a bicycle shop in Italy." Mr. Gibson laughed again, "All I said was that I love to ride my bicycle in Italy." They both burst out laughing.

"I've been there, sir. I've been there. They turn everything around."

"However, you know that may not be a bad idea. Not for me, Guyiser, but maybe for you. How are things going?"

"Mr. Gibson, the phones have not stopped ringing. We have all kinds of new accounts. In fact, Carla is talking to a big chain of stores now."

"Speaking of Carla, I see that you two are pretty close. She's a very smart girl. You look good together. But Guyiser, what about Cindy? I thought you two, well; I guess it's none of my business. Have you talked to her? How's she doing?"

"I guess she's doing okay. I don't talk to her very much. I've been busy and so has she. We have kind of drifted apart, but don't worry, sir. She's doing fine."

"Well, Guyiser, what I'm calling about is that Margaret and I are leaving tomorrow.

She has shipped everything she wants, and we want to see you before we leave. How about tonight?"

"That would be fine, sir. I'm sure going to miss you both."

"Guyiser, we're only a phone call away, but I know what you mean. We'll talk tonight. Now, go make us some more money."

"Yes, sir. I'll see you tonight."

Mrs. Spellman sat behind the large antique French glass-topped desk. "Yes, it is Guyiser. Mr. Spellman would sit here for hours. It is a beautiful piece. I hope you enjoy it. Here are the keys to everything—the guesthouse, all the doors in the house, the wine cellar, and the building out back. They are all yours now. There is also a safe over there. I'll show you." She stood by a large bookcase and pressed the last book.

The bookcase slid open, and the safe appeared. She handed Guyiser an envelope.

"Guyiser, would you open it?" He opened the envelope and took out a paper with numbers on it. He dialed the safe and opened the heavy door. "Thank you, Guyiser. Now take everything out." Mrs. Spellman put all the papers, some money, and a gun into a metal box.

"That's everything, Mrs. Spellman."

"Thank you, Guyiser. You can lock it now." Guyiser locked it, and Mrs. Spellman pressed the book again. The bookcase closed. "Now, that's how it works. Mr. Spellman had it put in. Shall we join the others now?"

Mr. Gibson was talking to Carla. Mrs. Spellman came into the living room holding Guyiser's arm. "Earl, I'm happy to say that everything is in Guyiser's hands now." They sat talking about Florence, Italy.

"It's a city rich with artwork such as <u>Madonna and Child</u> by Luca del la Robbia and works of other masters like Donatello, Gentile da Fabriano, Masaccio, and so many more. You two must visit us."

Guyiser and Carla smiled at each other. "We will, Mrs. Spellman. By the way, Mr. Gibson, what about your shop?"

"Sold, Guyiser. I've had people wanting that property for years. I bought the land and the building for $20,000.00 years ago. I sold it for $154,000.00." Mr. Gibson laughed, "Nice profit, don't you think? I'm going to miss that building." Mr. Gibson put his arm around Mrs. Spellman, "But, look what I have now."

Carla clapped her hands. "You're a lucky man, Mr. Gibson. I'm so happy for both of you."

Mr. Gibson kissed Mrs. Spellman's cheek, "Thank you, Carla. I think Guyiser is pretty lucky to have you. I still can see those kids' faces at your give-away.

Guyiser, my boy, we're leaving in the morning. It's been a long day for Mrs. Spellman. Is there anything we need to talk about?"

"No, sir." Guyiser looked at Mrs. Spellman and smiled, "Everything is in order. Again, I just want to thank you for everything. I still can't believe... well, everything you have done for me. I really love you both." They all stood and hugged and kissed each other goodbye. "Mr. Gibson, I'll take you to the airport and..."

"No, no, my son. That's not necessary. We would rather say goodbye here. We love you, son. You take care of yourself."

"I will, sir."

Carla hugged Mrs. Spellman again, "May I call you sometime?"

"Carla, dear, you had better call me. I want us to be close always. You're a very special person. Please take care of Guyiser."

Mrs. Spellman kissed her. "I will, I promise."

Guyiser had tears in his eyes as they drove away. There was a big empty feeling in his heart. He felt the same way when his father had died. Carla could feel his pain. She sat close to him and touched his hand, "I know, I know, Guyiser."

Three days had passed. Carla and Guyiser stood by the pool looking at the mansion. "Your guests will be arriving from out-of-town Saturday morning. Their rooms are all ready. Tom Maker is bringing the bicycles tomorrow. I have everything in order. Kate is taking care of the kids. By the way, I ordered a tuxedo for you, and..."

"A tuxedo? I've never worn a tuxedo before."

"Don't worry. You'll look handsome. I'll take care of you. The band can set up over there, and you and I will stand over here to greet everybody."

"A tuxedo? What color?"

"It's a maroon, crimson color with black pants and shoes and with a maroon country string tie. It's a power color with a country flare. I want you to look powerful and rich, besides, it matches my dress."

Carla had begun decorating inside the mansion. Mrs. Spellman had taken pictures from the walls that she had wanted. Carla had rearranged chairs, couches, tables, vases, flowers, books, and had given the house a much better look. Guyiser stood looking at all the changes. "Much better, now it looks much better. Carla, you never stop amazing me. Let's sit and talk a minute." They sat on the couch facing each other. Guyiser looked at the fireplace, "I like the couch this way facing the fireplace. Now, Carla, I've been thinking. I need you, and this is a big house. I want you to move in here with me."

Carla was surprised. Her eyes opened wide and her mouth opened, "Oh my, are you serious?"

"Yes, I am. I want to share things with you. What do you say?"

"I say yes, Guyiser." She hugged his neck and kissed him. "But one thing—I want to share your bedroom with you."

They laughed, hugged, and kissed.

"I was hoping you would say that, but I get the window side."

Carla smiled, "Mr. Blackman, you can have anything you want."

Hollywood could not have had a better party. Every detail was covered. Celebrity guests arrived. Kids played everywhere. James picked up guests at the airport. Butlers served food and drinks. Live music filled the air. Carla and Guyiser mingled with all the guests as more arrived during the day. They stood by the double doors of the mansion looking at each other. "Carla, you look like a fantasy, just fantastic, but there's one thing missing." Guyiser took a blue satin box from his pocket, "For you."

Carla opened the box and took a deep breath, "Guyiser, it's beautiful. I've never seen so many diamonds.

Oh, Guyiser, I love you."

This totally surprised Guyiser. He took the bracelet and put it on her arm. "Now, you're even more perfect. And, I love you, too." He stood gazing into her ocean blue eyes. His strong feelings for her had surfaced. There was no turning back. He knew then that Carla would be in his new life. Cindy was the one he had loved, but now that seemed to have been a lifetime ago.

"Now, let's go have some fun."

And they did! But, that's not all. Deals were made that night. New companies wanted the Blackie Bicycles. Celebrities had ideas for Guyiser. They wanted to endorse his bikes in ads and commercials. Mr. Levine had told him about the millions he could make on his patent idea. Sporting manufacturing companies wanted it. Japan wanted it. Mr. Levine had put the word out to investors and bankers. This new product would be a very big moneymaker. The 'blinking light speedometer' would be a big addition to the bicycle and sporting industry. Mr. Levine and Guyiser had discussed putting in bids for government contracts for bicycles. Cory told him about new investments in different stock. Oil prices were going up. The steel market had opened up. The airlines were growing. Real estate was booming. Guyiser was considering all of his options.

Carla impressed everyone. Her beauty had attracted movie producers. There were offers for movie rolls. The media call her 'The New Queen of Industry.'

It took a full day just to put the mansion back together. Guyiser, Carla, and Loaner sat relaxing on the couch. They were reading all the newspapers, giggling, and laughing at all the pictures and articles. Carla smiled as she cut out the pictures and articles about them. "What are you doing?"

Carla held up a picture of them, "It's for my scrapbook. I've got everything we have done together."

Guyiser just sat watching her enjoying herself. Yes, she was the one, and he was proud of her. "Say, why don't you take one of those movie offers?"

Carla looked at him and went back to cutting, "No, thanks. I'm not interested in any of that stuff. I've got everything I want right here." She stopped cutting and put her arms around Guyiser, "I've got you, this big house, friends, and a job I love. What more could I want?" She kissed him and went back to cutting.

"Miss Comings, have I told you that I love you?"

Carla thought, "Only twice—when you gave me the bracelet and now."

Guyiser grabbed her, "Come here, you." Loaner lay watching them playfully play.

The Dark Find

Part 13

Love is blind; hate is real.
It is in my mind like a piece of steel,
My eyes are closed, but I can see
All the things you have done to me.
If I could open my eyes, you would see
How much your death pleases me.
I sit in darkness, and here I dwell,
But you, my friend have gone to hell!

The sun streamed in the patio door. Carla was taking a shower when Guyiser called to her, "I'm going to the plant. Got work to do. I'll be back later tonight."

Carla stuck her head out of the shower, "Okay, hon. I'll wait up. Love ya."

Guyiser smiled, "Loaner, let's go."

He sat in the hangar by the doors talking to Buck. "Just a few more days and those puppies will be up and running. I understand that was some shindig you had at your place."

"Buck, I never met so many country stars. I have to go, my friend. I'll check with you tomorrow."

Guyiser walked around his apartment reading his messages Kate had given him. The phone rang on his desk. Loaner followed him to the office. "Yes."

"Mr. Blackman, this is Manning. I wanted to check in with you."

Guyiser sat down. "Good, I'm glad you did. What's going on?"

"Well, we've located your man. This is how it goes. He went to London for a while, left there, and went to Canada. He did some banking business. It seems he needed money. From there he headed down your way. He has a daughter living in Kentucky. I don't think he will stay there too long. He has a ticket back to London. I have the name and phone number of the detective who handled the murder case. It's..."

Guyiser wrote down everything, "Got it. What's the address and number of his daughter? Good, got it. Stay with him and keep letting me know all his moves."

This call had aroused Guyiser's instincts again. Instantly his intuition gave him a chill. Olsen was near. Guyiser dialed the front gate. Jim sat in the guardhouse reading a magazine. "Security."

"Jim? Guyiser. Is the other guard at the mansion?"

"Yes, sir. He will be there until four in the morning."

"Good, call him and have him watch the house, not the gate. Miss Comings is there by herself."

"Will do, sir."

"Thanks, Jim." This made Guyiser relax.

Clouds passed in front of the moon making the night even darker. A black car with its lights out slowly drove through the back gate. Loaner began to growl and bark. He ran down the stairs barking. Guyiser went to see what he was upsetting him. He opened the door and saw two men in the darkness. One man was standing on the plane pouring something from a can. They had saturated the aircraft with gasoline from several large cans. He heard one of the men call, "Let's go, let's go."

The man aimed his gun at the can and fired. The gas can exploded, sending flames high into the air and through the plane. It only took seconds for the plane to light up the sky. One man started running to a parked car.

"Stay, Loaner!" Guyiser chased after the man. The plane spewed gas from the left tank and a huge ball of fire rushed out. The explosion could be heard for miles.

The right tank roared and exploded with even more flames, throwing fire high into the sky. Guyiser was knocked off his feet. He could see a man's body lying on the ground. He got up and went to him. When he was almost there, a third more powerful explosion threw fire and flames all over Guyiser. He fell and rolled repeatedly. Jim was running as fast as he could, carrying a fire extinguisher and calling to Guyiser. He started to spray foam on Guyiser. In a moment, the flames were out. Guyiser lay crying with his hands covering his face.

Jim dialed 911. "This is an emergency. A plane has exploded and my boss is down. Send an ambulance now. You hear me? Now!" The explosion was so big that the fire station had seen the night light up and responded immediately. The paramedics instantly worked on Guyiser. With their sirens, they cleared a path to the hospital.

As they sprayed foam on the plane, a firefighter called out, "We have one dead over here."

Guyiser lay in the ambulance and grabbed the paramedic's arm. He cried out in pain, "I can't see! I can't see!" The emergency staff began to cool his skin. They gave him a shot of a sedative to relieve his pain. Two hours later, Guyiser lay in his room. His body was numb. He could hear a faint sound of a fan. He shook his head feebly, and the pain returned. His mind walked through a blind tunnel of silence and darkness.

"You're very lucky, Mr. Blackman." The doctor's voice faltered seeing that Guyiser was conscious.

"Very lucky." Guyiser lay on the hard bed. The image of the blast came to him. He remembered the heat, the smoke, the smell, and the pain. He heard panic in Jim's voice as Jim called to him. The last thing he remembered was the sounds of the fire truck's siren. The doctor touched Guyiser's hand. "Superficial burns but no lung damage. Mr. Blackman, you may have lost your sight. We will keep your eyes bandaged for a while. Then we will determine more about your sight. "Very lucky, Mr. Blackman."

The doctor's voice drifted away.

Carla touched his white coat as the doctor came out of Guyiser's room. "Doctor, is he...?"

"Stay only a few minutes. The tranquilizers will make him sleep." Tears fell on the white sheets of Guyiser's bed as Carla stood looking at the man she loved. She sat on the bed, touched his arm, and broke down sobbing. Carla sat by his bedside for several hours. Guyiser moved in pain. She quickly pushed the call button. The doctor came in within seconds. He checked Guyiser and turned to Carla, "His pain is natural. Do not worry. He is asleep."

"Doctor, his eyes, face, and hands—what, why?"

"A chemical fire like this one is very dangerous to the eyes. We can treat the burns, but the eyes are very delicate and sensitive. He may lose his eyesight. His young age is in his favor. His muscles are strong. Nevertheless, we will just have to wait. I'm sorry."

It was late the next day. Carla sat drinking the coffee the nurse had given her. Guyiser moved his head and tried to raise his arm. Carla instantly came to his side. "Guyiser, it's me. Can you hear me?" She touched him. He slowly turned his head to her voice.

"Water."

Carla pushed the call button. "Oh, Guyiser, I'm so sorry." The nurse came in. "He asked for water."

The nurse poured water and put the straw in Guyiser's mouth. "That he can have."

Carla took the glass, "I'll do that."

"Mr. Blackman, are you in pain?" Guyiser slowly turned his head no. The nurse looked at her watch.

"Well, that is a good thing. The doctor will be here shortly, Mr. Blackman. That's enough water for now." She left the room.

"Carla, I can't see."

She touched his arm, "You will." Tears came to her eyes. "I love you. You will."

The doctor came in and looked at Guyiser's chart. "Mr. Blackman, I have looked at your first X-Rays. There is some damage to the opening of the pupil of your eyes. But, and this is a big but, in time and care and after more X-Rays later tomorrow, we should know how to proceed. The tissue around your eyes is what is giving you pain now. We will change your dressing on your eyes, face, and hands and take the x-rays in the morning. But, Mr. Blackman, I do not want you to get your hopes up. Now get your rest. I will have the nurse bring your medication. Young lady, he will be out for some time. I suggest you go home and come back tomorrow night. Good night."

Carla touched Guyiser's hand, "I'm not leaving you, Guyiser."

Kate and Jim sat in the waiting room. Carla took a short walk down the hallway and saw them. "Kate, I'm so glad you're here."

Jim came to them, "I'm so sorry, Miss Comings. I did all I could."

"I know, Jim. I'm just glad you were there."

"Carla, how is he?"

They sat down. Kate held Carla's hands. "Not good. The doctor says that he may lose his eyesight."

"Oh, Carla, how terrible. We cannot let that happen. What are they doing for him?"

"Everything. The doctor is an eye specialist. He is giving Guyiser medicine for the pain. They will take more X-Rays in the morning. Oh, Kate, I'm so afraid."

"Don't be, we're all here for both of you."

A week passed. Guyiser was released from the hospital. His burns were beginning to heal, but his eyes were no better. He sat in a wheelchair. Carla knelt down by his side. "Do you need anything?"

"Yes, Carla, I need my eyes." His voice was very angry.

The doctor, who had come to the mansion, spoke to Guyiser, "Mr. Blackman, you must be patient about this. You are not going to get well overnight. It is going to take time. Miss Comings is doing all she can for you. You should be glad she is by your side. Do you know how many nights she sat watching you sleep? Now, I will be back tomorrow to change your dressings. Keep those bandages on and stay out of bright lights."

Guyiser had time to think after the doctor left. He rolled his wheelchair and bumped into the coffee table. Carla came to him with pills and a glass of water. "Guyiser, I'm here. Here, take these."

He reached and Carla put the glass in his hand. "Carla, I'm sorry I yelled at you. This is not your fault. I just feel so helpless."

Carla knelt down, "It's all right. Loaner and I are right here beside you."

"Carla, I need your eyes. I need your help. There's something I must do."

"Anything, Guyiser. You know I'm here."

He held up his hand, and Carla held it. "There's something you must do for me. Go to my office. In my desk, you will find a list of things Manning told me about. Get it. There is a safe behind the picture of a lighthouse. There is a picture of my father beside it. Inside the frame is the combination to the safe. Open it and you will see a newspaper, a tape recorder, and three tapes. Bring the tapes and recorder to me. Carla, this is something that no one must ever know about, understand? Just you and I."

Later that evening in the mansion, Carla and Guyiser sat listening to the tapes. Carla was shocked at what she heard. She looked at Guyiser's bandaged head and eyes. "Guyiser, do you know what this means? How did you get this?"

He rolled his wheelchair to her voice, "That doesn't matter. Find the detective's name and number."

She read it to him.

Carla looked over the papers. "Okay, I've got it. His name is Green, Ben Green. His number is 555-1212, extension 315."

Guyiser thought for a moment, "Good, now put a new tape in the recorder. I want to record this."

"Okay, now what?"

"Call the number and put the speaker on the phone. Then turn on the recorder. Carla, I just want to say I love you, no matter what happens. Now, dial the number." Many thoughts went through Guyiser's mind as he heard the phone ringing. He raised his hand and Carla held it.

"Detective Green."

Guyiser took a deep breath, "Mr. Green, you were the investigator of a case some twenty years ago.

To refresh your memory, it was a murder case of a woman at the home of James Olsen. Do you remember the case?"

Green tapped his pencil and thought, "Yes, I do. It was one of two cases I didn't solve. The burglar who killed the woman and shot Olsen got away."

"No, Mr. Green that is not what happened. Olsen killed the woman. There was no burglar. I have a tape recording of Olsen bragging of how he killed her."

"Who is this?"

"I'm just a concerned citizen who wants to see justice served. Would this tape help?"

"Well, of course. If he confesses to a murder, I would definitely check it out."

Guyiser tried to squeeze Carla's hand, "This is where he is right now."

Green wrote down all the information as Carla read it. "He won't be at this address for very long. You will have the tape soon. Be looking for it." Guyiser pointed to the phone. Carla hung up. He took a deep breath, "Now, that wasn't too bad. Carla, this is what you do— take the tape, wipe it clean of fingerprints, put it in an envelope, and address it to Green. Put 'Rush' on it. Disguise yourself and take it to the police station. Just hand it to the officer and tell him to get it to Detective Green and then leave. Do not say anything else. I don't want this coming back to us, understand?"

Within a few hours, Carla had delivered the tape. The early morning sun was shining through the clouds. "Call Manning for me, Carla." She dialed the number and put it on speaker. "Manning?"

"Manning here."

"This is Blackman. Where are you?"

"I'm still watching the house. Nothing has changed much. His daughter left the house, but he is still inside."

"Just keep watching the house. I think something might happen soon. Could be today or tomorrow. I don't know when, but it will be soon. My number is 382-7913. Call me if anything goes on."

"I will. I have a man with me. We are watching the house around the clock."

"Good. Let me know about anything, okay? Anything."

Two detectives sat with Green listening to the tape. They looked at each other. Green put the recorder on rewind and played back some of it.

The men listened closely to the tape. 'You killed her.'

'Yes, I killed her. She was blackmailing me.' Olsen laughed on the tape. 'And my bodyguard shot me to make it look good.'

Green stopped the tape. "Twenty years, but I think I have finely got my man. Get a squad car to go with us. We're going to pick him up for questioning. Let's go!"

It had been over an hour. Guyiser and Carla sat in the almost dark office. "Sweetheart, nothing may happen. You don't know what the police will do."

"Well, I know one thing. He did this to me, and some way he'll pay for it. Carla, I want to thank you."

The phone rang. Carla answered it and put on the speakerphone.

"Hello, this is Manning. Something is going down."

Guyiser leaned forward, "What's going on?"

"Mr. Blackman, there is a police car and a plain car coming down the street. This may be it."

"Stay there and tell me every move. Carla, dial Olsen's house."

The phone rang and Olsen answered, "Hello."

"Well, Mr. Olsen, I'm a voice from your past. I just wanted to let you know that you're going down— murder in the first degree."

"Blackman, how did you get this number?"

"Oh, that doesn't matter. Listen to this, Guyiser played the tape. 'You killed her.' 'Yes, I killed her. She was blackmailing me.'

There is a lot more. I gave this tape to the police. You're going to fry in the electric chair, you bastard." Guyiser laughed. "You fucked with the wrong country boy."

Manning came on the speaker phone, "Mr. Blackman, I think this is it. The cars stopped in front of the house. I see three plain clothed men and four cops."

Guyiser leaned back in his chair with knowing satisfaction, "Mr. Olsen, look out your front window. Tell me what you see."

Olsen quickly went to the window. He slightly pulled the curtain back and peeked out. He stood shaking. His heart was beating rapidly. Blood rushed to his head. He saw the men with their guns drawn. A plain clothed officer was giving directions to two of the policemen to circle the house.

"Manning, what's going on?"

"They have their guns out and are walking to the door."

"Well, Mr. Olsen, it won't be long now. You're going down. You're going to fry. You hear me, fry!"

"Mr. Blackman! The police are on the ground. There's been a gunshot." The line was quiet for a moment. "Now they are going to the door. One detective went in. Now all of them are in."

Guyiser could see all of this happening. "Olsen, are you there? Talk to me, you bastard." There was no answer. "Hang it up, Carla. It's over. Manning, are you there? Tell me what you see."

"Yes, I'm here. There are more police here. I see two T.V. trucks and some reporters. The paramedics took a body out of the house."

Guyiser smiled under his bandages. "Go home, Mr. Manning. Good job. Send me your bill."

The television studio was lit and full of energy. Jeff leaned on his desk talking to Cindy, "We have two-five second spots to do. This one, 'Join our team at Eleven' and this one, 'The latest news and weather on Good Morning. Okay, lots of smiles."

Cindy looked at the two papers, "Easy, let's do it."

Jeff's assistant came running to the set, "Here, boss. This fax just came in. Tom wants to air this right now. Our crew is on scene."

Jeff took the fax and read it,

"Interesting, here you go. A late breaking news story."

Cindy took the fax and read it, "Okay, I can do it."

"Good, let's do it first and get it out of the way." Jeff sat in the booth, "Cynthia, are you ready?" Cindy sat looking at the paper. The red light came on the camera. "Rolling, speed, and action."

Cindy looked into the dark lens. "We have late breaking news. Our team is on the scene reporting live. Detectives and police were serving a warrant at the home where James Olsen was wanted for questioning. As they approached the house, police say there was a gunshot. Upon entering, they found the body of James Olsen. He had shot himself in the head. Police said he was involved in a murder of a woman some twenty years ago. There will be more on this story on our News at Eleven. This is Cynthia Taylor..."

"And cut." Jeff came out of the booth and walked over to Cindy.

"That was great. Do you want to follow up on this story?"

Cindy looked at the fax. "No I don't think so Jeff, a twenty-year old story is history. However, there is something about it. Olsen, wasn't he one of the backers at a bicycle plant years ago? Interesting." She touched the necklace around her neck. Oh well, are we still going to Cuba?"

Jeff grinned, "If you want to, but Japan is nice this time of year."

Sandy came crawling on her knees and hugged Jeff's leg, "Me too, me too, Jeff, please, me too."

Carla leaned over Guyiser's wheelchair with her arms around him, "Are you all right?"

"Carla, honey, if I could see, I would take you to the moon. I'm in heaven."

"Guyiser, when I was in your office, I couldn't help but notice that there were no pictures of Cindy. But, I did see a picture of us."

Guyiser held her arms, "That's because there is an 'us'—just you and me. I love you, Carla. You are my future. That was my past. Now, would you go to the factory? I want to know how Buck is coming with those machines. Check with Tom Maker in Shipping and see if Kate needs anything, and..."

Carla laughed, "Okay, okay I get the idea. When I get back, I've got another idea; you and me up stairs."

Guyiser smiled, "You always have the best ideas. Hurry back."

The house was quiet. Guyiser held the remote control and flipped through the channels to find a news or weather channel. Suddenly he heard the voice of Cindy. 'As they approached the house, police heard a gunshot. Upon entering, they found the body of James Olsen. He had shot himself in the head.' Guyiser turned up the volume. 'Police say he was involved in a murder some twenty years ago. More on this story on our News at Eleven. This is Cynthia Taylor.' Cindy touched her necklace as the commercial came on. Guyiser shut off the T.V. "Well, well, Miss Taylor, you got what you wanted. I wish you good luck and happiness always. I hope you are as happy as I am."

Carla walked in with the doctor. "Guyiser, the doctor is here."

"I'm in here."

"Well, Mr. Blackman, how are you today?"

"I feel much better."

"Good. Let us take a look. Miss Comings, would you close those curtains? I need it to be dark in here.

Okay, now, Mr. Blackman, I have a small flashlight. It's on. Now, when I slowly take off the bandages, I want you to tell me what you see. Don't try to strain your eyes." The doctor slowly started taking the gauze off Guyiser's head. "Scalp! Looks good. Don't worry about your hair. It will grow back." He continued removing the gauze. "Not bad. Your face is healing well, but it will take time. Now, your eyes."

Carla took Guyiser's hand. "I love you."

"Okay, Mr. Blackman, do not open your eyes, but do you see any light?"

"Kind of, it's lighter."

"Okay, now the right eye. Any light?"

"About the same. It's lighter."

The doctor looked at Carla, "Now, your eyelids look good, but they are not healed, so this may hurt a little.

I want you to slowly open your eyes and tell me if you see the light. Slowly now, slowly. That's good, slowly."

Guyiser held Carla's hand tighter. The doctor waved the small light. Guyiser opened his eyes slowly. The doctor looked closely. The pupils were white. Carla saw the white in his eyes and closed hers. "Do you see the light?"

"I see light, but it's milky, not clear."

"Now, slowly close your eyes. That is good, slowly. Now, I am going to put this antibiotic ointment on your lids. Try not to blink. There, that will help heal and cool your eyes. Now, I will put new pads over your eyes. The gauze will hold them in place. There we go. Miss Comings, tear off some tape for me, please. Okay, I'm leaving your face uncovered. The air will be good for it. You can open the curtains now. Let's keep the bandages off your hands, too. They are looking pretty good. Miss Comings, put this ointment on his hands and face twice a day."

"But, my eyes, doctor. I couldn't see."

The doctor smiled at Carla, "But, you did see light. Even if it were milky, you saw light. Mr. Blackman, you are very lucky. You will not be blind. With today's technology and new forms of surgery and treatment, you will see again. However, it will take time. Now, I will be back in a few days to check your eyes again. I might tell you, I was concerned until you said you saw some light. I was afraid you might not. Still, stay out of the sun. Miss Comings, thank you for your help. I will see myself out. Good night."

There is an old saying, and I quote,
"Time heals all wounds."

That is what happened to Guyiser. Carla held his arm and Loaner lead him around. His surgery saved his eyes. He could see his factory grow and grow. Carla ran everything. He saw her making millions and millions of dollars in stock, real estate, and the Internet.

Anything she touched made money. One day she asked, "Guyiser, how much money do you have?"

Guyiser laughed, "The papers say I have a billion. I really don't know. I have trouble counting to a thousand. A million is impossible. A billion—forget it."

It was a year later as Carla and Guyiser lay on the white sands of Hawaii at a hotel they owned. "Well, what do you think?" Guyiser rolled over on top of her. Looking into her big blue eyes, "Do you think it is time to go back to work, Mrs. Blackman?"

"Yes, Mr. Blackman, but I have another idea. The room and the bed is fresh and waiting for us."

"You always have the best ideas Mrs. Blackman."

They rolled in the sand laughing as Loaner barked and smiled.

"The end of a perfect story."

Conclusion

The Blackman Empire grew. 'Blackie' bikes were known the world over. Guyiser and Carla bought factories in Japan, China, Italy, France, and London plus two more in the U.S.A.

Over a period of time, stocks and investments did make Guyiser Blackman a billionaire.

Carla Comings Blackman became a power in the women's movement for women and children's educational programs. Libraries were created in twelve countries.

Cynthia (Cindy) Taylor finished her dream of reporting and became the executive president and C.E.O. of the largest cable network for countries all over the world. She, her husband, and their beautiful daughter found their home in Santa Barbara, California.

Mr. Gibson and Mrs. Spellman lived their happy lives together in Italy.

Kate retired from the factory, but she worked with Carla on different projects.

When Guyiser, Jr. was born, Guyiser, Sr. devoted his life and time to his son. Carla watched as this father and son bonded. They would often visit the farm where Guyiser would teach his son about the trash and treasure of life. THIS WAS GUYISER'S SON.